DONS OF TIME

GREG GUMA

Fomite
Burlington, VT

ISBN-13: 978-1-937677-51-0
Library of Congress Control Number: 2013941205

Fomite
58 Peru Street
Burlington, VT 05401
www.fomitepress.com

Cover Art - Greg Guma

For JG, DG, JD, RL
and all the golden dreamers

Don, noun. 1. In Spanish, a title before a man's name; a lord or gentleman. 2. In Britain, a head tutor or fellow at a college; a college or university professor. 3. A distinguished or important person. 4. The leader of a crime family

Dons of Time

Contents

PART ONE

RETROCAUSALITY

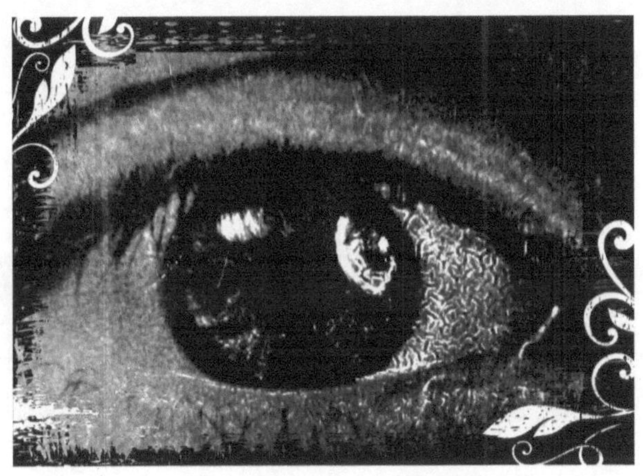

1
The Inside Track

Tonio Wolfe didn't like to think he was a wiseguy. On the other hand his father Senoslav – Shelley to family and close friends – was the head of a criminal syndicate that had successfully transitioned into a more-or-less legitimate international office, hotel and casino development corporation, buying and selling, building, demolishing and rebuilding along much of the Atlantic coast for the last few decades.

He had never shown much enthusiasm for the family business, although he did benefit from what it allowed him to do. At the moment he wasn't even comforted by that. He was in an emotional slump no amount of recreation or misbehavior seemed to relieve. And it was coming at the worst time, just as Shelley wanted answers about TELPORT, the company his wayward but fortunate son had been supervising on the family's behalf for the last three years.

The head of the Wolfe family had obtained a stake in Danny Webster's company by covering his massive losses on poker and horses and then summoned Tonio to the mansion in Wood-Ridge after he returned from a three-month backpacking trip across Greece. He remembered thinking at the time how much his father's new home looked like the set from De Palma's *Scarface* – a plush gangster palace with vaulted ceilings, parquet and slate floors and gaudy art.

Two of Shelley's goons were installed on a low puffy couch, one engrossed in *People Magazine*, the other deep into Grand Theft Auto

IV on an Xbox 360. Tonio yelled "hey" as he proceeded down the hall past the elevator and indoor pool to a dark hardwood door, took a deep breath and pushed it open.

Shelley's inner sanctum was like the executive chamber of an old world monarch. A pre-Raphaelite tapestry dominated the wall to the right of the entrance, flanked by vases and a bust of Alexander the Great on a pedestal. The suite featured a full bar in the corner near his desk, a huge, shuttered picture window, generous conversation pit, then an adjacent hallway leading to a workout room, bathroom with sauna, and game room beyond featuring air hockey and 70 inch home theater. It was a separate apartment within the larger mansion occupied by his wife, Tonio's aunt Vivian and her teenage daughter, a private world for the king and his cronies.

The head of the family was sitting behind his oversized mahogany desk warily watching Tonio approach from the security of a high-backed, red leather chair he had chosen for both comfort and intimidation. Shelley was fit for his late sixties, and had everything a decadent Baby Boomer could want: power, success, freedom, unlimited funds, a gorgeous trophy wife – not Tonio's mother – and apparent impunity from legal sanctions. Still, he exuded a restless low-level paranoia, like a besieged and suspicious dictator who believed a disaster, betrayal or attack capable of overturning his empire was just around the bend.

"Take a seat," Shelley said, waiting mere seconds before adding that it wasn't a request. "About the proposition we discussed…"

"You know I'm not interested," Tonio interrupted, continuing to stand.

"What are you interested in? Ruins, dead civilizations."

"Warm weather, hot women, ethnic food. That about covers it." He wasn't serious, but it might push dad's buttons.

"And you're satisfied with that?"

Satisfied was much too strong. The truth was that he shared his father's

unsettled nature. But Shelley dealt with discontent by projecting it onto anyone who stepped in his way, or happened to be in the vicinity, in the form of sudden outbursts and occasional deadly violence. At least Tonio was asking himself questions, he thought. At least he wanted to understand why he felt unfinished and superfluous, as if there were missing pieces in his life creating chronically unstable conditions.

"It'll do for now," he replied, finally taking a seat.

Shelley grunted but let it pass. "So, have you thought about it, what we discussed?" The offer was to chair the board of the digital tech business in which he'd obtained a controlling interest. According to *Wired*, Danny Webster could be the next Steve Jobs.

If he survives my family, thought Tonio. "Yes, I did consider it, and I appreciate the thought." He paused to find the best words but realized he needed only four. "I can't do this," he said.

"Can't do what?" He could hear contempt in the rising voice.

"This," he said, gesturing randomly at the décor. "Our thing, which is not my thing."

"Really? It's a little late for that. You're part of the family."

"Gianni didn't choose it," he snapped, "and don't give me that Godfather routine. I didn't either."

Bringing up his dead uncle was designed to shut down the discussion. Giancarlo Wolfe, Shelley's younger brother, had chosen the Army during Vietnam and managed to survive it intact. After the war, he made the leap to a post in the State Department. He had escaped the family and seen the world as Tonio grew up on the Jersey shore. He was Tonio's favorite relative when he was young, a sympathetic adult who wasn't around often but took a genuine interest when he was, a romantic figure who brought back exotic gifts from places like Jamaica, Angola and Pakistan. But he died unexpectedly when Tonio was ten, and neither he nor his father had ever completely recovered from the loss.

The Don rose slowly and circumvented the desk to confront Tonio at close range. "I understand," he said slyly, "but you didn't choose anything else. And you don't mind living off our success. Sleep okay at night, I assume?"

"Yeah," Tonio said. It wasn't completely true.

"Good." This contest of wills was beginning to feel like a draw. "And you're right: I run the family. I'm the one who's ultimately responsible. And you – you..." Shelley hovered between resentment and regret. Should he slap down the ungrateful snot, he seemed to be thinking, or clasp him in a bear-hug? Unable to resolve the conflicting impulses he moved over to the conversation area and dropped onto a sofa.

"When you said you didn't want in, I was all right with that," he said wistfully. "But you barely get into college and then get yourself kicked out – for beating your roommate half to death. I'd call that a career move."

"He almost raped my ex-girlfriend." It was a fact, but not an excuse. At the start of sophomore year Tonio had agreed to share a room with Roger Hilton, a psychology major who was also interested in coeds and murder mysteries. But when he found Roger about to screw a half-conscious Candy Newman in their room, after slipping a roofie in her beer, he instinctively weaponized a tennis racket and broke Roger's arm, skull, and several ribs before three members of the varsity football team pulled him off.

"A citizen calls the cops," Shelley concluded. "A criminal does what you did. I'm not judging, he probably deserved it. But that's reality."

"I know that."

It was hard to hear what came next. "You don't want to try another school, OK. You say, Dad, bring me in, I want to be part of the family. OK. But then three months later you move to Los Angeles and say you're an actor. I go along with that too. A few years of experimenting, that I can understand. You need to find yourself. But then all the trips to the ends of the earth – and the therapy. Tony, you're over thirty-five. You don't get to grow up and then go direct to the mid-life crisis."

Things were getting too close to the bone for comfort. "Your point?"

"That maybe you need a little motivation, something to keep you occupied." The suggestion implied that Shelley was trying to do his job as a father – for a change. But Tonio suspected it also suited the old man's personal agenda, despite his repeated assurances that "it's completely legit."

"I have hobbies," Tonio said dismissively.

"Hey, a little respect. Most people would kill for this kind of chance."

Tonio didn't want to admit it, but his father was right and his idea had merit.

"I get it," said the Don, deploying his trustworthy smile while placing a tentative arm on his son's shoulder. "You want something meaningful. Yes? So, check it out. I think you might like it."

A week later Tonio visited the TELPORT corporate office and took the meeting that changed his life.

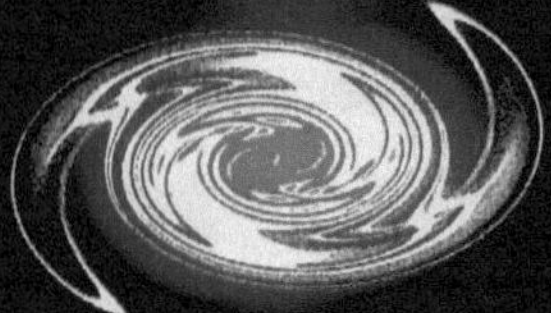
"Wherever you look
there you are"

Remote Viewing
Is Here . . .

TELPORT

TELPORT Tests 3-D Helmet Visors,
Plans Consumer Launch for Christmas

When the first Space Shield Tactical Fighter jets become operational, pilots will use visors produced by TELPORT, Inc. to simultaneously view the controls, holographic maps, and almost any location inside and outside the plane.

TELPORT is working with the military to fine-tune its new 3-D visors. Keeping the images clear and stable at supersonic speeds was a challenge, admits CEO Daniel F. Webster. But Webster, an inventor who was recently named a Tech Titan by Washington Magazine, claims that image clarity has been dramatically improved in recent months.

His company has received more than $20 million in contracts for virtual reality, drone operation and cyber-intelligence research.

"This is cutting-edge," Webster said Tuesday in an interview about the new visors, which can be adapted for use with most combat helmets. TELPORT already has requests to adapt them for use with F-35s and other aircraft. A consumer version of the visor is also being developed in association with the company's Locator, a recording and communications device scheduled for release in time for the holiday season.

"Like anyone working in this area we had 'latency' issues, the time delay you usually encounter in trans-mitting any images," Webster explained. The problems tended to intensify the faster the plane travels. But according to Webster solutions are "on the horizon" for instantaneous transmission.

TELPORT reacted early to concerns that military budget cuts would slow down research and lead to staff reductions. "That's one reason we're moving forward rapidly with applications for the general public," Webster admitted. "But military uses were never the goal for me."

He described the sequence interception locator (SIL) being developed by TELPORT as the first fully-functional 3-D telecommunications device. "We're combining GPS technology with next generation VR to create a remote viewing experience as close to real life as possible," he promised.

"The idea is to provide an affordable communication portal to the whole world," Webster said.

2
Appointments

"**D**id you nail her?"

The sound of Paulie Dragon's classless question echoed through parking level 4, followed by an amplified wall of collective laughter that faded by the time Tonio reached the Hummer. Sometimes driving around with these bozos was embarrassing. Still, he preferred being chauffeured to making his own way across the city, especially on a day like this.

They were teasing him about Marcia Siegel. He'd just finished an hour of therapy and sometimes did wonder why he came back each week. But there was really no place else to take his general state of confusion, and sometimes she stumbled on something that pointed in a useful direction. This week, for example, when he complained about not controlling key decisions about his own life, she simply asked who did. A reasonable question, one he knew he should try to answer seriously. But it made him uncomfortable, opening up a Pandora's Box of issues best left where they were. Plus, she made it sound like a judgment.

"Are you mocking me?" He'd kept his voice low but telegraphed his displeasure.

She hesitated, disoriented by the hint of a threat. "No, not at all. I was just suggesting you could do something. What about your friends, maybe they can help. "

"Not a chance," he laughed. "They really don't get it."

"What don't they get?"

A fair question. But if he had to list what those steroid-pumping, sex and drug-addicted "colleagues" of his didn't understand they would be here all week. Could anyone get it? As far as Tonio knew, he was no one's object of special sympathy, a 40-year-old underachiever who lived a charmed but emotionally stunted, and until recently pointless, life. Expelled from college, with little perceptible ambition, a social nomad who had drifted for years, never married or even close. The consensus among the women in his romantic life: he was emotionally inaccessible and a poor prospect for much more than athletic sex and preferred concert seating. He had to admit they had a point. He had jumped from one relationship disaster to another for almost two decades, as if he was a compulsive collector of broken toys.

Hey, they were broken when I got them, he told himself.

He did have a few natural gifts – solid recall, a quirky imagination, the ability to adapt to almost any social scene. Admittedly that made him a bit of a chameleon, but in comparison with the wild bunch waiting for him, he felt positively self-actualized.

"Keep it down, retards," he said, climbing into the front seat. Inside, it was thick with a mix of grass, cigarettes and after-shave. He grabbed a joint circulating behind him and took a long toke. "I needed this," he managed while holding his breath.

Paulie grinned and gunned the engine. "Sorry, man," he said. "We are just having trouble imagining what you do up there."

"Finding out some shit about myself."

"Ooh, a treasure hunt. Have you found her snatch yet?" That was Pesci, the group's muscle, so Tonio let it pass. His real name was Joe Mancini but he preferred his professional wrestling moniker. Pesci was known for unexpected, excessively brutal attacks during his bouts. Being a ticking time bomb had become his trademark and meal ticket.

At first Pesci would hang back in a fight, defending himself while giving the impression that it was barely holding his attention. But at some point his opponent would do or say something – it didn't actually matter what – just something Pesci found offensive, any excuse for him to immediately increase the level of violence to eleven.

While administering the blows he would shout his catch phrases. "Am I funny? Do I amuse you? Am I here to amuse you?" It was from his favorite scene in *Goodfellas*.

Audiences loved it.

The third member of the crew in the yellow bourgeois monstrosity was Ray Connelly, a black Irish lady-killer who was equally effective with firearms. Pesci, Paulie and Tonio had known each other for years. Ray-Ray was a more recent addition to the crew, courtesy of Shelley and possibly assigned, at least in part, to keep track of his son.

Of the three, Paulie was the one Tonio had known longest, and the only one he trusted. They had been kids together on the boardwalk, moved together into an East Village loft after Tonio's college period abruptly ended, and basically considered each other brothers from another mother. Still, some of the biggest events in Tonio's recent life were off-limits to his old friend.

"We're just concerned," Paulie said, obviously kidding. "We think you need to get laid."

"But if you're not interested, I'll take a run at her," Ray-Ray offered.

"Take my word, you don't want any of that. So guys, I need to stop at TELPORT."

"Shit," Pesci cursed, "not nerd-central!"

They were speeding uptown and the lights were green. Below the Empire State building on 33rd the electricity had been turned back on after a storm that left more than a hundred people dead and thousands without power in Manhattan, Staten Island, and across a large swath of Jersey.

"Not yet," Paulie added. "We got business first, for the old man. Plus, he wants to see you post haste."

"Now, tonight? Can we even get to him?" The entire region was one big traffic jam after what was being called the storm of the century.

"No rush. He'll send the chopper when we're ready. But the first thing, he wants it done tonight."

Tonio dreaded this aspect of the family business, the obligatory ride-alongs when the crew was told to collect a payment – or wreak havoc – on Shelley's orders. Sometimes he could persuade the boys to minimize the broken bones or furniture when handling this sort of assignment. But it couldn't always be avoided, and some of the degenerates, gamblers, grifters and addicts they tracked deserved a beat-down, at the very least.

After almost an hour in heavy traffic they were in the tony uptown apartment of a defense attorney who was avoiding calls about a $100,000 loan. Paulie took the lead, shouting his version of Samuel L. Jackson's jeremiad from *Pulp Fiction* as Pesci suspended the lawyer above the ground by the bathrobe, repeatedly smashing him into an abstract expressionist canvas that was rapidly losing its resale value.

Ray-Ray checked out a collection of vintage vinyl, casually tossing LPs across the apartment until he found one he wanted to hear. It was an original pressing of The Beatles' White Album, protected in heavy plastic. Ray-Ray broke the seal and slipped Side One on the turntable.

"You have been shirking your responsibilities, counselor," shouted Paulie as the state-of-the-art sound system kicked in, filling the room with the squeal and rumble of an airplane landing. "Is that the right word, T? Shirking?"

Tonio nodded. "Excellent choice," he said. "I'll check the office." He didn't want to witness the next part, and had noticed bookshelves on the way in. "Back in the USSR," harmonized The Beatles, a less-than patriotic choice to cover up any screams.

He started by sitting behind the desk, taking in the room from its intended power position, then strolled along the wall for a closer look at the titles. There was the obligatory collection of law books, but a more interesting section was biographies, starting with ghost-written hack jobs by politicians, players and presidents.

Some of the names were familiar – Giuliani, Clinton, Trump, Bush, Obama and Romney – then less so as the spines announced early American icons from Jefferson to TR and industrial titans like Carnegie, Rockefeller, and Morgan. One title on the shelf jumped out from the rest: Ignatius Donnelly.

What a handle! He pulled it out. The cover photo showed a proud, compactly-built man wearing a top hat, hands thrust confidently in his pockets, eyes gazing at a far horizon, full chin and a jutting jaw that suggested extreme tenacity. "Portrait of a Politician," announced the subtitle.

The book looked rare, a 1962 edition by the University of Chicago Press in mint condition. The subject was apparently an obscure 19th century populist from Minnesota. Next to it were other Donnelly titles. His interests evidently ranged from Atlantis to Shakespeare.

There was something vaguely familiar about the name even before he picked up the book. When he looked at the cover he was sure. He recognized that face! In fact, he already knew more about Donnelly than he possibly could.

He somehow knew, for example, that in 1888 he was disillusioned with politics. Why that year specifically? He had no idea. Tonio also knew, absolutely, that although Donnelly had been in the Minnesota state legislature and the United States Congress, what drove his deepest passion was offbeat research into the past. As he could see before him, Donnelly had written books asserting that a comet once struck the Earth and that William Shakespeare didn't write the plays bearing his name. But Tonio also knew that, in spite of such weird writing and pro-nouncements, most people didn't think Donnelly was a crackpot. They took him seriously as a political leader and thinker.

Around the country readers, supporters and fans of his day looked forward to his research and odd speculations. When visiting London he could draw a crowd including Oscar Wilde and the cream of the literary set to hear a deconstruction of their most revered writer.

How could he possibly know any of this? And was he right? Tonio had no clue, but he was certain that it didn't come from a classroom or any book he'd read. And even if it turned out he was wrong, the fact that Donnelly's name and face felt so familiar was enough reason to check it through the warehouse.

3
ORIENTATION

He called the office from the backseat as Paulie looked for a route off Manhattan. There was no answer at first. He was lucky to be getting a signal.

Almost a week after Hurricane Sandy large swathes of the tri-state area still didn't have power. A fourth of the city's cellular transmitters had been knocked out by the super-storm, a situation so severe that public phones were making a comeback. Tempers flared as drivers waited in endless gas queues. Opportunistic convenience store operators were charging as much as six bucks a gallon.

Train service was limited. Only a handful of buses circulated, and only through selected boroughs. Subways had reopened in upper Manhattan, but no lines operated below 34th Street. The Battery tunnel was flooded. Along the Jersey Turnpike cars lined up for miles to get fuel. In outer-borough areas, stations were sealed off with yellow caution tape. In Queens, rumors spread about the next fuel shipment.

But this was New York, the Big Apple, the country's financial hub, the city that didn't sleep even when partially submerged, so people were shaking it off and getting back to business.

"What you think? Does this work for Romney or Obama?" Pesci's question was apt. The occupants of the car, like the inhabitants of the country, were about evenly divided over who should win the presidential election on Tuesday. After four stubbornly polarized, near-Depression years Tonio and Paulie supported the president. But Pesci and Ray-Ray were gut-level libertarians who thought government was the problem and Obama was a half-black bleeding heart. About the only point on which they agreed was that the hurricane gave the incumbent the edge in a close race.

"He's lucky it hit where it did," joked Ray-Ray. "Blue states, New Jersey. Obama owes Christie big time." New Jersey's governor had just toured the devastated coast with the president and praised his performance. Not an endorsement exactly, but it looked like one to many casual observers. Republican apparatchiks were outraged.

"If it quacks like a Duck," Gianni used to say. His uncle had proverbs for such occasions, a catchy phrase to make his point. "Ronald Reagan is such a threat to humanity that the whole world should be allowed to vote." Despite his work for the government he'd frequently shared that nugget in the run-up to the 1980 election. Tonio wondered what he might have said about this one.

Gianni was his first mentor, a confidant and a trusted adult guide to life until he was ten. Shelley was too preoccupied building Wolfe Enterprises to take an interest, and his mother was busy finding herself through therapy and astrology. Gianni thought young Tonio was unique and gifted, and often told him so. When his uncle was suddenly gone Tonio became so depressed he spent months struggling with a life-threatening infection, a period so stressful and isolating that he had blocked most of it out, even some of the period before Gianni's death.

Danny called back in five minutes. "You rang?" He sounded cocky, even for an über-nerd primed to make billions on his invention.

"Yeah, we need to talk."

"Can it wait? I'm kind of in the middle…"

"No," he broke in. Whatever Danny was working on, it would be just as incomprehensible to him after an explanation. "I mean, maybe. But the main office is nosing around."

"Big Daddy, you mean? Still not satisfied? Does he know the rollout is way past projections?"

"He's impressed," assured Tonio. "But that's made him curious. He probably wants to know what's on tap. And there's something else."

"A breach?" This was Danny's main concern these days, what would happen if someone got wind of their off-book activities.

"No breach. But I may have found something, a familiar face." He picked up one of the volumes he had taken from the lawyer's office. "I need a search, and maybe some view time."

"Can we deal with it tomorrow. Please."

Tonio agreed and let him go, then told Pauli to forget about TELPORT, drop off the boys and take him home.

Not even Paulie suspected what Danny and he were doing. His friend knew only what the public had recently learned – that their remote viewing system was about to revolutionize mass communication with a combination of next generation GPS, holographic recording capability and portable virtual reality display.

MANHATTAN, 2009

Their first meeting began in TELPORT's corporate waiting room, an antiseptic, post-modern limbo. Rather than the usual landscapes or abstract kitsch, however, its walls were covered with quotations in bold distinctive fonts, formats and styles.

Tonio didn't recognize every name, but a theme was apparent. The quote in wrought iron near the entrance was from Theophrastus, successor to Aristotle at the Lyceum. *"Time is the most valuable thing a man can spend,"* the old Greek reportedly advised. And highly finite, he added.

He vaguely remembered the next quote in line, a scrolling LED homage to John Archibald Wheeler, a theoretical physicist who collaborated with Niels Bohr on fission and Albert Einstein on the unified field theory. In addition to coining terms like wormhole, quantum foam, and black hole, he once warned that *"time is what prevents everything from happening at once."*

Useful information, considering what Tonio had experienced since then.

The quilted quote from Tennessee Williams was quaint and lyrical. *"Time is the longest distance between two places."* So lamented the creator of plays that defined 20th century angst. Andy Warhol was more pragmatic in hard-edge acrylic paint. *"They say that time changes things,"* the father of pop art reflected, *"but you actually have to change them yourself."*

Kind of do-it-yourself butch, Tonio thought.

Benjamin Franklin went directly to the point in a huge linotype reproduction: *"Time is money."* An archetypically American viewpoint from one of the country's original celebrities. There was also a thought from one British celeb. *"Time is on my side,"* proclaimed a colorful mosaic installation, the words attributed to Mick Jagger.

"Which one turns you on?" Danny Webster was watching him. TELPORT'S founder looked only a few years younger, chronologically. In street smarts, however, they were miles apart. Danny's clothing was designer casual, his affect and words screamed ivy-tower egghead.

Danny had a doctorate in mechanical engineering from the California Institute of Technology and a master's from Virginia Tech. He was the inventor or co-inventor on multiple patents and patents pending. *Washingtonian* Magazine had just named him a Tech Titan. His company TELPORT had at least $16 million in defense contracts for virtual reality, drone support and cyber-intelligence work, and now was apparently developing portable applications.

"I should say Franklin, but I'm partial to Greeks," Tonio answered as they shook. "Actually, my mom is Greek."

"Iron, I like it, solid. And your dad…" Danny let the sentence dangle, the ambiguity intended to let his prospective board chair complete the thought however he wished. Tonio didn't bite and moved on to business.

"So, why all the time quotes?"

"It's what we're about – saving time."

"I thought you had the next smart phone."

"That's where we started, an affordable, fully functional picture phone with recording and playback capability. That's why we chose TELPORT, a telecommunications portal to the world."

"And how did that go?"

Danny's expression turned sly, then widened into a self-satisfied smile. "We did it," he announced. "But that was just the tip of the iceberg." His speech picked up velocity as he warmed to the topic. "We're into something much bigger. We've tapped into quantum functionality, GPS technology combined with next generation VR. This is going to change the basic way we relate to each other."

It sounded like bullshit. "Plain English," Tonio insisted. "So, it's basically a wireless phone and projection system?"

"That's one aspect. Let me show you something," Danny said, directing him past cramped offices into a conference room. It was empty except for a few chairs, a long table, and two objects purposefully positioned at its center. One was a shiny black metal box large enough for a pair of shoes. The other was a slim handheld computer, slightly smaller than a tablet but larger than a mobile phone.

"We calling her SIL, for Sequence Interception Locator. Or just the Locator."

4
COLD CASES

Tonio loved tales in which complex mysteries were spun or terrible crimes were solved. It started when he was young with TV shows, long before *Law & Order* and the rest of the franchise. He still remembered *Police Story*, a late 70s series set in L.A. that covered police work from multiple perspectives. One week it was the rookie cop, the next an undercover narc or an officer suspected of taking bribes. Joe Wambaugh, a real LAPD detective, came up with the idea. He even enjoyed the spin off, *Police Woman.*

About ten years back, after the bodies of local hookers started turning up around Gilgo Beach, Paulie and he had briefly become addicted to *CSI*. It was slick and quick and set in Vegas. But Tonio lost interest as the spinoffs proliferated. In the late 1990s a non-speaking role as a Baltimore cop on *Homicide: Life in the City* became the high point of his acting career.

Lately, he had been re-watching *The Wire* on Netflix. Tonio appreciated that it too was shot around Baltimore, an old stomping ground, which gave it undeniable authenticity. Like *Police Story*, it was created by professionals who based the stories on their ordeals and experiences with surveillance as a tool to bust up drug rings.

Beyond that, he followed real-life, unsolved murders – from JonBenet Ramsey, the beauty pageant child found in the basement of her own home, to Tupac and Notorious B.I.G. A special focus was on the dozens of serial killers who escaped justice for their crimes. Most people knew about the Zodiac killer, who obsessed some investigators and was frequently referenced in fiction. Tonio's "favorites" included the Long Island serial killer, the Freeway Phantom who had terrorized DC, the Alphabet murderer in upstate New York, San Francisco's Doodler and southern California's Night Stalker, the West Mesa murderer out of Albuquerque, the Daytona Beach killer and Philadelphia's Frankford Slasher.

For the past decade young men had also been popping up dead in bodies of water along the East Coast. Tonio rejected the official explanation – a series of accidental drowning incidents– and agreed with two retired detectives who suspected one or more serial murderers.

The mother of all serial killer mysteries was, of course, the case of Jack the Ripper. Tonio knew the basics by heart. England's legendary crime spree had begun on August 7, 1888 when the body of Martha Tabram was discovered near Batty Street in London's rough-and-tumble East End. The police investigated, but press reports about a possible serial killer didn't begin to circulate until weeks later.

On August 30, Mary Ann Nichols, one of thousands of London prostitutes, was brutally murdered in the same neighborhood. A week later, it was Annie Chapman. One witness suggested that the killer might have been a foreigner, possibly an American. Then, on September 30, a Sunday, Lizzie Stride and Catherine Eddowes were killed on the same night. In the weeks that followed, the crime spree set loose an international media frenzy.

The crimes were initially called the Whitechapel murders and became London's biggest news. Due to tax reform, an era of inexpensive publishing had just begun, including cheap mass-circulation newspapers and popular magazines like the *Illustrated Police News* that appealed to a working class audience. Together, the establishment and less respectable "yellow" press turned the hunt for the murderer, dubbed Jack the Ripper through a fabricated letter, into an unparalleled media event. Tales of grisly murder and a phantom killer were an irresistible, sure-fire circulation bonanza.

Most of the theories that had circulated since the Ripper's time sounded weak and unconvincing. But Tonio had reached the conclusion that it still might be possible to identify him, and spent considerable time on this coldest of cold cases. What drew his attention at the moment, however, was a less brutal mystery – why a long-dead politician from Minnesota seemed so familiar.

Instead of watching *The Wire* or trying to sleep, he skimmed through Donnelly's bio. In 1857, he and his young family had moved to the Minnesota Territory and settled in Dakota County, where Donnelly promptly tried to launch a utopian community called Nininger City with several confederates. An economic crisis doomed their attempt and left him in serious, long-term debt.

Many of the original settlers in this part of Minnesota were trappers and guides for the American Fur Company, or whiskey traders who sold to the Indians and soldiers at Fort Snelling on the Mississippi River. By 1838, however, the drinking and violence became such a local scourge that the post commander expelled all the civilians. Unfortunately that included a number of innocent bystanders, Swiss and German immigrant settlers living in or near the fort. They joined the banished traders in establishing a settlement nearby.

They named it Pig's Eye in candid recognition of Pierre "Pig's Eye" Parrant, the most notorious whiskey trader in the group. To the Dakota it soon became the place to get the Minne-wakan, the alcohol. Three years later, at the urging of the Catholic Church, the community's name was changed to St. Paul.

The Irish who came from points east saw it as a beacon of prosperity, a place where a resourceful man could get ahead and use his skills to good advantage, building a career and maybe even a political power base despite anti-Irish prejudice. One immigrant was Donnelly, originally from the O'Neil clan in County Tyrone. Turning from utopia-building to practical politics, the naturally charismatic and transparently ambitious young man was elected lieutenant governor of the new state in 1860, just three years after arriving, and became a Republican congressman within a few years more. In Washington he stood out as a reformer, pushing for a National Bureau of Education and improvement of the Indian Bureau. By the end of the Civil War Ignatius Donnelly was a rising political star. But he wasn't above striking dodgy deals to win, and made some powerful enemies along the way.

The rise of the Irish was closely linked to the prominence of the Church, and specifically to Archbishop John Ireland, and to the Canadian mogul James J. Hill, architect of the Great Northern Railroad. Hill was actually Protestant but used his friendship with the archbishop, a fellow empire builder, to shape the region's direction. Hill controlled the railroads, an integral link in the westward march that dominated the area's economy, and Ireland ran one of the most powerful dioceses in the country.

Virtually every aspect of the economy depended on Hill's railroad. His closest friends were bankers, other business titans, and Patrick Kelly, a grocer and Democratic Party boss who helped him seize control of the Minnesota machine. As Donnelly saw it, "Scratch the Democratic Party of this state and you will find Jim Hill." But Hill and his "Bourbon Democrats" saw clouds on the horizon, mainly in the form of a farmer and labor faction gaining a foothold in the party. Across the state the general impression was that St. Paul had become mired in Hill machine corruption. Among radical farmers his influence was considered as pernicious as the grain trust's hold over the Republicans.

In 1884 Donnelly campaigned for Democrat Grover Cleveland largely in the hope that his election might produce a little reform. After that victory, however, Hill passed the word to shut him out of the leadership. Instead, Kelly offered Donnelly a "mission abroad," an obvious ploy designed to remove him from the state's political landscape. He angrily declined.

Republican grain tycoon William Washburn, owner of Minneapolis Milling, shared Donnelly's distaste for Hill. But his reasons were related to strained business relations, not any political principles. Several years earlier Hill had declined an offer from Washburn to buy company stock in exchange for favorable shipping rates. That didn't mean Donnelly and Washburn were allies, in fact far from it. They'd been sparring for decades, ever since the 1868 House race in which Donnelly described Washburn as an "office beggar."

He was caught in the middle, locked in a political crossfire with two corporate kings.

So far, none of this rang a bell. But one of the books Donnelly wrote later in life related to a story first told to him by his uncle. "Reality is the lie we all agree on," Gianni had said the night they attended his first live Shakespeare production, a summer stock version of *Hamlet.*

"But what do we really know for sure? Take even this play," his mentor explained. "How do we know Shakespeare wrote it? One guy didn't think so and spent 20 years looking for a cipher in all the plays."

"What's that?"

"A secret mathematical code," he explained. "That's the core of cryptography. The guy went through every play using a formula to decode hidden messages that were supposedly concealed in the texts." Gianni even mentioned the book's name, *The Great Cryptogram*, the same title Tonio had noticed decades later next to Donnelly's biography on the shelf of a deadbeat attorney.

Now he cradled the huge, leather-bound antique in his lap. Along with the biography he'd taken it with him from the penthouse. The book was heavy, three inches thick, and contained almost a thousand pages, along with a decoded reproduction from the original folio that folded out from the center. The subtitle described it as "Francis Bacon's Cipher in the So-called Shakespeare Plays." Donnelly was also credited as the author of *Atlantis: The Antediluvian World* and *Ragnarok: The Age of Fire and Gravel.*

The Great Cryptogram had been published in Chicago by R. S. Peale and Company. Then he noticed the publication date –1888 – and made the connection; the same year the Ripper terrorized London, and the temporal link to Donnelly that had perplexed him earlier.

This is worth noticing, he realized. Nothing clear yet, but it resonated as synchronous and he would definitely pursue it with Danny, not to mention Angel. "There are no coincidences," he reminded himself. That was another thing Gianni used to say.

MANHATTAN, 2009

Tonio met Angel the same day he tested the prototype at the TELPORT office. Danny tapped her address and apartment number into the Locator and after a few seconds the face of an attractive, 30-something brunette popped on screen. Webster handed him the device.

"Hi, this is Angela Brancusi," said a seamlessly recorded version of her. "I'm sorry I can't come to the phone, but if you leave a message I'll get back to you. If you're calling about a production emergency, try my cell. Have a nice day." There was no pixilation or jerkiness, no buffering or out-of sync audio, just a high-definition video message that looked eerily like the real thing.

"This is good," said Tonio, moderately impressed.

"That's nothing. Wait for the beep and tell her to pick up. I know she's there."

"You can see and record?"

"Exactly. Here, let me…" Webster grabbed the device and held it a foot away. "Angel, pick up," he announced. "It's the meeting I mentioned yesterday."

The next thing he saw was a screen saver of Angel kickboxing at the camera. After a few seconds the image dissolved, replaced by Angela herself, wrapped in a towel as she faced the screen and dried her hair. What impressed him most was the image quality – and her figure.

"Damn it, Danny," she said. "This was supposed to be later."

"Change of plans. I needed to show our new partner what we have." He shifted the angle. "Antonio Wolfe, meet Angel Brancusi, director of operations."

"Tonio," he interrupted, grabbing the device for a better look. "Hello. I'm sorry. It's a pleasure to – see you."

Angel was frosty. "So, you're the Goomba whose daddy builds casinos? Can't say I'm impressed."

He already liked her. "Also hotels and malls," he answered, taunting back.

"Just so we're clear, I'm not happy with this arrangement. But it's not up to me, is it?" Then a glare that contained a challenge. Prove me wrong, she was telling him.

"Let's talk it over," he said. "Maybe I can change your mind."

She gave Tonio a long look before answering."Rain check, nice jacket though. Bye." Then dropped the towel and gave him a peek before the image dissolved.

The screen saver returned, ending the transmission with another recorded kick. He couldn't help feeling she was aiming at him. Talk about your mixed messages.

5

Demonstration

New York Times, October 5, 2012

Group Buying Long Island Estate for Tesla Memorial
A dream of 16 years came true for science enthusiasts on Friday when they struck a deal to buy a dilapidated estate on Long Island and transform it into a museum and educational memorial to Nikola Tesla, an eccentric genius who lit the world with alternating current but died penniless.

The Agfa Corporation, which owns the heavily wooded site and once operated a factory there, agreed to sell the estate to the Tesla enthusiasts for an undisclosed sum after they succeeded in raising $1.4 million through a Web campaign.

Before that day at TELPORT the name Tesla was no more than a historical rumor to him, some inventor a century ago, possibly real, conceivably a fictional character, who did risky experiments with electrical current. Tonio remembered David Bowie playing him in a Christopher Nolan film, *The Prestige*, the one in which two magicians compete over the world's best teleportation trick.

Now he knew a bit more. He had learned, for example, that Nikola Tesla was a visionary electrical and mechanical engineer, a physicist and a futurist, prime mover in the development of alternating current, inventor of the induction motor, neon lights and remote control, a showman and the holder of multiple patents who bet the farm on global wireless transmission eighty years before it happened.

"This is all Tesla," Danny said.

"Whatever," he replied, not yet getting the significance of Webster's explanation. "She could see me too?"

"True that. And it's saved."

"So, a kind of picture phone and camera."

Webster shook his head and giggled. "You're still missing it. Those categories aren't relevant anymore. First of all, that wasn't a phone call in the traditional sense. It's closer to Skype. You key in the place, almost any street or geographic location, an address, a landmark, a field in the middle of nowhere, even in many cases just a longitude and latitude on the map. There are icons for the different modes. Radical, no?"

"How was she seeing me?"

"In this case, on her TV screen. It could be a Locator, a computer tablet, almost any monitor or device, depending on the carrier deals and the package the consumer purchases. Add CCTV and you get pretty broad coverage. But there's more. We wanted to incorporate two more elements – a one-way GPS-based retrieval capability and a virtual reality experience. Look at this."

Tonio had forgotten about the black box, which Danny now slid to the edge of the long table, giving him a look that telegraphed "I'm about to blow your mind." Inside, cushioned in white foam, was a set of heavy-rimmed black sunglasses that looked like they had been crafted for a *Men in Black* or *Matrix* knock off. The frames were thick, apparently to accommodate wires connecting to dangling earplugs.

"It can be disorienting at first," he explained. "Some people get nauseous. We're still working on that, plus design, fabrication, everything. It's just a prototype. You use the Locator to find and select where you want to visit, and the Visors to see and hear it. The important thing is, no sudden moves. You'll want to, but don't. It disrupts the image at this point, and you'll trip over the furniture."

Tonio held the glasses gently in both hands and slipped them over his eyes. The view went black.

"Too soon," said Danny, amused by the eagerness. This made Tonio uncomfortable, and he removed the glasses to hand them back. Danny demurred and apologized. "I just mean, first you need to input the location. Think of it this way: You're getting in a car that can take you almost anywhere. The Locator is your console, the Visors are your eyes and ears. But first you need to decide where you want to go. So, where to?"

"Anywhere I want?" This was over-selling. There must be some kind of archive. "How about the top of the Empire State Building?"

"Easy-peasy," said Danny, activating the GPS function. He explained the options while selecting settings. "See, major buildings are accessible by name and floor. County or zip code is usually enough. For businesses, homes, most private structures you need a street address, some defined starting point. You can also use cartography mode, especially for outdoor locations. But for that you need to choose the elevation. So, ready to go?"

"Hit me," he said and slipped on the visors again.

The darkness was brief, followed by a flash of daylight, a frozen birds-eye view of Manhattan Island, followed after a second by a dramatic plunge at increasing speed. He almost fell before Danny steadied him.

"Jesus, this is live?"

"Absa-fucking-lutely."

The experience was total, enveloping, a breathtaking combination of surround sound and three-dimensional picture covering the entire peripheral field. It made 3D feel like 1950s television. The velocity of descent slowed until he settled onto the observation tower with a view of Manhattan on a windy afternoon. He could hear faint sound from the street far below, and noticed the subtle changes of light as clouds moved across a luminous sky.

"Now I'm impressed," he said, reaching out to touch the wall. He couldn't see his hands until Danny took one and put on a glove. When Tonio lifted it again into his field of vision the tip of each finger glowed. The Locator was also visible and he could input commands, or use a finger to move the cursor, visible as a blinking red dot.

"Try something else," Danny urged, an overgrown kid eager to show off his new toy.

"How about my father's place?"

"Outside or inside?"

"Are you kidding?" He abruptly removed the visors. "How are you doing this?"

Danny started by explaining that Tesla's reputation as a mad scientist was probably a cover story invented by the government to conceal the fact that many of his inventions were seized and pursued after his death. "You've heard of DARPA, right? Defense Advanced Research Projects. They did Total Information Awareness, that surveillance program under Bush – until word leaked out and Rumsfeld had to disown it. I heard it was re-launched. Anyway, they work in the same basic ballpark."

Little of this had made it onto Tonio's radar, but it sounded plausible enough and DARPA was a familiar acronym.

"The point is, we've been following up on high voltage power, what Tesla called radiant energy, using earth resonance and magnification. He worked out most of it in Colorado and on Long Island, in Shoreham, just after 1900. He was looking for the key to a world system for power generation and instant communication, cheap and plentiful. Can you imagine? But most of the money for the research came from financial figures like Astor and Morgan.

"He ran early tests out in Colorado using huge copper coils as magnifiers. Tesla realized messages and information could be transmitted anywhere without wires. But he was also close to a breakthrough on the collection and distribution of massive amounts of energy. He was looking at the electrical properties of the Earth. In Colorado Springs he shorted out the town's power during one of his experiments. But he had confirmed that the planet itself has a resonant frequency and could be used as a carrier.

"He published an article around that time, 'The Problem of Increasing Human Energy.' Some of it was strange, grandiose, borderline delusional. There was even some stuff about detecting bases on Mars and receiving radio signals from outer space. His rivals pounced, pushing out the madman theory. But his basic theory was sound and many of the leads we followed began right there. He discussed the Colorado experiments, and he claimed to have proof not only of global wireless but also that it was possible to generate millions of volts of electricity, cheaply and renewably.

"Tesla was already worrying about pollution and future energy supply. Morgan wanted to control transatlantic telegraphy – that's as far as he could see – and he recognized the value of Tesla's wireless patents. But he knew the guy was financially strapped after Colorado, so he was able to strike a bargain giving him 51 percent of both the wireless patents and 'cold light,' the name Tesla used for radiant energy."

Tonio urged him to get to the point.

"Ok, ok. So, he built the tower in Shoreham – a magnifying transmitter, almost 200 feet high, with a shaft deep in the ground and iron pipes hundreds of feet beyond that, all of this to tap the earth's potential. But he told Morgan it was mainly for wireless, you see, and then, at the end of 1901, when he was almost ready for a demonstration, Marconi succeeded with transatlantic wireless and Morgan got cold feet. Then Tesla came clean about the real purpose of the tower, his dream of cheap and unlimited energy. Right after that Morgan ended the partnership."

"Why?"

"He had an enormous stake in the electrical power grid being developed at that moment, and already controlled Tesla's patents. The theory is that he didn't want competition from a technology that could undermine his other investments."

"Motherfucker!"

Tonio recalled the conversation as if it was yesterday. The next day he had returned to Wood-Ridge and accepted Shelley's offer to become Chairman of TELPORT. He assumed that it was supposed to be a tax shelter or potential laundry, or both. But the old man didn't provide details or specific instructions, instead simply asking to be kept informed, picking one of his accountants to be CFO, and wishing Tonio luck – most of which made him suspicious.

He already had a few secrets of his own, of course. And more of them after Danny explained what else Tesla's theories, papers and plans had allowed the company to accomplish. The launch of the TELPORT Locator, in time for a last-minute holiday marketing push, would whet the public's appetite for the release of Visors about a year later. It would be a game changer in the tech sector. Investors were already knocking and orders were through the roof.

There was no need for Shelley to know, now or perhaps ever, that the technology could also be used for more explosive applications.

He was almost unconscious when the phone rang. "You up?" said Angel, more an order than an inquiry. "Webster says maybe we have a breach. What happened to you tonight?"

"Danny needs to chill," Tonio yawned. "Jesus, what time is it?"

"I don't know."

The clock said 3 a.m.. "Don't you sleep?"

"No, actually."

"Oh. Well, anyway I didn't say that. I just recognized someone and think it could give us something, an entry point, a location."

"Who?"

"This guy, Ignatius Donnelly. What a name, huh? Imagine the razzing in school."

He felt more relaxed with Angel than almost anyone except his mother, especially now that they were supposedly past their "relationship issues." After their first encounter on the SIL prototype, he thought she was arrogant, a stuck up bitch. But he still wanted to get her into bed.

When they finally did sleep together almost two years later, it was great for a few weeks. But he eventually couldn't handle the condescension that often crept into her attitude, and she came to see his crew, his use of marijuana and cocaine, and his unwillingness to break cleanly with Shelley's world – or even to discuss the issue, as evidence of a fundamental flaw. After several arguments, including one that almost turned physical, they mutually agreed to keep it professional and work at being friends.

"Want me to begin a search?" she asked helpfully on the phone.

"You read my mind."

6

TARGETING

TELPORT had two labs now, one to refine the technology and launch commercial applications like the Locator that Tonio tested in 2009, the other to pursue "field tests" and R & D. The former was open to the stock-holders, located in midtown, and used to test and tweak various iterations of the Locator and Visors. The latter was in an unmarked 77,000 square foot warehouse in Nutley, New Jersey, purchased surreptitiously in 2010, where they experimented with refining and navigating within the holographic projections produced by Danny Webster's invention.

As far as Tonio knew, no one in Shelley's orbit knew more than what was offered up in press releases. They needed to keep it that way.

Due to the storm it wasn't possible to reach the building until early the next week. On Tuesday most people were preoccupied with voting and the presidential race, an opportune moment to drop out of the loop for several hours. Angel's search had turned up plenty of information in the meantime to suggest that tracking Ignatius Donnelly might bring them closer to identifying Jack the Ripper. The writer had visited England at the time of the murders on a book tour for *The Great Cryptogram.*

"What have we got?" Tonio shouted at the phone as he reached the suburban parking lot.

The warehouse was at the far end of an industrial park that hadn't survived the country's economic meltdown. It shared a cul-de-sac with the remains of an abandoned radio station and its tall, latticed transmission tower. Few people knew the facility existed, and less than six had been inside since the remodeling and arrival of key parts fabricated and assembled in China.

Inside, the ground floor featured an antique cafeteria, dressing area and storage room at one end, and an elevator and wide stairway in the center leading to a mezzanine. A long hallway at the top was lined with offices on an outside wall and led to a large room that had been converted into their control room. It has also been extended to create a triangular observation deck providing a birds-eye view of the space below. Supported by stilts and located in a corner it was accessible via a ramp built into the wall. The remainder of the building was devoted to a cavernous space the size of a football field, with 40 foot clearance and enough room to contain much of a 19th century village. Thousands of coin-sized sensors were installed along the walls, ceiling and floor at 33-inch intervals.

By the time Tonio entered the Image Retrieval Chamber, also known as the View Room, and ascended the ramp, Angel was pulling up highlights of the dossier material she'd found since their late-night conversation. Tonio gave her a peck and flopped onto a couch facing the largest of several wall screens used to display feeds, photos, and research.

He loved this aspect of the job: instant access to a vast array of information gleaned from cyberspace, elite libraries, private collections, closed-circuit systems, and documents seen by just a handful of people. Better still, Angel provided the briefings. Tonio felt like the head of a clandestine intelligence group or a high-tech detective on a case.

"You already know something about his politics," she began. "Basically farm populism. By the early eighties, however, Donnelly thought his career was over and wrote the Atlantis book, then the other one about a comet hitting Earth. He tried to build his cases like a lawyer, you know, a rational assessment of various arguments. But he rarely challenged his own sources and was mainly synthesizing the crackpot science of the day, mixing in some progressive reform ideas and his personal religious thoughts.

"The newspapers christened him the 'sage of Nininger.' It wasn't really a compliment, Nininger being the name of his utopia, a well-known regional fiasco.

"He had balls, you have to give him that," she went on. "He obviously knew that writing a book claiming Shakespeare's plays were written by someone else would open him up to more ridicule. The man wasn't a fool, though potentially bipolar, so you do have at least one thing in common." He let that pass. "The Atlantis book sold well. But it was out there, and this one was an even bigger reach.

"The main reason he wrote it, I think, was a kind of obsession. He spent years deciphering secret messages he thought Francis Bacon had hidden in the text of the plays credited to Shakespeare."

Tonio had to know how Donnelly even came up with such a strange notion.

"I blame it on a rough winter," she joked. "Seriously, one winter he was trapped in a blizzard and he said the isolation led to him writing a lecture on whether Shakespeare was the author of the plays. Remember, this is Minnesota – and 1873 for fuck's sake. Cabin fever or creative breakthrough, you decide. After that nothing shows up for years. But we know he followed the debate swirling in English intellectual circles. He eventually became convinced that Shakespeare just didn't have the education – some researchers said he could barely read – while he considered Bacon a 'profoundly wise and great man.' That's from the Atlantis book.

"Who was Bacon?"

"A British statesman, philosopher, scientist and author, an actual renaissance man, Lord Chancellor for a while. More significantly, he's considered the father of the scientific method. Inductive methodology, empiricism – it used to be known as the Baconian Method. He's also supposedly connected to the Freemasons and Rosicrusians, though I have my doubts about that. In any case, you can make a case that he's the philosophical godfather of the industrial age. Jefferson called him one of the most influential people in world history.

"So, capable of it? Possibly. But to accomplish everything he did and also write the world's greatest plays, plus insert cipher messages and keep it absolutely secret. I enjoy a good conspiracy but that's a stretch, don't you think?

"Also, Bacon's book about Atlantis is possibly the first one in print. But his was called "New Atlantis" and was really about America. He predicted that the colonies would one day replicate the grandeur of the original Atlantis and become a perfect, golden society. So, we know he wasn't able to predict the future.

"Donnelly claimed at one point to have first discovered Bacon's cipher in 1882. However, there are references in his letters from years before. Basically, it looks like he set out to discover a secret code, and eventually he did. But keep in mind that other people were on the same wavelength. Here's Appleton Morgan, a railroad executive who wrote a related book, *The Shakespeare Myth*. He was the one who announced Donnelly's cipher to the world. After reviewing the evidence he concluded that either it existed or else Donnelly's discovery represented the world's most extraordinary coincidence."

"There are no coincidences," said Tonio.

"We'll see. I found an early mention of Donnelly and Shakespeare in *The New York Sun*, which said he risked becoming a 'ridiculous and despised figure in literary history' by pursuing the cryptogram. But we also have *The New York World,* which hired a mathematician who came away impressed with the computations."

"Is this going somewhere?"

"Just background, in case we want to view or retrieve something. He left for Europe on March 17 after a week promoting the book in Chicago. We know he was under pressure at the time, from the farmer-labor alliance to run for governor and the banks to pay debts. The night before leaving he stayed at Astor House on Broadway and composed a will. Then he boarded the Etruria, a steamship he described as small and dingy.

"He was definitely worried about money. The family needed at least $20,000 to hold onto the farm and repay lenders. Some of the letters sound desperate. In the will he left the rights to the new book to his wife." The ship docked in Liverpool on March 24th. A few days later he moved in with friends at 20 Duke Street in London, a nice second-floor flat in the city's "aristocratic" section.

"Does that match with the murder dates?"

"All but the last one. He was in Europe twice that year between March and October, mostly in London." Angel finished summarizing and then displayed a letter opening with "dearest wifey." It mainly described Donnelly's visit to an old church built with black flint. He wrote that the place looked as if it had been subjected to a form of intense volcanic action.

"What's the connection?"

"Don't be impatient," she teased. "I like the image. That was in late March, just days after he arrived. A few weeks later he spoke at Westminster Town Hall, one of his main engagements. We have a time and location for that, April 17, 1888, about a week before Shakespeare's birthday.

"And we care because?"

"Because we also have a letter to wifey in which he describes an encounter with someone who fits the Ripper profile."

7
SECRETS

NASA Aims for Space Settlements

WASHINGTON, DC, 11/5/10 -- A senior NASA official has promised to deliver a spaceship that will travel between alien worlds "within a few years." Speaking at a conference in San Francisco, NASA official Simon Worden said his division has started a project with Defense Advanced Research Projects Agency called the "Hundred Year Starship."

The project was kicked off recently with funding from DARPA and seed money from NASA. The hope is to use new propulsion ideas being explored by NASA. Worden said the space program was "now really aimed at settling other worlds."

"Twenty years ago you risked getting fired if you said, 'I think we'll be on the moons of Mars by 2030 or so,'" he explained. "Larry Page asked me a couple weeks ago how much it would cost to send people one way to Mars and I told him $10 billion, and his response was, 'Can you get it down to 1 or 2 billion?' So it's just a little argument over the price."

WOOD-RIDGE, 2010

The conversation was bland until coffee and dessert. Against his better judgment, Tonio accepted an invitation to attend dinner with the family over the Christmas holidays. But the latest stories about kids, vacations and home improvements were followed by inevitable arguments.

As a child he'd enjoyed family rituals, despite the disputes of the era – Carter and energy prices, the hostage crisis and Reagan, the meltdown at Three Mile Island and the nuke plant in East Shoreham near Long Island Sound. They would gather in Bayside at the palatial home where Shelley, Giancarlo and their three siblings grew up. Among Tonio's earliest childhood memories was Roman Wolfe presiding at a bountiful Christmas table in the formal dining room.

Tonio didn't remember much about two of his uncles – Alek and Georgie – both dead when he was around two. But he was close with Gianni and appreciated the sunny disposition of his aunt Vivian. After dinner they would spend hours opening presents, one by one, enjoying each reaction and anticipating the next surprise.

But this was Wood-Ridge and not Bayside, and Shelley was not the man his father was, a war-hardened Croatian immigrant who left Yugoslavia in the fifties with little but knowledge of construction, the phone number of a family associate in New Jersey, and a flexible attitude toward the use of illegal means and violence to achieve the American Dream. By the time Tonio was born, Roman Lupinjak, who changed his name to Wolfe, was the owner of Wolfe Enterprises, a construction business that concealed involvement in pornography, prostitution, money laundering and murder.

To Tonio he was Grandpa, the benign family patriarch who distributed candy and provided unconditional love.

Even then, however, death was no stranger to the family. In 1974 uncles Al and George perished in a plane crash during their return flight from a Florida construction site. Inconsolable, Roman deteriorated and suffered a fatal stroke in 1977. Tonio was only five years old at the time. Five years later uncle Gianni died. He never accepted the official explanation of that, a sudden heart attack at forty-two while on his regular jogging route.

Over coffee Tania, one of Vivian's kids, brought up Wikileaks, the whistleblower group that had released a slew of State Department documents shortly after Thanksgiving. "All their dirty little secrets are out," she chirped, "all in one big, stinking dump."

"Tanny, that's disgusting."

"That's what they call it, mom, a document dump. They released over 250,000 cables. Now we know the truth."

"Oh really," Shelley sniffed. "What truth is that, honey?"

He was asking for trouble. Tania, a college junior majoring in political science, was prepared to defend her position.

"The truth? Our embassies around the world are involved in spying, that's one. Also, we've bribed countries into accepting detainees in exchange for aid, and then let them be tortured. Or how about this? Did you know we support the Kurdish Workers Party in Turkey? The Turks and the US say it's a terrorist group. I mean, total hypocrisy.

"And oh, in 2003 the CIA kidnapped a German citizen, and they took him to a secret prison in Afghanistan, and they tortured him and held him there for months. And when they were done they just dropped him off on a hillside in Albania. Afterward, they pressured the Germans not to prosecute the agents who did it."

She was just getting started but Shelley's hand wave said enough. "Where are you getting this?" It came off as an accusation.

"Newspapers, Julian Assange. Where have you been, gramps?"

"Oh that one, he should be in prison, that one. It's treason, what he did."

A few years earlier Tonio would have said nothing. More accurately, he would have had nothing much to add. But what he had learned since taking on the first serious work of his life made it more difficult to accept Shelley's knee-jerk blustering. Tania was being provocative but she was on the right track. Tonio was no longer so willing to swallow his feelings or conceal his contempt.

"Sunlight is the best disinfectant," he said, "that's what G used to say.

And he worked for the State Department." He glared at Shelley. "It was State, right? I agree with Tanny. We need whistleblowers. We wouldn't know about the secret prisons without them. And the body armor – we had troops in battle without decent armor until someone said something. Some things need to be secret, no argument. But the reason some of it stays secret is because it's embarrassing, or against the law."

Shelley wasn't happy. "It's a free country so we can have a civil discussion here," he offered, trying to sound flexible while simultaneously playing Alpha dog and family patriarch. "But I say he has blood on his hands, Assange. I like Steve King's idea – treat him like an enemy combatant, get him and take him to a military tribunal."

Tonio hit back, "So, you'd rather not know what the government is doing?"

"In our name," Tania added supportively.

"Don't be naïve," Shelley snapped. "Things need to be done, in business, in government, in private. Not everything belongs on the Internet. Gianni knew that, by the way. He was a patriot. And he would have been the first to go after an anarchist like that albino. He worked on important projects.

"It's always better to surprise your enemy than be the one who gets surprised," he finished. "G appreciated that."

It was accurate, as far as it went. But working with Danny and Angel had introduced Tonio to a more complex and cynical view. For decades, he'd learned, various federal agencies conducted secret operations, questionable experiments and selective assassinations that had little to do with the public platitudes of political leaders.

He now knew, for example, that DARPA, the agency supposedly launched in response to the Russia's Sputnik, was really an R & D wing of the military industrial complex, engaged in everything from hypersonic research to lightweight satellites. In recent years it had been working on high-energy lasers, advanced aircraft, automatic target recognition, submicrometer electronic technology, electron devices, the Strategic Defense Initiative – also known as Star Wars – and a congressionally-mandated particle beam program directly related to Tesla's original research. But Danny said the publicly-acknowledged projects represented only a fraction of what the Defense Advanced Research Projects Agency had been doing for the last half century.

One example among the many was the suspected use of children in a series of top-secret experiments known as Project Pegasus. The name had triggered the memory of a trip with Gianni to Nutley, and standing in another cavernous room with a gang of kids to see what was described to them as the latest innovation in 3D filmmaking.

Shelley had mentioned his brother's "important" work. "What projects," Tonio asked, "do you know?" He had been waiting to pose the question for months. In hindsight, the likelihood that his uncle worked for the State Department looked slim. He wasn't the type for purely diplomatic missions. More like a field operative, a guy you sent in with a team to rescue hostages or conduct sabotage.

"He couldn't talk about it," barked Shelley. "And he didn't. Like I said, he was a patriot. He followed orders. Loyalty, duty – that used to make a difference."

"Did he ever talk about DARPA?"

Shelley flinched but tried to conceal his reaction with a joke. "Yeah, I remember him dating somebody with that name."

"It's a government agency," Tania injected.

Now Tonio knew Shelley was holding back. One of his own companies was a subcontractor involved in building the agency's new headquarters in Arlington, just a few miles from the Pentagon. Shelley's clumsy evasion added to the growing suspicion that his uncle never completely left the military, and instead went into a defense project like DARPA. It was even possible that the official version of his death was a cover up.

When he brought the suspicions to Marcia Siegel she suggested he might be clinging to the past. He'd begun therapy after a series of nightmares in which he was huddled with other children in a middle of a high-tech battlefield. For some reason, however, none of the bullets or lasers whizzing past injured anyone in his group. In another dream he was in a space station, gazing out a porthole at Earth in the distance. After a few moments he had to gasp for breath.

Danny encouraged him to record the dreams. They might mean nothing, or they could be distorted glimpses of repressed memories. It sounded like psycho-babble, but he also provided more reasons to think that DARPA was a piece of the puzzle he needed to complete.

"You see it mentioned in fiction and films all the time," Danny said. "Self-aware computers, super-bombs, experimental planes. That's all DARPA and they use the real acronym. The only one close to reality is that TV show *Numb3rs*. But it's all basically a public distraction, part of the cover up. They want the agency's image to be so out there you'll just think, 'Oh, that couldn't possibly be real. It's all science fiction.' Meanwhile in the real world, DARPA has a budget of more than three billion dollars – that's only what we know about – but a staff of less than 300 people. About half of them are technicians. They like to think of it as a covert network of geniuses connected by a travel agent.

"They collect talent like action figures," Danny joked. "That's how they stay at the cutting edge."

A few days after the Christmas debate Tonio got a call. Danny wanted to rendezvous in Nutley, where work was under way on their off-the-books lab. The idea was to run tests on a holographic remote viewing system that would, hopefully, be ready within a few years. It would ultimately be possible to view and explore distant locations without wearing visors, to stand in a field of super-charged particles and be virtually transported to another place. Hypothetically, with enough storage capacity, you would be able to record and replay an entire "visit."

The warehouse windows had been blocked off. Surveillance cameras installed on all sides of the building swept a vacant parking lot, entry corridor and radio tower across the lot. Before Tonio reached the door Danny hailed him through a speaker above the key pad. He heard a buzz before the lock released and the door opened.

The main chamber seemed empty. He looked past the support poles, up the ramp at control room. He could see Danny waving from behind plate glass. "Stay there," he announced over the PA.

"Are we running a test?"

"Yes, though we can't stabilize it for very long. But that's not why you're here."

"Is there a problem?"

"I'll come down." He said something to Angel off-mike before sprinting down the glass-shielded gangplank recessed in the wall. "Ok. We've found something…new. We think it must be related to alignment of the shaft and pipes, or possibly our location. We were following the plans from Wardenclyffe, Tesla's generator and tower. We retrofitted and extended the radio transmitter next door and based our generator on his radiant energy plans. Below us is a hundred foot shaft, and 16 pipes down another 300 feet beyond that."

Danny paused, his brow furrowed as he struggled for the right words. Tonio had seen that happen so seldom it made him uneasy.

"You have to use visors. We haven't worked out full-spectrum projection. But I think you'll get the point." He handed Tonio the dark spectacles, which had gone from clunky to aero-chic in two years. "Remain in one place, Ok? But you can look around to get the whole 360. I picked the location because of the talk we had about the Ripper. Angel did the workup."

"Can't wait," Tonio said.

Danny ran back up the ramp yelling, "Remember, it won't last long." Then, before slamming the control room door, "Stay put! Find a spot and wait. We have to scan you."

Tonio was alone, just about to put on the visors, when the room went black.

8
Theories

The experience was so overwhelming he had to catch his breath. For about twenty seconds Tonio was on Whitechapel High Street in London, standing in front of a pub with a hanging sign that read White Swan. It was late in the evening, after 10 p.m. but warm, and he was on a narrow, shabby thoroughfare watching middle-aged prostitutes teasing potential clients in uniform.

He was careful not to move but turned his head gradually to take in the panorama of a rough, active neighborhood lined with pubs and clubs, half-timber cottages, bow front homes and jerry-built hovels. If asked he would have called it a ghetto. In a few seconds he noticed drunken sailors, gaudy whores, incoherent tramps, hunkered-down immigrants, and a few slumming gentlemen in capes and long over-coats. Stifling smoke and gas fumes filled the air and a stream of dirty water ran down the rough street.

Everything looked and sounded absolutely real. The only obvious difference he noticed was the absence of smell to match the squalor he saw and heard.

This wasn't the London he had visited as a tourist. It was a place he'd only read about – the same neighborhood in which Jack the Ripper had stalked victims more than a century ago. He was there, he said to himself, although he rationally knew that he was in a New Jersey ware-house. Looking down, it was disorienting not to see a body or arms, just manure-spotted cobble stones.

He knew this place from movies and books, but none of that prepared him for the intensity of the poverty and overall atmosphere of degradation. He also thought he recognized one of the prostitutes. Not tall or especially young but attractive, with dark hair and a dusky complexion. She was wearing a black bonnet and a long black jacket over an old green skirt, a brown petticoat and stockings below that. The outfit was finished with side-spring boots. She was obviously drunk and laughing a bit too loudly. One of the sailors threw a possessive arm over her shoulder.

It was Martha Tabram, possibly the first victim of the most notorious killer of the 19th century. She was murdered nearby within hours of this moment on August 7, 1888, on the first floor landing of George Yard, a narrow corridor off High Street leading to Wentworth. She was stabbed thirty-nine times.

As Martha and her John walked away Tonio forgot Danny's warning not to move and attempted to follow. The projection immediately shuddered and the chamber filled with a squeal that lasted about ten seconds before abruptly ending. The moment froze, then went to black and left him alone in the center of the empty warehouse.

"Trippy, right?" Danny sprinted down the ramp as the lights came up, Angel close behind him.

"Where did you get that?" Tonio demanded. "It must be a recreation. What? Is James Cameron doing *Avatar* meets *Sherlock Holmes*?"

"No, man. You were there, in London, in the exact place on the same day that Martha Tabram died. The first victim, right? Or more accurately, London was here."

Tonio didn't believe it. Capturing and projecting a three dimensional feed from some distant location was one thing, this was something else entirely. He hesitated to even use the words. "Time travel?"

"Not really travel," Angel corrected. "You didn't go anywhere. That would involve teleportation. This was just an advanced form of image retrieval and holographic reassembly."

"No, no, that's not all this is. But the question right now is how? Or why?"

Danny had ideas but no definitive answers. "Tesla said that radiant energy is pervasive in the universe and has the latent capacity to bend time-space," he offered. "But that was theoretical. The problem is that information can't travel faster than the speed of light, at least that's what we've believed. So the first question becomes, how can information sort of 'get there before it gets there?'"

"One possibility is tachyons," said Angel, "particles that travel faster than light and backwards in time. But I think the answer has more to do with quantum entanglement. When you entangle two particles, their properties are no longer independent of one another. They're linked, even if you separate them in space. That means if you can measure a particle and discover its properties you instantaneously also discover the other particle's properties, even if it's very far away."

Danny picked up the thread. "Einstein called that idea 'spooky action at a distance.' He wasn't really a fan of quantum theory but the phrase caught on. It relates to the idea of quantum teleportation. This isn't teleportation in the traditional sense of actually moving a person or some object through space or time. But information is being moved in a form of superluminal communication. And that's pretty close to retrocausality."

"You've lost me."

"We're all flying a little blind here. These are open questions in science. Retrocausality would imply a fundamental change in how we understand gravity as well as physics. Is a closed timeline curve possible? Under most scenarios no. But what if? What if the energy source and environment here resonate to create a traversable wormhole? Then retrocausality can't be ruled out.

"On the other hand, Hawking talks about chronology projection conjecture, which would eliminate the timeline curve before someone could use it," Danny added. "So, I certainly don't claim to have the last word. But the fact is, we've stumbled onto something, a quantum window to remote view not just a distant location but an entirely different time."

Almost two years later Danny still had lingering questions about all the parameters and variables. But now a holographic projection of the past could be stabilized for at least an hour before collapsing. They could also explore without visors and move around the huge warehouse. Tonio could anyway, Danny preferred the control room and Angel repeatedly declined to try.

During the same period, by keeping a record of his dreams, Tonio continued to recover images from his childhood. The most disturbing conjecture was that Gianni probably did have some connection with DARPA, or had volunteered him, at around eight, as a test subject in something. He clearly remembered visiting a facility where he and other children took what felt like intense, often confusing and sometimes terrifying fantasy vacations. He remembered Gianni saying he was so special that he'd been chosen to try out new thrill rides and effects. There would be tests after each, but it would be fun anyway and the best rides would be used at Disney World or another amusement park. So, he was helping to pick rides for the rest of the children. He felt honored at first.

One ride involved entered a brightly-lit chamber, waiting a while and then sliding down some kind of soft, twisty tunnel that seemed to open out of the floor. But instead of ending up in the water, he found himself standing in a scene from history. One time he witnessed the signing of the Constitution, another he watched Lincoln deliver the Gettysburg

Address. After each trip, he went through a physical exam and debriefed with a woman in uniform who asked a lot of questions about how he felt and what he remembered.

Other rides were futuristic. He visited a strange city on a weird gassy planet, he watched Earth in the distance from the bridge of a space station, and met beings that combined the traits of humans and something else entirely. Some experiences were frightening even thirty years later. For some tests, he was asked to wait in a small, tightly-sealed chamber that felt like solitary confinement. Eventually, a cavern would open and envelop him, inducing extreme dizziness as he was propelled through an endless tunnel and almost blacked out. When he regained consciousness he was standing alone in the middle of a boiling, desolate landscape. After a few seconds, just enough time to panic, the cavern would reopen and pull him back through the tunnel to the starting point.

When Tonio described these experiences, Danny said it reminded him of Project Pegasus, which allegedly involved gifted children. In Greek mythology Pegasus was the divine horse, an offspring of Poseidon, who brought lightning and thunder from Mt. Olympus. "Symbolically it relates to energy access, some kind of godlike power," he explained.

In New Jersey, New Mexico and other places, Danny claimed that DARPA had gone over the technological rainbow with experiments that studied the physiological and psychological effects of remote viewing and other para-normal processes. Some researchers were convinced about the Montauk Project, psychics trained in mind control, telekinesis and manifestation, or the Philadelphia Experiment before it.

The government denied rumors when necessary, and perhaps some of this was urban legend or wishful thinking. But Tonio knew that strange things were indeed possible and, in fact, little of this was completely new. References to remote viewing, even physical teleportation, appeared in ancient literature and religious texts. In Kabalistic writing "Kefitzhat

Haderach" was the term for "contracting the path," a reference to traveling between distant places in an abbreviated period of time. Examples also popped up in the Talmud and other Jewish texts. The concept was often linked to clairvoyance and E.S.P.

Much of what he had "recovered" might simply be suggestion, stimulated by his work with TELPORT and their recent discovery. But he also respected his hunches, and one taking hold was that his favorite uncle had volunteered him as a guinea pig in some highly secret, probably unethical and potentially dangerous experiments.

9
THE VIEW STREAM

Launching the Locator exceeded expectations. Angel thought the marketing push was a bit much, but she couldn't deny the buzz. Production was humming. Danny Webster was in such high demand that he didn't have time to accumulate new debts buying techno-kitsch or placing bets. Beyond such encouraging signs, so much money would be made on Locators, Visors, applications and accessories that no one would notice an out-of-the-way R & D facility in New Jersey.

At least that was the plan.

Tonio had come up with the name, convincing Danny and the team that it didn't matter what SIL meant or if sequence interception was at the heart of the patent. Eventually, everyone was on board with Remote Viewing. Despite associations with CIA mind control legends and forms of E.S.P. it vividly described what distinguished this from any other handheld device on the market, while the slogan promised freedom and instant gratification. They could play endlessly with the initials RV and VR as they rolled out Visors, modifications and, eventually, the ultimate virtual reality experience– the full-scale View Room.

They decided to base the slogan for the rollout on an old hippie saying: *Wherever You Look There You Are.* He even had a catch phrase for the VR campaign next year:

You *can* be in two places at once.

Since his first view of Whitechapel there had been other trips as they extended the period for which a projection stream could be captured. Danny eliminated the need for visors and overcame the disruption initially caused by movement. But there was a difference between using a Locator to contact someone else who had one of their own, or even retrieving a live stream from another place via sequence interception in your home, and standing in the View Room examining the stream from another time period.

The ability to view the past was linked to the starting location. While both recording the stream and playing it back was ultimately a question of memory, it only worked inside the warehouse. There was some process at work that not only amplified the available power but created a closed timeline curve. However this occurred, it helped create the conditions for retrocausality. The View Room was a one-way wormhole window. The person watching was a phantom, invisible at the other end. It didn't actually teleport you to another place or time; instead, the place or remote time somehow wrapped itself around the present, limited by the physical boundary of the SIL sensors.

"How long will I have?"

Angel ran the numbers. "Two hours max, probably less," she announced minutes later. "The letter says that they originally met on the Etruria, sometime during the trip over. That's why he noticed the man at Westminster and mentioned it. No name, but he made an impression. The second encounter was at the reception right after the lecture."

"Is there some description, something to identify him?" Tonio already knew that the person described by Donnelly was a doctor, an American or Canadian who made a good living selling a cure of some kind. He had a business, most likely based in New York, but had set up a branch operation in London.

"Tall, close to six feet, big moustache, in good shape. Also, he was wearing a cape when Donnelly saw him at Westminster. He wrote that it looked almost like a costume, vaguely military, but it was impossible to tell whose army."

What made it a serious lead was the letter's reference to the "museum" of anatomical specimens he had shared during the voyage to England. Donnelly couldn't forget the glass jars in which he kept a collection of female organs, sexual and otherwise. He called them the "matrices of every class of woman." His apparent disdain for females made it all the more repulsive, and worthy of note when the same character showed up at his talk.

Donnelly wrote: "I found it especially disquieting, that this dandy, a man with such disdain for women, would travel with these specimens, but also the way he spoke of them. He could not bear to have women near him, or so he claimed. He charged them as universal imposters responsible for all the troubles of the world."

It read like the profile of a sociopath, a man who absolutely might carve up women in the dead of night. Tonio's idea, one he hadn't yet discussed with the team, was that they could accomplish something revolutionary and historic – identify the world's most notorious perp. They could bring back photographs and perhaps catch him in the act. It would be quite the hook for a product launch. When they went public, he wanted to do it with dramatic proof that also suggested a serious social purpose – solving crimes.

Anything could be faked with digital tricks these days. But if this worked, it would someday be possible to show who really killed Kennedy or Martin Luther King. Jr.

Angel thought he was being naïve. She was savvy enough to respect the significance of the breakthrough, and saw little harm in letting Tonio – board chairman, but more importantly the only effective buffer between TELPORT and Shelley Wolfe – pursue his hobby while they worked on why the project had taken such an unexpected turn. But she was also seriously worried. Angel saw more potential that remote viewing would be used for control and illegal spying than for police work and unlocking historical mysteries.

In the wrong hands, it could be dangerous, she warned, an enormous threat to civil liberties. Far beyond just observing people in public, the technology could be used, by whoever ultimately controlled it, to violate the privacy of everyone, spying on their past and even changing their futures. Libertarian doubts about whether it should be released reinforced her natural hesitation to try it for herself.

Danny stayed out of the debates about politics or the moral implications. He was having too much fun being a media wunderkind. Still, Tonio heard the rumors via Paulie. The young wizard was also placing bets at the track again, nothing major yet but a red flag suggesting trouble ahead.

They agreed that the view stream should be opened at exactly 9:00 p.m. Greenwich Mean Time, on April 17, 1888, a Tuesday, at latitude 51.498545 – longitude 0.134951, 24 meters (or 79 feet) above sea level, just outside Westminster Town Hall on Caxton Street. Not far away a young Winston Churchhill had just spent his first day at Harrow. Four miles from the spot, Joseph Merrick, the Elephant Man, was entertaining friends at London Hospital on Whitechapel Road, in the same neighborhood where the Ripper would soon be stalking his victims.

Angel's best estimate was that the lecture began around 7:30, with the reception following in the same location. He would have no more than two hours to explore, in an area containing most of the building and as much environs as could be contained within the boundary of the warehouse walls. He would be an uninvited ghost, unable to interact but free to eavesdrop on anyone he saw.

To overcome the problem of elevation – the projection was solid and three-dimensional, but insubstantial – flexible wires were installed in the ceiling so that he could "fly" to an upper floor or higher elevation when necessary. He no longer needed visors but wore a mike to communicate with the control room. The stream looked translucent and confusing, a faded jumble of overlapping surfaces and figures with an overgrown Peter Pan dangling in its midst, intermittently shouting orders to shift position.

"Let's go there," he shouted, testing the wires with an energetic leap. They adjusted automatically to lower him back to the ground.

Tonio heard a low hum as the observation lights faded. It was dark but he could pick out the sensors. Then the glowing dots sprayed the space with light and he was outside a late 19th century building at the corner of Caxton and Palmer Streets. The red brick and sandstone façade looked new in the gaslight glow. It was dark and foggy but he was in the right place. Everything looked solid and real, just slightly faded in comparison to him.

Pulling on the wires while giving directions, he floated through the front door. There were two primary public spaces inside, Great and York Halls. He knew Donnelly was in Great, the larger of the two, normally the place for concerts. He was already speaking when Tonio entered. The audience was in the hundreds and seemed mainly literary, religious or middle bourgeois. But they looked fatigued, and in some cases confused, after struggling with Donnelly's dense, complex arguments for two hours. Some had already left.

Donnelly was short, a solid man with keen blue eyes. He looked like a merchant but spoke like a natural motivator in a pleasant, carefully-modulated voice. He wore a black coat, vest and turned-down collar, and addressed the room with jovial charm. Most of the audience had come at the invitation of the Bacon Society. Still, they were having trouble with his intense hostility to the man most Britons called The Bard.

After more than an hour going through the cipher with diagrams and math, he turned to a withering deconstruction of Shakespeare's humble beginnings, "menial occupations in early life," and limited education. The real Will Shakespeare had no legal training, he explained, while the plays displayed the broad knowledge of a learned man who was most likely a lawyer. Bacon was the logical choice, a highly literate gentleman who was the acknowledged father of modern philosophy. When Shakespeare grew up, he reported with disdain, there weren't even books in his home.

He also suggested, with some heckling from the floor, that Ben Johnson and other literary lights had engaged in "a common fraud" designed to deprive Bacon of his copyright "in favor of the butcher boy." Sensing resistance, Donnelly wound up with a more persuasive argument.

"There is a battle underway in the world, between intelligence and concentrated ignorance," he proclaimed. It was now almost an hour after Tonio arrived. "Here, and in America, open-minded people have begun to reconsider this question and other traditional beliefs. We live in revolutionary times, my friends, with expanding networks of transportation and communication, large and dominant corporate enterprises, and a looming transformation in business management and worker relations.

"I understand the strong attachment of Englishmen to their Shakespeare, author of the world's most extraordinary body of literature," he said. "I ask only that you give this matter due and fair consideration. Your *Daily Telegraph* has taken it up, and numerous articles and informative letters have been published. I now add my own thoughts, the result of 15 years of steady and careful research, and offer them to the public with overwhelming documentation and arguments that have yet to be answered.

"This old and cherished belief may be obsolete," he concluded, "but

The Bard, whoever he was, remains an Englishman and the greatness of his contribution to the world is unchallenged and unchanged."

The applause was respectful but brief. As Tonio scanned the hall most of the audience moved toward the exit and a few hardcore Baconians collected Donnelly's charts, covered with figures and computations. The speaker remained at the lectern, still brimming with energy as he exchanged random views with sponsors, a few journalists and those invited to meet him.

No one fit the description in Donnelly's letter.

"How did you originally get the idea there was a code hidden in the plays?" The question was from a woman about Tonio's age, probably a reporter. She was petite, with a sweet face and blonde hair just beginning to show specks of silver. Rather than an evening gown, she wore a short plain skirt that skimmed the top of thick, laced boots. In place of a choker necklace or other jewelry she draped a bright red scarf around her neck.

"I have been looking at Bacon as the possible author since the early seventies," Donnelly answered. "But it was just five years ago that I learned that, among his many accomplishments, he also invented one of the most complex ciphers ever written. That sent me back to work. In the end, I discovered that the first folio edition of the plays contained the arithmetical cipher, based on a peculiar way of paging, hyphenating and italicizing."

"But didn't you worry that it might damage your political work?"

Donnelly was thrown off guard by the bluntness of her question. Tonio loved it.

"My dear lady," he replied defensively, "my supporters in the Farmers Alliance are not influenced by reviews. They know where I stand."

President Watts attempted to cut off the exchange on behalf of the Baconians. The reporter ignored him and pressed on. "Sir," she insisted, "you have been an important spokesman for labor and farm groups, a builder of national coalitions, a bulwark against the lumber interests and a defender of reform."

"You've done your homework, I see."

"I'm a journalist and an advocate," she said. "And I know the value of one's public image. And that's my question: Why do you risk the high opinion in which you have been held for decades with such speculative theories, especially one bound to alienate some of your natural allies, one that will have no impact on the struggles of today?"

Snap, Tonio thought. The girl has game. Too bad she's not really here.

Angel's voice in his ear announced that time was running out and asked whether he had seen anyone of interest. "No serial killers who enjoy the odd talk on obscure cryptography and literary conspiracies?"

"Nothing yet, but I see someone I'd like to meet up close."

"Typical."

The reception was winding down. It was possible, he had to confess, that someone might have slipped past him since most of the men wore virtually identical frock coats or ditto suits, a standard three-piece out-fit with vest and trousers. A few wealthier gentlemen were dressed in cutaway morning suits with dress shirts and ascots, or dark tail coats. Maybe it was a dead end, a historical wild goose chase. What was he doing anyway? Hanging in the middle of a warehouse waiting for a long-dead villain. This began to feel ridiculous.

But Donnelly was clear about the encounter, and there was a late arrival entering the room. He looked tall enough, with a dominant black moustache, dark eyes and uncommonly clear complexion, a dandy in a long cape and officer's cap, and he strode forward as if he was the person they had waited to meet.

Interrupting the conversation, he took command with a partial apology. "I have missed the main event, I fear, but it was a great success, am I right?" The accent was American. "Or am I right?"

Donnelly seemed uncomfortable but extended a hand. "Sir, a pleasure to meet again. The pimple cure, is it?" The man nodded. "Yes, we had a frank and serious exchange."

"I'm sure, despite any nay-saying," he added, staring down at the journalist.

"Dialogue," she corrected. "Civil discourse."

"Quite right," said Donnelly, stepping between the two. "And I certainly appreciate that priorities and opinions will vary. I must make my case in the court of public opinion, and let me just say, I trust the jury."

It was close to 11 and President Watts was ushering people to the exit. Tonio stayed with the cluster around Donnelly, listening for a name or clue to the man's identity. The discussion had turned to American politics and Donnelly revealed that he might re-enter the fray, despite his passion for writing and history, once the book tour ended.

"We look forward to that," the reporter said. "We need something radical, a new fellowship to challenge the landlords and the corporations, reform the workhouses and reduce the hours of toil."

"Just the claptrap you would expect from the female of the species," said the stranger.

"None of it." Donnelly beamed. "Well said, my dear. Just ignore him. For whom do you write?"

"The Link," she told him. "A half-penny paper, the true voice of the people."

The man in the cape retreated, chastened, but watched the conversation from the edge of the group with a growing, transparent contempt for the views being expressed. After a few more minutes he gave a shallow bow in Donnelly's direction and turned to leave.

Tonio followed, hovering ahead of the stranger as he exited the building and strolled down Caxton Street. But the boundary of the projection didn't reach the corner. He slammed into the warehouse wall and had to watch helplessly as his target passed by and vanished into the fog.

"Shit," he shouted. "It could be him. We're recording, yes?"

Swinging back rapidly he reentered the Great Hall in time to catch more of the conversation. Now the reporter was briefing Donnelly about the Fabian Society and the Socialist League, demonstrations in Trafalgar Square and the general brutality of the police. Donnelly made it clear to the few people still listening that, although he was certainly sympathetic, personally he was no socialist. Then he thanked his informant for the summary and asked for her name.

"Annie Besant," she replied with a firm clasp of his hand.

Tonio floated closer. Almost a century before he was born, he thought, and this woman shows more guts – and makes more sense – than most people he knows. If only he could really, physically go back and see if they have any chemistry.

10
SITE VISIT

Remote Viewing (RV) Visors wouldn't be released to the consumer market for at least a year. Meanwhile, the TELPORT staff was constantly testing and improving them. The new lenses could be adjusted to balance remote projections with the proximate environment. You could view someone or someplace as a three dimensional projection, and also keep track of what was directly in front of you, either by adjusting the intensity or assigning the remote stream to one eye.

There were only twenty-five prototypes at this point. Tonio made sure that Paulie received a pair. They had been seeing less of each other and he wanted to share what he could. Without GPS capability Paulie couldn't do much except surf the web, sometimes while driving, and call a few people equipped with other Locators. But he could do it in VR mode. His old friend was thrilled.

A week after Tonio's remote time viewing (RTV) in Westminster Hall they caught up over beer and a bong, then took a helicopter ride across the city out 60 miles to an abandoned estate on the north shore of Long Island. The hurricane devastation he saw along the coast was a shock, billions in damage, homes and businesses under water, a half million people still living without power.

The media said it had helped re-elect Obama and brought the conversation back to climate change. "Ray-Ray says the weather was manipulated by the government," shouted Paulie. "You know, to help the Democrats. He saw it on the Internet."

"Ray-Ray is an idiot," Tonio yelled back over headphones.

Shelley was waiting for them in front of a crumbling brick building not far from the shore. He had arrived separately with three of his men, an obsequious architect and his trophy wife, Lisa Margret Wolfe, a former runway model a few years younger than Tonio.

"Isn't it fabulous?" Lisa gushed. She waved at the once-attractive, early 20th century structure and overgrown property surrounding it. "It's going to be the best, most talked-about museum in the world. New buildings, world-class exhibits, working labs and the best interactive experiences for children and families."

He had to admit it wasn't the worst location, about 15 acres close to a local post office and fire station. Much of it was overgrown and the building needed serious rehab, but there was room for additions and parking, and the Italian Renaissance architecture of the existing structure provided an anchor that suggested a certain old-world charm.

Still, something didn't add up. "We're building museums now?" he tested. "Did you have some kind of political rebirth last week?

"More like a near death experience. I'm still trying to figure out what Karl Rove did with all my money. But I thought you should see this place," Shelley said. "I'm getting into philanthropy. The economy here could use a lift and this project has been stuck in the mud for a while. AGFA put the land and this place up for sale a few years back. Friends of Science, local do-gooders, launched a web campaign that raised a ton of cash. But now they gotta develop it, which takes time and a lot more money…"

Lisa cut him off. "And Shelley thought, with all his success putting together hotel projects and so on, why not help them make this happen?" She patted his arm as if her husband was a child who had turned in a strong effort on his test. "And this building has such a great history. Do you know who built it?" He had no idea.

"He's famous, like Lloyd White." She meant the architect Frank Lloyd Wright. "He was in that movie about the showgirl and the black man who wants the police to repair his car, and then he blows up a museum. The architect, the one who designed this building, was in the movie, and he was killed in the middle of Madison Square Garden – which had a real garden then – in the middle of a huge party by a crazy husband from Philadephia. True story."

"*Ragtime*," he said. "That was the movie, great film. You must be talking about Stanford White. Norman Mailer played him in the film."

"That's him. I get them confused. This is the one with the showgirl, and her husband killed him."

Unlike the other one, Tonio considered saying. In Frank Lloyd Wright's case, his second wife was the one who ended up dead when a deranged servant killed her and set fire to his dream house. He also knew about White, a legendary and ultimately tragic figure in New York high society's golden age, and realized that Lisa was right. Stanford White had created the original Madison Square as a business block on the corner of Madison and 26th, with an open-air rooftop theater and gleaming tower topped by a bronze Diana. His architectural firm had also built Pennsylvania Station, mansions for Tiffany and Vanderbilt and other members of the ruling class, the Farragut Memorial and the Washington Arch.

The main reason Lisa knew about him was his high-profile death and its roots in his seduction of another celebrity, the young Evelyn Nesbit. The most famous face at the turn of the 20th century, she was the original "it" girl, a photographer's model turned theater starlet, America's Dream Girl, and White had seduced and deflowered her, reportedly at age fifteen. Four years later her husband, Harry K. Thaw, an obsessive and deranged heir, walked up to White in his Manhattan rooftop garden and shot him three times during dinner.

Tonio thought White basically deserved it and asked, "Will there be an exhibit?"

"Don't be smart," Shelley chided. "It's not about architecture or some murder. The point is, we're trying to help get something off the ground. Friends of Science and the local high school got the project moving. The basic deal is made. But they will need help with feasibility, the site plan, possibly corporate partners, and of course long-term advice on contracts and options."

"What's the angle?" There had to be one. Shelley didn't invest his time, not to mention his money, without calculating the payback. And he wasn't doing this merely to satisfy Lisa's desire for respectability or bizarre interest in the building's provenance.

"No angle the way you mean," Shelley claimed, "though I obviously wouldn't mind building some of it. Believe it or not, this is straight up. There's a foundation and a board. I just wanted you to have a first look, kind of a before picture. The idea did come from your guy Webster. He knew about the property and consulted on the museum idea."

"Can we look inside?"

"Not at the moment, but let's take a walk." Shelley led him a safe distance from Lisa, Paulie and the goons, supposedly to tour the property. "There are several rooms in the original floor plans, an old machine shop, a laboratory and a room for instruments, plus space for the boiler and a generator," he said. "They apparently brought in all kinds of equipment – transformers, generators, X-ray machines, all that stuff, glass blowing for the lights. On the other side of those trees, originally there was a wooden tower, about 200 feet high, with some kind of rounded top made of steel."

This was sounding familiar --the location, the tower. He suddenly realized they were at Nikola Tesla's lab, the place Danny had mentioned, where the experiments with wireless communication and radiant energy had been conducted. It made sense and he appreciated the idea of a science center that would showcase Tesla's ideas and contributions. All the same, Shelley's motives were suspect.

"I thought we should get some things straightened out," his father said. "You've done an excellent job on that tech thing and I appreciate it. Very promising. You remember, I said it would be a good fit."

"One point for you."

Shelley sighed. "See, that's it, always sarcasm. I'm trying to have a serious conversation. I'm trying to say you are my only son, damn it. And we should be able to talk, and be open, and disagree without insulting each other, or turning it into a competition or judgments."

Tonio was surprised to see his father show insecurity, yet simultaneously amazed at how easily he glossed over what they were arguing about. It was simple: Shelley was the head of an enterprise that operated as though extortion, bribery, money laundering, tax evasion, pollution, arson, assault and sometimes even murder were nothing more than interchangeable tools in a corporate arsenal. It wasn't entirely his fault. He had inherited Roman Wolfe's empire, perfecting its metamorphosis into a construction and leisure development corporation. On the other hand, he'd done nothing to mitigate its basic criminal tendencies. As a result Tonio now privately thought of himself a gangster by default.

"Things have to change, I know," Shelley whispered. "It takes time."

"Ok, I'm sorry," Tonio said, trying to mean it. "The RV rollout has been great, and I do enjoy what I'm doing." He knew Shelley had summoned him in part for an update on TELPORT, so he ran down the business plan for the coming year, stressing the promise of the Visor, but avoiding any hint that they had stumbled onto more. Then Tonio pivoted to his own agenda.

"Openness is good," he said. "So, let me be frank and admit I've been thinking more about Uncle G and what you said about his work for the government." Shelley's charm offensive might provide the opening to learn what he really knew about Gianni's secret life and sudden death. "I know he worked for the Defense Advanced Research Projects group in the late seventies. It makes sense that you didn't want to acknowledge that."

Shelley said nothing. But he didn't deny it, which felt like an admission. By this time they had turned the corner. Shelley checked to be sure no one was watching and pulled out a cigar. "Havana," he bragged and lit it. "You don't mind. She thinks it smells."

Tonio chuckled. "It does, but be my guest. I've also been remembering incidents from around that time. I think G took me to a government facility." This was harder to bring up than he thought it would be. "I don't remember much. But I saw some things, and I wondered whether you know anything about that."

"Not much," Shelley shrugged. His clenched expression suggested otherwise. "Enough to be unhappy. He did it without permission from Athena or me."

"Where was it? Was it DARPA? And when exactly?" He couldn't contain the flood of questions.

Shelley shook his head vigorously. "I don't know," he said, "I'm sorry, I never knew. That was the point. He couldn't tell me or Athena. Maybe DARPA, but it could be almost anything connected to Defense. Everyone does business with them, of course. We do. Your own company gets millions in contracts for research. We stopped the visits as soon as we knew, but yes, you were involved in some…advanced government testing. You were bright." He paused. "But he shouldn't have done it."

"And mom knew?"

"At some point. She was very upset too. But it was hard to stay angry with G, and you loved him so much. Then we lost him, and you were sick, so we never brought it up again. I thought you'd forgotten all about it."

"I had," he said. "But it's coming back. You and mom separated not long after that."

"Three years, but yes. She'd been spending time in Sedona. Eventually it became permanent."

"I remember that."

My first long-distance relationship, he thought. Shelley had insisted on joint custody – to limit Tonio's exposure to all the "weirdos" and "tin-foil hats" out there, he told a conflicted teen. Nevertheless, some of Tonio's positive memories from the period were hikes with Athena in the red rock hills, getting high with friends on trips to Tucson, and thrilling days of white water rafting along the Colorado River.

He and Athena remained close via phone calls and later, e-mail. But visits to the southwest became less frequent after he gave up on college and became a part-time actor and full-time hedonist. During his "lost" years she followed her bliss from yoga and hypo-therapy to Buddhism and Wicca before finding evolutionary consciousness, her current path to self-awareness. Tonio adored his mom. But he couldn't completely reject Shelley's view; she was a beautiful, creative and stimulating companion who could be frustrating, unreliable and disconcerting in her malleable beliefs.

Why did the women in his life seem unavailable, in one way or another, and somehow extreme? Had it started with her? There was Cathy, the environmental activist who spiked trees to protect them from loggers, disrupted meetings of the World Trade Organization, and ended up in federal prison for taking down a cop while resisting arrest at a protest before the Iraq war. And Michelle, a dance therapist who liked bondage and left him handcuffed in a motel room for twelve hours. In 2004 he had moved to Amsterdam to live with Jana, a lab technician who introduced him to polyamory and group sex before deciding that she preferred the company of Tereza, whom they met together at an orgy in Berlin.

And Angel, smart and sexy, a focused professional who was also, unfortunately, highly judgmental and inexplicably insecure. After the Westminster RTV, for example, she noticed his interest in Annie Besant and immediately began reacting, belittling her behavior, politics and dress. She was unconsciously competing with a hologram for the attention of someone she considered an uneducated slacker. She had called him that not so long ago.

They were almost back within view of the others after circling the building. Shelley stopped before the final turn and stubbed out his cigar on the building wall. "What else have you remembered?"

"Nothing definite, random images," Now Tonio held back. A little openness probably wouldn't do much harm – but nothing about the warehouse. "I get the feeling there's more to come," he said.

"That sounds like Athena. When I would ask her something and she didn't want to answer she'd say, 'Bad timing, dear, but more to come.' I hated it, now I kind of miss it. Interesting woman, one of a kind."

"Want me to tell her that?" In a few days he and Paulie would leave for Arizona, with plans to stay through Thanksgiving. Plenty of time to find out what mom remembered about his time as a government guinea pig.

"No," Shelley mumbled, "no message, just give her my best." Then he checked to see whether Lisa Margret was listening.

11
HOMEWORK

They caught a flight to Phoenix on the Monday before Thanksgiving and rented a car for the drive north. Since meeting in elementary school, Tonio's parents had treated Paulie like part of the family. His burly wing man – technically head of TELPORT security – was buoyed by the prospect of seeing his surrogate mother after a decade. Excited as he was, what pumped him most was a planned excursion to Roswell, a day's drive over in New Mexico. He was determined to photograph a UFO before the end of their visit.

"I think there's actually a UFO tour in Sedona," Tonio suggested.

"They have sightings?"

"I think so. Let's ask mom."

Paulie was one of those people who wanted to believe that aliens (and angels) were real, huge alligators lived in the sewers, and General Motors repressed the development of a futuristic Stardrive car that ran without gas and could go from zero to eighty in seconds. Yet he couldn't imagine his own life being any different and accepted, usually without questions, whatever lame justification Shelley offered when he was ordered to intimidate a local organizer or sabotage a competitor's work site.

"For some reason they prefer this part of the country. You heard about those lights over Phoenix. There are great pictures on the Internet."

Tonio was half-listening as they drove up I-17, moving from sea level to two thousand feet before passing Agua Fria. He had explored the area's river canyons, petroglyphs and abandoned pueblos as a child. If Martians existed, he thought, they might find the place familiar.

"Hey, T?" his friend asked. "You think they'll ever tell us the truth? They've had those ships for years. Teleportation, the super-airplane – the one they've seen near Edwards and Nellis." He was talking about the Aurora, a rumored top-secret spy plane that may have incorporated alien technology – if it existed, obviously. The Air Force flatly denied it.

"I doubt it," Tonio replied absently. As Paulie fleshed out his own theory – basically that the Air Force had a UFO, knew how it worked but was keeping it a secret in the name of national security -- he paged through the dossier he had begun on Annie Besant.

After the Westminster trip he had debriefed for hours with Angel and Danny, re-watching the stream repeatedly, and discussed potential next steps. Danny thought viewing time could be extended with programming tweaks, recalibrated sensors, more powerful computers and more energy from the Tesla generator. Angel suggested that, if the goals were to perfect RTV and solve the Ripper case as a dramatic way to demonstrate it, they ought to visit and record all the crime scenes. They might notice something the authorities missed, or even "catch" the killer.

Tonio also had a suggestion – improve the process of observation. He didn't relish spending the next months dangling from wires in a warehouse. He also suggested a search of every available database for matches to the captured image of the stranger in the cape. But despite a growing desire to make Annie a separate object of RTV attention he didn't bring that up. A file assembled by Angel would be more thorough than anything he could build. However, the prospect of an interrogation made it more time-consuming, but less uncomfortable, to find out what he could on his own.

He had discovered, for example, that he and Annie Besant were about the same age and she was more than a journalist. She was the most famous female speaker in England, a socialist organizer who, not long before Tonio saw her in Westminster Hall, had led a massive protest against unemployment.

A series of demonstrations had begun the previous October. Workers associations, unions and reformers like Annie were mobilizing for job creation and against the abysmal wages and working conditions of those who had them. The Fabian Society was attracting prominent intellectuals who supported a gradual evolution of British society into a social democracy. Their clearest evidence of the need for change was London's East End, infamous for its poverty, overcrowding, disease and crime.

At this point Annie had been on her own for more than a decade, writing for the *National Reformer,* speaking and recruiting on behalf of the Secular Society, an ardent advocate of Irish home rule and liberal causes, a world-class firebrand for fairness, reform and freedom. Her appearance had changed since leaving Lincolnshire. As a young church wife she had worn gowns that showed off her figure. Tonio had seen her in more modest garb, a working class uniform she had adopted in recent years. Whatever the attire, the independent spirit, the fierceness and hunger for liberation, were unmistakable and enormously attractive.

She was born Annie Wood in 1847, into a comfortable family with Irish roots. But her father died when she was five and left the family destitute. Her mother made ends meet running a boarding house for Harrow School boys, while Annie came under the tutelage of Ellen Marryat and received a strong religious education. Occasional travel in Europe added a taste for ceremony. She also developed a sense of duty to society, and caught occasional glimpses of what an independent woman could achieve.

In 1867, at the age of 19, she nevertheless married a 26-year-old clergyman, Frank Besant, an evangelical Anglican who on the surface seemed to share her values. He was posted as vicar of Sibsey in Lincolnshire and they soon had two children, Digby and Mabel. The marriage failed. The decline apparently started after Annie began writing short stories, children's books and articles. Frank appropriated all the money she earned. Married women had no right to own property. Politics further deepened the tension. Annie supported farm workers fighting to unionize and win better conditions. Frank was a Tory who sided with the landlords and farm owners.

Around 1874, after refusing to take communion in church, she finally left Frank and moved to London, taking her daughter along. Her doubts about her faith led her to various churchmen for advice, among them Edward Bouverie Pusey, leader of the Catholic wing of the Church of England. But her disillusionment only deepened when he defined her basic problem as a tendency to read too many books.

Ultimately ending this chapter of her life, after a final attempt to repair the marriage, she found herself by earning her own keep with a column for the *National Reformer*, the paper of the National Secular Society. In the years that followed she became one of its most popular public speakers. Crossing the country she lectured on many pressing issues of the day and developed a close friendship with the leader of the Society, Charles Bradlaugh.

The two of them became household names in England when they published a book by the US birth-control campaigner Charles Knowlton. Its appearance so offended English churches that Annie and Bradlaugh were arrested, tried and convicted. The case was ultimately thrown out on a technicality, but the scandal cost Annie her daughter. Frank had persuaded the court that she was an unfit mother.

By the early 1880s Annie had built solid contacts among the Irish home rulers, supporting them in her journalism and meeting regularly with movement leaders like Michael Davitt, who hoped to mobilize peasants for a Land War. In 1883 she started editing *Our Corner,* a publication that projected her ideas for the next six years. She also became close with George Bernard Shaw, Irish author and leading light of the Fabian Society. At one point she offered to move in with him but Shaw declined.

Annie also wrote for the Fabian Society and helped popularize its social democratic ideas. By 1888, however, she was starting to question some of her own beliefs. Only months before attending Ignatius Donnelly's lecture she agreed to a new partnership with William T. Stead, controversial editor of *The Pall Mall Gazette,* with whom she shared a righteous hatred of oppression.

Hero to some, irresponsible muckraker and huckster to others, Stead had just announced his latest radical insight: the need for a new, secular church that would teach social duty and create a true commonwealth. Annie felt much the same. "We need a church of our own," she told the Rev. Stewart Headlam, a Christian Socialist leader in her circle, "one that includes everyone with faith and love for humanity."

More unexpected still, she and Stead had reached the same conclusion despite the fact that he was a Christian and she'd become an atheist.

Not all her friends shared her enthusiasm. Shaw considered Stead a Philistine and couldn't forgive him for fabricating a story about child prostitution a few years earlier. Stead claimed to have personally witnessed the sale of a young girl. Such transactions happened often, but were silently tolerated and difficult to prove. This time, however, the transaction turned out to be a hoax, arranged to buttress Stead's published charges with a so-called "proof of purchase."

Fraud didn't stop the exposé, "The Maiden Tribute of Modern Babylon," from becoming a national sensation. Millions of copies were sold, legally and in unauthorized reprints, thousands rioted, and virgins wearing white marched through Hyde Park to demand legislative action. Stead's story was the perfect combination of moralism and titillation. Deploring the violation of children, it simultaneously provided readers with a borderline pornographic opportunity to read all about it. As far as Shaw was concerned, the story proved that Stead was an opportunist, a boor and potentially a confidence man, an unpleasant, crass and ignorant person who, as he put it bluntly, "would not work with anybody; and nobody would work with him."

But Annie apparently could. She and Stead had launched *The Link*, the half-penny paper Tonio heard her mention to Donnelly in April. Atheism meanwhile freed her from believing in a God who seemed unjust. But Tonio sensed that it also left an empty space in her life that Stead, who acted like a substitute father, was quite ready to fill.

12
Convergence

Evolutionary consciousness is a psycho-spiritual movement integrating mind, body and spirit. It combines the earliest esoteric knowledge with the latest scientific discoveries, and draws from disciplines ranging from quantum physics to alternative medicine. To participate, you only need the desire to know more.

There is no bible or sacred text. The key is being attuned, with an open mind and positive energy. By joining together to examine the universal truths underlying advanced science and spiritual traditions we can create the conditions for a more fulfilling and sustainable life on this planet.

—2012 brochure, Center for
Evolutionary Consciousness

Sedona was a magnet for all manner of New Age seekers and enlightenment hucksters, a former small town at the base of the Colorado Plateau that had become a destination resort second only in the southwest to the Grand Canyon. The area's otherworldly landscape, eroded red rock monuments rising sharply into a bright blue sky, had made it a Mecca for millions of tourists, many of them searching for something transcendent.

The traffic was backed up on Route 179 through the hotel zone and the Village of Oak Creek when they drove through, but thinned out after the Y, Sedona's main intersection. The road north led through Uptown, the original downtown, and from there on to Oak Creek

Canyon and Flagstaff. Paulie turned left instead onto 89A and headed for West Sedona, taking them past plazas and trading posts, bistros and boutiques, high-end galleries and more crystal shops per capita than anywhere on the planet.

Athena Metsova, once Mrs. Shelley Wolfe, was meditating in her Zen garden behind a low-slung, spacious home as they pulled into the drive. She had come a long way from childhood in Astoria, from public schools and working the perfume counter at Bloomingdale's. She was only eighteen, almost a decade younger than Shelley, when they'd met at the wedding of a mutual friend.

Their first conversation was a flirtation revolving around politics. She condemned the Vietnam War and expressed reluctant support for Hubert Humphrey. Athena was still deeply unsettled by the death of Bobby Kennedy in June. Shelley was backing Nixon, and his brother was an active duty soldier. Despite the political divide he was captivated by her intelligence, wit and positive energy, and asked her on a date.

Over forty years later her views hadn't changed much, leaning liberal but with a mitigating pragmatism. Don't let the perfect be the enemy of the good, she would tell him. However, a profound shift in her world view began after Tonio's birth. First it took the form of talk therapy and yoga, then a combination of homeopathic cures and advanced astrology that required a regimen of drops and capsules. As he struggled through puberty she was visiting various sacred sites around the world, networking and meditating with other Aquarians who believed a new era of global harmony and love was about to commence.

In 1987, she was in Sedona for the Harmonic Convergence, which burnished its reputation as a spiritual center and sacred spot, and one of the millions who embraced the prophecy of Jose Arguelles. The Earth would shortly begin to slip out of its "time beam," Arguelles warned, and possibly spin off into space without the united psychic energy of humanity. It would be a time of increasing déjà vu and extraterrestrial epiphanies, he predicted, the beginning of a New Age – that is, if enough people gathered to concentrate together at sites of power around the world.

The planet's time beam slip was averted, apparently. But for Athena the summer marked the birth of a new life.

"**M**y boys are home," she gushed after rising to hug and kiss them. "You must be exhausted. Have you eaten?"

An hour later they were served a gourmet vegetarian dinner prepared by two tanned and well-toned young women whom Athena introduced as her interns. Afterward they stayed at the large handcrafted table on a veranda behind the living room, sharing stories and taking in a stunning view. She wanted to hear about the hurricane back east, especially concerned whether anyone they knew had been affected, and if enough food and water was being delivered to the victims.

After Tonio provided a rundown she concluded, "Well, I guess now we know that government isn't always the problem. Mother Nature has spoken."

He didn't disagree but sometimes found her tone insufferable. "So, is Arizona seceding now that our Muslim president is back in the White House?"

"Hardly. This state can't even run an election. They're still counting votes in some places. But I know what you mean. It's like one big gated community with anger management problems. Did you hear about the woman in Phoenix? After she heard Obama won she ran her husband down in a car?"

"What? Why?"

"Because he didn't vote! I've been here twenty five years but don't ask me to explain the place. I call it the State of Denial, not that there aren't others. But with a Republican super-majority in the legislature anything can happen. Last year they actually passed a law to protect Arizona from a UN invasion. The way things are going, they could require every resident to carry a gun."

Waving away the state's politics she inquired instead about TELPORT and he told her about the launch. Later, when Paulie brought up UFOs, she was ready with advice. "I've started – re-birthed really – a publication that covers all the attractions and changes going on in the region. That's what the girls usually work on. We're online and also have a quarterly print edition."

She tapped her Android and went to the *Earth Harmony* website, quickly coming up with The UFO Experience, a commercial road trip to a local UFO hotspot that featured two hours of scanning the night sky. "It says they go to a triple Vortex location, which probably has something to do with all the sightings." She scrolled down and summarized the highlights. "They provide night vision goggles, and the leader says he was abducted. There's a bus, but you can caravan on your own. Cameras are allowed, and they recommend comfortable shoes. Also, dress warmly. It gets cold in the desert at night."

"And you see UFOs?" Paulie asked.

"They say at least ten sighting on every tour." She handed Paulie the phone and turned to her son. "And what are you planning for your stay?"

"Visit with you, talk about the good old days. Maybe take a hike and catch up on my reading."

Athena reached for a lacquered jewelry box and retrieved a perfectly-rolled joint. "And what are you reading these days?" After asking she took a deep drag.

Tonio wanted to talk about Gianni, particularly what she knew about his death, as well as his own secret testing as a child. But he wasn't ready to share everything with Paulie; plus, her question was apt. "Actually,

I'm reading up about someone you may have heard of," he said. "She was fairly famous in England in the late 19th century. Annie Besant?"

Athena broke into a broad, blissful smile. "I adore her."

"I thought you might."

"Absolutely, she was one of the mothers of the New Age movement. A leading Theosophist. She practically raised Krishnamurti."

"Remind me."

"The world teacher. She believed that an emissary was coming, a torch-bearer of truth who would guide the evolution of our species, and she thought Krishnamurti was him. At the time he was just this boy from Adyar, in southern India, living near the Theosophical Society center there. Later, they had a break up, I think when he rejected the idea that he was the emissary they were waiting for. But he never stopped loving her.

"During World War I, she went to jail for Indian Home Rule. She actually helped to launch the first political party in India that demanded real change. And the British blinked. Her arrest created so much pressure that they had to make concessions."

Somehow the description seemed both consistent with what Tonio already knew and had witnessed, yet different in signifcant respects. The woman he had seen was a political radical, an atheist and a socialist, not a spiritual dreamer who believed an Indian street kid was going to save the world.

"Interesting," he said.

"And what brought you to her?"

Here he would have to fudge. "It's a background research project, connected to the work we're doing at TELPORT." It made no sense but what else could he say? Oh, I met her recently while visiting the 19th century? "But what I really want to talk about is uncle G."

"Yes?"

He took a drag and passed the roach to Paulie. "I've been doing some thinking and remembering things. First of all, he was only 42 when he died, not much older than I am, and he was in great shape, right?"

"Yes, he was healthy. He exercised and ran." Athena's mood was changing, from curious mom and eager teacher to something closer to bereaved widow.

"So, were you surprised?"

"Uh, yes. I was, we all were. It was so…" She hunted for the word. "Unexpected. But why dredge all this up, honey?"

He considered not telling her the truth but decided it might be the best way to provoke a spontaneous response. "Because I think he was killed."

She caught her breath. "Why would you think that?"

"You serious?" said Paulie, jolted from his own research by the news.

"Call it a hunch. I've been having some interesting dreams. I'm digging into my experiences during that period. And dad has confirmed what I know that you know – which is that G worked for the government. But not the State Department, like he said. He worked for some agency involved in advanced defense research."

"Yes, I knew that."

"I know you did. And you also knew that he got me involved in some secret testing program."

She blanched and nodded uncomfortably, as if caught stealing.

"What I want to know is what you remember about that time. Did you talk about the tests? What they were, when or where?"

"It was the beginning of the eighties, no later than eighty-two, but they may have started earlier. And it was somewhere in northern New Jersey. He didn't talk about it much, obviously. Does it make any difference now?"

"If he was murdered it does. If he was killed because of something he was doing for the government."

"That's what you think?"

"I don't know." He sighed, relieved that he had finally voiced the suspicion out loud. "But things are coming back, memories."

She took his hand in both of her own. "That's really good, dear, and healthy. While you're here you should work on that. How about visiting a vortex? I know how it sounds, but seriously, they are very special places, energy centers that enhance our spiritual and psychic powers. It made a real difference for me. I was pretty lost, you know, and desperate after leaving your father. But waking up near one of them, wow! It really opened my chakras."

Tonio had heard it all before. As the ocean receded millions of years ago layers of sandstone and limestone had been left behind, eventually covered by Iron Oxide to create Sedona's gorgeous red rocks. But vortexes weren't created by mere wind and water, rather by a spiraling energy that made them powerful locations for meditation and healing. True believers thought the sites facilitated the flow of energy on multiple dimensions and resonated with each person's inner being.

The craze had taken off at the time of the Convergence, when thousands of believers descended on the small community. Now there were tours in Sedona priced at up to $500. "Maybe," he managed, concealing his skepticism.

"I understand. But if you're doing dream work you should really drop in at the center and talk to Ryan Crown. He's in residence for the winter." The Center for Evolutionary Consciousness was one of Sedona's many "educational foundations" catering to affluent spiritual shoppers with an assortment of seminars, intensives, massage, group meditation, guided excursions, a line of merchandise, and, in this case, guided personal sessions in channeling and past life regression. "I'm a sustaining member, so there should be no problem getting an appointment."

He wanted to decline. On the other hand, he knew that if he showed respect for her beliefs and her eccentric colleagues she might open up a bit more about events surrounding Gianni's death.

"Sounds good," Tonio said. "How about after Thanksgiving? We're here until early December."

"Perfect. I'll make the call."

13
ERUPTIONS

Three emails arrived from Angel before he woke up the next morning. She had found time during a conference on advanced manufacturing to review the Westminster feed more closely and noticed that Donnelly mentioned something about a pimple cure business. Some people considered acne a sign of immorality at the time, but popular treatments had come on the market.

"It was the golden age of quack medicine, so this may not be easy," she explained in the first message. "I checked out some of the snake oil salesmen of the time. William Radam – the Microbe Killer – initially looked promising. He was operating in the states and the UK. But he was a German immigrant, so the accent seems to rule him out as our man. There are other leads to check.

"P.S. When are you due back and how's life in the land of fruit and nuts?"

The second was a remote view schedule for the coming months, with a list of precise times and places in London between August 20 and November 9, 1888. The last was an initial summary of an 1894 report prepared by Sir Melville Macnaghten, who became Chief Constable in the Criminal Investigation Department less than a year after the murders, and statements from his boss and the chief investigator.

At the end she said, "miss you (not really), AB."

The memo explained that Macnaghten disagreed with his chief, Sir

Robert Anderson, who thought the killer's identity was well established. Anderson claimed to believe it was a Polish Jew named Kosminski, a known lunatic with a homicidal streak and a hatred of women. They never charged him but committed him to an asylum.

Macnaghten suspected a 31-year-old doctor, M.J. Druitt, who disappeared after the last murder and was found floating in the Thames two months later. Macnaghten claimed that the good doctor was a sexually deviate and even his family suspected he was the culprit. Many experts still considered him the prime suspect. However, that was based mainly on Macnaghten's report and he had little solid evidence to back up the claim. More likely, Druitt was just depressed and committed suicide after losing his job at Blackheath School for some odd, unspoken, conceivably homosexual behavior.

Inspector Frederick Abberline, who led the Ripper investigation on the ground, said years later there was nothing to the suspicions surrounding Druitt, no evidence to incriminate him beyond his coincidental drowning, and Macnaghten really knew little about any of the suspects. Abberline classified it an unsolved mystery, and felt it was nonsense to claim the villain was dead.

After scanning the material he sent a brief reply and shared his plans for the week – sleeping late on Thanksgiving, exploring the ruins in Red Rock Pass, taking Paulie to the Montezuma Castle monument, and an obligatory meeting with Ryan Crown at the Center. He promised to be back by early December, ready for more tests and the next phase of the investigation.

Hundreds of messages were stacking up. Clearing out the spam he noticed several emails from occupytheplanet@flashpoint.net, not a familiar screen name. But the subject line of one email caught his eye: Shape up Sherlock. Only one person used that nickname and he hadn't seen or heard it in twenty years.

The brief message read: "Too busy to reply? Or just scared? I wrote as a courtesy, but from what I can tell you're a lost cause. Respond or reap the whirlwind. Peace, Harry."

He didn't appreciate threats, even from Harry Atlas, but after checking out the rest of the messages he had a better sense of why this ghost from his brief time in college now held him in low esteem. Harry had noticed his name in a story about TELPORT's product launch.

"Swimming with the sharks now?" he wrote.

Tonio's reply was brief and cool. "Great to hear from you but sorry you feel that way. It took me years to find my place in the world. Not sure this is it. But I believe TELPORT can make a positive contribution. What have you been up to?"

Once the mail was done he showered and joined the others for brunch. Athena said she and the interns would be busy updating the Earth Harmony website for a day or so. Perfect timing for a road trip, he decided. Visiting the Center would have to wait until after the holiday since Ryan Crown was conducting a weekend workshop in Prescott.

That afternoon he and Paulie took the five-mile hike along Boyton Canyon trail in the Red Mountain Secret Wilderness. Paulie was so tired by the time they returned that he passed out before dinner. The next day he declined a visit to the Palatki and Honanki ruins, so Tonio went alone.

Athena had introduced him to the region's history, the time before the Spanish came, when hunter-gatherers roamed the Verde Valley and native people lived in stone villages and on mountain cliffs. Driven off at some point by a volcanic eruption, they returned and built the pueblos. By 1250, however, they vanished, leaving behind only carved remnants of a civilization more advanced than Europe's at the time. And no one knew why – war, famine, plague, drought? There was no written record.

When he came back into wireless range Harry's reply was waiting. He had subtracted Sherlock from the original subject line and added three new words, "READ THIS, ASSHOLE!"

They had last seen each other in 1999, when Harry was "The Voice of Atlas" on KLAR, a California radio station that aired a mix of eclectic rock, health shows, public affairs and syndicated programs like Democracy Now! He was the late-night guy who took calls from strange people and rambled on about oddball theories. But Tonio knew him from a decade earlier, when they met at the University of Vermont.

Harry was two years ahead, already developing his style on campus radio, but then more mainstream liberal in his interests and political views. Before Tonio tuned up Roger Hilton in college and got himself expelled they had bonded over pool, pot and a shared obsession with criminal investigation procedure. Tonio soon became Sherlock Bones and Harry was Doctor Wheed-Love – a nod to Doctor Strangelove, Doctor Who and weed – a whacked-out, cold case detective duo that made unscheduled appearances on the show.

Why had he turned up now and where the hell had he been all these years? Tonio definitely had questions. But the threatening tone suggested the possibility of exposure. Harry was well aware of Wolfe Enterprises and that Tonio was Shelley's son, which potentially could be damaging if the target of his anti-corporate anger was TELPORT. However, he also had to know that if he really went there, well, the response could be terminal.

"Your reply suggests that either a) your head is up your ass and you don't know who you're in bed with, or b) you're a corporate whore and deserve whatever you get," the message began. "Take your pick. If you still have a soul, get in touch. I remember you wanting to improve society, at least not make it worse. This threat to freedom will not stand! Stop the Surveillance State."

He's raving, thought Tonio. But what exactly was the accusation, or the nature of the threat? He composed a brief reply. "I'm hurt. But I don't get what you mean. Who do you think I'm working with? How does TELPORT threaten anything? Isn't more and better communication what the world needs? Suggestions are welcome, insults not. Can we talk?"

Thanksgiving passed without more from Harry or Angel. The next day he continued reading up on Annie Besant in the morning and then went shopping, quickly realizing that he'd chosen one of the busiest days of the year. As he strolled past the Uptown shops, searching for a piece of native jewelry that might appeal to Angel, his smart phone sang.

"Where are you?" The full, resonant voice was unmistakable.

"Harry! I don't believe it," he said. "Great to hear from you. Where are you these days?"

"Nowhere anyone can find me. Where are you?"

Tonio laughed. "I'm in Sedona visiting mom. Are you a fugitive or something?"

"Just careful. You know, you should be a little more careful too – about the company you keep. Those boys play hardball."

"What boys? What the hell are you talking about, Doctor?"

Harry's tone softened. "Haven't been called that in a good long while," he said. "Right. Cool. Well, I'm talking about THEM. You remember THEM."

"Sure I do. But we were twenty then. We thought the entire federal government was the enemy of humanity." He asked whether Harry had specific evidence for what sounded to him basically like paranoia.

"Clearly I do, but I'm not discussing it on a cell phone. Or any phone. Or online. The Internet is a bulletin board. Anyone can read it."

"How then, drumming? By the way, how did you get this number?"

"Gotta go. I'll work out a way to connect. But meanwhile, I need to tell you one thing." The pause that followed was so long that Tonio thought they had been disconnected and almost hung up.

"You call it remote viewing," Harry broke in at the last second, gig-gling. "Can't believe you did that. I mean, watch your back, man. If this is what I think, they've got plans for you. And they're already watching." He followed that bombshell with another pregnant silence.

"Elementary, my dear Sherlock" was his sign off. Once he discon-nected it took Tonio several minutes to recover enough composure to finish shopping.

14
DIRECTIONS

The truth is different for every seeker, but our philosophy recognizes that the basis of growth is honesty, acceptance and will. The goal is mastery of ego, the development of unconditional love for all beings, and an active harmony with your inner self.

– Center for Evolutionary Consciousness

It turned out to be a quiet weekend. Paulie had his Locator for amusement and prepared for the UFO hunt next week. Athena drove to Prescott to hear Ryan Crown, and the Earth Harmony update was done, so the interns went to be with their families.

For a while Tonio restlessly prowled the house and tried to lose himself in re-runs of *Criminal Minds* and *The Mentalist*. But he couldn't stop processing the call. Did Harry know something or had he finally gone insane? And why the obsession with surveillance? He'd always been on the paranoid side and open to fringe thinking. But he never said people were spying specifically on him. On the contrary, he said the world was too big, and there were too many decent people fighting the system for the NSA or whoever else to watch and listen to everyone.

That was more than a decade back, however, before the millennium, Bush's election, 9/11, an endless "war of terror," the age of cyber war and executive action by drone strike. They hadn't talked in years and attempts to locate him had led to a dead end. No address, no phone listing after 2007. The emails suggested that he was working with the

Occupy movement. That made some sense. But it also meant he could be anywhere, even another country.

He felt uneasy and didn't know why. But he finally tired of re-running the events of the last few days and managed to distract himself by returning to the material on Annie. There wasn't a decent biography, but enough to reveal a complex, intriguing woman.

Annie and Stead had launched *The Link* in January 1888, about four months before Donnelly's lecture. The mission statement, published in the first issue, was a quote from Victor Hugo: "The people are silent. I will be the advocate to end this silence. I will speak for the dumb. I will speak of the small to the great and of the feeble to the strong. I will be the Word of the People. I will be the bleeding mouth after the gag is snatched away. I will say everything."

Talk about direct action, not to mention big ambitions. They saw their modest little paper as a way to build a new community, one dedicated to the service of humanity. "What we want to do," they announced in a joint editorial, "is establish in every village and in every street some man or woman who will sacrifice time and labor as systematically and as cheerfully in the service of man as others do in what they believe to be the service of God."

In fact, Annie knew it was just a small periodical. She wasn't delusional. But she believed in shedding light in the darkness, and exposing injustices inflicted on the poor, especially the starvation wages being paid to women who worked ten hours or more a day. Since the paper's launch they had begun to make good on their pledge by exposing greedy landlords and workhouse abuses. They also promoted the formation of Vigilance Circles to take on the abuse of children.

In a column Annie explained the stakes. "It has been thought, in these days of factories and of tramways, of the shoddy and of adulteration, that all life must tread with the even rhythm of measured footsteps, that the glory of the ideal can no longer glow over the greyness of a modern horizon. But there are signs that the older heroism is beginning to stir men's breasts, and that the passion for justice and liberty, which thrilled the world's greatest in the past, and woke our pulses to responsive throb, has not yet left the hearts of men.

"The quest of the Holy Grail exercises its fascination," she wrote. "But the seekers no longer raise their eyes to heaven, nor search over land and sea. They know that it waits for them in the suffering at their doors, that the consecration of the holiest is on the agonizing masses of the poor and despairing. The cup is crimson with the blood of the people."

A grim and militant vision, thought Tonio. But he could also see Annie's faith and optimism – her sense that right and justice could overcome the growing mountain of ignorance and evil she saw around her in a cruel modernizing world. It could replace the darkest clouds with a rainbow of hope, she believed, and somehow make life worth living.

The months before Westminster were stressful, however. After editing the *National Reformer* with Bradlaugh for thirteen years, she had resigned. An issue released on October 23, 1887 went out with only him as editor. Annie didn't stop writing and stayed involved, but things weren't the same. She was no longer a partner and now considered herself a mere contributor.

She and Bradlaugh had parted company on labor and many other political questions. But the real problem was that when she started out at *The Reformer* she wasn't a socialist, she was a newly emancipated, still relatively naïve young woman trying to make her way in a man's world. Now she viewed socialism as the necessary and logical outcome of the paper's mission.

It was a matter of practicality, she decided, different theories leading to different actions and prescriptions. In any case, a publication should have a single, clear program. The idea was to resume her old post and keep *The Reformer* clear of responsibility for anything she did going forward.

She still admired him. For more than thirty years Bradlaugh had spoken for the little man, questioning authority, standing with Polish and Irish nationalists, with the Italians against the Austrians and the Pope, for atheism and birth control. A decade earlier he and Annie had defied the British government together and published the American birth control tract that had led to their trial. In the end the jury didn't think their motives were corrupt. But they unanimously said that *The Fruits of Philosophy* was "calculated to deprave public morals." It took an Appeals Court to overturn their convictions and keep them out of jail.

As an atheist she also admired his defiance of the State in refusing, as a Member of Parliament, to swear the oath to God required of all public officials. The government's reaction was to lock him in the Clock Tower for violating an obscure medieval law. But each time the House of Commons tried to punish him the people of Northhampton returned him to office. Ultimately, despite the intrigues of a Cardinal and blustering of Tory pols, he had prevailed and taken the oath without mentioning a deity in whom he didn't believe.

Yet her old friend had a blind spot when it came to socialism. He resented the spread of collectivist ideas and the agitation it was promoting. Annie found the same ideas uncommonly attractive. "Foreign ideologies" would lead to violence, he charged. She saw a promising, perhaps inevitable, transformation.

"You are giving excuses for coercion," Bradlaugh warned, "you are trying to lead my people wrong, and therefore I bar your way."

Reluctantly, she recognized that their friendship would have to evolve, perhaps even end. She no longer attended his frequent public meetings and slowly slipped into the background of his world. It was time again to move on.

The buzz of his phone wrenched Tonio back from London. It was Athena, still in Prescott but due home the next day and eager to share that a personal session with Ryan Crown had been arranged. They could meet on Tuesday at the Center and "take it from there," she said.

"What does that mean?"

"Nothing," she said, "I've just told him a bit about you, some of your issues and what you're doing in the world."

"Thanks. It's just talking and having a tour, right?"

"Absolutely. Nothing too heavy."

He thanked her again and went back to his papers.

Two days later, in the late afternoon, she drove him to the Center for Evolutionary Consciousness. Paulie had taken the SUV to the mountains for his alien encounter. The Center was a few miles from West Sedona, down a flat gravel drive that opened onto a high-desert plateau. The "campus" was a complex of buildings connected by stone stairways and winding walks. The dominant structure was a huge apse, a semi-circular dome facing an amphitheater lined with rows of long benches.

They stood at the top and gazed out at the setting sun.

"Ryan Crown," said a tall, bald man climbing toward them from the stage below. He looked around sixty and seemed unnaturally confident. Tonio noticed the hint of tattoos peeking out from his collar and one sleeve. Athena smiled and waved an arm jangling with bracelets.

"Greetings. You like this place? It's similar to Arcosanti," Crown explained. "You should go, remarkable accomplishment though obviously still in process." Tonio did know the place, an alternative settlement beyond Cordes Junction where Paulo Soleri had turned his architectural ideas and a philosophy called arcology into an intentional community that looked like a resort near Tatooine.

Crown gave her an intimate hug and said, "Let me take it from here." They agreed that she would return in two hours, in time for dinner.

After a storm of her exit air kisses Crown led Tonio to a modest office located behind the Apse with a decent view of the canyon.

"Let's talk," he started. "We can do the tour later."

Tonio gave a noncommittal nod and took a seat. Instead of sitting behind the desk Crown chose a spot near him. He didn't immediately speak. Instead he simply sat in silence with his guest, apparently his way of conducting an assessment.

Then, "I understand that you're involved in important work in the technology sector," Crown said. Tonio agreed but provided no further details.

"Can you tell me something about it?" He smiled. "No, let me tell you." What followed was a crisp rundown of TELPORT's corporate profile, most recent audit, and the Locator roll out they had just completed. "Good so far?"

"Accurate. You considering an investment?

"Not really. I just wanted you to know, before we go any further, that I understand," he said, pausing before he added, "what you're telling people."

"Meaning?"

"That your remote viewer isn't the limit of the research underway. Relax. There's no danger of industrial espionage, though you might want to give it a bit more attention. The point is that it's fairly easy to connect the dots and conclude that your company is pursuing what we call exo-scientific experiments. How do I know? Because before I turned toward the light I had some personal experience in this area."

He stopped a moment. "Because I was part of experiments in remote viewing."

Tonio tried to interrupt. "Please, let me lay a foundation. From 1980 to 1990 I was attached to INSCOM, the Army's Intelligence and Security Command, first as a training officer and eventually as a remote viewer. But we weren't using high-tech equipment like yours. We were part of a program that focused mainly on the development what they were calling then 'para-normal' abilities. I worked with General Albert Stubblebine. He was looking for people with special potential, trying to turn psycho-kinesis and other latent powers into military assets. Remote viewing was one of the main areas of research."

At this point Tonio couldn't resist interrupting, "Did it work?"

"About 55 to 60 percent accuracy wasn't uncommon," Crown said matter-of-factly. "In the sessions the viewer would find a location with simple descriptors, spontaneous drawing, latitude and longitude and so on. Afterward photos of the actual location would be matched with the information to check. I was involved in hundreds of sessions."

"But you left the program."

"Yes. I can't say that ego wasn't involved. In this kind of research there are delicate mental states, and very large personalities. I wasn't the only one who went private. Ed Dames formed PSI-TECH and trained so-called viewers for large sums of money. Dames claimed to have perfected the process. That's bullshit, no one I know has ever been one hundred percent accurate. David Morehouse claims that he hunted down Pablo Escobar using remote viewing techniques, but who really knows?"

Most of this was news to Tonio. He'd heard the general legend about a secret government program involving the cultivation of psychic abilities. The association, often depicted in films, was part of the reason he had pushed for the term "remote viewing" in developing the brand. But he assumed it was a fantasy kept alive by conspiracy nuts.

"Why are you telling me this?"

"Trust," he said. "Full disclosure. Your mother says you're looking for answers, about your family, your uncle, your own past. I think I may be able to help you."

"How's that?"

"By helping to develop your abilities in this area. Interested? "

Tonio wasn't sure. He sometimes felt that he could sense things, his hunches, but then again so could other people. This sounded like Athena's vortex blather.

"Not convinced?" Crown smiled. "That's fine, skepticism is healthy. But let's begin with the basics. First, the biggest barrier – fear. I'm talking about our primal fear of the unknown. But as the unknown becomes known this kind of fear can be overcome."

"Fine. No fear."

"It's not that simple, but let's come back to that. Next, you have to give yourself permission. This means getting in touch with your inner self and accepting who you are. You can access all the resources you need – if you let yourself. And finally, patience and persistence – the keys to cultivating your will. That can take some time. Clear so far?"

He wasn't convinced that Ryan Crown was more than a motivational speaker with a bizarre back story. On the other hand, what the hell.

"Ok, let's begin. Get comfortable." Tonio adjusted himself in the chair. "Look around the room for a moment. Good. Now close your eyes." He followed the instructions. "Imagine the room, as clearly and distinctly as you can. Take your time."

Tonio summoned an image of Ryan Crown's office in his mind's eye, the cluttered desk, the view out his window, shelves filled with books and artifacts, the chairs in which they were seated.

"Good. Now, visualize yourself moving to the desk. Look at what's on it, try to recall precisely. Can you see it?"

"Yes."

"Excellent. Now touch the desk. Are you touching it?" Tonio nodded. "How does it feel?"

"Like wood, smooth wood, and papers, photos."

"Can you see your hands?" He was surprised that he could."Ok. Now move to where you see yourself standing. And when you get there look back, look back at yourself. Are you with me? How do you look? Do you look comfortable, peaceful?" Tonio nodded again.

"Great. Now, can you see out the window, can you see the mountains?" He could. "All right, I want you to move. I want you to move through the glass. I want you to move and keep moving. I want to you keep moving until you reach the mountains. Now, are you moving?"

Tonio nodded, flying closer to the mountains as he watched the crimson sky.

15
CONTACT

"**M**an, it was totally awesome." Paulie couldn't stop gushing the next day about his big night in the desert. "They were in a triangle formation, moving fast," he said, thrusting both hands forward and up to demonstrate. "I was getting pretty frustrated, you know, since we'd been there like hours and nothing. But this was definitely worth waiting for."

"Dude, that's great," said Tonio, struggling to pay attention.

"They call them bogies. We saw at least twelve, I think, and I'm going back tonight. They come up suddenly, you know, usually in twos and threes, lights moving all together, with kind of strobing, but definitely flying in formation. The amazing thing is the changes in direction, like whoosh and then they zig the other way. Or just stop. One second they're streaking across the sky like a bat out of hell and next they're frozen. Then after maybe twenty seconds, off they go again. I mean, it's crazy, right? You've seen them, mom."

"Many times," Athena nodded. "But it's hard to say what they are. There are many possibilities."

"Hank – the guy who runs the tour – he's been abducted."

"So he says." Tonio couldn't resist poking a little at Paulie's blind enthusiasm.

"Right. Well, it's pretty clear we're talking about something not from this Earth, some extra-terrestrial power. But good or bad, that we don't know."

Whether or not any of that was so, Tonio had other things on his mind.

His encounter with Ryan Crown had been startling. It felt as if he actually left the building and looked back at the Apse and Crown's office from somewhere far away. Meanwhile, Crown's references to his experiences with the military and remote viewing suggested that Danny's description of DARPA's dark past could be more accurate than he thought. But that was decades ago and, whatever they were looking for, the focus eventually had moved on to more technologically reliable projects.

Crown ended the session with an offer to meet again. He had openings, he said, to teach him more techniques and discuss any other issues that came up. Tonio was intrigued but especially eager to hear more about Crown's experiences with INSCOM and anything he knew about DARPA.

While Athena did errands he caught up with email. More Ripper tidbits had arrived from Angel, peppered with flashes of insecurity and veiled doubts about the potential uses of the discovery. There were also photos from Lisa Margret from the visit to Shoreham, along with a stilted note of appreciation. He was about to dig back into his Annie B file when Athena returned with a package.

"Did you order a book?" It was addressed to Tonio, in care of the Earth Harmony editor, and picked up from the local PO box. He hadn't ordered anything and the question gave him a sudden chill.

"Maybe? Let me take a look."

"You don't know if you ordered a book?" She was skeptical but handed over the package, postmarked from Old Time Book Peddlers in Cambridge, New York. It certainly felt like one. Still, for a second he entertained the possibility that it could be dangerous – booby-trapped with Anthrax or even a bomb. But why would that be? Maybe because his imagination was lurching wildly these days between threat and anticipation.

Taking a long breath he ripped it open. Inside was a receipt indicating payment received, along with a paperback edition of *A Study in Scarlet*, the first volume by Sir Arthur Conan Doyle, the detective story that introduced a new hero to the world – Sherlock Holmes.

Tonio knew immediately it was from Harry Atlas.

But what was the message? He knew the book from high school. Conan Doyle had written it in less than a month while he was a doctor in Portsmouth. After numerous rejections he eventually sold the story, under a different title, to *Beeton's Christmas Annual* for 1887. It appeared in book form with its final title about six months later, in July 1888.

The book begins with Dr. John Watson, a retired soldier who takes a Baker Street flat with Sherlock Holmes, an eccentric "consulting detective." Holmes shows little interest in pursuits like philosophy and politics but has impressive deductive powers and a useful knowledge of disciplines like chemistry, geology and botany. Together the new duo proceeds to unravel the case of Enoch Drebber, a murdered Mormon who took part in the killing of another church member many years earlier. After the crime, Drebber forcibly married the victim's daughter – who was in love with someone else – and inherited the family farm. She died of a broken heart.

Drebber's killer, it turns out, is the long-suffering boyfriend with the unlikely name of Jefferson Hope, who tracks him from Utah to London and takes his revenge before dying from an aneurysm – with a smile on his face – the night before standing trial. At one point Holmes tells Watson, "There's the scarlet thread of murder running through the colourless skein of life, and our duty is to unravel it, and isolate it, and expose every inch of it."

The job itself is "a study in scarlet," the detective colorfully proclaims.

It occurred to Tonio that the novel was published shortly before the Ripper began his spree. But there was no actual Sherlock Holmes to examine the crimes scenes with his preternatural powers of observation and identify the villain before he struck again. In any case, Harry Atlas had no way of knowing who he was pursuing.

Flipping through the pages he found a postcard-sized promotion for Oaxaca, a popular Mexican family restaurant in town. Written by hand on the reverse side were tomorrow's date and an hour, along with the words, "Watson Come Here" followed by the initials W.C.

Clever but extreme, he thought. He was telling Tonio where to have dinner, and had even given a specific time to be at the pay phone near the bathroom and await a call.

"Watson Come Here" was a play on the words Alexander Graham Bell reportedly said when he first demonstrated electronic transmission of speech in 1876. In that first phone call Bell actually said "Mr. Watson" and added "I need you." But in this case Tonio was being cast as Watson rather than Holmes, and he needed Harry rather than the reverse. It also seemed to be a reference to a phone near a W.C., otherwise known as a toilet.

What he still didn't get was all the subterfuge. Harry obviously didn't want anyone knowing about the call and had taken pains to select what he considered a secure phone. The next day he invited Athena, Paulie and the interns to join him for dinner at the restaurant and made a reservation for 30 minutes prior to the hour listed on the card.

Enough time, he assumed, to place an order before excusing himself.

Oaxaca was a sprawling place built in exaggerated adobe style. Comfortable seating on enclosed decks provided views of Uptown and the jagged, dramatic landscape beyond. They settled in at a table in the back dining room. By the time they finished ordering it was only minutes before the designated call time.

Tonio feigned an upset stomach and hurriedly left the table. Luckily, the phone was free. He picked up the receiver and dialed, then disconnected and waited, concealing his hand while silently cursing Harry for the cloak and dagger routine. Looking at his watch he decided to remain no more than a few minutes past the assigned time.

The ring gave him a start when the call arrived precisely on schedule.

"Sherlock Bones I presume," said Harry, "the doctor is in. I knew I had to be on time for this. But you have to admit, the tradecraft worked. Low tech. No one is watching Old Time Books and you're pretty safe on that phone. Just keep track of any loiterers."

"Fine, I came here, and I went along with your tradecraft or whatever." Harry's threats and intrigues had gone far enough. "So you owe me an explanation. Why should I be concerned about surveillance? And beyond your politics and generally paranoid perspective, what do you have against my company?"

"Fair enough," he said. "We can get started. First of all, the question is why wouldn't you be concerned about surveillance? If they could get General Petraeus' emails and bring him down, what makes you so special? He was the freaking head of the CIA, and all he was doing was screwing his biographer."

"You mean the FBI then? Why would they…"

"Not necessarily, lots of acronyms to choose from. The point is that you're connected, already in the web of the military-industrial-intelligence complex. Your corporation receives millions in defense contracts. You don't think they do security checks, you don't think they know exactly who you are and all about your father? Why wouldn't they watch you? That's one good reason.

"Second, this research, remote viewing, it clearly has military applications. My bet is on the NSA. They're the eyes and ears, and they already have Crypto City." Tonio tried to interrupt but Harry was on a roll. "It's in Maryland, schmucko, check it out. Supercomputers, connected to everything – spy satellites, subs, aircraft. They have listening posts around the world and over thirty thousand employees, bigger than the CIA or the FBI. Your Locator, that's in their wheelhouse – phone calls, emails, any form of communication.

"By the way, there's a long and sordid history of spying on commercial communication, eavesdropping to win contracts or stay on top of the next big thing. If you compete with or challenge any significant elite interest that can easily become a matter of national security.

"And there's no problem monitoring your email, warrants are simple and not always necessary. They can also capture keystrokes and monitor images from your computer. You don't have to be online. They call that little trick Project Tempest. Check out 'Compromising Emanations: Laboratory Test Requirements and Electromagnetics.' It's an NSA paper describing how to capture information from a computer – through radio waves or the phone, a network, or the power cables connected to the wall."

Tonio wasn't sure how to respond. Instinctively, he checked to see that he was still alone.

"So, you can understand my caution," Harry continued. "But the good news is, I can help – if you're ready to make a commitment."

"To what?"

"You're in an interesting position, potentially you have inside access." You have no idea, Tonio thought. "I've been working with some people who, let's just say, are preparing to put a cyber-wrench into the system. You know OWS? Occupy? We're not with them officially – much too much process – but we coordinate and act in the same spirit of resistance."

"Sounds righteous," said Tonio. "But what do you need, what can you do for me, and by the way, I still don't see why I should be so concerned." He was more convinced than he admitted, but felt a need to push-back and hoped it might shake loose more information.

"OK, I can say this." He could hear Harry breathing at the other end of the line. "We hacked the Department of Defense and your name came up."

"What? Why?"

"It's a list." He paused again. "A request for the results of security checks on various people. It also indicates that subjects may be the target of further investigation. Which begs the question, what are you doing that might attract attention?"

Tonio had a few ideas but couldn't tell him right now, even on the most secure of telephones. He desperately wanted to trust someone and Harry was a strong prospect. But he had to be sure.

"It may just be the technology underlying your device," Harry speculated. "As I explained, what you are doing has clear applications for surveillance. And that's my point, man. We aren't going to let this be used to erode personal freedom any more than it has been. You have to step up, man, seriously. We can help, and I will help. But you're going to have to prove you can be trusted.

"If not," he warned, "friend or not, mob or not, we'll burn your business down."

Despite the threat Tonio thought it over. Maybe Harry was what the project needed – a conscience and some bigger balls. He knew technology and he knew the street. And once he saw, he would understand the social significance of what they were doing. He could also help Tonio handle Shelley. Harry didn't want the government to control a technology that could be used to invade personal privacy or threaten freedom. Neither did Tonio. But he didn't want his father to control it either.

"Meet with me," he said. "I'll be back East next week."

"I don't do meetings."

"Do this one. It's private and very secure. Less than six people even know it exists."

He waited. Silence on the line, but Harry was listening.

"Actually, it's a perfect job for The Doctor and Bones." This was a bit sweet but it somehow felt right, an honest appeal to friendship and basic solidarity. "I promise you, we're not working with any government agency. This is off radar, completely, and needs to stay that way for a good long while. But maybe we can improve the firewalls and look at the mission. At least let me reassure you, let me show you. You may also be able to help me with..."

It was too soon to bring up the View Room or his hunt for Jack the Ripper. "Some historical research," he decided. "I need you."

Harry waited only a few seconds before giving in.

16
Outbreaks

He looked up from the maple trees lining the street and stared at the shimmering lake. It was far below him in the distance, a blue world dotted with islands and a mountain range beyond. Close to where he was standing he could pick out buildings, a wide boulevard and closer still, the edge of a modest park. It was afternoon and traffic moved at a leisurely pace.

"Do you see any signs, maybe the name of a street or store?" Ryan Crown was sitting beside Tonio under a tent at the Amitabha Stupa half an hour before dawn. The gate of the popular prayer, meditation and healing spot, set among the pinion and juniper pines, didn't open until the sun came up but Crown had made special arrangements. They followed one of the winding trails with a flashlight, past the smaller Tara Stupa and up to the 36-foot monument, a rare example of sacred architecture in North America.

Crown and Tonio had met a second time in his office, and based on his success with preliminary exercises agreed to improve the location. In daylight enough seekers stopped at the site to make it insufficiently private. This early, however, they could be completely alone in the middle of West Sedona, not far from a Circle K, at a place people were calling another vortex.

It's better to sit than lie down, Crown explained. The point is not to get too comfortable, to relax and expand awareness rather than drifting into sleep or dreaming. He had led Tonio through the process, helping him find a specific place he wanted to explore and gradually freeing his consciousness to go there.

"If you're having trouble just look down at your hands." Tonio nodded, his eyes closed, sitting on a prayer mat with his legs crossed. "Good. Feel yourself there. And listen for sounds, voices. Are people talking? What are they saying?"

He strained to hear. Tonio had moved down the hill to the park and proceeded up a path that led to an artificial pond. He picked out a steady distant burble but couldn't catch the words. "I hear water," he said.

"Are you on the water, or floating above?"

"I'm on the ground, there's a fountain."

"This is good," said Crown, increasingly impressed as he continued to guide. "Can you find a newspaper? Or a street name? What are people doing?"

"They're shopping," Tonio said. "And I think I'm losing focus."

"Stay as long as possible. Know you are there, know you don't have to try, as if you're watching a favorite home movie."

He held on for a few moments more, then opened his eyes.

"That was excellent. Where did you end up?"

"Burlington, where I went to college. It felt good," he said. "Pretty real."

"Just keep practicing. Things will come into better focus. And have fun with it. But remember: the difference between this and dreaming is that here the place – where the viewing takes you – has its own existence. In a dream you can alter your surroundings. But with this you aren't the creator. You're an observer, gradually pulling what you see into sharper and sharper focus."

Interesting as it was, Tonio wanted to hear more about Crown's past life. He hadn't brought it up since their first meeting. "Thanks," he said. "It's amazing. Where did you learn these, uh, techniques? Was it in your INSCOM period?"

Crown nodded. "As they say in physics, it was the same – only different. The techniques are similar but the intentions and the context were another matter entirely. This was in the military, in the Cold War. It wasn't a relaxed process at an optimal time. It was trying to figure out where the Red Brigades were holding General Dozier, locating not only the city – which turned out to be Padua – but the exact building. A bit of pressure, you could say.

"In most cases we ran a tape recorder with the viewer. He would describe as much as he could while someone else created the preliminary sketches, unless the person had a talent for automatic drawing. Afterward, we'd go through them all and produce primary images that could be matched with an actionable location."

"You mentioned a general."

"Stubblebine – Albert, the third. Chemical Engineering from Columbia, head of INSCOM for the first few years I was there. He ran the Army's intelligence school in Huachuca, worked with Tony Robbins on neuro-linguistic programming. The ideas obviously pre-date him, but Albert really pushed the idea of psychokinetic ability as a weapon."

Tonio thought he recognized the description. "He's not the guy from *Men Who Stare at Goats?* The only who tried to walk through walls."

"According to Jon Ronson's book. I never witnessed that and anyway, I'd say it misses the point."

"Did you ever run into my uncle?" It was a random question, not calculated for a particular response.

"Certainly," Crown answered casually, "We knew each other for several years. It's a fairly exclusive community. I thought you knew that."

"No," he said, taken aback and more curious than ever. "So, you knew he worked for Defense."

"Actually I think he was Agency, CIA, and liaised with them. But that wasn't public."

"So he was a spy? He traveled enough."

Crown made a snap decision in favor of candor. "No, he must have been in the Office of Technical Services, but also with Defense. The Agency had an interest in possible E.S.P. applications as far back as Word War Two, but OTS didn't get actively involved until the early sixties. Two physicists, Targ and Puthoff, pushed the research. Eventually, a joint project was launched between OTS and the Office of Research and Development. That was in the seventies, the real Golden Age."

"What about DARPA?"

"They weren't interested at that point," he said. "They had their own priorities, more oriented toward distance communication and space exploration, as you know."

"As I know what?"

"Athena said you've recalled some your experiences there." Once Tonio nodded agreement he added, "They really thought it would be the right move, given your natural potential."

Tonio stopped him. "Wait, what? Who thought it would be the right move?"

"They did – Athena and your uncle."

The words hit him like a brick. His mother had lied. She'd known about the tests from the start. In fact, if Crown was remembering it right, she and Gianni had decided to make him a test subject together. And most likely they hid it from Shelley.

What really happened? What else had she withheld? It was time to find out.

Athena put down the phone as he burst into her bedroom. In the short time it had taken him to drive home Crown had called to prepare her for the reaction.

"Mother, we have to talk," he demanded from the foot of the bed.

"I know. But I think you misunderstand what happened."

He was far beyond accepting any of her usual excuses and rationalizations. "No, *you* misunderstand," he shot back. "You said you didn't know about the program Gianni put me in. But you did, didn't you?" he shouted. "From the beginning, you knew. You and Shelley dropped me in that nightmare."

"You mean Gianni. Your father knew nothing about it. That is, until the end."

"Mom, it was child abuse," he shouted, feeling his temper rise. "What were you thinking? Were you thinking?"

"You were a gifted child," she pleaded. "We could all see that."

"And so you enrolled me in a project to do what? What?"

"I don't know!"

"Well, I do," he screamed. "Your own twisted fantasies about nature and the Earth spinning out of alignment. What was going to happen? Was I going to heal the planet, mom!"

"No," she objected, wiping back tears. "We just wanted you to reach your true potential."

"So, what happened?"

"Shelley found out," she said, "so it had to stop."

They had reached the question he'd been waiting for weeks to ask. "And did taking me out of that program have anything to do with G's death?"

She seemed genuinely surprised. "I don't think so. You think the government had him killed, for removing you?"

"It's possible," he said. "It could have been because of me."

"No, it couldn't. And Gianni was valuable. They had no reason to do that."

The response was supposed to reassure him but instead made him more suspicious and set off another series of questions about the events surrounding his uncle's death. "Is that so? What else don't I understand? Tell me, now. Or do I have to wring it out of you."

She jumped at the threat and tried to brush past him, but he pushed her back forcefully and pulled a photo from his shirt pocket. "Look at him," he sneered and shoved the old picture of Gianni in her face. "I've carried this with me for thirty years. Did you know that?"

The rage of years was bubbling to the surface. "He was the one who really raised me, the one who cared. And they murdered him, I know it. He got in the way or met the wrong person. Tell me, tell me what happened. I'll hunt them down, I swear."

Athena gasped. "You'll get yourself killed, or end up committed." Determined to prevent the worst, she tried to make a stronger argument. "How do you even know anyone killed him? How do you know he was murdered at all? And even if it's true, couldn't it be someone else? Think it over, who else might have had a reason?"

He grabbed her roughly by the back of the neck. "You tell me. What do you know? Do you even care who did it?"

"I care," she said, her defenses crumbling. "I always did. There hasn't been a day that I haven't missed him." She pushed him away and collapsed across the bed.

Tonio stepped back as a troubling idea began to form. "What? Were you two…

Exhausted by hiding it she confessed. "Yes," she sobbed, "I'm sorry, yes, I loved him."

His reaction came in stages. For the first few seconds he stood perfectly still, seeming to rationally process what he'd just heard. But then he rose and loomed over her. "So did I! What were you thinking? Is everything in this family a lie?" He felt a momentary surge of rage but pushed it back. "I can't believe all the bullshit I listened to." Next came sarcasm. He turned away, trembling, and growled, "Could you be more selfish? You like Buddhism, so shave off your hair and become a monk. Or how about this, a vow of celibacy? Maybe you can work off some karma. Just no more men, you're just too risky."

When he turned back Athena was sobbing at the other end of the king-sized mattress. "Don't worry about that," she said. "No more danger, I'm gay."

Despite his rage the revelation stopped him. He stared at her, still processing other details from the last thirty minutes. His mother and his uncle were lovers, and together they'd plunged him into a secret government program. The immensity of it took his breath away. And now she announces that she's gay?

He wandered over to a window, stunned, staring blankly out at the garden for a long while. "Did dad find out?"

"About the gay?"

"Stop it. No, that you were screwing his brother."

Yes," she admitted, "it came out when he heard about the tests."

This sparked the next suspicion – that his father might somehow be behind the deed. He recovered enough to conceal this reaction but an idea began to form. If he was going to uncover the truth about his uncle's death – how it happened and who was responsible – he would need a more calculated approach. What he didn't need was his mother reporting to his father that he attacked her for sleeping with his uncle.

The first step was a small act of contrition. "I'm sorry," Tonio managed, "it was just such a shock. But don't say anything to dad, okay? We have plenty of issues already. It certainly won't help if he finds out what happened here."

Athena was shaken and short of breath, but relieved that the worst appeared to be over. "All right," she agreed. "What are you two at odds about?"

"Nothing major," said Tonio, "just company business." Before this would have been one more minor lie, told merely to prevent Shelley from finding out about the warehouse. Now it was the beginning of a strategy to uncover the truth.

17
The Vortex

They drove along the Rim Road and stopped at a turnout to walk the edge of the Colorado Plateau and take in the valley below.

The Yavapai and later the Tonto Apache were drawn to this area more than a millennium ago. But the Army drove them off in the 1870s after gold was discovered near Prescott. Tonio remembered the story. In the summer of 1882, not far from where they were standing on the Mogollon Rim, the high escarpment of the plateau that ran across central Arizona, the Apache had made their last stand.

After the argument in Athena's bedroom Tonio wandered aimlessly until noon, finally returning for the car and a drive back to the Center. He still wanted answers and thought Crown might have some, if not about Gianni's death at least about why the government experimented with children thirty years ago. He felt violated and betrayed by everyone, by the affair between his uncle and his mother, by their arrogance and selfishness, and he was determined to known whether their actions, however misguided, had anything to do with Gianni's death.

In that context, his reaction to what he had learned about his mother's current sexual preference was downgraded to a mild surprise. He was also beginning to think that Harry was quite right. It was foolish to assume that the government had no interest in TELPORT, or in him for that matter. Even without knowing about the experiments in New Jersey they could already be assessing the commercial applications and had to see the intelligence implications.

Crown was waiting and suggested that they find a private spot for a frank exchange in what he called a "beneficial environment." The drive itself was soothing, and when they reached the plateau ninety minutes later Crown began with the tale of Nock-ay-del-klinne, the Apache medicine man who had set the Mogollon Rim battle in motion. Nock-ay-del-klinne had begun a ghost dance cult, he said, and predicted that dead Apache warriors would return and lead them to victory. The army was worried enough to send almost two hundred soldiers from Fort Apache to arrest him. In the shootout that followed the medicine man was killed and the troops were slaughtered. But the uprising ended when the army tracked a band of Apaches to the rim just north of Payson and killed most of them.

The Yavapai and Apache recognized the natural energy of the area, Crown said. They didn't need shiny scientific toys to sense that powerful forces were at work. He talked about the abundance of Iron Oxide, which gave the soil, the rocks, even the bark of trees their reddish hue. That and other metals and minerals common to the area helped to focus the earth's geomagnetism, produced by its molten outer core. Below the surface quartz was embedded in the sandstone. Years of research with Fluxgate magnetometers and induction coils confirmed the intensity of the resulting electromagnetic activity, he explained.

As stimulating as Tonio found such ideas he couldn't turn off the other questions collecting and colliding in his brain or the roiling emotions they reinforced. Crown recognized the problem and shifted the conversation to a more immediate topic. He acknowledged that he knew about Athena's affair with Gianni. But he had judged it a private family matter and decided he wasn't the best messenger. Then he quickly pivoted on to a recap of government experiments with paranormal abilities, beginning with hypnosis in World War II. The classic Hitchcock movie *39 Steps* turns out to be pretty close, he said. Hypnosis was used with couriers, apparently splitting their personalities so that one could remember a secret message while the other wouldn't be aware of it or crack under pressure.

Hypnosis was also used to increase endurance and reduce sensitivity to pain, a useful ability if a spy was captured and tortured. This was an early inkling of the deadly dream, Crown explained, the goal of creating super-soldiers. The Nazis tried it without success, and ironically enough, many of the same training techniques were also used traditionally in Shamanic rituals. One example had been put on public display in *A Man Called Horse* when Richard Harris was suspended from hooks in his final test for admission to the tribe.

In 1983, while Crown was recording the images of remote viewers, the Army was pursuing the Jedi Project. Visualization, positive rein-forcement and suggestion became tools to increase concentration and willpower, he recalled. They were keys to higher performance in battle, while Neuro-linguistic programming accelerated the training.

Over time, however, Crown lost faith in the government's intentions. He accepted the need for a strong national defense, even the use of hypnosis, remote viewing and other paranormal abilities, but he began to notice a determined shift to the dark side – aggressively preemptive methods – as well as a tendency to classify political opponents as threats. Remote viewing as reconnaissance was one thing, and telepathic pro-jection was another. Research was underway on how to exert remote influence on blood pressure, respiration and other functions, and how infrasound and ultrasound could be used to kill.

He claimed to have no direct knowledge of what DARPA was doing then, or of the specific tests Tonio had undergone. From his descriptions and Crown's own knowledge of the agency, however, he speculated that it was probably connected to aerospace research. Children were considered good test subjects because they reacted more spontaneously and had fewer preconceptions. They might also have been looking for kids who showed above-average potential for NASA or other space program projects, perhaps trolling for the astronauts of the future.

That made it sound only slightly less offensive.

Once they were back from walking the Rim for an hour, Crown suggested that Tonio could use some time "off the grid," a period with no email or calls, time and space to get centered. It sounded like the right idea. Although he wanted a progress report from the lab and wondered whether Harry had been in touch, what he needed most at the moment was to be on his own.

"When?"

"Right now. I have gear in the trunk, sleeping bags, food, everything we need." Tonio hesitated. "Be prepared, the scouts have at least one thing right."

He didn't need to be at the airport for three days, and he wasn't ready to see Athena. Of course, Paulie would be worried, but Athena could handle that. Unable to find a good reason not to agree he jumped in the car.

That night they camped at the foot of Schnebly Hill, a high plateau with views of Sedona and Oak Creek Canyon. After dinner Crown turned the discussion to what he had learned since leaving the government. The techniques he and others were attempting to control in the service of national security had existed for millennia, he said. In ancient Mexico Aztec dream interpreters used sleep deprivation and drugs to sharpen their minds and, so they claimed, travel through space to spy on enemies. Remote viewing, Crown suggested, might be a modern version of what was once called soul traveling.

He explained that human beings specialized in mastering their power to reason, and also gave considerable attention to their emotions. What they did not practice nearly enough was the control of dreams and will. The focus on reason reinforces our ordinary perception of the world and the "rules" we believe govern it, he said. But it is also possible to transcend reason and mobilize the will.

Beyond the personal level, he said, there are places that can amplify natural abilities, some of them conducive to introspection, others more helpful with skill development or expanded consciousness. Schnebly Hill was such a place, he said, a center of energy that can heal and purify.

Tonio wanted to object. He had heard Athena enthuse about Sedona's vortices, places where the earth's energy is somehow enhanced and helps with self-awareness and health. Tourists treated them like spiritual hot tubs. As a teen he had witnessed hundreds of believers, his mother among them, waiting at Bell Rock in 1987. They had convinced themselves that the top of the rock would open to reveal an alien craft. The fact that nothing happened failed to prevent people from believing that the area was a vortex buffet.

Sensing the skepticism Crown returned to basics – the spinning motion around an imaginary axis known as vortical flow. He pointed out that vortices exist in numerous forms – stirred liquids, smoke rings, whirlpools, hurricanes – and move in complex ways. Their most evolved form is the spiral. He had selected their campsite because of its location near a magnetic inflow vortex, where the energy flowed toward the earth. This tended to generate pensive reactions and a cleansing focus that could help with introspection or on a spiritual quest.

Tonio had to admit he felt "heavy" since settling down for the night. Not depression, but definitely an increased intensity in the air.

"What are you afraid of?" Crown asked. "Not superstition or personal secrets, the real deal. Do you know?"

He thought about it before answering, "Being trapped, I suppose.

That I can't escape my circumstances or change anything. Also, that there may be no answers out there, that there's just chaos."

"That makes sense. You remind me of Stephen Daedalus, from *Ulysses*. Joyce has him talking with a teacher who believes that history is moving toward one goal – the manifestation of God. But Stephen, who is Irish, thinks history is filled with chaos and violence – to begin with, the violence of excluding people who don't believe in God. And he thinks people who are responsible for terrible violence too often get away with it."

"I agree."

"Yes. So, he's feeling pretty hopeless. But he also feels that his personal history must somehow be overcome."

"I can identify."

"And so he says 'history is a nightmare from which I'm trying to awake'."

"Can't argue with most of that, though I don't accept the chaos part. At least I hope he's wrong."

That night he slept soundly for the first time in almost a week. The next day Crown made them a hearty breakfast before suggesting it was time for another step in the training. While the goal of most government remote viewing experiments was to locate people or places, he explained, it was possible not only to choose a specific destination, but also to find people and places not on any map.

To do that, however, they should move to a better location, an up-flow vortex where the energy moved away from the ground rather than toward it. Crown said he had just the spot.

The drive took several hours. When they arrived Crown led him to a spot midway up a ragged hillside and sat beside a twisted juniper tree. He explained that the energy of a vortex interacts with what people bring with them, amplifying and magnifying their intentions. In general, the stronger the energy the more twisted the branches and trunk.

He told Tonio to close his eyes and find a dark speck of indeterminate size, then think about the spark of creation, the very beginning, until he saw a crack emerge within the speck, then split into parts. The parts looked identical at first, but slowly differentiated themselves. At Crown's instruction he picked out one of the specks and moved closer. Eventually, he could pick out the details of the warehouse lab and Angel in the control room at a computer. He could tell she was upset, worried about her reputation in New York and Washington business circles, concerned about being blamed if their warehouse experiments were exposed, and skeptical about Tonio's interest in Annie Besant.

Instinctively nervous, he backed away and selected other specks to examine. One led to the abandoned museum on Long Island, another to the old family home in Bayside. One took him to London, where he picked out Annie Besant by her red neckerchief. She was leading a procession along a narrow street toward Trafalgar Square.

The police were waiting. When the protesters reached the square the cops charged in on foot and horseback, striking out wildly, thousands of them backed up by armed soldiers.

Horse police waded into Annie's group as men and women fell away like ninepins. Tonio watched in horror, struggling to hold himself there as the coppers struck out at people with truncheons and cut through the crowd. He saw Annie running to a wagonette and jumping on board, begging the driver to block the road. The man refused and drove off as she leapt out and ran back to the Square.

Then he saw the cavalry, relentlessly trotting forward, shouldering the crowd apart, and after them the Scots Guards, bayonets fixed, marching in, assuming control. The protesters shouted "Go home," but began to retreat as Tonio's view dissolved.

When he opened his eyes it was almost sunset and he was alone. His first reaction was a momentary flash of fear. It dissipated quickly as he remembered where he had been. He stood up, stretched and looked at his watch. He had been sitting for five hours. Yet he didn't feel stiff or tired. In fact, he was energized, ready for anything.

He had no idea where he was. But he wasn't frantic or even upset. In fact, things were as clear to him as they'd been in years. He would return to work and solve the mysteries confronting him, finish the Ripper investigation and uncover how his uncle died. If the CIA -- or even his father -- was responsible, they would pay.

Somehow he would also arrange a way to see more of Annie. And he would work with Harry and the team to make sure their discovery stayed secret and secure.

Closing his eyes again, he guided himself through the steps Ryan Crown had taught him. The immediate goal was finding a ride home. Step by step, he moved from the hillside, checking his hands along the way and occasionally glancing back to make sure he was still sitting there. Not far away he could pick out a car.

He pulled back further, rising higher in the air for a commanding view. From there he could see mustard-red buttes and mesas, and subtle chains of light criss-crossing the vast landscape. Where the chains crossed, their intersections gave off a slightly stronger glow.

Descending back toward the ground he found the car again and moved closer. It wasn't Crown's. Tonio could see him building a fire not far from where he was sitting. He shifted to another angle for a look at the driver.

Inside the SUV he found Paulie on the phone. Tonio struggled to eavesdrop on the conversation. Unfortunately, it was a skill he hadn't mastered. How had his friend found him? Or was he just out hunting for a UFO? Not likely. The only way anyone could have located him was by physically tailing them for days.

And if that was true, only one reason made sense. His father had given the word.

PART TWO
THE JUMP ROOM

18
Tensions

The team met "face-to-face" for the first time around a hardwood table against the backdrop of a rustic cabin in central Vermont. They had shared a few e-mails and held conference calls after Tonio returned from Arizona. He also approached each person separately about their role in a revised R&D plan. Yet by early February they hadn't all spoken in person.

The first item on the agenda was the View Room schedule. Angel's proposal to visit the Ripper murders, create an audio-visual record, search for additional clues and perhaps get a look at the killer, was reviewed and ultimately accepted. Harry was the only dissenting vote. His subsequent report on security upgrades, encryption and digital self-destruct protocols impressed everyone. Next, Danny offered a primer on projection stream analysis, and then Tonio reminded the group of the demonstration deadline in March.

All that faded into the background once Angel made her announcement: she had identified the man in the cape at Donnelly's Westminster talk. His name was Francis Tumblety, owner of a patent medicine business called Tumblety's Pimple Destroyer. They finally had a name for their suspect.

"He lived at 79 East 10th Street in New York at the time," she said, "but made frequent trips to London, which was a promising market for his cure. He was there within the August through November time frame, so we have opportunity. We also have Donnelly's letter as a clue to motive, his hatred of women. And we have a newspaper account of him in the *New York World* published in December, 1888.

"A reporter interviewed a business acquaintance who worked with him several years before the murders. This guy, Martin McGarry, said Tumblety claimed to have been born in Dublin and had a diploma to prove it. However, it may have been forged. He also told McGarry he was a surgeon during the Civil War, and showed him a testimonial from Ulysses Grant to prove that."

"I don't get it," Harry interrupted. "What makes him the man?"

"Wait, she's building a case." Tonio was already alert to the potential for an argument between the two of them about virtually anything. They'd been indirectly picking at each other's competence and covert agendas since Harry joined the unit.

"It's really the whole picture," Angel explained with an edge of contempt. "But what really makes him our best candidate, aside from Donnelly's information, is that Scotland Yard thought he was guilty. They just didn't tell anyone. By October they'd contacted the police in San Francisco for a sample of his handwriting. And less than a month later, a few days before the last murder, they took him into custody."

Tonio blurted, "What for?"

"Initially the charge was gross indecency. It appears he had a taste for young men, not an uncommon proclivity obviously, but seriously frowned upon in 1888 – technically against the law, depending on who you were. It was kind of like getting Al Capone on tax evasion. That was on November 7, a Wednesday. But he was released on bail the next day, and Mary Kelly was murdered less than 24 hours later, sometime early on November 9. The following Monday, they re-arrested him, this time as a suspect in the murders. The Central Criminal Court Register record described him as a 56-year-old American physician.

"The problem was that the evidence was too circumstantial to hold him. So, Plan B was to charge him with a separate offense under a law to prevent child trafficking. It was passed a few years before, after some newspaper exposé." Tonio remembered it from his Annie research, the sensational story by her friend Stead with the false "proof of sale." A partial hoax had produced a constructive result.

"The Criminal Law Amendment they called it, an omnibus bill covering sex crimes," Angel continued. "Beyond regulating prostitution and procuring, it increased the age of consent from thirteen to sixteen. And made sex between adult males completely illegal. Based on that, Tumblety was charged and arraigned for trial. But they still had to release him on bail. Two alleged friends – I say alleged because one knew him for only a few days – came up with the money."

Danny asked whether Tumblety was convicted of that or any crime. "You're dreaming," Angel said. "What happened is he skipped the country at the first chance. From the little anyone knows he caught a ferry to Boulogne within days, then a steamer from Le Havre under an alias. By the end of November he was back in the States."

Harry was still skeptical. During Angel's report he'd left the table briefly to pour himself tea. Upon returning he apologized for not sharing, his idea of an inside joke.

"We're not there yet," Danny acknowledged with a twinkle, "but I'm on it." Within a few years, he predicted that major corporations, hospitals, universities, basically any institution or individual with enough money to afford the installation price, would be able to use view stream technology to conduct a meeting like this one. People would convene from multiple locations, as they were doing at the moment, and interact as if in the same room. Rather than watching one another on a computer or TV screen they would talk "face-to-face" with holographic projections of their colleagues in a pre-selected location.

In this case they had chosen Harry's Vermont cabin, which turned out to be an extremely secure location. The warehouse ran the operating system, making possible a virtual conference between Danny and Tonio in Nutley, Angel sitting in her mid-Manhattan office, and Harry in his Green Mountain hideout. Harry and Angel wore RV visors.

"For the sake of argument, let's assume this Tumblety is our guy," Harry suggested. "If that's true, why have we never heard about him?"

Angel expected the question. "Because it was a major fuckup. They lost their man, their main suspect and they didn't want it to get out. You could even argue it was actively suppressed, although there was some early coverage in the New York press. Check this."

She called up a story from the December 4, 1888 edition of *The New York Times* for projection. It mentioned Tumblety by name and said that Thomas Byrnes, who headed the New York Police Department, had assigned two men to watch his apartment. There was also a reference to an English detective. On the other hand, it stated that Chief Byrnes "does not believe that he will have to interfere with Tumblety for anything he may have done in Europe, and laughs at the suggestion that he was the Whitechapel murderer or his abettor or accomplice."

Angel speculated that Byrnes may have downplayed Tumblety as a suspect at the request of Scotland Yard. That said, two police officers did follow him from the dock to his New York flat. The British detective assigned to the case, a little fellow with huge side whiskers, according to *The New York World*, meanwhile set up a surveillance post at a local saloon down the block and plied the customers for information.

"Are you saying Francis Tumblety is Jack the Ripper?" Tonio wanted a clear answer to at least one of his questions.

"The newspapers asked Chief Byrnes the same thing. After all, he put a tail on the guy. But he claimed not to know enough, and described Tumblety only as a fugitive from justice 'for a nominal offense.' For me this plays as another tell that he was working with the Yard and they didn't want the connection between Tumblety and the murders advertised. This became an even larger issue once he disappeared."

"Are you kidding? He slipped out from the stake out?" Harry sounded impressed.

"Exactly. He apparently did a disappearing act more than once. Scotland Yard said they thought he'd gone to Canada; they looked for him in Montreal and Toronto. But Inspector Andrews, the detective they sent over, refused to answer questions while he was there. The truth? No one knew where the hell he was."

Tonio asked how the American investigation was covered back in England.

"It wasn't, despite the fact it was a hugely popular international story. The only report I've been able to find in the British press about the American pursuit was in *The Pall Mall Gazette*. It said the search had moved to America and detectives were in New York. But it didn't mention Tumblety by name. It's obvious: Scotland Yard didn't want the details out, especially the identity of their prime suspect – someone they and the Americans had lost. Everyone was embarrassed, so they agreed to cover it up."

Tonio was encouraged by the evidence, a genuine breakthrough that might ultimately help to solve the case. They also knew the exact location and approximate time of each murder. If Tumblety was the Ripper, they were closer than ever to catching him in the act. The objective was to visit each murder scene and possibly capture the crimes for later replay and study.

"Okay, I get it," said Harry. "We go back and we get all this evidence. We solve the crime of the century. We catch Jack the Ripper. Then what?"

"What do you mean?" Tonio was thrown off by his skepticism.

"I mean, once you've done it, what happens?" The tone was more than a touch sarcastic. "What's the point? Are you trying to become Sherlock Holmes?"

Tonio was hurt. "This is not about me. It's about this," he said, motioning at the projection stream in which they were meeting. "The potential of RTV. Can you imagine it? Being able to solve crimes – no matter how cold the case is, to uncover the truth about, well, you name it. The power to know, absolutely, what actually happened at any given point in the past. Talk about accountability. This is radical, Harry, can't you see that?"

Harry sighed. "As a revolutionary I hate to say this, but that's what worries me."

That stopped the conversation flat until Angel broke the silence. "And I hate to admit it but I have to agree with Harry," she said. "The civil liberties implications alone are enough to give me doubts about where we go with this."

Harry turned toward his friend. "Bones, I don't think you can go public. The feds would be so far up our asses, and fast. Frankly, I think they'd probably seize it as a security threat, ship your warehouse to Area 51, and send us to black sites in Eastern Europe. For some people this is the real WMD – a weapon capable of destroying their monopoly over history."

Until this point Danny, as often the case, was only partly engaged, instead focusing most of his attention on tweaking and monitoring their projections. But the concerns emerging about the risks of the project brought his attention back to the table.

"Hold on," he objected. "We're engaged in research, nothing political."

"Everything's political," Harry shot back.

"Ok, but each time we use the View Room we learn and improve something. Look: right now we're having an experience most people would love to have, but would call impossible. Like on Star Trek, we're exploring to where no man has gone before. And we really don't know where it leads. So we're just exploring the possibilities -- of the past. Meanwhile, we have a hot new product on the market, one that can underwrite the research for years, and with Harry on the team we have improved security. So, I give government intrusion a low probability, at least as long as we prevent a breach."

Everyone had to agree, Angel a bit grudgingly.

"But I do have a concern," Danny continued, "our silent partner – your father."

"I'm on it."

"Yes, but he's getting suspicious."

It was true, and Tonio hadn't even confided that Paulie had tailed him for Shelley in Sedona. That would involve discussing things he was having trouble explaining, specifically the remote viewing with Ryan Crown. But he had mentioned the fact that Shelley was a bit too curious about TELPORT.

"We may need to do something about that," he acknowledged. "Harry and I can work on it." His friend agreed. "And I have questions too. We're in uncharted territory. But as for the Ripper, what better place to start? Solving one of history's great crimes."

"With due respect, I think we need to set some priorities," Harry countered, staring hard at Tonio's projection. "I came into this, at your request, because you made a commitment. Remember? You said we would prevent this company's invention from being exploited, especially by the government."

"And I meant it."

"And you also promised we would use it to bring some real-live perpetrators to justice. Not dead serial killers, live corporate and government scum. You know where I think we should start."

"Enlighten us," Angel snapped.

Tonio cursed to himself. Not this, not now.

"Well, I'd say start with what happened on September 11, 2001, the truth about the attacks that launched the whole fucking War on Democracy. To start with, the fire theory doesn't stand up. FEMA said the steel beams of the twin towers buckled. That means the fires had to reach 2,800 degrees, but jet fuel only reaches 1,700. On video we see black smoke billowing, but just at first, which proved that most of the jet fuel burned up in ten minutes. Everything after that points to controlled demolition."

Angel cocked her head. "What are you saying?"

"That it was an inside job, baby. And building seven across the street? It wasn't even hit by a plane and there were just these small fires on a few of the floors. Yet the firefighters, the medical workers, they were all told the building was coming down hours before it happened. Shit, they were ordered to move five blocks back. So how did the 9/11 Commission deal with all that? By not mentioning building seven in their report."

"I'm not listening to anymore of this," Angel said. Moments from removing her visor and leaving the visual field she turned on Tonio. "You brought him in," she accused.

He sighed, "Let's not do this. Sit down, please."

"And you, with your dream girl," she sneered. "You talk like a truth seeker but it's pretty obvious what really has your attention." She was fuming. "And Harry, if you're so worried about security risks, what about the risk you pose? I mean, what better reason could the government have to come after us? The biggest threat we face right now is you."

Alert to the risk of an early, irreparable split, Harry opted to remain silent. Danny retreated to his computer.

Watching their holographs stare at each other Tonio had no choice but to accept responsibility for this fiasco; not the most promising start. But he would make it work, since he saw no other way forward. Meeting with Harry two months ago, and what happened afterward, had convinced him of that. Just like the rest of the team, his friend's involvement had become essential, and therefore worth any stress and personal conflicts they would have to endure.

19
ROAD TRIP

A dusty snow blanketed Vermont's Green Mountains the day before he left Sedona. It had been quite a while since his last visit.

After leaving college Tonio sometimes returned to Burlington to spend weekends with Harry. Beginning in the late nineties he'd also made an occasional excursion to Killington and other ski areas, but mostly for the great romantic backdrop. As a result, when he changed his itinerary at the last moment, adding a connecting flight to his return from Phoenix, it attracted little notice.

Paulie did want to tag along at first. But Tonio effectively discouraged that by stressing the supposed reason for the trip: to see a play directed by a college acquaintance. That worked, and it was partly true. He'd received a mass e-mail and the production was directed by Sam Sargent, an acquaintance from college days. Sargent had modernized and staged Upton Sinclair's long-lost drama, *The Millennium*, replacing the radiumite explosion that Sinclair had invented to kill almost everyone on the planet in Act One with extreme weather that wipes out the East Coast. Despite the grim scenario, according to one review, Sargent was reportedly managing to retain both the original's satirical tone and Sinclair's underlying optimism about society's future.

In the original play a group of survivors, trapped in a skyscraper as the crisis commences, argue about life without servants or luxuries until

Billy Kingdom, a resourceful outsider attending a gala celebration on the eve of the year 2000, leads a group of survivors in building a new society. Sinclair wrote *The Millennium* in 1907. The Broadway production never opened, and every copy of the play was reportedly lost. Almost twenty years later Sinclair re-wrote the story as a novel – from memory. Sargent's version used a combination of live actors, pre-recorded video and paper-mache puppets to convey the scope and humor of Sinclair's post-apocalyptic vision.

The untrue part was what Tonio didn't say – the real reason he was making this trip. He suspected that the invitation was another message from Harry. There was no way a local production company in Burlington had his email address at TELPORT. That meant Harry wanted him there.

His remaining doubts evaporated the next day when Athena handed him a printed promotional flyer for the same production, addressed to him at Earth Harmony. She wondered why he was using her PO Box as a mail drop.

"I'm not," he replied icily. "It's just data mining. We are still related."

VERMONT, DECEMBER 4, 2012

Emerging from the airport baggage claim late the following afternoon he crossed to the taxi stand for a lift into town. It would be only minutes to the Hilton and a comfortable room with a commanding view of the waterfront and Lake Champlain. But then he heard his last name being called and noticed a wiry-haired kid holding a cardboard sign with the word "Wolf" on it.

"I'm Wolfe," he said, "Tonio, or T. You here for me?"

"I guess so," the kid shrugged, "this way." He grabbed Tonio's bag without asking and led him into the parking garage, boarding the elevator for the top. When they emerged and Tonio saw the vehicle, a faded blue cargo van more than two decades old, he began to suspect he'd made a mistake. Before he could do anything, the side door slid open and three more young guys with scarves over their faces invited him inside.

"I hope you're with Harry."

Rather than answer they handed him a scarf and asked him to blindfold himself. "Just for now," one of them apologized. These definitely weren't Shelley's people; their greeting would not have been so civil. The government was also out. It didn't use rusty vans or operatives who dressed like hippie Zapatistas. This had to be Harry. Still, why the drama? Despite his explanation over the phone it didn't compute.

The ride took two hours, at first on paved streets and the Interstate, then on local roads, and several minutes at the end over rough gravel and dirt. When the van finally rolled to a stop and it was time to remove the blindfold, he could have been anywhere from the Canadian border to New Hampshire.

Harry was waiting at the cabin door. He had always enjoyed costumes and preferred facial hair. This day he looked like a cross between a pirate and a panda. "You have questions, I know," he announced. "Thanks for coming."

"It better be good." Tonio shook his hand and followed.

The cabin was larger and more functional than it looked from the driveway, part tech center, part mountain retreat. Computer terminals covered one wall, screens running data, charts, and video streams. Three college-age hackers monitored them. The rest of the main room was taken up by a large oak table, several couches and thrift shop chairs, a hard-working woodstove, all facing several unmarked doorways and an archway that opened onto the communal kitchen.

Harry flopped down in a ratty lounge chair, and said, "It was necessary, believe me. Not on my end, in this case. We have good reasons to play it safe with you, my friend. You may already be a person of interest."

"That's extreme," Tonio objected, "but I do believe Shelley had a tail on me."

"That's not what worries me." He pointed up with a finger, as far as Tonio knew meaning either God or spy satellites.

"What does worry you? More to the point, what's happened to you, man? Last I knew you were a radio personality."

"A personality, right, I remember when I had one of those," Harry mused. "Last time I saw you we were about to take over Seattle, right? Blocking the WTO, now that was a demo. Things looked promising in '99, didn't they? Even after the coup – that's what I call W's first term – we totally derailed that FTAA deal in Quebec. But they were already starting the crackdown. After the attacks…well, you know that story, Patriot Act, wiretapping, secret searches, the whole deal. Plus, for the first time the CIA gets a direct role in deciding who gets rounded up or hit. It was the first stages of drone justice."

That still didn't explain why he was hiding in the woods, and Harry knew it.

"I was operating above ground then," he reminisced. "But things were changing. It was an eavesdropping bonanza. The intelligence budget hit $60 billion after 9/11 and thousands of new private contractors got into the game. It was a very lucrative club in a very growing industry. And Fort Meade, that was the Gold Rush zone for masters of the data stream.

"I still had the show then. But instead of the usual stuff I started talking about the surveillance state, what the government was really up to. Big mistake as it turns out. In 2007 I tried to board a flight to DC and found out I was on a no-fly list." After more than an hour of interrogation Harry was released. But not his laptop, cell phone, camera and USB drive.

As Harry outlined the rest of his path from radio host to underground man Tonio heard more than he wanted about Crystal City and the Wiretappers's Ball, a secret annual gathering where experts shared their latest toys and competed to create the ultimate bugging device. Harry had managed to infiltrate it and bring out pictures. He also talked on the air about Verint Systems and Narus, major private eavesdropping operations that reached most of the planet. They made it easier to block websites considered politically or culturally threatening to those in power.

The next flashpoint for Harry came after the Democrats capitulated on amendments to the Foreign Intelligence Surveillance Act. He explained that the changes gave the telecoms legal immunity while providing a go-ahead for the NSA to target almost anyone classified as a terrorist. Obama, who was running for President at the time, opted to support the amendments. Once he was in office, the move toward mass surveillance launched almost a decade earlier continued to escalate. Obama's Justice Department invoked "state secrets" to stop citizens from suing the government for spying on them. In fact, it argued that the feds had immunity from litigation for any surveillance that violated the law.

"You thought I was being ridiculous about emails, right?" Harry reminded him. "There's a reason, Sherlock, the CIA. They've invested heavily in Visible Technologies, which analyzes social media. It can look into half a million websites a day. But the biggest reason we're here, instead of enjoying room service on your tab, is because in 2010 they demanded all the visitor information from Truthsquad. I mean everything, and we weren't supposed to tell anyone about it under penalty of prosecution for impeding a federal investigation.

"The IFC – that's the Internet Freedom Center – challenged the subpoena." He was winding down. "But it was obvious where this was heading. They'd already jailed Bradley Manning for the Wikileaks cables and Julian was under house arrest. The handwriting was on the wall. It was only a matter of time 'til that knock on the door and I'm a suspected cyber-terrorist. That was two years ago, shortly before we set up here. Just in time it turns out, since now I'm on the terrorist screening database. Drone bait -- if they ever find me outside the country."

"But we're safe and secure?"

"Like a frog's ass, baby. Acoustic dampening, the latest in encryption. We just added self-destructing e-mails and encrypted cell phone calls, anything you send digitally. By next year there will be a commercial self-destruct app on the market, but ours is better. My rule of thumb is either that the message is destroyed after it's read, or else no more than an hour or two after sending it goes poof, like Mission Impossible. But your current security, not so great."

Considering what he had just heard Tonio wasn't surprised Harry felt that way.

After a break for dinner the other members of his collective left the room and the conversation resumed around the woodstove. Now it was Tonio's turn to explain. He started simply, talking about his early thirties and what he'd learned since meeting Danny Webster, his reasons for accepting Shelley's offer to chair TELPORT, and, with as much technical language as he could muster, the company's goals and on-the books plans. His intention was to work up to the secret they had kept for two years. In the process he described Angel, holding back about their relationship, and casually mentioned, without much detail, some of his recovered memories and suspicions about his uncle's death.

When he finally reached the pay off – the discovery of remote time viewing and his personal pursuit of Jack the Ripper – Harry was less shocked than worried and amused.

"It's true," Tonio insisted, uncomfortable being the one who sounded crazy.

"I believe you. The question is, does the Don know?"

Tonio assured him that wasn't possible.

"Are you sure?"

Choosing frankness over defensiveness, he admitted that he wasn't absolutely certain, in fact that it was part of his reason for being in Vermont, and that even his oldest friend Paulie might be watching him on Shelley's orders.

"As long as it's Paulie I think we're safe," Harry said. They'd met during a ski trip. "But Wolfe Enterprises isn't what it used to be. That's why I ask." Tonio's frown said: tell me more!

"Daddy has satellites now, three so far. It's still a young industry, and about five years ago Wolfe Enterprises bought E-Global, which builds and launches satellites and sells images to a wide variety of businesses – agro-cartels, oil companies who need to check on rigs, fishing fleets that want info on the best feeding areas, normal corporate shit. Live stream or images, whatever you want from their cameras in the sky. You just need the bucks."

He paused briefly before continuing. "The trouble is, they also work with the feds. It's synergy, a public-private partnership. The government's satellite operator has a program, NextView, which shares the costs of satellite development with the private sector. From what we know it covered about half the cost of E-Global's most recent model, GlobeWatch-3. And among its tasks is to provide surveillance for the Department of Defense."

Harry speculated that Shelley's takeover of TELPORT might in some way be related to other moves he was making in tech and aerospace. "Fuck man," he added to hammer his point home. "He could be watching us now, the building at least."

"But he's not, right?" This was as good a time as any to make his pitch. "That's why I need you. Look man, we know remote viewing could be exploited, any technology can be. The Pentagon invented the Internet, right? You told me that. But Danny isn't doing this for the military or the Agency. He's just a nerd inventor creating his dream and offering it to the public."

"With a weakness that's already been exploited," Harry reminded him.

"Yes, but I run the company, the RTV end is totally insulated from the other units and anyway, no one knows what happens in Nutley except the three of us – now you. Danny runs the lab, Angel handles operations. What we need is help with strategy and tactics, plus your cyber skills. From what you said I can see that security and prevention need to be a higher priority."

"I could do that. What's your job?"

"Staff guinea pig."

Harry laughed. "Right man for the right task."

"Seriously, we need you. I need you. I need someone who has my back. Also someone I can level with, and work with to figure out what went down with Gianni. I'm almost positive it was a hit."

"And the candidates?"

"At the moment? The CIA and Shelley."

"Hard to say which would be worse." Harry leaned back in his chair and took a series of deep breaths, considering the weight and shape of the information. "And what can you do for us," he asked, "for the movement?"

"Underwrite it?" The lack of response told Tonio that wouldn't be enough. "All right, how about this? Either we go public with RTV or no one gets it."

"Good start."

"And if we use it ourselves," he added, struggling to reflect what Harry might want to hear, "if we do, we use it to get some real truth out there, no matter whose ox is gored."

"Right on," replied Harry, pumping a clenched fist in mock salute. "So, where do we start?"

On the trip Tonio had come up with a list that covered the gamut. But now that he was in the cabin, near a warm wood fire, safe and relatively comfortable with a trusted old friend, he didn't feel like discussing security firewalls at midnight. But he did want to know what Harry thought about his uncle's death. After briefly explaining the evolution of his suspicions he asked for ideas on what to do next.

To Harry the answer seemed obvious, "Find out what the man was doing that could get him killed." It sounded like the right place to start. Unfortunately, sleeping with his mother was the first clue that came to mind.

20
Flight Plans

His room with a view was waiting when Tonio checked in a day late. The snow had melted and the temperature was approaching 50 degrees, incredible for northern New England in December, yet another sign that the weather was changing. He gazed at the lake and, for the first time in years, felt a sense of personal responsibility to do something about it.

Damn it, he cursed, what a time to grow a conscience.

Tomorrow he would be back in the city. Everything he'd left behind was waiting for him. But much had changed since Athena's confession and the realization that Gianni – idol of his youth – had betrayed his trust, altered the course of his life, and perhaps set his own death in motion. Suspicions were even deepening about his father's role.

Thanks to Ryan Crown, he had meanwhile discovered something liberating about himself, the ability to focus his will and expand his vision without any technical or pharmaceutical assist. Had he imagined it, or had he really traveled a great distance across space and time? For the moment at least he decided it didn't matter what really happened. Whatever he experienced, it had altered his world view. Getting high had become a letdown.

He was also sorting out Harry's revelations. That was going to take more time. Yet getting him to join the team was reassuring, despite the pledges it had required, while what he'd learned about Shelley's investment in satellites raised unsettling questions.

That night as planned, in case someone was indeed watching, he attended *The Millennium*, Sargent's cheeky adaptation of Sinclair's century-old novel. Despite the update, some of the dialogue retained an old-world tone. In the third act, once a socialist utopia is created after the environmental catastrophe, most capitalist stragglers embrace the new world disorder. But one person resists and is left behind in the devastated city, a former building manager named Tuttle who attempts to seize control of food production from the new Cooperative Commonwealth.

Despite his anti-social behavior other survivors pity poor Tuttle, and Billy ultimately returns to the city to rescue him. In the final scene Billy comes home and announces solemnly that the last capitalist is dead. Tonio had trouble keeping a straight face.

"But he was only what we made him," the hero proclaims, "a product of our past."

It was charming and hopeful, but he couldn't see the basis for such optimism.

NEW YORK, DECEMBER 6, 2012

He hadn't shared his whereabouts or responded to calls in days. As a result, no one was at Kennedy Airport to meet him the next night. As soon as he entered his building, however, he noticed familiar faces in the lobby. His first impulse was to flee. But at some point he would have to face the music.

"You moving in?" he shouted to hail their attention.

Pesci shrugged and pulled himself up. "The boss wants to see you."

That didn't sound promising. Shelley had apparently assigned these two bozos to track him down, and they had come without Paulie, his usual wingman. For all he knew they might have been waiting since the trip in Burlington. Consider the bright side, he thought. At least they weren't inside the apartment.

He asked where they were going and Pesci shrugged again. When he moved toward the elevator, they followed and flanked him.

"Let me take that," Ray-Ray insisted, grabbing his bag a bit too quickly.

Ten minutes later he was in the front seat of the Hummer on his way back to the airport. "What's been happening, guys?" The worst thing he could do was show any nervousness.

"Not much," Pesci answered without conviction.

Ray-Ray took the seat behind him and combed his hair. The right place to be; that is, if he was the mark. "Hey, it's all good," Ray-Ray bragged. "Like a stripper in heat."

"Not too hot, I hope. What have I missed?"

Pesci gave him a bearish grin. "Nothing much. Just the usual."

He was feeling safer by the mile. "That's usually how it looks just before everything goes to shit," he joked. "But I gotta say, you two don't look happy. What's wrong? Is somebody getting whacked?"

"If that was happening I'd be smiling," Ray-Ray replied – Tonio thought a bit ambiguously – and extended his lip in a fake pout. He had reached the conclusion long ago that Ray was a head case. Still, he felt relatively sure that he wouldn't be killed tonight. The question was, where the hell were they taking him?

"Pesci repeated, "Yup, just the usual."

"The usual? That's good. What's the usual? Usual bullshit, usual lies." As he said it he worried he'd gone too far. But maybe this was how to play it, draw them out by pretending to have an identity crisis. Crazy could work for him too.

Pesci reacted exactly as he hoped. "Don't talk like that, you worry me." The ex-wrestler was concerned. "What happened to you out there?"

Tonio whispered the answer solemnly. "You might say, I took a good long look at myself."

"I don't get it." He was taking the bait. "You think too much."

"You're right, I do. But don't you ever get depressed or have bad dreams?"

"Sure," Ray-Ray injected. "But the way I see it, a dream is just a blocked wish." He'd heard the line in *Analyze That*, the mobster comedy about a boss played by DeNiro who goes into therapy. "So I figure out what I wanted in the dream, and then I go for it. Bada-bang."

"Sounds like a plan." It actually sounded dangerous.

"It is, if you let it." Pesci pressed his own point, "Just stop thinking." And why wouldn't he think that? It had worked for him for years.

"Excellent advice," Tonio said. "But I can't help wondering, why am I here? Is this all there is? You don't ever worry about that?"

The car went silent as the two wiseguys made eye contact in the rear view mirror. Several seconds passed before they answered together, "Nah."

Try something else, maybe a direct approach. "Level with me, guys, where are we going? You're lurking in the lobby when I arrive. Seriously, if I'm not being whacked, what's up?"

"What can we tell you?" Ray-Ray was apologizing, eyebrows up, shoulders forward. That also said he wasn't being killed. But there was still something missing.

"Anything, as long as it's true," he tried. "You're leaving something out. I see it in your face, man."

Pesci emitted a growl, never a good sign. "What do you see in my face?"

"Down boy. I'm just saying, we're friends and friends watch out for each other. If I'm heading into something and I should be worried, you'd tell me, right?"

That seemed to calm him, but also propelled him to action. Despite the fact that they were in traffic on the Long Island Expressway he swerved into the emergency lane and screeched to a stop. Then he opened the driver's door and extracted himself, motioning Ray-Ray to follow, and walked to a spot about twenty feet away. Tonio watched their brief, animated discussion but couldn't catch the content over the traffic's roar.

Once they were back inside he didn't wait a second before demanding an answer.

"Virginia," Ray-Ray announced with some guilt. "We're going to Virginia. And the Don *is* upset with you. Fuck man, you disappeared for days."

Fair enough. But he still couldn't trust two family goons with what he was doing, who he had met with, or what he'd found out. What he needed was a cover story that could plausibly pass for the truth. "I've been pretty depressed lately." That worked, something they already believed they knew from his therapy.

"Maybe it's just turning 40," he said, "or it's the environment. God knows. Things feel screwed up, out of whack, as if nothing fits the way it should. I mean, look at what's happening out there." He pointed out the window. "We're running out of time. Did you know, if the average temperature rises another two degrees we're screwed. I mean seriously screwed. The way things are going with global emissions, well, that looks pretty fucking certain. The oil, the gas and the coal companies, if they use too much of their reserves we're definitely toast. Who's going to stop them?"

He widened his eyes, going for a borderline hysteria effect, a man on the edge of a nervous breakdown. "And then I think, if only we could all go back and see where we're heading, maybe people would make different choices, maybe at least admit we're responsible for what's coming. It's definitely coming!"

Pesci couldn't suppress a giggle. "Man, that's weird" was all he said.

Tonio seized the chance to turn the tables. "What's so funny?" he grumbled.

Thrown off guard his minder instinctively apologized. "I was just thinking about it," he said. "Going back and seeing all the foul shit you did. I sure wouldn't want to."

Tonio considered continuing his impromptu performance, but then another idea hit him. Pesci was actually right: most people wouldn't want to face the worst moments from their past. It was something to consider, possibly the kernel of a plan. He stored it away and lowered the volume, nodding acceptance of the musclehead's amens.

"Let's go," he motioned. Pesci was relieved and gunned the engine. But Tonio couldn't resist adding one more thing, his own spin on the concept. "Good point," he said, "sometimes it does take a shock to get a decent confession."

GORDONSVILLE, DECEMBER 6, 2012

In the 1930s the Department of Commerce established a network of small airfields for use in emergencies by commercial aircraft traveling between major cities. One of them, known as Gordonsville Airport, began operating around 1938 northwest of Richmond. Known as Intermediate Field #50, it was located about five miles southeast of town along the Nashville to Washington corridor.

At the time the airport featured a modest hangar, one rotating beacon and two sod runways arranged in a T-shape, but no services, fuel or amenities. It remained in service for about twenty years, longer than most emergency landing sites, but it was ultimately abandoned at the end of the fifties as commercial flights became more commonplace and reliable.

Once they were cruising at 500 miles per hour in Shelley's Learjet it took less than half an hour to get there from Long Island. The plane was a midsize model with space for about seven. As they landed, Tonio noticed the construction underway, along the two runways and around a wing-shaped structure sheathed in metal and covered on the runway side with huge panes of glass. A hangar nearby looked empty but ready for occupancy.

"What is this place?" No answer from the peanut gallery, but from the smug expressions upon disembarking near the unfinished terminal he surmised that they weren't totally unfamiliar with it.

"The boss is up in the control room, I think," explained Pesci, pointing in the general direction of an immobile escalator that led to an observation level. "He said the elevator's working." They walked down a wide concourse, past a check-in section that looked like a hospital waiting room, an empty restaurant with vast kitchen at the near, and a series of stalls for future concessions.

Once inside the elevator and rising he noticed the view; a wide runway headed out more than a mile, farmland surrounding it and a highway beyond. This isn't your normal airport, he thought. What was his father up to now?

"Welcome to the Jefferson Spaceport." The words echoed through the halls. Shelley was waiting for them in a control room that looked like the bridge of a movie space ship. It was a large oval, the near wall covered by screens with semi-enclosed workstations below, the front side covered with huge windows that looked out the runways and hangar. Below the windows was a curving row of consoles, stationary chairs and a central podium with an elevated command post at the center.

"Well, beam me up," he said.

The Don was ensconced on the oversized chair, holding a microphone as he gazed out at the view. "It's a work in progress," he said. "Sit."

This was very different from their meeting on Long Island just a month earlier. Out of the house, away from Lisa Margret and the family, Shelley was another man, in control, confident to the point of unnerving arrogance, more like the mercurial tyrant Tonio remembered from childhood. It made him wonder whether the other version had been an act.

"What is this? An airport for V.I.P.s?"

"I said sit." He barked it this time and pointed to one of the chairs below his throne. "There. We're going to have a conversation. I'm going to ask you questions and you are going to tell me the truth, for once. I understand your confusion. To you, I'm some old fart, out-of-touch, ancient news. You tell me anything, or nothing, what do I know?"

"Dad, I'm just asking…"

"Shut the fuck up. I'm talking. You asked me a question: what is this? Well, I'll tell you what it is. The future. Do you know where we are?"

"Virginia?"

"Don't be smart. That's right. Near Richmond, and just two hours from Washington, DC. Two hours! And yes, we will cater to some of the most important people. But you weren't listening. I called it a spaceport, not an airport. We're not going to be shuttling people from here to Vegas or Miami for a few hundred bucks. We're going to give them the ride of their lives – right into space, at least close. I'm talking about suborbital flights, to the boundary of the atmosphere at three thousand miles an hour.

"That's four times the speed of sound," he bragged. "And then the real fun begins. They become weightless for ten minutes. They're fucking astronauts. I mean, if that isn't worth $150,000 a pop I don't know what is."

Tonio was stunned. He hardly knew where to start. Was he actually doing this? How long had it been in the works? What was it costing? Could it really happen?

"Close your damn mouth," Shelley said. "It's called space tourism and it will take off – pardon the expression – by the end of this decade. We'll be ready in less than five years. The low estimates say more than two hundred thousand passengers per year, just to start. That's a five hundred billion dollar market. Our piece could be up to 20 percent of that, one hundred billion a year. Up-front cost is around three hundred million – but the feds will underwrite fifty percent. I never got that deal with a casino, and we can add a hotel later.

"Virgin Galactic expects to charge two hundred K for a flight out of New Mexico. We can do it cheaper and we'll be on the East Coast. Aside from California and Texas that's where most of the market is. And talk about your V.I.P.s. We've got DC and New York. Those Wall Street assholes, old money, new money, senators, high society, they'll all line up."

"That's why we're in Virginia?"

"It helps. But the big reason is insurance. When Branson set up in New Mexico he missed something. They had passed a state law exempting his flights from liability for five years, but not his suppliers. We need to protect the suppliers from liability or the thing will never happen. You know, in case of mishaps, like a crash or something blows up. Virginia is one of four states with permanent exemptions for carriers and suppliers. It works like informed consent at a ski area. You waive your right to sue when you buy your ticket. We've got that locked up."

"I also call it Jefferson Spaceport because we're in Virginia. There are about nine other companies with projects like this in various stages, but most of them are at existing airports. This one will be stand-alone, and the best – a total experience. We'll have high-end flight training by former astronauts. We can also sell it to the general public, with or without the flight, at affordable prices. For passengers the training will be two days right before you go up. Got to be sure everyone is fit to fly.

"Then you board the Space Wolf. I like the sound of that. We'll have Space Wolf One, Two, Three and so forth. Each one will take eight passengers and two pilots. Everyone gets a seat with a great view out the side and overhead. You climb fifty thousand feet to – they call it the Kármán line – then the rocket engine goes off, whoosh, and there you are at zero gravity. We expect to take in at least $1.2 million per flight, three hundred million per plane per year."

He rose from the oversized chair and circled his son. "But that's not why you're here. You're here because you've been hiding shit, and because you disappeared in New Mexico, in the ass end of nowhere. And then you did it again in Vermont when you got back."

"I'm sorry about that." As Shelley spoke Tonio worked up an excuse. Before he could offer it, however, his father caught him off guard with a sharp slap across the face.

"I'm not interested," he said. Tonio resisted the urge to deck him. "Now, what are you and your little friends doing in Nutley? You thought I wouldn't hear about that? This is what I mean, no respect. What am I, an idiot?"

"No, sir."

"That's right. But you, you think small. You're wrapped up in your dramas. Ooh, I have no control over my life. Daddy didn't love me, Mommy went away, I didn't choose this, I didn't choose that, poor me, wah, wah, wah."

The old man is pushing it, he thought, as a fat finger poked at his forehead.

"And those little schemes, rattling around in there. Forget about it. And take a good look." He extended his arms in a grand gesture meant to encompass the site. "This is just the beginning of what's possible. Think about it: Wolfe Space Adventures. We'll dominate tourism and entertainment."

By the end of the monologue, Tonio was forced to admire the sheer audacity of the vision. On the other hand it sounded delusional. But what his father knew about the warehouse experiments still wasn't clear and the mere fact that he was aware of its existence required fresh tactics. Virtual teleconferencing and other advances being made with basic remote viewing might have to be revealed early. Whatever it took, he decided, as long as no one outside the team found out what the View Room could do.

Watching Shelley strut around the control room like a starship captain he saw a man losing touch with reality, yet wealthy enough to impose his will and sustain his fantasies, and prepared to do it by whatever means were necessary or convenient. When caught he was much more likely to turn on his accuser than admit the smallest lie. Tonio and others had learned the hard way, sometimes painfully, that you didn't call out Shelley if you valued your dignity. Combined with what Harry had told him about the Wolfe Enterprise investment in satellites, he was starting to suspect that even his own entry into the tech sector might not be as accidental as it appeared.

He apologized several more times and offered up a thorough, although selective rundown of progress with holographic remote viewing and public plans for the next few years. He even offered a tour of the warehouse, while continuing to downplay its significance, and promised to arrange a demonstration as soon as the glitches were ironed out. How long? Not more than a few months.

Mollified for the moment Shelley called him over to the window and adopted what he considered a fatherly tone. "What happened with your mother?" It came off like another threat.

What could he say? That he knew about the affair with Gianni and almost attacked her. How about the fact that Shelley was one of the leading candidates for killer? The trouble was that he didn't know how much his mother had already said. The thought of being caught in an outright lie sent a shudder through him. It also re-sparked the anger that had been building since he was forced to make this trip.

"We had an argument," he offered. So far so good. "You know I have questions about G's death."

"You're still on that," Shelley snapped. "People die, grow up."

"Yeah, I know. Anyway we had a fight and I said some things." He paused, checking again for a reaction. "She was worried I was getting obsessed and might get into trouble."

"Listen to your mother." He grabbed Tonio by the arm and shook it. "You hear me? There's nothing more to know about that."

'Yes, sir."

"Focus on business," Shelley issued the order as he returned to his command chair. "Do your job, eyes on the prize. We're about to put a mark on this ball, a very big one."

Tonio smiled and nodded. The Don took the gesture as submission. But the smile was only for the bullet he'd just dodged, while the nod meant that he understood what was being required. How he responded from here was another matter entirely.

21
GRAVITY

Two days after Angel's outburst Tonio invited her out for drinks on a Sunday evening. As soon as she sat down he thought there might not be a reason to worry. He also considered rekindling their brief but intense affair.

"Nice choice," she said with a conciliatory kiss, and drank in the view from the fourteenth floor. He had picked the Ava Gardner lounge at Dream New York, a designer hotel in a classic Beaux-Arts building within walking distance of Central Park and Times Square. The enclosed rooftop, in fifties style with touches of the Riviera, provided great views of the skyline and Hudson River.

"Do you feel like a star yet? That's the general idea."

"It's working. I'm really, really sorry about that freakout the other day. It was un-called for, unprofessional."

"Forget about it. We're on track and you made a valid point."

Feeling more comfortable she briefly reiterated her worry that remote viewing, not just the warehouse, posed a potential threat to personal privacy. But she didn't linger on that. Instead, she rapped excitedly about several new financing prospects while apologizing repeatedly for talking shop. She also reaffirmed her commitment to what she called his "passion project" and summarized her latest finds.

"Turns out he was a Canadian, technically," she explained. "Francis

Tumblety was born in 1833 somewhere on the other side of the border. But he mainly grew up in Rochester, youngest of eleven kids – two brothers, eight sisters. The Tumbletys lived on Plymouth Avenue, pretty close to the center of town."

"Great. Anything else?"

"He left Rochester at seventeen, but came back about ten years later. By this time, about 1860, he was already calling himself a big-time doctor, and was seen walking around town dressed like an aristocrat. Quite a sight from what I've read, parading in public with a couple of huge greyhounds. Several stories were published while he was in the news, and reporters tracked down a few friends. From what they said, the only medical training he ever had was working in a drug store as a teenager."

"So, a con artist."

"Among other things. He evidently carried it off in Buffalo, Detroit, Washington, all over the country really, even overseas. Patent medicines were his main angle. And he hit the jackpot with the Pimple Destroyer. I say that because afterwards he tended to live in a pretty high style. And there's even more."

"Terrific. We'll begin visiting scenes in a few days."

"Wow, that soon. I also wanted to say, the more I get into this the more I see why you're obsessing about 1888."

"I'm not obsessing."

"Right, whatever, why you're so highly motivated then. There is something about the year. And I'm not just talking about your girlfriend." He wanted to object but she claimed it was just a joke. "The inventions alone – cameras, celluloid, the dry cell battery, the first electric streetcars." She conjured up more examples. "The first windmill to generate electricity, refrigerated boxcars, coin-operated phones. I mean, even the first successful computer."

"All in 1888?"

"It's something, right? I'm just getting into this." She sat back and nursed her drink while looking him over. "Why are you doing this?'

"Doing what?"

"The Ripper thing. It's not just to demonstrate the value of remote viewing. Why do you care about murders before you were born? It's not as if you can do something about it."

He often wondered himself. It was more than fascination with unsolved crimes and investigative procedure. "I'm not sure," he admitted. "I think it has to do with people getting away with things. If we can show that you can't – that even decades later the truth catches up – that would make a difference, wouldn't it?"

"I suppose," Angel mused.

"There's so much we don't know, and some of what we think we know is lies or fairy tales we tell ourselves to feel safe. Now we can find out. We can go back, record it and show it to the world. Think how that would change things."

"Would it?"

"That's what I'm counting on. There are mysteries in every family, on every street, right around the corner. And they shape our lives."

As he spoke her expression shifted from amusement to something closer to admiration. "So, what secret is around this corner?"

"This one?" He considered, thinking he had probably overstated the case. Then it came to him. "I'll tell you," he said smugly. "The murder of Arnold Rothstein."

"Who's that?"

"The guy who fixed the 1919 World Series. A professional gambler, but really more than that. Rothstein owned buildings all over the city. He was also a fence and a bootlegger. You read *The Great Gatsby*. Gatsby's business partner, Meyer Wolfshiem, that's him. They never actually proved he was behind the White Sox fix but everyone thought so. They also never found out who shot him around the corner from here."

"Really? When?"

"In 1928, just before the November elections. Rothstein lived further uptown but he'd been sitting in at a floating card game near here. Afterward he was walking down the street right below us when someone walked up, and pop, pop, pop, several times in the stomach. It took him two days to die.

"And still, when they asked him if he recognized the shooter he refused to say a word. A few weeks earlier he'd announced he was giving up gambling, supposedly he was going to focus on his real estate investments. As if. But there was also a rumor circulating that he owed big for welshing on a bet. Other guys said he was about to collect a million for betting that FDR would win the race for governor. All we know for sure is he didn't live to collect."

Angel shook her head. "How do you know all this?"

"It's gangster history," he said. "Rothstein was a king in this city. But even a king can get too smart for his own good. The secret isn't who killed him. It was probably just some hired thug. The question is why."

NUTLEY, FEBRUARY 7, 2013

It took practice to adapt to the improvements. One of the main problems with RTV was how to deal with the overwhelming amount of data captured by thousands of sensors, each one processing and projecting from a different position. You could isolate and review the stream from any one of them. However, to locate a person or witness a specific event you needed to know exactly when and where to look. Running facial recognition software provided a shortcut for many "conventional" uses, but there was no image archive for people who were dead more than a century – and had never been photographed even when they were alive.

"The NSA has basically the same problem," Danny explained as he made adjustments on Tonio's outfit. "They've been drowning in useless data for years. Keyword spotting has improved, but they're a long way from separating massive collection and efficient extraction of useable intelligence. There's still no substitute for Humint."

Having Tonio observe events from inside the stream began to address the "human intelligence" problem. Danny built on that by developing a biodegradable roaming sensor that could be attached to any item of clothing and angled up to ninety degrees by pointing a wired finger. The result was a record from a unique point of view.

Addressing freedom of mobility in a large area and a three-dimensional stream took more time, creativity and cash, and highly-classified information from a contact at NASA's Jet Propulsion Laboratory in Pasadena. The spark came when Tonio described Shelley's spaceport and mentioned the plan to simulate weightlessness as part of pre-flight training. Tonio expressed amazement that people would pay so much to be in zero gravity for less than ten minutes.

The story gave Danny a related idea. Several years ago, he recalled, NASA conducted a series of microgravity tests, successfully levitating small animals with superconducting magnets. This was what they needed, some type of anti-gravity capability – a weightlessness effect that might be simulated with diamagnetism.

"You just made that up," Angel teased.

"No, Michael Faraday made it up two centuries ago. He realized that every material responds to an applied magnetic field, either as a para-magnet or a dia-magnet. The idea dates back to the discovery that certain elements were repelled by magnetic fields. The effect is weak in most materials, but superconductors intensify it."

Common materials with diamagnetic properties include water, organic compounds like petroleum and plastics, he said, but also mercury, gold and bismuth. In theory, a superconducting magnet cooled to the cryogenic level can handle more current and produce a greater field than the strongest electromagnet.

Once his instincts were confirmed, Danny wasted no time. Before the end of January he had supervised the installation of new electro-magnetic coils with liquid nitrogen-refrigerated, superconducting wire. Tonio meanwhile began testing the other outcome of their conversation. They called it the B-Suit, a custom-made jumpsuit with enough Bismuth in the weave to assist with lift off. It wasn't only the most naturally dia-magnetic element, it was safe, non-toxic and used in glazes, lubricants, paints, acrylic fibers and even X-ray shields. The combination created an extraordinary effect. It was close to the experience Shelley hoped to market, although it required some practice to maintain your balance.

Given the obstacles and the odds, Danny was understandably proud of the results.

"We should call this extreme viewing," Tonio joked as he suited up.

LONDON, AUGUST 31, 1888

Latitude 51.519722, Longitude 0.060812

The last time anyone saw Polly Nichols alive was around two-thirty in the morning. The previous evening she had walked Whitechapel Road for hours, trolling for johns as she wandered from pub to pub. She was forty-three and the last decade had taken a high toll.

Her given name was Mary Ann, the daughter of an English locksmith named Edward Walker and his wife Caroline. At nineteen she married William Nichols, a local printer, but they didn't move out of her family's home in Walworth for ten years. Eventually, after the birth of three chil-dren, the couple finally found a place of their own on Stamford Street off Blackfriars Road. But after two more children the marriage ended badly. Young Mary Ann had become middle-aged Polly, a depressed and desperate alcoholic willing to screw for a drink.

Since 1881 she'd been in and out of various workhouses and infirmaries around London. Again and again she tried to clean up. But desperate circumstances and the pull of alcohol proved too strong. Earlier in 1888, from May to July, she had work as a chambermaid in a lovely home on Rose Hill Road. That ended badly when she ran off with some cash and all the clothes she could carry.

For the last three months she'd been staying primarily on Thrawl Street in Spitalfields, either there or at a doss-house on Flower. Shortly before two in the morning on August 31 she was in the common kitchen, drunk and pleading with the night manager to hold a bed open until she could come up with the fee.

Half an hour later she was on the corner of Whitechapel and Osborn, alone.

From where Tonio was waiting he couldn't see her. But she was less than half a mile away, by now likely having an argument with Ellen Holland, an acquaintance who stayed at the same house. She saw that Polly was dead drunk and attempted to persuade her to return to Thrawl. But Tonio also knew that Polly would refuse and head his way, down Whitechapel Road to the turn for Buck's Row.

The church clock chimed two-thirty.

They'd picked a spot between the railyard and the street, less than ten feet from Buck's Row #2. There was little light and a dim projection spread out around him, from the railroad tracks and a stable yard down Buck's Row almost to Whitechapel. The B-suit was working well, gently levitating him with help from a set of climbing ropes dropped from the ceiling. This augmented the weightless effect by giving him a way to propel from point to point or remain in place by holding the closest rope. In the control room, as well as Harry's cabin, they could monitor the stream from the censor on his suit.

Over the next forty-five minutes he rotated occasionally, waiting to see someone arrive from another direction. It was almost impossible to tell. But there was sufficient moonlight by around three-thirty to identify the outline of a woman strolling unsteadily in his direction. The sound of her boots clicked on the stones.

He saw her, and then someone else, moving stealthily along a wall across the street not far in front of him. Tall, wearing a long cape, he stopped before reaching the corner.

Tonio swung around for a better view, looking for an angle with sufficient light. Now he had both of them in sight, Polly in the distance stumbling, her stalker closer, just beyond her notice. He heard the metallic sound of a blade slowly sliding from a sheath and glanced down to see its glint in the moonlight. The clouds parted slightly and light struck the face.

It was him! Frank Tumblety, the man who would soon be known as Leather Apron, the Whitechapel killer and Jack the Ripper, and eventually as the most famous serial murderer in history – just moments before one of his crimes. He was tall, strong, determined, a pale middle-aged man with oil-dark eyes and the outsized mustache Tonio had first seen at Donnelly's lecture. Looking icily committed and yet clinically detached Tumblety was primed to pounce.

Suddenly it wasn't enough to watch and record. Tonio felt himself tense involuntarily with rage, a frustrated hunger to leap out and stop it. But he was powerless, a witness to the inevitable.

As Polly reached #2 she staggered a bit and reached out for a wall to catch herself. Tumblety heard the falter and sensed his moment to strike. Leaping out he swung the long, slim blade and caught the edge of her throat, closing in quickly for a second slice, this time deep across her windpipe. The blood didn't spurt. Instead, she gasped as the wounds slowly opened. He moved closer still, steadying his victim as he pointed the knife at her abdomen, watching her terror before plunging in the blade. He held her there as she died, suspended like a ragdoll as blood seeped from the wounds.

Tonio felt weak, on the verge of vomiting, and fought an urge to turn away.

She was dead when Tumblety lowered her body to the ground and prepared for the next phase. Out of the folds of his cape came a small medical bag, which he opened methodically and placed down beside him. Next he laid a cloth and selected his instruments. Tonio changed the censor's direction.

Tumblety leaned in, gripping Polly's jaw in a gloved hand as he stared into her dead eyes. Then back to business. This was not like any operation Tonio had ever seen: it was abrupt and brutal, a series of slashes that married a killer's unfettered anger with a working knowledge of anatomy. He cut her open and began ripping into her genitals.

Tonio could barely watch. At the same time he had a clear sense that the grotesque ritual wasn't over. Fortunately, other people were already approaching. He heard them before Tumblety did, two men walking toward them from the other side of the tracks. Tonio knew what came next, witnesses discovering the body. Tumblety heard the noise moments later and emitted a growl of frustration. But he knew the risk and wrapped his tools in the cloth before returning everything to the bag. Then he stood and inspected his work.

Suspended in the stream a few feet from him, Tonio was revolted yet compelled to watch. The killer stepped away from the body and the censor caught his face. The eyes were blank, the windows vacant. But the mouth gaped open, twisted into a self-satisfied and carnivorous grin.

22
DOUBTS

As the stream collapsed Tonio floated to the floor and rushed from the chamber, no longer able to contain his nausea. Afterward, without removing the B-suit or saying a word he jumped in the car he rented to avoid questions from the crew and headed nowhere in particular until he noticed an entrance to the Garden State Parkway.

He ended up on Long Beach Island two hours later heading down a deserted main drag through Beach Haven, a tiny resort he remembered fondly from his teens. The place felt abandoned in the dead of winter. Less than two blocks wide and directly on the ocean, it had been hit hard during Sandy. But somehow most of the old Victorian homes, remnants from a time when it was a prime vacation destination for wealthy Philadelphians, survived without extensive damage.

Parking in the public lot at the end of the pavement, he bundled up in an overcoat and walked the shoreline toward land's end.

During the drive images of the crime replayed and re-triggered the same emotions. As they flooded back they sparked tough questions. What was the point of witnessing such horrors? What exactly did he hope to achieve? To prove he wasn't superfluous, that he had a purpose in life? Maybe Harry was right and he was just on a twisted ego trip, trying to become a modern Sherlock Holmes? Why go after Jack the Ripper rather than address more pressing concerns?

For years he had been content to drift through life, detached, basically disinterested, watching events unfold like the scenes of a home movie. That had changed with Danny's discovery. Still, what was he trying to accomplish? And why did he suddenly feel responsible to make a difference in the world? Better to stop now, before life became too complicated -- and more dangerous than usual. Just bail out and get back to Greece.

A Mediterranean island sounded about right. But he'd been hiding for years, hiding out and asleep, numb to pain but unable to experience real joy. Did he prefer being numb to the feelings set loose by what he'd seen?

On the other hand, there was little point in trying to catch a killer in the act if he was no more than a puppet, dangling in the dark while a sad and desperate woman was disemboweled.

He walked to the farthest point on the island, a rounded plateau at the end of a sandbar surrounded on three sides. Watching waves roll in calmed him down. Yet as a child Tonio witnessed deep terror strike even this place. The monster then was a shark, and the impact so shattering that it inspired a book and a blockbuster, and seared a new word into popular consciousness – Jaws.

Tonio had vivid memories of that long ago time. The idea of Jaws prowling the waters offshore terrified him as a child. A few hours earlier that night he'd felt the same terror. In London he had gazed into the face of death incarnate, a force so terrible it paralyzed his reason and gave him a glimpse into the abyss. Maybe that was what he felt compelled to confront. Or maybe this – the attraction to terrible crimes and his gnawing need to solve them might reflect a desire to face some darkness within, to expose and somehow harness it.

Looking back, it occurred to him that the feelings had begun to emerge after his uncle's death, triggered by his sense that everyone was lying. What he was being told simply didn't sound plausible. His first reaction was unfocused anger, followed by denial and depression. After his illness the emptiness was finally replaced in his teens by a morbid fascination with crime and death -- including his own. What was the point, he often asked himself, of the wrong people dying and the bad guys getting away? Where was justice? Where was love? All he saw was cruelty, manipulation and lies. What about rules and law? Some jokes, he thought, just a sham, mass deceptions in wide circulation.

For several years he gave suicide serious consideration, but eventually rejected it as a cop out.

Get a grip! He scolded himself, gradually becoming aware of the drenching wind and sea spray. Somebody needs a reality check. He was cold and damp and too close to the water.

"Is it safe?" Harry was using a bad German accent, not to disguise his voice but to see if Tonio caught the reference.

He had driven back into town and found a pay phone at the Engleside Inn. "Marathon Man," he answered. "Lawrence Olivier as the mad Nazi dentist. Yes, it is safe, I'm following your damn rules. You said this number was okay."

"It is. So, how did it go?"

"Gross. I barfed."

"That means you're normal. Your eyes saw more than your soul could take. But you got your man, you know who it is now?"

"Yeah, we do." He described what he'd witnessed, Frank Tumblety stalking and murdering Polly Nichols, providing just enough graphic detail to establish why it was so upsetting. "But I'm beginning to feel like this is meaningless. What I really want to know is who killed uncle G, who and why? Then I think that's just as pointless, another goose chase up my own ass. How do you do it?

"What?"

"Not say fuck it all."

"Sometimes I do." This was unexpected. Harry wasn't the doubtful kind or one to share confidences. "I told you I was with OWS for a while, the Occupy movement," he began. "Everyone knew what was happening for years, massive and growing inequality. We're at the point where the 400 richest people have as much money as half the population. But no one was talking about it until we lit the match. It was awesome, man, hundreds of cities, everywhere. The Tea Party became yesterday's news and everyone was talking about the one percent."

"I noticed that."

"And it happened at the right moment. It allowed Obama to define Romney as a one percenter before he had the nomination. The guy never would have won a second term without it."

"It's a theory."

"It's a fact! But nothing changed, that's my point. The Democrats were toast and we made it possible for them to win. And what did we get? Tear gas and rubber bullets. They cleared out all the encampments, a coordinated campaign right across the country. Still, I admit we didn't do ourselves any favors. We got hung up in process. We confused ends with means. It seems to happen every time."

"Democracy is messy, isn't that what you say?"

"Messy is okay. We were like Congress. But what I'm saying here is you buy your ticket and take the ride. Make a commitment, whether it's to some cause or to yourself. You're always taking a risk. And you could fail. Or you could discover that you were after the wrong thing. But you don't get to control the outcomes, or what you learn on the way. It doesn't work that way."

As therapy, this left something to be desired. Tonio wasn't particularly comforted. But he did feel a bit stronger. He appreciated what Harry was telling him – stop second guessing and stick with the plan.

"So I continue? I thought you wanted us to go after something… what's the word?"

"Relevant," Harry replied. "We will. I'm holding you to that. But meanwhile…"

"Back in the saddle?"

"Finish what you started. Nail the fucker."

"And what about Gianni and the bigger picture?"

Harry also had some ideas about that.

MANHATTAN, FEBRUARY 9, 2013

Street noise wasn't keeping him up. Over the years he'd become accustomed to the cacophonous soundtrack of everyday life in the city. Neither did New York's perpetual light prevent him from shutting down when necessary. But that night, even after two hours driving back from the shore and reaching his apartment bone cold and exhausted, he couldn't stop thinking.

He had filed away the most disturbing images. Now he was speculating about Harry's cyber warriors, the Truthsquad collective, which would begin looking into the life and untimely death of Lt. Gianni Wolfe. Harry would meanwhile work up a dossier on Shelley, one that did more than "follow the money." It would be another kind of profile, personal and psychological, the basis for a special presentation.

Harry's idea was to turn the promised demonstration of next-level virtual reality to their advantage by making it a Rorschach test for its audience. If they learned enough in advance and selected the right locations they could confront Shelley with his past and monitor his reactions. It would be a form of interrogation, a holographic journey leading step by step to his brother's death.

They could hardly wait for the show to open.

Tonio's time in old London had another effect. After weeks it brought him back to thoughts of Annie. He hadn't forgotten that first sighting or what he learned about her in the weeks following. But eventually he told himself there was really no point, especially when the infatuation bothered Angel. She hadn't mentioned it lately, but why rock the boat? Just one reason: he needed to know Annie better.

During the Sedona vortex expedition he had seen her a second time. Of the infinite choices available to him in that moment he had found her in the midst of a crisis. Could it be an accident? What did it really mean? A least it was possible to isolate the moment – November 13, the climax of a series of demonstrations that had been building for months.

The dispossessed of London had begun to protest unemployment. The term was new, just coined. The police response was predictably harsh, often resulting in injuries and arrests. Even the press wasn't safe.

For those in charge the problem was mainly tactical, a question of how to maintain public order. That meant stopping the protests in Trafalgar Square. Demonstrations had become an almost daily occurrence there. It was the most convenient place in the city for an outdoor gathering, and a central refuge for the homeless. Hundreds of men and women slept in its nooks and crannies, joined in daylight by thousands more, the ragged denizens of the city's notorious East End.

Trafalgar was also near Westminster and Buckingham Palace. As a result Lord Salisbury, who often saw threats to public safety where there were none, ordered the chief of the Metro Police to take care of it. Perhaps the Square should be ringed with fences, the security conscious Lord advised. That way, if trouble came at least the trouble-makers could more easily be rounded up.

Annie was also thinking about tactics. To that end, she had organized a Socialist Defense Association so those in jail could get legal help. Many of the charges were being trumped up. She also assembled a group of well-to-do supporters who would show up night or day in response to a telegram and bail out anyone unjustly arrested.

The boiling point finally came on November 13. The Radical Federation had called for a major march and rally that Sunday in response to three abuses of power. One was the imprisonment of a Member of Parliament, another was the ongoing repression in Ireland. But the primary focus of the day was the notorious Coercion Act, which had suspended civil rights indefinitely. Annie was invited to speak.

Four days before the rally Sir Charles Warren, the Home Secretary, issued an order forbidding meetings in the Square. However, he simultaneously offered private assurances that "legitimate political gatherings" would not be disrupted. On Saturday, he changed his mind again and issued a final order banning all processions.

Delegates from the labor and radical clubs, the Fabians, Social Democratic Federation and Socialist League met that Saturday night. There was little time to deliberate, however, so in the end they opted to move ahead. They would gather at various places around the city in hopes of disorienting the authorities by approaching the square from several directions. What they didn't know was that spies had tipped off the police and the place was surrounded before they arrived. Backing up the coppers were squadrons of "life guards" with bayonets. It looked like what it was – a massacre in the making.

He had seen it go down remotely in the desert. Annie wearing her usual outfit, the neckerchief, short skirt and boots that had captured Tonio's attention, leading a procession from Clerkenwell Green along the city's narrow streets. Thousands more marching in from Holborn, Bermondsey and Deptford.

Before the riot was over thousands of citizens were injured, many of them newcomers to protest and police violence. Just south of Trafalgar, a young writer named Alfred Linnell was fatally injured by a horse. The next morning, still dazed and traumatized, dozens of decent people were sentenced to jail in Bow Street Police Court. Stead quickly launched his own defense fund and raised enough money within days to free everyone on appeal. Annie defiantly led them out of Millbank Prison, bruised and battered but unbowed.

More cynical than most, G.B. Shaw called it "the most abjectly disgraceful defeat ever suffered by a band of heroes outnumbering their foes a thousand to one." Then again, no one considered it a rousing success. Three people had died. And what was gained? Nothing as far as Tonio could tell.

Within days it was known as Bloody Sunday.

The riot became a turning point for Annie. Due to her identification with the march she moved from being well-known to famous and, in some circles, notorious. It also confirmed what her old friend Bradlaugh feared and deepened the break between them. Not only had she joined forces with the Socialists, she hadn't even consulted him before leading the disastrous march. Fighting for freedom was one thing, but to Bradlaugh this looked like an invitation to slaughter.

Annie agreed in one sense. The situation was dire, possibly deadly, and having faith in the legal system felt increasingly naïve. But she had reached the conclusion that more radical action was required. At least Stead and the socialists were prepared to fight back. In private moments, however, she wasn't so certain. Neither socialism nor atheism seemed to offer the real answers the world needed.

Their differences were vast, yet Tonio admired her. Beyond her courage and obvious charisma, he was drawn to her independence and strength of purpose, her powerful focus and ability to inspire, and her innate need to bring people together in pursuit of a great goal. He was also beginning to think they might have a few things in common.

Annie's current beliefs, like earlier ones, might simply be a stop on a longer road. Despite her defiant public image and passionate speeches she wasn't that sure about much of anything. Tonio felt much the same way. Both of them were groping in the darkness, struggling toward visions they couldn't quite see.

23
DESPERATION

LONDON, SEPTEMBER 8, 1888
Latitude 51.519736, Longitude 0.065242

Hanbury Street was like most in Spitalfields, unpaved, runny with mud when it rained and never quite free from the scent of horse manure.

The population of the East End had exploded since its days as one of the peasant villages north of the Thames and east of the wall. For more than a century immigrants had been migrating here, displaced people looking for work at the port, Huguenot refugees, Irish, Russians and Jews. On some streets in the overcrowded inner-city the English language was barely spoken. The poor lived cheek to jowl, jammed into hovels, eating, sleeping and reproducing in the same room. The few who were lucky enough to find steady work managed a bit better, but many people did much worse. They slept on stairways or huddled in squares with the rest of the city's homeless.

In the waning years of the Gilded Age the neighborhood had become a world-famous hell-hole, one of the roughest places on the planet, a breeding ground for crime and disease. Liberals and radicals complained. Protesters took to the streets. But nothing changed, and for women like Annie Chapman there was little relief and no safety net.

Short, stout and never very attractive, this Annie hadn't started life planning to be a whore. In fact, decades earlier she had married a respectable coachman with steady work on a farm in Windsor. Three children followed. But her daughter died and both of her sons ended up in institutions. Whether it was the grief or just the strain of life in general, both she and her husband became drunks. It ultimately killed John Chapman in 1886. The marriage was over almost a decade earlier, although John did continue to provide a ten shilling a week allowance until he died.

During her last eighteen months of life Annie Chapman was basically penniless, often sick, and drunk whenever possible. When she had enough money she would buy a bed at someplace like Crossingham's Lodging House on Dorset Street. On the second Saturday in September, she didn't have enough money for that after a drinking binge nearby.

"We got rules, you knows that," said Tim Donovan coldly. He was in charge after dark and saw no reason to make an exception in her case.

Earlier in the week Annie had visited the infirmary at St. Bartholomew's Hospital. They looked her over and suggested that she spend more on food and less on ale. She ignored them and by Saturday night felt weak and feverish. Donovan could see it but offered no aid.

Turned out at two in the morning, she wandered Spitalfield's fog-filled streets. A hard veil hung over the rooftops as she stumbled down Commercial Road looking for anyone willing to spend a crown or two on sex. With any luck she might get paid without actual penetration, just a few minutes with someone's cock between her thighs. Many johns went home satisfied with that.

Four hours later she was dead. The scene of the crime was the yard behind #29, an open space reachable from Hanbury Street via a narrow passage through the building. The area had a shed and cellar entrance, and was separated from the surrounding backyards by a five foot fence.

Shortly before five in the morning John Richardson emerged from the building and went into the yard. His mother owned the place and rented several rooms. After making sure that the cellar door was locked young Richardson checked the perimeter before sitting on the steps to trim some leather from his boots. When he finished he went back in.

About thirty minutes later, as Annie turned the corner from Commercial onto Hanbury heading east, a tall man dressed in a cloak and cap approached her from the opposite direction. He greeted her politely in English with an American accent. They were less than a mile from Buck's Row, the site of Polly Nichols' murder eight days earlier.

"That's him," confirmed Tonio as he watched from across the road. He had arrived half an hour before and used the time to "walk" the area. The goal this time was to provide a broader context. They already knew the killer's identity, now he wanted to focus on the victim and the wretched conditions that contributed to the crimes.

If he had to witness another brutal murder at least he wanted to understand how Annie Chapman lived. Assuming that their estimates were correct, he might even have time left to capture some of the initial investigation. After the murder it would be only minutes before an elderly renter discovered the body.

On the sidewalk Annie finished the preliminaries and moved on to the price. She knew the area well, she explained woozily, pointing toward the doorway. "It's private enough, sir. I've used it before."

Tumblety leaned down and whispered a question, "And what will you give me?"

"Anything you wants," Annie replied with a slur.

"Is that right? Hmm. Let's find out."

Once he checked to be sure no one was watching he followed her down the dark passageway into the yard. She was already waiting when he arrived, her back up against the fence, legs parted slightly as she tucked the heavy hem of her skirt into her belt.

"So, what'll it be?"

He cocked his head and looked her over as if considering options. When he was a foot away, however, he took her by surprise with a solid punch to the side of her face, then grabbed her by the throat with a gloved hand and squelched her scream with the other. Annie fought back as well as she could in a drunk and weakened condition, striking out randomly while attempting to push him away. One of the blows caught his cheek with a ring and drew blood. It only added to his grim determination.

He had come prepared for mayhem. With one hand continuing to squeeze her throat he beat Annie unconscious with a series of sharp blackjack blows. Once she was flat on the ground he brought out a narrow, eight-inch surgical blade and slit her throat. What followed was the orgiastic mixture of violent mutilation and hasty surgery he'd been denied after murdering Polly. Now there was more than enough time. Before daylight he'd cut her open and crudely but methodically removed several organs, including her vagina and womb.

When he finished, he wrapped up what he had extracted and draped a leather apron he noticed in the yard over the corpse. That concealed most of the blood. Next, he placed Annie's hands across her chest in a mock gesture of self-protection, re-arranged her feet so her knees fanned out, and wrapped a handkerchief around her throat. Anyone seeing her from a distance might conclude she was sleeping.

Before exiting through the passageway and back the way he came, Tumblety also positioned several clues – a patch of muslin and two small combs, arranged to create a triangular shape. Even though they now knew his identity the message remained cryptic.

Inspector Chandler was the first to view the body up close. Several workingmen had noticed John Davis, the elderly tenant who saw it in the yard, running down the street as he yelled incoherently. Once Chandler reached the backyard and looked over the hideous remains for himself he ordered one of the men to fetch the nearest division surgeon, more coppers and an ambulance. While waiting for them to arrive he conducted a preliminary search and identified anything like a clue. This included not just those left behind intentionally, but also the leather apron Tumblety used and random items scattered around the yard that revealed nothing.

Dr. George Phillips arrived at 6:30 to officially examine the body before releasing it to Whitechapel Mortuary. From the way Annie's organs had been removed his off-the-cuff conclusion was that the killer had detailed anatomical knowledge. The same had been said about Polly Nichols' killer. But Phillips also informed Inspector Chandler that Annie had been dead for at least two hours. Tonio knew personally that was off by half.

Drawn by the ambulance and police presence a crowd gathered and rumors began to spread. With minutes a hundred gawkers had blocked the street. Some speculated that the killer must be a religious fanatic dispatching whores in a private battle with sin. Others saw vengeance for some real or imagined offense. As word circulated fear and paranoia spread with it.

Chandler learned little from John Davis or the three working stiffs who had seen him raving. But Albert Cadosch, who lived next door, claimed he heard a voice around five-thirty, followed by the sound of something falling against the fence. Awakened by the escalating noise Elizabeth Long, who rented a room across the street, opened her window and inquired about the ruckus. "Murder," someone yelled.

Several minutes later, when Chandler stopped by for a statement, Tonio tagged along. A layer of dust and soot coated everything in the shabby room. The only highlight of the décor was faded, mildew-stained wallpaper. In some places, where the paper was crumbling or gone, he could see the plaster beneath. The light through the window panes, covered with a layer of grime, cast an otherworldly pall over the space.

Mrs. Long said that she had trouble sleeping and had woken up around five-thirty. Peering out her dingy window she'd noticed the outlines of a man and a woman having a conversation on the sidewalk near the corner. She couldn't pick out the words or see the faces, but he was tall, looked like a "foreigner," and wore a long coat and a deer-stalker hat.

After listening Chandler thanked her and said another inspector would be in touch to follow up. However, Tonio could immediately tell that he didn't take her information seriously. And why? Simply because this eye-witness account conflicted with the medical examiner's "professional" estimate that the murder was committed earlier.

They certainly needed someone like Sherlock Holmes. Having received an excellent description of the killer by the last person to see the victim alive this limey lawman chose to ignore it, he thought. Given this sort of gross incompetence it was really little wonder that Tumblety felt free to strike so boldly or assumed he could get away with it. It also explained why poor old London might get hysterical.

And the media circus hadn't yet begun.

24

NEGOTIATIONS

WASHINGTON, DC, FEBRUARY 15, 2013

When it came to business Angel Brancusi could be as ruthless as any man and more persuasive than most with the right audience. Before two headhunters hired by TELPORT found her in 2006, she had spent more than decade after Princeton with the Renaissance Equity Group, a former merchant bank making a name in private finance.

Rather than operating out of New York or Chicago, REG was based in the Capital and had a roster that included former Cabinet secretaries, ex-prime ministers and career diplomats. By the time Angel was thirty she had worked with them on billion dollar deals. It was a heady environment reinforcing her belief that anything she desired was ultimately within reach with the right pitch.

The move that made her career was with LinkUSA, one of several companies competing at the time to build a fiber-optic cable infrastructure for e-mail and phone calls over the Internet. To make it work she used an approach that became standard – financial incentives, including generous stock options for upper management and decent bonuses for others. Every employee also received training in how to manage their newfound riches. With key staff effectively incentivized, expenses dropped as revenues rose by more than 30 percent in the first three years that REG owned it.

By 1999 most of the debt from the buyout was repaid and LinkUSA was ready to go public. The initial offering was $2.3 billion. Renaissance Equity was entitled to half, meaning that its original $150 million investment had turned into more than a billion dollars.

"If you ever get tired of New York there's a corner office and parking space with your name on it," said David Simon, the REG co-founder who had hired Angel and nurtured her like an Olympic athlete.

"For now I'll settle for lunch," she teased. "Maybe afterward I'll see things differently."

Simon had requested the meeting and said there were two people he thought she should meet. Angel asked Tonio to come along, insisting that as board chair he needed a deeper understanding of the business landscape, players and choices TELPORT faced. The success of Remote Viewing meant potential partners and suppliers would be lining up and more meals and meetings like this one were on the horizon.

The other two at the table were Lucy Gershon of FABRICO, a leader in on-demand digital production, and Peter Lynch, who listened attentively but said little after Simon introduced him as an assistant to the Undersecretary of Defense for Acquisition, Technology, and Logistics. According to Simon, DoD needed to keep an eye on any new tech with potential security applications or implications.

"It's basically about turning data into things," explained Gershon. "First generation rapid prototyping brought down the price of computer-controlled manufacturing. Now we can make almost anything, and make it anywhere." Catching Tonio's perplexed expression she provided a brief primer.

The first "fab lab," shorthand for both fabrication and fabulous laboratory, was launched in Boston by Mel King a decade back, she explained. School girls were among the first to use it, in their case to hold a high-tech craft sale and earn extra income. Now there were more than a hundred, from South Africa to Detroit. She called the process the leading edge of a new industrial revolution. It meant that a design could be created and sent anywhere for production, eliminating most shipping costs.

"Sounds promising," offered Tonio. "Futuristic actually."

"To be honest, it's not a new idea," Gershon admitted. "Humans have cell structures called ribosomes, which makes other proteins. It's pretty much the same. Or say like assembling LEGO pieces, except that we're developing 3D assemblers that also build things. We can already fabricate 3D integrated circuits, electronic boards, and components for your Locators and Visors."

Angel broke in. "I heard some guy has made parts for an automatic rifle."

"True. They've also fabricated unique keys. You just X-ray the lock with a CT scanner, build a model and produce the keys with a combination of milling, 3D printing and molding. We can do the same things for you with visors, accessories, and so on."

"But there may be restrictions," Lynch injected, "particularly on the 3D printing side. Remember what happened when color laser printers came out. Next thing you know they're being used for counterfeiting. I'm not saying you can't use it to manufacture, but there could be some legal limitations down the line."

Simon chose to focus on the positive, specifically the prospect of federal legislation to create a National Fabrication Project with an R&D grant program, national research center and a network of Fab Labs. His proposal was a partnership between TELPORT and FABRICO, with Renaissance leveraging the capital, using this new form of inexpensive production around the world to make remote viewing a major mass communication competitor.

Tonio felt in over his head. But he didn't mind it, since the occasion provided a prime opportunity to watch Angel impress corporate Alphas with a combination of her business acumen, ease with tech talk and knock-out looks. Yet Lynch was resisting. He seemed to have a reason for attending other than the deal. Tonio began to think it might be him.

"Aside from the concern about illegal fabrication," he probed casually, "how does the administration, from what you know, feel about our plans?"

Lynch smiled. "From what I know? That's interesting." Obviously there was something this guy wasn't saying or couldn't. "I'd call it a wait and see attitude."

"Waiting for what?"

"Whether you're the next Apple or just a novelty act."

"What else?" The follow up telegraphed a challenge.

"Well, we like to know the players. Wouldn't want this kind of opportunity wasted, or the enterprise in irresponsible hands, would we?"

Simon didn't like where the conversation was heading and steered it back to happy talk. "We're confident," he said, "very confident. For Renaissance this is a natural fit. That's why I wanted you and Lucy to meet now. It's early days, but I think you see the potential for synergy. TELPORT has the hottest product since the cell phone and FABRICO can produce it for the world market."

"I'll drink to that," said Lucy, lifting a glass. Angel and Simon followed the lead and clinked, but Lynch just wished them luck.

Tonio added his glass at the last moment, his attention staying squarely with Lynch. Those "spontaneous" comments, especially from someone with DoD, didn't seem off-hand at all.

He was in the hotel suite watching *Dexter*, his favorite TV crime series at the moment, when someone knocked insistently. Dexter Morgan, the sympathetic Miami serial killer whose internal struggles drove the storyline, was on the verge of falling in love, or murdering his girlfriend's father – or both. Turning down the volume he peeked through the pinhole, saw Angel and considered not answering. Once he opened the door just slightly she pushed it wide and brushed past him.

Angel was high on being in her element, but also on the prospect of catapulting TELPORT into the global game. In the years since leaving REG she'd often questioned her decision to "actually produce something" rather than continue making mega-deals. It seemed finally to be paying off.

Pacing the room she speed-talked through the main points of the recent sit down, projections, her hopes for the deal, global branding and distribution, tie-ins with other products, unlimited merchandising possibilities. "It's perfect," she kept saying. As a result, Danny would be free to pursue the "pure research" side without worrying about cash flow or prying eyes, and Tonio could conduct his personal "investigations." They could even break free from Wolfe Enterprises, she said. There was no limit to how far this could go.

He felt the contagious energy rush when she was in such a mood, somewhere between euphoria and mania. Leaping between topics, she managed to connect them all with the force of her blind enthusiasm and create a detailed portrait of a future that wasn't merely possible but, as she conceived it anyway, positively inevitable.

She could even summon obscure details from the new finds on Frank "the Ripper" Tumblety, the result of assigning an assistant to locate every published mention in New York, Rochester, Toronto, Boston, Pittsburgh, San Francisco, St. Louis and Washington, DC between 1860 and 1890. "We know he operated in all those places," she explained. "In the early years he was constantly facing prosecution, or fleeing from it. Around 1857 he was arrested in Toronto for attempting to perform an abortion on a prostitute. A story in, I think the *Montreal Pilot*, christened him the Prince of Quacks. Great handle.

"One of his patients actually died," she added, "in New Brunswick, I think. He was found guilty of manslaughter on that, but by this time he was long gone, off to Boston."

Tonio interrupted to say that she didn't have to explain all this tonight and he probably wouldn't remember most of it anyway.

"But I haven't gotten to the most amazing thing."

"What's the most amazing thing?"

"They thought he was part of the Lincoln assassination."

"That is amazing. Who said that?"

"But it's wasn't true. The thing is, during the Civil War he offered to serve as a surgeon and got a pass to move around freely. He never actually joined up, supposedly because of a sudden, very convenient decline in his health. But he hung out with the general staff and attended parties. Of course, he also claimed to have hobnobbed with Lincoln at White House receptions.

"After the assassination he was staying in St. Louis at the Lindell Hotel, the largest hotel in the world at the time. Seven floors! Anyway, he was arrested there and held for two days as a suspect in the assassination. You have anything to drink?"

He opened the mini-bar. She grabbed two small bottles and kicked off her heels.

"So, why was he a suspect?"

"Mistaken identity. They confused him with another herb doctor, Blackburn I think, but Blackburn was with the rebels. The suspicion was that, at the time Lincoln was killed, Blackburn was working on a plot to infect the north with yellow fever. So they ordered his arrest and got Tumblety instead. He was held a few days, but from what I can see he never got over it. Strange, huh?"

"Very," he said, propped up on one of the beds to watch her pace and ramble. "I'm kind of tired. Could we do this –"

"Sure," she agreed automatically, "but I have to tell you one more thing." She took his shrug as permission to flop down at the foot of the mattress. "It's about that year, 1888. There was definitely a lot going on. Here in DC, for instance, the National Geographic Society was formed. The German emperor died, electrocution became legal in New York, and I told you about all the inventions. But there's also a Tesla connection."

That got his attention.

"I mean, it was the year of the speech that changed his life." She crawled up and stretched out beside him. "You know Tesla worked for Edison after coming to New York. But Edison was building power stations for direct current and Tesla was working on AC. He eventually resigned and made this presentation to the Institute of Electrical Engineers. When was it? May 1888, his big game changing moment. In that speech he told the world that alternating current could generate millions of volts and travel hundreds of miles from a power station. Edison could only transmit power a mile or so at the time. But Tesla also saw how motors and lights could work with the same electrical system.

"It was a radical breakthrough," she said, "like what we're doing." Finishing off the second bottle she let it drop and grabbed a pillow to cuddle closer. "So, did that guy Lynch spook you?"

"Not exactly. But I do think he was trying to tell me something."

"Well, if you were spooked that would be appropriate, since David says he is one."

Tonio expressed mild surprise but also felt vindicated – with a fresh dash of insecurity.

"You don't have to worry," she said, now tired, tipsy and openly flirting. "It's like rock, paper, scissors." He had no clue what she was talking about. "He looked like a snippy little spook, but you're my rocky little gangster. Rock can crush scissors, isn't that right?"

She took one of his hands and placed it over her breast, then put her own over that. "But I'm paper," she said, "and paper smothers rock."

He knew this drunken invitation wasn't her brightest idea. Trying to sidestep a decision and distract himself, Tonio constructed a quick mental list of the reasons why he shouldn't reach into her blouse and slide down to kiss her. Then he went ahead anyway, deciding to settle for a less rational approach. After a big day and for that matter a rough month, both of them deserved a time out.

25
Struggle

LONDON, JULY 11, 1888

Latitude 51.498912, Longitude 0.125098

The House of Commons was a model of architectural symmetry and political pragmatism. When the chamber was full during parliamentary debates, government supporters took the seats to the right of the speaker's chair. Opponents and others sat on the left. Senior members from both camps, the so-called "front benchers," occupied seats closest to the center. Separating the opposing sides was a gangway, known as the Floor, measuring the distance of two swords.

The original reason for the gangway was to prevent duels from breaking out.

Located at the north end of Westminster Palace on the banks of the Thames, the ornate chamber was originally called St. Stephen's Chapel, part of the royal residence until the "lower house" moved in from Westminster Abbey. Over the next few centuries the medieval look faded and finally vanished until the entire palace was remodeled in the early nineteenth. Less than a decade later, an accidental fire destroyed both chambers of parliament and most of the residence.

The next round of renovations took twenty years, this time a controversial mixture of Sir Charles Barry's conservative Gothic style and the neo-classical approach becoming popular in the States. The work wasn't done until 1860, just as a young Charles Bradlaugh, then emerging as one of the country's leading freethinkers, launched *The National Reformer.*

Almost thirty years later, in the same chamber, he and two other MPs were waiting as Annie Besant arrived with a delegation of matchstick girls. Most were under sixteen years old.

After years of resisting the oath of office and repeatedly facing jail and disenfranchisement, Bradlaugh had finally succeeded in winning the right to speak and to vote in parliament in 1886. Since then he and Annie had parted ways over Socialism and Bloody Sunday. But they were on the same page about the matchstick strike.

Tonio had selected the moment carefully. For months, in secret, he'd assembled his profile and concluded that this was the best opportunity to see Annie at the peak of her political career in London. In June, after attending a talk by Clementina Black at the Fabian Society, she had interviewed some women who worked at the Bryant & May match factory and published a searing account in *The Link*. They called the story "White Slavery in London."

"Born in slums," Annie wrote, "driven to work while still children, undersized because under-fed, oppressed because helpless, flung aside as soon as worked out. Who cares if they die or go on to the streets, provided that Bryant & May shareholders get their 23 per cent and Mr. Theodore Bryant can erect statutes and buy parks?

"Girls are used to carry boxes on their heads until the hair is rubbed off and the young heads are bald at fifteen years of age. Country clergymen with shares in Bryant & May's, draw down on your knee your fifteen year old daughter; pass your hand tenderly over the silky clustering curls. Rejoice in the dainty beauty of the thick, shiny tresses."

Using hard facts and compelling imagery she drove home the extreme working conditions and the severe, often deadly effects of the phosphorous used to make matches. Hair loss was just the start. The skin of many girls turned yellow over time, then green and black as they succumbed to a deadly form of bone cancer known as phossy jaw. The use of phosphorous in manufacturing was banned in the US and Sweden, but Britain's government considered such a restriction a dangerous restraint of trade.

The girls at Bryant & May worked fourteen hours a day for less than five shillings a week. At times they didn't even get that due to a draconian system of fines that covered things like talking or taking a toilet break without permission. The fine for arriving late was half a day's wage.

Shortly after her article appeared Bryant & May management circulated a statement along with a demand that workers sign. The statement basically said that the undersigned were satisfied with their conditions. Several workers refused, organizers were fired, and before the end of June more than a thousand girls were out on strike. The Salvation Army soon joined in the call for better factory conditions.

The Times blamed Annie and other agitators for the labor "unrest."

On July 4 she received an anonymous note. "Dear Lady," it began, "they have been trying to get the poor girls to say that it is all lies that has been printed and trying to make us sign papers that it is all lies; dear Lady nobody knows what it is we have put up with and we will not sign them. We thank you very much for the kindness you have shown to us. My dear Lady we hope you will not get into any trouble on our behalf as what you have spoken is quite true."

Annie was moved to tears, and soon action.

Two days after the letter arrived, all work at the Bryant & May factory ground to a halt and a delegation of one hundred women approached her for help. A strike fund was quickly established, with Shaw, Beatrice Potter and Sidney Webb distributing the funds collected. Stead and others used their newspaper outlets to increase the pressure and launch a boycott.

But the striking girls also wanted a union and Annie was their first choice to lead it.

Bradlaugh brought two allies with him to the meeting. Samuel Montagu, a member representing Whitechapel, was the son of a Liverpool watchmaker who had become a successful banker and philanthropist. He was also an Orthodox Jew and had recently founded a Federation of Synagogues in the East End. The third MP was James Bryce, a liberal jurist and historian who represented the city's Tower Hamlets before moving to South Aberdeen.

Once the girls sat, Annie reviewed the issues involved in the strike, her role and their demands. "After my story appeared I was threatened with libel," she recalled, "but it was easier to strike at the girls. That's why we are here. Although we appreciate Mr. Bradlaugh's support and the questions he is asking, this won't be settled until we can sit down with management."

"Mr. Bryant is a reasonable man," offered Bryce. "What's his response?"

"He don't like publicity," one girl snorted. "But he ain't said a thing."

"What could he do?"

"Improve the air is one thing, sir," an older girl replied bluntly. "After they added that upper floor to the place, the ventilation didn't work no more. The fumes is so thick you can barely breathe. That's the real reason we get sick."

Annie pointed out that since the girls took meals inside the factory, phosphorous was also being ingested with their food. If someone complained about the pain as their teeth rotted from the poison, foremen had them pulled, often by brute force and without permission.

"We need Mr. Bryant to stop listening to his foremen and meet with us," she said.

Bradlaugh called the company's actions intolerable, but admitted that, no matter how many speeches he and others made, a legislative solution would take far too long, if it came at all. "Your power is the public's good opinion," he advised, "more effective and timely in this case than any action by this chamber of cowards."

Some of the girls gasped, shocked by his candor and condemnation of both colleagues and his class. None except Annie had ever been inside the intimidating room before or witnessed a parliamentary debate.

After listening quietly for twenty minutes Montagu joined the discussion by posing a larger question. "What concerns me, beyond addressing the egregious conditions you have brought to the nation's attention, is the ultimate goal of the movement that appears to be underway. As I see it, there are two schools of thought – gradualism or revolution.

"So, is it to be the Fabian's path or Marx and Morris?"

"If not the one it will be the other," Annie replied. "Are we asking so much? The right to organize collectively, to take meals in a separate room to prevent contamination and illness, the reinstatement of those who have been fired, an end to the arbitrary fines and unfair deductions from wages. All of that, yes! We also want to bypass the foremen and bring the grievances directly to management. If they hadn't prevented complaints from being heard for so long," she scolded, "many girls could have been saved."

Although Tonio had insisted on this precise time and place, the matchgirls' strike, even the opportunity to witness this unique encounter, wasn't the ultimate reason for his timing. It was a destination of opportunity. Even with a device that could take you to virtually any place or time you still needed to choose exactly when and where. You could visit London through the View Room forever and never run into the person you wanted to see. But on this particular day, Tonio knew where Annie would be. His only concern was what would happen if Angel found out.

Annie strode toward the gangway to address the girls huddled to one side and the old men on the other. "Where is the real cure for our sorrow? How will we rescue the world? Do we seek more? Absolutely! But the road is long and has many turns. Today we fight for health and fairness, tomorrow perhaps for a common room, a refuge for girls who never had a proper home, a welcoming atmosphere and a bit of comradeship. If necessary, Mr. Montagu, yes, we are ready for revolution. The poor, after all, have little to lose. But at this point I still hold out hope for gradual improvement, a peaceful path to liberate the enslaved and change the world.

"What we need is a movement of love and self-sacrifice," she said, "inspiring us to give rather than take."

A few days before, Tonio had seen Angel, the other woman in his life, take control of a meeting. She was equally adept at persuading groups and bending powerful men to her purposes. At times that included him. But her style was not as direct and rested on charm rather than argument. After all, she'd recently maneuvered him into bed with a combination of ego stroking, infantilism and alcohol. It was hard to imagine Annie resorting to such subterfuge, though he did wonder whether he would mind.

He was preparing to press Home on the mini-locator he carried in a pocket of the B-suit when he noticed something he didn't expect. At the far end of the room, concealed by darkness and the Speaker's Chair, someone else was watching the same group. He pulled on a rope and propelled himself across the chamber. Now he could see a man, tall with brown hair and dark eyes, a long nose and drooping mustache that framed his pale face. He wore a long overcoat and was holding a cane.

Although there in the flesh he seemed ghostly, a phantom witness almost as invisible as Tonio. He wracked his brain over who it could be;

not an MP or a member of the delegation, yet someone able to enter a restricted area at the heart of the empire and eavesdrop.

Could it be Rachkovsky? Tonio recalled seeing the only known photograph of the infamous spymaster. Aside from a missing hat and goatee it looked like him. Born in the Ukraine, Peter Rachkovsky had clawed his way up the ladder of the Russian police system as an undercover agent and eventually taken control of the Okhrama, an international network of provocateurs and agents that specialized in infiltrating and disrupting radical groups, using deception and terror to destroy them.

Reports were circulating that Russia's revolutionary underground had moved its headquarters from Paris and was hatching plans in England to assassinate the tsar. That was the chatter at least, certainly enough to bring Rachkovsky to London in June and lead him to hire Wladyslaw Milewski, a Paris case officer who crossed the Channel to recruit new agents. Together they were building contacts within the Special Branch, and hoping their usual tactics – surveillance, fear and intimidation – would work again and convince a frightened, gullible public to see radicals, immigrants and Jews as the enemy.

Annie's work with the matchstick girls had evidently been effective enough to make her a person of interest. The strike was demonstrating, in England and beyond, that young girls with no education, political power or previous organizing experience could join together and bring a powerful company to its knees. They might even win the fight, an outcome that could force changes in business policy and deliver a needed victory for the labor movement.

That was more than enough to make her a threat and a target.

26
ALLEGATIONS

Was it better to know about a threat – even if you couldn't do anything about it -- or not to know? Impotent knowledge or blissful ignorance – in Tonio's mind it had become a relevant choice. After noticing Rachkovsky and realizing the potential danger to Annie he returned to New Jersey more frustrated and anxious than ever. Just as when he observed a Ripper murder for the first time he had barely controlled the urge to leap at someone who wasn't there.

Knowledge without the freedom to act felt like a trap. It reinforced the sense that he still wasn't in control of his life or much else. What had he gained from learning about Annie Besant or discovering Jack the Ripper's identity? Could he report the murderer to Scotland Yard? Could he prevent an attack on Annie or the death of the next prostitute? For that matter, what had he gained from recovering the lost memories of his own childhood, or finding out about Gianni and his mom?

The answer to all his questions seemed the same – nothing yet. When he finally sent Harry an e-mail making that case, after struggling with doubts for a weekend, the response was a shock. Less than twenty-four hours later his friend was knocking at the door.

"I wasn't that depressed," he joked.

Harry laughed and pulled off a ski cap, part of his current disguise. Since he'd also shaven his beard he opened the conversation with congratulations for recognizing him without a hint. "I thought you could use a reality check," he said.

Tonio brought him up to date – the DC trip, Renaissance Equity, FABRICO and the cryptic Peter Lynch, sleeping with Angel and his obsession with a 19th century woman he could never meet. When he was finished Harry asked for a drink.

After some vodka, he said, "I don't know whether to get into this or distract you with something that could be worse. Two things actually."

"Great," snapped T. "Is this a good news bad news situation?"

"The good news is that I'm here and you do have choices."

He accepted that with unconcealed skepticism. "And the bad news?"

"Where do we begin?" But Harry actually needed no time to decide, having brought along the findings of the Truthsquad's research. He opened his laptop and pulled up the files. "Gianni Wolfe, Department of State staff beginning in 1975. This was the tail end of the Kissinger era," he reported. "Saigon had fallen. Every day brought some new horror story about the FBI or the Agency. Committees in the Senate and House were looking at covert ops, the Pike Committee, Church Committee, Rockefeller Commission. That's the overall context.

"You wouldn't think they'd be launching new covert shit in this environment, but they were. And from the files and cables we've retrieved so far, plus your suggestions on dates and places, we place him in Angola, Jamaica and Afghanistan at key points."

"What are you saying?"

"We think your uncle was a spook, an intelligence agent of some sort with a cover at State." Tonio wanted to reject the idea. Unfortunately, the longer Harry spoke the more it bordered on the obvious.

"First Angola," Harry summarized. "The roots of that go back to the sixties and opposition to Portugal as a colonial overlord. There was the MPLA under Agostinho Neto and the FNLA, led by Holden Roberto.

We don't know whether it was official policy or a rogue operation, but someone decided that Roberto was the horse to back.

"By the mid-seventies the situation had escalated into a full-scale civil war. The US was still behind the FNLA, by then the most violent of the groups. So was China, by the way. Meanwhile the Soviets were sending large arms shipments to the MPLA. In July the CIA started doing the same for its guys. But they went further; they launched a major covert operation that included mercenaries, recon and supply missions, and disinformation back at home. And your uncle was in the middle of it. He was one of the Kissinger boys sent over to advise and recruit. The trips to Zaire and South Africa coincide with military and propaganda operations."

"What did he do?"

"We believe he was involved in a disinformation scheme to create panic around the idea of Soviet advisers. One story was that a group of Russians and Cubans had been captured. Another alleged rapes committed by Cuban troops. The reports were bullshit but that didn't stop them from going global."

Harry paused, checking on how Tonio was taking the news before continuing.

"I'm fine, I get it. He was a Cold Warrior."

"That's one way to look at it. I would say stone cold psy-ops specialist, at the very least." Harry opened the folder labeled Manley_Jamaica. "In 1976 he made several trips to Jamaica, but not for the ganga. It wasn't just a big election year in the US. The Jamaican Prime Minister, Michael Manley, was also running. We know that Kissinger visited with him in December of '75 and threatened to 'review' US relations unless certain policies were changed. 'Review' meant watch it, buddy!

"So, what was Manley doing? One thing was publicly expressing support for the MPLA, one of Kissinger's obsessions. He was also making nice with Cuba and the USSR, and generally advocating democratic socialism. But his worst crime was demanding increased payments from US-based transnationals for mining bauxite. If you don't know, bauxite is aluminum ore. Not only did Manley impose a production levy, he was persuading other countries to do likewise. He was even working with Mexico and Venezuela on an independent processing center.

"Okay, now it's early 1976 and US aid to Jamaica has basically come to a halt. But the US Embassy presence increases. And what happens? Arms shipments to the opposition, and strikes by key unions – transport, telephone, electricity. Also arson, bombings and several political murders."

Tonio protested. "Are you saying he was involved in that?"

"Yes, we just can't be absolutely sure which ops. But the overall goal was certainly destabilization and he was a key player. By June things had seriously escalated. Shipments of staples like flour were being poisoned with insecticide. Anti-government groups and demonstrations were on the rise. Given his military background, we think Gianni recruited most of the Army and security personnel, and took part in one of three attempts to assassinate Manley."

"Shit! Is there more?"

"Afraid so. But the thing is, his attitude changed over the next few years. Did you notice anything?"

"I was pretty young. What happened?"

"Well, something seems to have occurred in '79, in the run up to the Afghan war. The official line has always been that the Soviets invaded and the US responded. But the thing that gets lost is that Hafizullah Amin, who became prime minister in a coup, was probably recruited by the CIA while he was a student, either at Columbia or in Wisconsin.

"So, Amin takes power in September and the US *charge d'affaires* assures him not to worry if the Soviets sound unhappy. And what does he do? He purges the officer corps and discredits his own party. And publicly requests military help from the Soviets. At the time it made no sense. But it does if you know that Amin is a US puppet, covert US aid to the rebels has already begun, and that the CIA is training fighters in Pakistan and beaming in radio propaganda. Basically, the Soviets were set up. Brzezinski admitted it eventually. They intentionally suckered the Soviets into Afghanistan. The idea was to trap them in their own Vietnam. It clearly worked. Ten years latter, no USSR."

"But Gianni may have shown some scruples. We have a memo suggesting that he was sent home after expressing reservations about the Afghan play. I guess that ranks as good news."

"Jesus, are you sure about all this?"

"Mostly. It's a murky world but he was deep in the game for more than five years."

The revelations had succeeded in distracting Tonio from thoughts of Annie, the Ripper, Rachkovsky or Angel. On the other hand, it was depressing to find out that the man he idolized once upon a time was so different than he imagined.

"What does all this say about why he might have been killed?"

"I'm not quite through. You get the picture so far. He was a soldier, but somewhere along the way he lost faith in the mission. Now, you say he died in late September, 1982."

"Right."

"That was shortly after he returned from a trip to Egypt. Only it turns out he wasn't just in Egypt, he was also in Syria and Lebanon. Israel had just returned Sinai to Egypt under a peace deal. However, in early June someone, possibly Abu Nidal, tried to kill the Israeli Ambassador in London. That was followed immediately by a major Israeli bombing campaign on Lebanon, PLO rocket attacks in reply, and within days an Israeli invasion, which in turn sparked the formation of the Lebanese branch of Hezbollah. All in all, a first-class clusterfuck."

"Yeah, what about G?"

"Wait for it. In late August Bashir Gemayeel became President of Lebanon. Three weeks after that he was assassinated with a bomb detonated by a Syrian intelligence agent. Or maybe not a Syrian. The next day Israel invaded West Beirut."

"What are you saying now? That Gianni was involved in that?"

"He'd grown a conscience and it got him killed, that's what I'm saying. He knew the truth behind the invasion. During the Afghan operation he saw how screwed up a covert policy can get. He'd made those feelings known. And he was with Gemayeel the day he died. The day after the Beirut invasion Israel let Lebanese Christian Phalangists march into two Palestinian refugee camps and massacre hundreds of civilians. He saw that too. I think he'd just had enough. The last memo shows it, he was threatening to resign and go public. It's a solid theory anyway, the timing works, and the Agency can be very effective making murder look like natural causes.

"Bottom line, your uncle knew where some of the bodies were buried," he said grimly, "and it looks like he joined them. We'll keep digging, brother."

Harry had other reasons for leaving his Green Mountain lair. The message from Tonio was alarming, but he knew his friend's mood swings and tendency toward the dramatic. He'd also come to the city to pursue several leads, he explained, but declined to be specific. When pressed he would only say it might be blackmail.

The next day he took off after breakfast and Tonio went uptown for a session with Marcia Siegel. There was obviously much to process. In recent weeks she'd helped him open up about his family. He talked about the collapse of the marriage, his bonding with Athena as a teen, and his later rejection of what he considered her spiritual tourism. He also admitted to feeling an instinctive hostility toward his father, something that went deeper and back further than the break up, and described his anger with Shelley after the recent summons to Virginia.

On the other hand, he hadn't as yet brought up Athena's dangerous liaison with Gianni. And he hadn't talked about his recovered memories for several months. But it was impossible to completely sidestep the latest revelations about his uncle's secret life. Claiming that they were sparked by his memories just sounded safer than the truth.

"We sometimes call this the expectation effect," Marcia said. "You know, context has an enormous effect on our memories. It's certainly possible that this is genuine. But it's equally possible that you saw or experienced something that acted as a cue and created an expectation that feels as if it has been remembered."

"That's not it," he objected. "I'm positive about what happened."

"I know. The problem is thinking you were repressing something and somehow now it's been recovered. Despite what we might feel there's no laboratory evidence to support that idea."

"What are you telling me? That I haven't remembered it because I didn't repress it in the first place?"

"Well, you can't prove a negative, but yes. You also can't prove that ghosts don't exist."

"What about memories brought back from hypnosis?"

"They're a combination – some truth, but also some fantasy. It's really more a state of enhanced suggestibility. I wouldn't place too much faith in it."

It sounded plausible. Still, something about the whole argument made him feel that she was steering him away from understanding his past rather than toward it. Why would she do that? All he'd said was that he remembered, as a child, that his uncle mentioned being a spy and going on adventures to places like Africa. The fact that he was fudging how he knew was beside the point. Marcia sounded invested in the stories not being true.

"What have I been doing, lying to myself?"

"Distracting yourself. People tend to focus on past traumas, even if the memories are false. You can become so focused on it that you ignore real problems in your life."

"And what real problems am I ignoring?"

"You tell me." He waited. "What about your relationship with your father? You obviously have strong feelings there. But this preoccupation with your dreams, memories, whatever they are, lets you off the hook. You blame your father, but instead of dealing with that you veer off into fantasies about spies and conspiracies."

What had she just said? "I blame him? What do I blame him for?"

Marcia stared, suddenly less sure of herself. "For, uh, making you feel inadequate."

"Excuse me! I don't feel that way." This was rapidly getting weird.

"Sure you do. You've said it yourself. Small, you said."

In a flash it hit him. She had the conversation backward. It was Shelley who had said it about him! But he hadn't told Marcia, and the only other way she could know was if she'd talked to Shelley. Then he remembered what his father said to him that same day, ridiculing his sense that his choices weren't his own. It was the same thing he and Marcia had talked about several months earlier.

She wasn't a therapist, she was a snitch. And he was paying her.

"No, Marcia," he snapped. "That was my father." Seconds later he was inches from her face, pressing against her chair and using both arms to prevent her escape. "Tell me. What are the perks of being the mob shrink?"

"What are you talking about? This is –"

"Inappropriate? You're inappropriate."

"Let me up! This session's over."

He grabbed her with one hand and shushed her with the other. "Let's think this over. You can yell and maybe attract attention. But you also have to consider that I may be armed. You know how distracted and strange I get. Plus, we do have ways of disposing of bodies, and enough cash to make charges go away, or just buy the jury. So, what's it going to be? You tell me something useful, something true, or I…act crazy."

She glared at him, then nodded and surrendered. He looked her over and let her go. As soon as he did, however, she shoved him as hard as she could and knocked him over. Before he could recover she lunged over the desk and pulled open a drawer. Tonio recovered and leaped, pulling her backward as she came up with a Glock 19.

"Shit, I was just kidding!" He grabbed her gun hand and smashed it onto the desk. Once more and the pistol dropped, which he followed quickly with a left that sent her into the coffee table. She landed hard and stayed there, conscious but down for the count.

Tonio grabbed the gun, released the clip, and tossed both back in the drawer. "Now it's over," he announced heading for the door. "Say hi to dad, and bill me for the damage."

27

Break Time

It had taken more than a year to complete the renovations, converting the abandoned industrial shell into a state-of-the-art lab. He strolled through the old staff cafeteria, now a well-equipped kitchen, and on into the gym. Beyond were showers, dressing rooms, a row of lockers, a sauna and massage alcoves. You could live in the building for weeks.

Angel was working on a punching bag as Coldplay blasted from the wall. She acknowledged his arrival and stopped. He asked casually how she was doing. They hadn't spoken since DC and he wasn't sure how she felt about it. An out-of-town interlude, away from friends and the usual inhibitors, didn't have to produce serious aftershocks. Then again, it might have.

Her lack of response was the first hint of trouble. Instead, she flipped off the sound system, went into the bathroom, stripped off her sweats and stepped into the shower. If she was sending him a message he couldn't quite read it. Was she issuing an invitation or giving him a "you-can't touch-this" brush off? With Angel it was sometimes hard to tell.

Tonio decided not to assume and returned to the kitchen to wait. Ten minutes later she joined him, but didn't say much while heating some coffee.

Eventually he couldn't resist and asked, "Is there a problem?"

"You could say that." Her tone was cold and snappy. "But let's not talk about it, there's enough going on. So what's the target this time?"

"The big one," he said, "September 30." Half of him wanted to know what was bugging her. Their reunion was sweet but she might have taken it too seriously. The other half was focused on the task at hand, bringing back proof that Tumblety brutally murdered Elizabeth Stride and Catherine Eddowes on the same night.

Stride, known in the East End as Long Liz, died shortly before 1 a.m. in Dutfield's Yard near the Jewish Socialist Center and International Working Men's Club. Less than 45 minutes later Eddowes' body was discovered by a police officer outside an empty house in a corner of Mitre Square in Aldgate. The locations were less than a mile apart and about the same distance from the previous murders. In fact, all the crimes were committed within two miles of one another.

Despite the physical and temporal proximity it would take two separate trips to record the "double event." The retrieval chamber was huge, almost 60,000 square feet, but that wasn't enough to reach from Dutfield's Yard to Mitre Square. He would have to return after the first murder and wait for Danny to recalibrate.

"No side trips this week?"

He immediately knew what she meant, his visit to the House of Commons. "About that," he began. "It's historically significant, a key moment in the midst of the biggest strike of the period."

The explanation made her laugh. "You're a historian now? I thought you were trying to be a detective and solve the crime of century." Her tone of voice had shifted quickly from concealed disgust to blatant hostility. "At least be honest."

Tonio was hurt. "What are you accusing me of?"

"Of being a liar. You went there to see her again. Admit it."

Embarrassed, he shrugged a confession. "Did Danny tell you?"

"I didn't need him to say anything. All I needed to do was check the log. If you're going to sneak around at least be professional. I thought you guys knew how to hide evidence."

It was a low blow. She knew he didn't enjoy being lumped in with the rest of Shelley's organization and wanted to land a shot.

"Yeah, we do," he said with mock pride. "If I really didn't want you to know I could have made sure of it."

"I suppose you could. Too lazy then?"

"Watch it!"

"Or what? You'll have me whacked?"

"Enough. I'm sorry. I'm just, well, interested in her. What can I say?"

Angel shook her head. "Pathetic," she said. "Know what you're becoming? A stalker. You'd screw her if you could, right?"

He didn't deny it. She was raving, but not completely wrong.

"History? Don't kid yourself," she sneered. "You're a tourist. This project, I think it's another excuse for you to escape reality and fixate on a shiny, unattainable object. Meaningless. Face it, you're no better than any schmuck who gets off following a woman he can never have. Only you do it in a spacesuit flying around a warehouse.

"Basically you're a stalker," she said. "You just lurk around in the past."

Up in the control room Danny prepared for the meeting. Since Harry had returned to Vermont after turning up at Tonio's they needed to convene remotely. The agenda included the DC meeting with Lucy Gershon, David Simon and Peter Lynch, and a pre-view stream discussion of how best to handle the events of September 30, 1888.

Even before powering up, Danny expressed his doubts about the terms of the financing being proposed by Renaissance Equity. Rather than welcoming the opportunity to leapfrog into global distribution he seemed to be resisting it.

"But on-demand production," objected Angel. "That would make it possible to radically bring down the cost and have production outlets all over the world."

"I get that. But we don't need to grow so fast. The technology is still in its infancy. There's still a lot we need to study. You've raised questions yourself about the social and political implications."

"Since when do you care about any of that?"

"Chill," Danny replied. He seemed amused rather than offended. "I care, I invented this. I'm simply saying we don't need to rush into anything, even if it looks attractive."

"Yes we do," she insisted. "If we don't seize this now we'll lose it."

Tonio asked why.

Angel sighed, "It's basic. Timing and marketing are key to acceptance of a new technology. The PC was a great product but some other company could have challenged IBM at the start. It was their timing – and the 16-bit processor. The decision to work with Intel and Microsoft let them harness incredible energy and helped them set the standard."

Danny didn't argue but wasn't convinced or much interested. Instead, he retreated to the window overlooking the View Room and checked his watch.

"I get that," injected Tonio, "but if you pick the wrong partner you end up getting screwed."

"You're the expert!"

After checking the time Danny waved down to the space below, as if trying to get someone's attention. Once he had it he pointed excitedly at his watch.

Tonio ignored Angel's insult, but Danny's odd gesture made him check the time himself. It had just turned 3:30. Then he said, "Didn't Bill Gates eventually leave IBM in the dust?"

"Sure, in the end. IBM was still thinking mainframe computers in the early eighties," she said. "They also developed products through a company-wide consensus process, which turned out to be unworkable in that situation. But the biggest problem was their previous success with a traditional approach to engineering. It just wasn't right for an emerging fast-paced market. It's all about adaptability."

She thought for a moment and then added, "Sometimes I wonder why I ever left finance."

Danny suggested that they continue the discussion during the meeting. "Harry may have another take on it."

"Great. Just what we need," she snapped, "the nutball factor."

While Danny finished prepping Angel pressed her point and Tonio opted to return to the ground floor. At the moment he preferred being alone in the empty chamber to remaining in the same room with her. It also allowed him to talk with the others without wearing a visor.

When a hologram of the control room above materialized around him, however, T noticed that he couldn't see anyone's eyes. This struck him as telling, symbolic of their underlying situation. Everyone seemed to be concealing something at the moment.

The first point – start times and physical parameters for the two projection streams – went smoothly enough. They would visit Dutfield's Yard, arriving about 30 minutes prior to the estimated time of the murder and staying long enough to track Tumblety afterward as far as possible. The second stream would pick up from there. However, the latitude and longitude would change to encompass all of Mitre Square about a mile away and several streets leading back toward Whitechapel.

Then came more discussion of FABRICO, Renaissance and whether the deal on the table was worth pursuing. Angel made her pitch and Danny reiterated his reservations, stressing that he wasn't saying absolutely no, just not yet.

But Harry's response was unequivocal. He considered it a terrible and totally unacceptable proposal. Equity firms like Renaissance cared only about raising capital for buyouts and selling the companies for huge profits, he said. It was a form of vulture capitalism. "In this case," he added ominously, "We could even be dealing with a front group."

Angel objected, "A front for what?"

"The Washington, DC base, a staff with deep political connections around the world, military companies in the portfolio, you tell me."

"You're talking about Renaissance, the place I worked there for ten years! What are you saying?"

"We don't know who we're dealing with, and there are major red flags. Maybe they're spooks. But even if not, do we want to be in bed permanently with people who trade in missiles and jets and who knows what the fuck else?"

"This is absurd. Do you believe the shit you're saying?"

Harry laughed. "That's why I say it. Are they as bad as the Carlyle Group or Bain Capital? Possibly not. But will they loot the company and feed the carcass to corporate vultures if that seems like the most profitable option? Absolutely, that's the nature of the beast."

"You'd rather be owned by the mob."

Now Tonio objected. "Wolfe is not the mob and anyway, Shelley is hands off. We need to grow, obviously. But the balance sheet is fine, we don't have a liquidity problem, and we're having a great quarter. I liked Lucy Gershon's production ideas, maybe we should go that way. I just don't see the urgency."

"So, you're a business analyst now? I have trouble keeping all your roles straight." She glanced around to see if anyone else found his attempt at managerial competence as unconvincing as she did. "Let me put it this way: you don't know what you're talking about. Danny, you brought me into this company because you had a vision and wanted to put it out there with as much impact as possible. I brought you millions in contracts and that helped to finance the early research. Now we have something that can transform the mass communication landscape."

She paused for effect. "But you're choosing to surround yourself with a neurotic wiseguy and a paranoid lunatic. Why is that? And because of that you're going to squander an enormous opportunity right in front of you. It's tragic."

"Not your usual corporate pitch," Harry snarked. "Very motivational."

"Fuck you very much Harry."

"Boardroom bitch," he shot back.

She threw down her visor and looked directly over to Danny in the control room. This was just between them. "Is this what you want? Because if it is." She let it hang there.

"It's the best thing, for the moment," he said apologetically. "There are reasons."

"Really? All I've heard is bullshit and procrastination." She rose and walked to the door. "And it doesn't work for me."

Tonio watched her exit with a mixture of regret and relief.

The View Room was a huge space, occupying more than seventy-five percent of the former factory. Outside, the building had two loading docks at the back and a bland façade facing a parking lot in front that could accommodate 120 vehicles but was normally almost empty. Most of the windows were cosmetic and blocked. Inside, the walls were covered with a smooth blue material, speckled with censors at precise intervals on all sides.

Tonio rose from the lonely, spot-lit chair in a painted circle at the center of the room. He glanced up at Danny, standing at the observation window high above. Maybe Angel was right, he thought. Maybe he was holding them back. Was he just afraid to step out from under Shelley's wing? Was he really what she said, an escape artist, the neurotic son of a crime boss just playacting his way through life, an emotional tourist, and a potentially-violent stalker who was fixated on something he could never have?

He tried to meditate to calm himself. A few minutes was all he could manage in this mood. Then he noticed it was almost five, and crossed the chamber to the door. From the main hall he returned to the fitness center to pick up his coat. He no longer even wanted to see London again. What was the rush? It wasn't as if a day mattered.

By the time he was back at the foyer Danny was moving down in the lift. "Let's do it tomorrow or next week," he shouted. "I need to go to the shore."

"Wait! We have to talk." Danny pulled open the faux-antique door. "Look, she's basically right. I like Harry but he's not seeing the big picture."

"Then why…"

"Come with me." He led Tonio back into the chamber and across the length of the space to the center of the back wall. Meanwhile, he explained that one reason Angel might be pissed is that Danny himself had requested that she look for new financing. In the long run, to advance, he did agree with her that they would have to move beyond the boutique operation TELPORT was likely to remain in the hands of Danny and a few small investors. Backing from Wolfe Enterprises could change this, but it came with a steep price. .

"The thing is," Danny said, and then freed a latch to slide open a hidden partition, revealing a room about the size of a prison cell that looked like a futuristic vault. "There are some aspects of this we haven't talked about.

"I've explained about sequence interception, using global positioning for location, and Tesla enhanced current. The coils and the transmitter next door were retrofitted to magnify the electrical charge. The receiver is tuned to the same frequency as the transmitter and the current flows between them. This gives us a boost. Frankly, if we didn't, we'd blow out the power grid. We're running the fourth largest collection of super-computers on this coast, plus a chilled water plant to keep them from melting. But location is a major factor in the time displacement effect."

"You said that was just a theory."

"About that, I ought to revise my statement."

"So revise."

"Okay, I'm talking here about the Earth grid and vortex-gravity research. The government has been pursuing it for years at several locations, normally under cover of atomic research. The first site was either Alice Springs in Australia or Los Alamos, but a lot of work has been done down at Brookhaven, near the museum project in Shoreham. It's a great location, right on the Hudson River flow."

When Danny talked this way Tonio had trouble staying focused. But some of what he heard sounded similar to what he'd learned in Sedona. The point was that the selection of this particular New Jersey warehouse was not at all accidental.

"Our location is really the main reason we've been able to create what amounts to a wormhole effect," he said. "It's like a bioelectric trigger. We've known about this potential basically forever; we just usually choose not to do much about it. Shit, the pyramids were on ley lines – flow lines of energy built into the structure of the planet. And we, my friend, are located on a ley line grid point right here.

"As far as I know the first modern observations of grid point impacts on gravity and time displacement were recorded at the eastern end of Lake Ontario. It's a very active point. Daniel Home, the nineteenth century psychic, used it to perform what his witnesses called levitation. Somehow the place let him get, well, very high. Now, if we jump ahead we come to a series of plane crashes and disappearances in the same area in the forties and fifties, along with UFO sightings and assorted strange reports. That's when people started calling it the Marysburgh Vortex and The Other Bermuda Triangle. The one I like is 'gateway to oblivion.' Sounds like a vacation spot in Middle Earth. Anyway, we're sitting on an active grid point and we have the capacity do much more with it than I've shared with anyone up to this point."

"No one?"

"Not this," he said opening the metal door. "To tell the truth, I'm a little scared. It's not the kind of wine you release into the world before it's time, and this one hasn't been tasted yet. I've done trials with objects of different sizes and a few small animals. There's video of all that."

"I'm still not sure what we're talking about."

"Well, you know how in the image retrieval chamber, the View Room, we create a one-way window, a form of superluminal communication. We capture the other place and time. We capture, transmit and reproduce it through the censors around us. Well, this is the reverse. What is scanned and captured inside this – let's call it a Port – is sent and reproduced at the other end."

At this point it sounded plausible enough. "Is it like the digital fabrication thing we were talking about?"

"It's more like UPS – but faster. It's teleportation, man."

In a flash, the name of Danny's company had a new meaning: TELPORT. He'd obviously been aiming at this long before remote viewing came along. The goal had been sitting in front of him all along, hidden in plain sight.

"And I have the slogan: It's Go Time!" Tonio didn't like it. "No? I'll work on it. But meanwhile," Danny said, stepping into the chamber and beckoning, "Come on back."

Tonio took a cautious step over the lip of the entrance and felt himself resisting. A small, confining space wasn't his idea of a fun trip. In fact, cells featured prominently in the memories that kept seeping into his consciousness. This one looked like a man-sized safe.

"It's simple, no risk," Danny promised.

Yeah, right. "Have you tried it?"

"Not personally, I have to run the program and monitor the process. My cat has, though, and she's fine. I also did a chimp. He was disoriented but alive and intact."

Tonio walked a few steps to the rear and turned, extending his arms to almost touch the walls. The censors were the same as those installed throughout the View Room, but these covered every surface except the floor with just inches between each. When he moved toward the exit Danny blocked his path and asked, "Can you do me a favor?"

"Maybe. What kind?"

He hesitated. "The big kind," he said. "I really want to run a brief human trial. How about making a jump? It would only take a few minutes."

28

THE COMMANDMENTS

The jump would be brief. Danny stressed that he wouldn't even leave the building. He would automatically return to the same spot after three minutes and would feel no ill effects, except perhaps a mild vertigo. Eventually, he was persuaded to stay inside as the door closed and several emergency lights activated.

He had no idea what would happen next, yet felt relieved at least not to be totally in the dark. Not that he minded some alone time.

Tonio had experimented with sensory deprivation in float tanks out West. He usually lasted a couple of hours and emerged exhilarated. But this wasn't like lying in a sealed pod immersed in shallow salty water, listening to soothing sounds and attempting not to think. That was chilling out. This was being locked in a small, confining chamber and it triggered an automatic fear response. For him it was more frightening than being "transmitted and reproduced."

"Trapped in the closet," he sang in a weak attempt to play it cool.

The instructions were simple. Don't move and don't touch anything, at least until phase one was complete. He would know because he would be standing in the middle of the warehouse, close to where he was during the meeting. The circle painted on the floor was his destination.

Once there he would be free to move for a minute or two to make sure it was real and not a holographic effect. However, he had to be standing back inside the ten-foot area to complete phase two –

returning to the departure point. Once he was back, the door would automatically re-open.

The short time it took for Danny to reach the control room and establish the coordinates felt like an eternity. Eventually he considered banging on the door before remembering that it violated the "no touching" rule. Then it began to feel like the room was expanding, opening wider, and pulling him into a deepening whirlpool of energy. It made him dizzy to the point of blacking out before the whirlpool itself opened and he felt as if he was descending effortlessly into a tunnel, moving slowly toward the vanishing point.

And then he was there, wobbly but on his feet, in the middle of the warehouse. At one end he could pick out the vault, at the other the door to the hall. He touched himself to be sure he was conscious and in one piece. This wasn't possible! He looked up at the observation window. It seemed as if no one was there. Then Danny appeared behind the glass, looked down and checked his watch.

He waved at Tonio and gestured at his wrist as if making an urgent request. Was this part of the experiment? Tonio wasn't sure but checked his wrist in response. It said 5:30. Then he checked the clock on the wall. That one said 3:30. Was this teleportation or something else?

He walked a few feet, thinking that he could join Danny upstairs and ask what had happened. But the test wasn't over yet. He remembered the three minute time limit and the instruction to be back in the circle. Time was almost up.

Before the deadline he heard voices from above, the sound of people having an argument. The woman shouted "Great! Just what we need – the nutball factor."

My god! That was Angel, which meant he had been here before, two hours earlier. Then the room contracted as the whirlpool reformed and pulled him back in. A moment later he was back in the metal closet.

"Technically it is teleportation," Danny explained after Tonio ran out of initial questions. "You moved instantaneously from point to point. But for some reason I can only use it in, well, let's call it reverse. It can be minutes or centuries, but it only goes backward from whenever you begin. And time passes here while you're away.

"Basically, the longer you stay the longer you're gone. Kind of makes sense."

"How long have you been working on this?"

"Since I was twelve," Danny admitted. "I was always fascinated with the nature of time, ever since physics. Quantum mechanics blew my mind – tunneling, time-energy uncertainty, decay times, delay times, jump times. But you don't get grants for proposing a time machine, you become a research subject. So I pursued areas at the margins and applied what I found out. Once we had the warehouse I could work on prototypes. The view stream proved it was possible to create a wormhole effect. The next question was whether anything could go through it and survive."

"This is amazing. I mean, I can't get my mind around it. Who knows?"

"No one except us," Danny said nervously. "Look, when I started this I was just a science geek with a vivid imagination. But this is real, and scary. We've been arguing about the civil liberties implications of remote viewing. If that's dangerous what's this? People would kill us for this, literally. That's why I'm delaying on the Renaissance deal. Any partner will be curious about the research end. They always have to know what's next. It's only a matter of time before someone noses around and finds out about this place and what we've been up to."

He saw Danny's point. He was concerned enough about what Shelley would do with RTV if he only knew it was possible to eavesdrop on past events. Who knew what could happen if he discovered you could go there.

On the other hand, this also meant he couldn't just solve crimes. He could potentially prevent them and even catch sick fucks like Tumblety.

"I already know what you're thinking," Danny said. "You're thinking you can go back and change things. 'Make right what once was wrong.' That's the first thing everyone thinks. Wow, I'll go back and kill Hitler and prevent World War II."

"Why not? There's no reason why those women have to die because of a freak."

"I know how you feel. And I know you want to go back and catch this killer and the rest of them. By showing you this I'm dangling that possibility."

"I know. So, let's do it," he said.

"We'll see. Before that we have to talk about the rules."

Danny had boiled it all down to a simple list. "I call them commandments but they're really guidelines since we have no idea what will happen."

"Are there ten?"

"Of course. I thought a biblical analog might convey the serious intent." He pulled out a TELPORT business card and handed it over. "Check the back. I figured we might need this someday."

Under the headline "Time Commandments" the card advised:

> 1) Remember the Entry
> 2) Stay in the Stream
> 3) Check Your Watch
> 4) Remain Inconspicuous
> 5) Avoid Yourself
> 6) Avoid Friends and Relatives
> 7) Don't Discuss It
> 8) Don't be a Hero
> 9) No Killing
> 10) Don't Change Things!

It seemed like a joke, a cross between strange social etiquette and updated rules for Fight Club. Danny wasn't kidding, however. "If we're going to run tests outside the lab you need to understand the risks and implications." he insisted. "I've given this a lot of thought."

The briefing took several hours. At the beginning they talked in the kitchen after microwaving dinners. Each item on the list had a well-argued rationale based on science, experience with the View Room and previous lab experiments, and lore accumulated from literature and film.

"The entrance is the exact location of your arrival," he said, "like the circle we used for the test. You need to know where it is and how to get back there in order to get home. Maybe it works beyond that specific area, I don't know. Let's not take any chances."

"Check."

Next he explained that the small chamber and the View Room were linked. As a result Danny would be able to observe the destination using facial recognition to locate Tonio and select the best angle. "But that will only work if you remain within the zone encompassed by the stream. So stay where we can see you – within the view stream."

"How do I know that?"

Danny handed him an antique pocket watch, a platinum octagon connected to a foot-long chain with a medal at the end. "Wear this," he said. "And don't lose it. It originally belonged to my father, but it's had some upgrades. See the inset clock on the bottom? The numbers go to 2000 feet. You designate a radius distance upon arrival. When you get close it vibrates. That means stop, you've reached the edge of the stream. I've set it to 125 feet, half the width of this space. It isn't digital so you won't attract attention when you use it."

That brought him to Commandment #3 – Check Your Watch. "This gets into a grey area," he apologized. "We don't know how far it's safe to move from the entrance or how long you can stay. Be cautious. Don't go farther than necessary and don't stay more than two hours."

"How do I return?"

"When you're ready – that means you're back at the entrance – press the winding mechanism. That's recall. We'll also have a default, based on how long the stream has stayed open in past runs before collapsing. That will be two hours. Be back at the entrance by then at the very latest. The timer is on the other inset clock."

He led Tonio through the exercise room to the lockers and retrieved an old, smelly overcoat. "You should wear this," he instructed. Tonio sniffed and asked why. "Number four. Camouflage. If you were going back a day, even a decade, it might not matter what you looked like. But you want to visit a time where someone dressed like you would stick out immediately."

Glancing in the mirror he saw the point. The boots might pass but his leather jacket, silk shirt and designer slacks would raise questions. "You've been preparing for this, haven't you?"

"Forever. But I figured you might want to jump back to the same location and time we've been visiting. I just didn't have your sizes. This should be enough for a short trip. But it's not just a question of appearance. Resist the temptation to draw attention to yourself."

Tonio tried not to take offense. "What's going on with number five?"

"Here we get into a somewhat speculative area. It's called the exclusion principle, also known as the Pauli principle for the physicist. In 1924, Wolfgang Pauli showed that no two electrons in the same atom can have an identical set of quantum numbers, which means that no two identical objects – a gas, magnet, person, even a star – can occupy the same space. We don't know what could happen, it probably wouldn't be pretty. But we shouldn't have to worry about it in this case. You'd be going back beyond the point of your own birth and wouldn't take anything that existed in that time. The main point is it's never good to run into yourself."

"Why avoid relatives? Couldn't I just say hello to Gianni, find out what the fuck he was doing before he died?"

"Not advisable. This gets into areas we haven't covered yet. One risk is that you could get in the way of your own birth, clearly a problem. It's known as the grandfather paradox. As far back as the forties Rene Barjevel talked about it in *Future Times Three*. The idea is that if you were to go back and accidentally kill your grandfather – or your father when he was young – you'd never be born. But it also relates to any contact that could prevent you from going back in the first place. Making contact with a member of your own family, actually anyone you know, can have blowback effects.

"This leads to number seven. It would obviously be tempting to talk about it with people you meet in the past. Hey, I enjoyed *Midnight in Paris*. Who wouldn't want to go back a century and regale Hemingway or Picasso with tales from the future? I suspect Gertrude Stein would love the idea. But they might talk about it and that might not be good for you or them. Worst case scenario – the *12 Monkeys* effect. Talk about a cautionary tale. In that film, if you recall, Bruce Willis goes back in time to find out why a plague almost wiped out humanity. But he talks about it with Brad Pitt and his therapist Madeleine Stowe in a mental hospital. It doesn't work out well for them.

"So, if you do get caught knowing things you can't reasonably know, my advice is to come up with a plausible alternative."

The next commandment – Don't Be a Hero – was especially hard for Tonio to accept. One of the reasons he was willing to contemplate going back into that cell was the possibility he might be able to save the victims of the Ripper and other murderers. He knew when and when they would die and he could stop it.

"Forget about being noble and courageous," Danny warned.

"What about just doing the right thing?"

"I understand. It feels wrong. But it runs into the consistency principle, basically a kind of universal course correction mechanism. The fact is, they would die anyway, just some other way. That's the theory. The exception is if the crimes are happening in the present. You might be able to go back a short time and use information to prevent another bombing or whatever from happening. It's an application we can look at, call it enhanced detection. Aside from that, my sense is that heroics can create drastic unintended outcomes.

"The same goes for killing the bad guys. I'm not being a moralist. It's mainly the risk of creating a temporal paradox. Let's say you go back and you kill that bastard Tumblety and he doesn't murder any of the women, or maybe just the first one. It sounds good. Here's the rub. Then he wouldn't become the first internationally famous serial killer and you wouldn't be motivated to track him down.

"I see. It's a paradox."

"It doesn't end there. As you of all people know, this was a watershed event, the first international media frenzy involving a serial murderer. The Ripper is suspect zero in society's fascination with psychopathic killers. Without him we might never have become so obsessed with crime stories. Jack the Ripper gave birth to an entire genre of literature and movies. Billions of dollars have been made, with untold social impacts. Without the Ripper there probably wouldn't be a Dexter or any of the other Serial Killer TV you love."

"Would that be bad?"

"It wouldn't change my day. But what I'm saying is that the implications of such a change are impossible to measure. They could be vast and the consequences worse. It's like Godwin's Law."

"You mean Murphy's."

"No, I mean Mike Godwin. It's also known as the Law of Nazi Analogies, but it's just an argument. Godwin noticed that the longer any online discussion continued the higher the probability that a comparison would be made to Hitler or the Nazis. The topic didn't seem to matter. Whatever it was, eventually someone would go there."

"I can see that."

"Here's the corollary. The more you try to change history the more likely it becomes that the Nazis win World War II. Or put it this way: things tend to get worse when you screw around with the past. There's even a theory that Germany was originally winning the war and that was somehow changed, and now history is somehow attempting to change it back. I don't buy it for a minute. But since we know it's possible to travel back in time, can we really say with full confidence that it's impossible that someone returned to the forties and, for example, convinced Hitler to invade Russia, thus setting his ultimate defeat in motion?"

"What are you saying? Someone from the future got to Hitler?"

"No! How would I know? I just set up shop. That's not the point. If you try to change the outcome of an event it could end up worse."

"Worse than millions of people dying?"

"Who can tell? You want to risk it? Are you ready to play God? That's why I included Number Ten. Please, if we go ahead, try not to intentionally change things. Theoretically, even the smallest alteration could change the course of history. Of course there's also the possibility that you can't change anything. That's known as the immutability principle. It says that if you go back in time you merely create the past that has already happened. It's related to displacement theory and the theory of relativity, which suggests that you can't do anything which would affect your own life. It's comforting, but not proven.

"But I say, if God doesn't play dice with the universe, who are we?"

"I'm a little lost."

"Einstein said that about Bohr's early quantum mechanics approach – it works, he said, but it doesn't reveal the true secrets of creation. The

Old One doesn't play dice. There is some order, we simply don't see it. Basically it boils down to this. Maybe you can't change the past. But if you can and you don't want to risk coming home to a world dominated by apes or lizards, please obey the commandments."

It was almost 10 p.m. before Danny finished the briefing and suggested that Tonio sleep it over before making his final decision. They could meet again over the weekend without attracting attention and, if he was willing, conduct one or two jumps.

Once Tonio realized what was possible, however, he never entertained an option other than moving ahead as quickly as possible – before he lost his nerve.

"Is there anything else I should know?"

Danny told him to empty his pockets. "Money, smart phone, keys, pens, mace, that blackjack, anything that could cause trouble or influence events if left behind. It all stays here. Also, if you talk with anyone be as vague as possible, which shouldn't be a big problem in your case. You can ask questions, but don't talk too much about yourself. If anyone asks, you're a visitor from America. You came over on a steamer, by the way, not a plane. Keep it simple."

Tonio stuck the list of commandments in a pocket of his pants and hooked the watch to a buttonhole on the overcoat, then put the coat on.

"What's the destination?"

"You know. Midnight on Sunday, September 30, 1888. We've already discussed the coordinates." It was the neighborhood surrounding Dutfield's Yard in Whitechapel. He would go there to find Long Liz about fifteen minutes before her death, and also Frank Tumblety as he stalked and killed her.

Research revealed that she was living on Devonshire Street with her boyfriend, Michael Kidney, a drunk and a brawler. They'd fought just a few days earlier. Elizabeth Stride was about 44, tall and still pretty despite her own drinking problem and aggressive tendencies. The strapping daughter of a Swedish farmer, she left home at 16 and became a domestic servant in Gotherburg. By 1865, however, local cops listed her as a prostitute.

When her parents died she moved to England, and in 1869 married a carpenter named John Stride, who died a decade later. After that she began turning tricks and living in an East End workhouse. Until the early Sunday morning nine years later when she ran into Francis Tumblety on Berner Street.

"Keep a safe distance away," Danny warned as they approached the Jump Room. "I'll be tracking you. You don't want to be noticed or get in the way of events. Just let things unfold – no matter what you see. Can you do that?"

Tonio nodded. "I'll have to. Wouldn't want to come back and find the lizard people in charge."

"Some people say they are."

He laughed and took a step into the cramped container. "Two hours."

"Right. But if it gets hairy, if anything feels wrong, get back to the entry point and hit recall. If that doesn't work – or you miss the deadline for some reason – I'll re-open the jump stream every three hours starting at 3 a.m GMT for as long as it takes."

Tonio agreed and then asked, "Why aren't you doing this yourself? You created this frigging thing. Don't you want to experience it?"

"I'm not sure," Danny admitted. "It's one thing to imagine and build it, but you have to be a little bit nuts to actually use it. Anyway, avante! Just don't forget the commandments."

Tonio gave a jaunty salute as the door closed and locked, triggering the lights and a minor epiphany: Harry had it right again. He was the man for the job.

PART THREE

GILDED NIGHTS

Time Commandments

Remember the Entry
Stay in the Stream
Check Your Watch
Remain Inconspicuous
Avoid Yourself
Avoid Friends…
  and Relatives
Don't Discuss It
Don't be a Hero
No Killing
Don't Change Things!

29
SCENES OF THE CRIME

LONDON, SEPTEMBER 30, 1888
Latitude 51.516663, Longitude 0.062435

He crumbled to his knees as the vortex deposited him in a back lot connected to the alley behind Batty Street. The first thing he noticed was the smell, so strong it stung his eyes. It permeated the neighborhood, from factory chimneys, tons of horse manure ground into the stones and untreated sewage running beneath them to the Thames.

Next was the fog, suffused at night with a sickly yellow wherever there was light. The combination made him feel smothered and queasy. He began to understand why so many people were ill and even cattle suffocated at exhibitions. The choking fumes, the rancid sewage, the shit and straw under his feet.

Tonio checked the yard, secluded and potentially large enough for a safe, unobserved return jump. He set the timer on Danny's watch, along with the location needed to establish a stream boundary. The plan was to stay within 125 feet and be back here by 2 a.m. It sounded like enough time to witness a murder and collect some fresh evidence.

The gateway to Dutfield's Yard was only a block away, off Berner Street in the heart of Whitechapel, less than a mile from where Annie Chapman had been killed three weeks before, and about the same distance from where Catherine Eddowes would die in less than an hour. He found a spot to observe without being seen in the shadows of the

Jewish Socialist Club down the block. From there he could see the half-open gate to Dutfield's Yard and the wall leading down Berner. The area was quiet except for a hawker, some passing dock workers and a couple strolling home.

Long Liz made an impression as soon as she came into view. Taller than most women, with a rugged but intriguing face and a soft Scandinavian accent, she wore a black skirt and dark velvet bodice under a long jacket trimmed in fur. The outfit was accented by a red rose with fern hair in her lapel and a checkered neck scarf, and topped by a black bonnet. Walking unsteadily beside her was a shorter, younger fellow in a frock coat. He looked like a clerk apprenticing to a barrister. They were headed past the gateway and seemed to be having a spat. He couldn't catch most of the words, in part due to the distance but also because the accents were virtually indecipherable.

A thought crossed his mind; in this case an alternative theory could turn out to be correct. Maybe the Ripper didn't kill Liz after all and the double murder was just a myth. Some people did claim it was her boyfriend, who in turn claimed that he hadn't seen her in days. But this fellow was too green to be the strapping Michael Kidney.

On the corner to the left, someone else was watching them while puffing on a pipe. It looked like Sherlock Holmes. But despite the non-threatening appearance Tonio immediately thought it could be Tumblety.

Liz and the young drunk were yelling. "Because I don't want to, that's enough," she said and moved to leave. He grabbed her by the arm and swung her against the wall. She yelped, tripped and slipped down.

That brought Tonio to attention. Before he could do anything, however, the man with the pipe rushed to the rescue. The clerk wasn't up for a challenge and decided to back off, slurring what sounded like a grudging apology. They watched as he stumbled out of sight in the fog.

Liz thanked her champion, brushing mud from her dress as he moved closer and spoke in a low and friendly voice. He was apparently making an offer that she seemed willing to consider. Her customer then glanced around to make sure they were alone.

Tonio noticed the knife before she did. A second later, when Long Liz looked down and gasped, the blade was already poking at her neck. The man whispered something and pressed his free hand against her chest, backing her slowly through the gate and shutting it behind them.

A moment later she screamed.

It happened too suddenly. He'd imagined Tumblety methodically stalking a victim until the perfect opportunity presented itself. But this felt like spontaneous mayhem, and he wasn't even certain it was the same man. Tonio moved into the street for a closer look. Unfortunately, he didn't notice Louis Diemschutz, the social club steward returning from a hard day of hawking cheap jewelry at the Crystal Palace. As Tonio shifted position Diemschutz' pony rounded the corner, noticed him and shied away.

That was just enough. The gate flew open and Tumblety burst out, scanning the area for the source of the interruption. He noticed the horse, the hawker and the man nearby in the pungent gaslight just as Tonio glanced away. When he checked again Tumblety was already down the block, moving briskly in the direction of Mitre Square.

Without thinking Tonio moved to follow. But Diemschutz stopped him, pointing his whip hand at something he saw across the way, just beyond the gateway. From where they stood it seemed like a pile of discarded clothing. Once they were across and close enough Diemschutz poked at it and lit a match. The flame flickered just long enough to pick out a bloodied face.

Long Liz had put up a fight and he had severed her windpipe. But the sound of the horse had prevented him from finishing the job. Now he was on his way to complete the ritual. Tonio felt he had no choice but to follow. The official plan was to visit each location separately, viewing as much as possible and analyzing things later. But that was before. He wasn't in the View Room, he was in London. He could go where he wanted, beyond the boundary of the stream if he wanted, and it only meant breaking one of Danny's commandments. The real problem was that there wouldn't be a record or any witness to what he found.

On the other hand, with each passing second a murdering bastard was getting farther away and closer to another victim. Could he really let it happen? So far this wasn't going anything like he planned. By the time he reached a decision Diemschutz had run to the Jewish club. Its door flew open and the sound of singing poured into the street, followed by several club members who rushed over for a look at the body. Two of them then raced off to spread the alarm and find the police.

Within minutes a crowd had gathered.

Danny did say his commandments were only guidelines. Tonio repeatedly reminded himself of that fact as he hurried to reach Mitre Square before the Ripper struck again.

About two blocks from Berner he felt the watch vibrate, meaning he had reached the edge of the stream. From here on he would be working without a net. When nothing changed as he crossed the invisible boundary he couldn't resist laughing. Commandments, my ass!

Evidence suggested that Catherine Eddowes, known recently as Katy Kelly, was murdered shortly before 12:45 and found only moments later in the southwest corner of the square just outside an empty building. Tonio made it with only minutes to spare after becoming disoriented along the fog-bound streets, dark roads and narrow alleyways.

Like other Ripper victims Katy was in her forties. The daughter of an English metal-worker, she never legally married but had raised three children with a common-law husband. For the last seven years, however, she'd lived with John Kelly, her boyfriend and possibly her pimp. Along the way she became a drunk.

Was Katy a whore? Irrelevant, he decided. She was innocent, just a woman struggling to survive and kill the pain in a grim world. The estimate on prostitutes in London ran as high as eighty thousand. The more successful in the massive sex industry could be watched and hired at Covent Garden and in the theater district, where they vogued for potential customers during intermissions. For most women who walked the streets, though, the "gay life" wasn't so pleasant. No, it was an assembly line of brief, anonymous, potentially risky and debasing sexual encounters bound up with bad luck, unrelenting poverty, a cruel capitalism and the illusion of escape provided by alcohol.

Earlier that night Katy was nabbed by a City copper and charged as drunk and disorderly. When asked simple questions she'd fallen into the road, dead drunk. They took her to Bishopsgate station and let her sober up in a cell. At one in the morning they released her, however, about the same time Long Liz was being murdered nearby.

Forty minutes later Tonio had found his way to the outside of Mitre Square on the east side and was taking a dark alleyway labeled Church Passage, entering a large area rimmed with pavement and high buildings. He could see almost nothing, just a lonely streetlamp across the way that revealed little but the rancid fog. He stopped to listen. It was supposed to happen somewhere very near.

He walked the perimeter, remaining on the pavement and close to the building walls. After a minute he reached a corner and made the turn. Around another turn he reached the Mitre Street entrance. Beyond that, past a group of empty houses in a dark alcove he noticed something on the ground. Katy was just in front of him, on her back, her head turned left, her arms at her sides, her palms up, dead. A thimble had been placed on one of her fingers. Her face was grotesquely disfigured and her throat was slashed. Her clothing was cut away to reveal her body from stomach to thighs.

This time Tumblety had completed his grotesque operation. He had opened her corpse from breast bone to genitals like a laboratory specimen. Tonio noticed that whole sections had been removed, along with several organs.

Why hadn't he been there? Commandments be damned, not making things worse wasn't enough. His basic instinct was to track Tumblety down right now, tonight, and kill him with his own knife at the first possible opportunity. But that was trumped by the realization that he might be discovered standing over the corpse. Officer Ed Watkins was just moments away.

Watkins was making his usual rounds. It normally took him fifteen minutes to get from Duke Street to St. James and back. The route went from Heneage to Bury, and from there to Creechurch Lane and Leadenhall. That brought him to Mitre, where he walked the square's perimeter before continuing on his way. He'd been doing the same route for hours.

Knowing that, Tonio carefully snuck away from the entrance, hugging the wall and staying as far from the light as he could. All he needed was to become a suspect.

He had about forty minutes to get back to the yard behind Batty Street and he'd already reached the conclusion that being a real-time eyewitness wasn't the best surveillance strategy. The first crime was so sudden he almost missed it, and leaving the stream to be at Mitre Square for the second turned out to be a mistake. He did have proof that Tumblety committed both murders. But beyond that he had to ask himself, what had he achieved?

Finding his way was another problem. Signs were hard to locate in the dark and the street grid was different than he remembered. He stopped at a narrow street marked Goulston and headed through, then stopped again. About thirty feet ahead he could pick out two men standing in front of a doorway. One was in the midst of writing on the wall, the other appeared to be his superior and issued instructions about the work in progress. A few steps further and Tonio could pick out the one in charge – Rachkovsky, the same man he had seen lurking in the Commons. The dark eyes, prominent nose, distinctive overcoat and cane left an indelible impression.

What was he up to, in an alley, in the dead of the night, blocks from a murder scene? Was the other his man Milewski or a fresh recruit? He pressed close to a building wall and waited until they were gone, then rushed to the same spot.

A message had been left at the front of the passage leading down to 108-119 Model Street. It said:

> *The Juwes are*
> *The men that*
> *Will not*
> *be Blamed*
> *for nothing*

On the ground, below what seemed like a manufactured clue, they had deposited a second one, part of a woman's apron strained with fresh blood. So, that's the game, thought Tonio. I know this play – planting false evidence.

The Russian spook was setting a disinformation campaign in motion, using the murders to make his case for what the good people of London and Great Britain ought to fear – immigrants, extremists and especially Jews. It was a perfect opportunity. The murder of Long Liz had happened not more than a mile away, right across from the Jewish Socialist Club. Dutfield's Yard was also next to the International Working Men's Club. In the past few years Joseph Lane had opened at least a half dozen radical clubs in the neighborhood, places for immigrants, activists and others to gather, speak freely and hear Sunday speeches from revolutionaries like Kropotkin.

The strange spelling in the message seemed purposely cryptic, as if implying a Masonic link, while the grammar pointed to either a Frenchman or someone less educated. Rachkovsky was planting seeds of suspicion, just enough to link this to the murder while remaining a mystery and playing on anti-Jewish sentiment.

He was almost back at Wentworth when Rachkovsky returned, this time leading a patrolman. They walked to the doorway, where the spymaster pointed out the "clues." It was obviously a set up. Resentment and blame, mused Tonio, always a good bet.

The closer he got to the Jump Room entrance the busier the neighborhood became. In the hour since he exited the stream – breaking Commandment Two – and visited Mitre Square hundreds of residents had gathered to gawk and gossip about the murder at Dutfield's Yard. Officers were prowling the streets, moving door to door, asking if anyone had seen something.

He thought about pushing through the crowd to watch the police surgeon examine the corpse or see how Superintendent Arnold handled the crime scene. That might be risky, though, since he could end up drawing attention to himself. What if Deimschutz was still around and pointed him out as the one who had spooked his pony? He had no time to be detained and interrogated. That would definitely break Commandment Four.

With only minutes to spare he walked toward the alley next to 22

Batty Street, turning back for a final look before going home. The orange glow of the lanterns tinged the yellow fog with warmer highlights. People gathered in small groups at various doorways, talking to neighbors and cops from upper floor windows. It was still dark and early, yet almost as lively as in daylight.

In the downstairs apartment at Batty #22 an argument was in progress between the landlady and one of her tenants. She was standing at his doorway complaining as he removed his overcoat and began changing out of the military outfit beneath. Tonio leaned in for a look and was instantly reminded of what he already believed: There are no coincidences.

Frank Tumblety was standing just twenty feet away in the midst of a landlord-tenant dispute. The owner, a stout German woman with a thick accent, had seen something on his clothing, possibly blood, and was asking questions in her poor English. It was obvious she considered him a dandy. Had he been caught red handed by an old woman? Tonio listened more closely.

"Madam, this is unnecessary," the killer objected. "I am a businessman, as well as a respected surgeon. I was simply making a call. You said nothing about noise issues when we made our arrangements."

"This house mine," the woman replied, "and we don't need fancy men who comes and goes at every hours."

"I understand, I assure you, it won't happen again. Now please, I need to prepare for a journey."

She backed away. "We go now, but you watch it. This is proper house."

The location was perfect, right in the neighborhood he was terrorizing. He was slumming, common among gentleman who wanted to keep their public and private lives separate. It provided access and time to scout locations or observe future victims. No wonder he seemed so spontaneous and premeditated at the same time. He had a familiar hunting ground where he could roam at liberty, effectively camouflaged and apparently above reproach. But now someone was becoming suspicious, which meant that he might kill her – or move.

This was excruciating. He knew the killer and had personally witnessed at least one of the crimes. Yet what could he do? Still nothing. Tumblety was armed and he wasn't. On the other hand, if he filed a report with the police one of the first questions would be why he had been following a gentleman around. He looked like a vagrant in Danny's damned coat. And imagine the reaction if they saw the clothes beneath.

No, it was time to leave. At least he had the satisfaction of knowing that he had solved the crime of the century. He knew where Tumblety was staying and how he operated. The only thing not completely nailed down was the motive. All in all, he rated this pretty impressive for an amateur. He had even uncovered an international plot, orchestrated by Rachkovsky with the possible complicity of the Special Branch, to exploit the Ripper murders in order to stoke fear and suspicions of Jews and immigrants.

What a TV documentary it could make someday.

The landlady bid Tumblety good morning and waddled along the alley to the yard. But she didn't return to bed. Instead, she complained to herself in German as she opened the cellar door, disappeared inside and emerged with a load of laundry. Continuing to eavesdrop, Tonio began to think she might be demented. He watched from the corner as she strung up a line and rambled on as she hung underwear and shirts.

He checked his watch: only a minute to go. Then he decided it might work from where he was watching; just press recall and check. When nothing happened his next thought was to walk immediately to the yard and wait. In theory, Danny was watching in the control room. But they were close. Would the woman come with him? And what would happen? One thing for sure: he wasn't touching her.

He retrieved Danny's list. It offered nothing helpful for this situation. Finally he decided to take his chances and proceeded, as inconspicuously as he could, to the general spot where he had landed. He tried not to attract attention, but kept a safe distance from everything. He checked the watch and waited for the whirlpool to form.

The deadline came and went. After a few more seconds he pressed recall. Nothing.

"What you want?" the landlady barked. "You got money?"

Shit! This could be a one-way trip, he realized with a heavy gulp. At the same time he just had to wonder, how many commandments did I break?

30
IMPROVISATION

What he experienced as the sun rose was nothing less than awe, the heart of the Empire beginning to beat faster as the city slowly came to life. During the murders he was able to pick out the sound of a single cart or carriage rattling through the empty, uneven streets. Now he heard a symphony of traffic, the clop-clopping of horses pulling hansom-cabs, London's local gondolas, and the wheels of hundreds of carts, drays, vans, landaus and broughams of countless shapes and sizes.

The streets gradually thickened with people and, due to all the horse shit, an army of shoe-shiners fanned out to make some coin. In this part of town they dressed mainly in blue jackets and set up their small chairs wherever they could, providing periodicals for gentlemen to peruse as their footwear was restored. To keep the walkways clear crossing sweepers dodged between traffic, dangerous work for seven shillings a week. Others set up shop on the curbstones, selling everything from walking sticks and shirt studs to self-composed topical songs.

After his recall button failed and Tonio was left standing in front of the landlady, he loitered in the area as long as possible in hopes of returning to try again. The laundry took longer than he hoped, however, and by six a.m., the next jump time on the schedule, there were simply too many people. He had no choice but to wait for a better, more private chance.

Heading generally toward London Bridge he passed shops selling fresh bacon, dairy goods and groceries, cheap-jack hustlers with knives and baubles, costermongers hawking fruit and vegetables as they made their way to Billingsgate for the day. At the edge of the river he saw the mud larks, pitiful boys under twelve scrounging in the muck for coal, rope and nails.

Then he took stock of his own situation: no money, no connections, and no idea how long he would have to stay. At the moment he looked like one of those fellows who slept near the docks. Well, at least he spoke the language, although the accents and dialects were so thick and diverse he had to concentrate to keep up.

By mid-morning he'd devised a short-term plan. Assuming that whatever hadn't functioned earlier would soon work again – in short, that Danny could bring him home – he reasoned that he had a twelve hour daylight window to explore the city and experience what no one in the twenty-first century ever had. Knowing the future might actually provide an edge. What he needed at the moment was food and friendly faces.

Turning from London Bridge he went further west on Cheapside until he saw the criminal court building, Old Bailey, then back toward the river and beyond Blackfriars Bridge. He was headed for Fleet Street. The destination seemed obvious – 34 Bouverie Street just off Fleet, the office of the only weekly paper where he already knew the editor.

The sign on the door gave the name and purpose: The Link, A Journal for the Servants of Man. And beneath that the name of the woman in charge: Annie Besant, Proprietor.

"So sorry," explained the red-head with his feet on the desk after Tonio asked if she was available. "Saint Anne is off saving the world somewhere. And Mr. Stead, well, he's off raising money. So you'll have to settle for two smart and devious gentlemen."

"Are you American?" The question was from the second man, perched on a table piled high with books and newspapers. "I'm sailing there in a week," he said extending a hand. "Sidney Webb."

And who was he supposed to be? Tonio just sounded wrong, a bit too Jersey Shore for this situation. He had worked out a basic persona and occupation for the role but had forgotten to choose a name. "Sinclair," he blurted. "Upton Sinclair, over from New York researching a new book."

"You've come to the right place," Webb assured, pointing to the thirty-something gentlemen who had answered first. "This is the most talked about writer in London..."

"Only London?" teased his associate.

"I'm not sure what they're talking about in New York. We'll find out soon enough. Paris also needs work, I understand, even after your book. In any case, you are talked about here, almost as much as you talk about yourself."

"Shaw," interrupted the red-head. "You can call me Shaw, or GBS.

"George, don't be an arse."

"Don't listen to him, he's a bookkeeper. You're here to see the proprietor?" Shaw continued, "I mean the editor, obviously. She will return shortly I believe. In the meanwhile, we were discussing whether the latest atrocities are part of a larger design. Have you formed an opinion yet?"

Tonio struggled to catch the thread. "The atrocities in..."

"The killings, man, two murders in one night. That's all people are talking about. Haven't you heard?" Without waiting for his answer Shaw recapped what was being reported and heard around town. The Whitechapel "fiend" was back, they all said, and the police were baffled. Sir Charles Warren had shown up at one of the crime scenes after Tonio left, but that added little light to the proceedings. According to the papers the East End was becoming lost in a "frenzy of horror and alarm."

Shaw read from the copy on his desk. "Look here, this one writes, 'Philosophy is helpless.' There's a concept. 'There is still an utter absence of conventional motive for the crime. We are constantly driven back to the old theory that the butcheries are the work on a madman with homicidal propensities.' Brilliant. They also claim he was almost caught. But the main concern of police, they claim, is 'an outbreak against the Jews.' An outbreak? 'Precautionary measures are being taken.' So, what do you say?"

How to respond? He didn't want to play the ignorant American, but having too much information might be suspicious. There was also Commandment Ten. With what he knew he definitely risked altering history. And he was talking with George Bernard Shaw, someone with the political and creative intelligence to make the story resonate through the ages.

"It's very disturbing," Tonio began. "Are there suspects yet?"

"Many and none. We have no trouble finding candidates to blame. Newcomers are always suspicious, don't you find? Anyone who's different really."

"George likes to kid," offered Webb.

"Irony, I know. But I understand your point and agree that some people have a motive for focusing on certain suspects and not others."

"There is an even darker theory," Shaw continued. "I'm not endorsing this view, but I've heard it said that the murders are really meant to frighten the whores, a means for those in charge to simply clear the streets for a bit. A triage purge."

"My God, really? I doubt that."

"As do I actually. Even the Branch isn't that devious. But that's the beauty of terror, isn't it? You don't know, you don't know who is ultimately responsible, or what he or they want. You just know you should be afraid and suspicious of anyone you don't know or understand."

Tonio tried to shift the discussion. "Mr. Webb said you've written a book?"

"About five years ago, but it was just published last year. *An Unsocial Socialist*, decent title," he noted, issuing his own review. "You might call it a middling social satire. As you can tell my hero is a socialist. But his trouble is more matrimonial. It was largely a platform to discuss the issues of the day rather than a fully developed tale. I expect to do better. And what are you working on?"

Tonio had prepared for this question. "My book? It's about a British detective in America."

"Like that Conan Doyle character in the serial?"

"Right, like Sherlock Holmes, but different."

"Will he be tracking more Mormons?" Tonio was confused. "Like Holmes and his friend whats-his name."

It took him a second to connect the reference to *A Study in Scarlet*, the Holmes book. It had been published a month earlier after appearing in serial. In part two of the book version, called The Country of the Saints, the story moved back in time and across the ocean to Utah for the story of John Ferrier and Lucy, his daughter, who were rescued by Mormons but forced to convert. Years later, when Lucy and Jefferson Hope, a non-Mormon, fell in love, her father was threatened by Brigham Young before being murdered by a band of Mormon vigilantes. Lucy was kidnapped, forced to marry and prematurely died. That was the motive for the murder Holmes ultimately solved.

"It isn't finished yet," Tonio said, opting to sidestep for the moment. "Bit of a superstition."

"Ridiculous." Shaw was determined to draw him out. "Then you can certainly tell us about your last opus."

He ran with the first ideas that came to mind. "It takes place during a war – the Civil War – and the South has just won a victory. They're losing in the long run, but they've won for now, and they're chasing Yankees out of town. And in this one grand house there's a beautiful young lady, the daughter of the major who won the battle." He was free associating, improvising his way through.

"What's she like?"

"She's excitable, very proud of her father and her fiancé – who is also a soldier – and wrapped up in her noble image of the South. She's dramatic and full of contradictions, also strong and has high ideals, but she's insecure and has doubts."

"Sounds like comrade Annie," Webb said.

"Quite right," Shaw added, "except that Annie has never in my presence expressed a doubt about an idea. Do continue."

Tonio imagined the next scene. "Later that night, she's awakened by gunfire. The army is tracking down stragglers. Suddenly one of the enemy soldiers bursts in. He's on the run and needs a place to hide."

"Excellent opening. What's it called?"

"War and Peace." The first title that came to mind.

"I'm afraid a Russian has already used that," he advised, "something about Russian aristocrats, French invaders and the deep ocean of philosophy."

"Actually we changed the name before publication. The new title is… Man of War."

Webb asked, "You mean like the ship?

"No, actually…

"It also refers to a venomous jellyfish," said Annie. She had been listening from the door for a few seconds. Now she entered and looked Tonio over. "Are you in a play?"

"Ambiguity, not bad," Shaw concluded. "Is it a comedy?"

31
SOCIETY

Officially, the evening was hosted by Beatrice Potter in support of trade union organizing underway at the docks. But Shaw saw it as a chance to network and recruit for the Society. Since Tonio – now Upton Sinclair – was a member of the writing fraternity, he promised that a last-minute invitation wouldn't be difficult to swing.

"I'm not sure I can stand it," Annie protested. "Not you, Upton, I mean Beatrice. She does so much but –"

"She has so much," Shaw finished. "Thousands of pounds a year, from what I hear, from Canadian railway stocks."

"I do respect her support for the cooperatives and unions," Annie said. "She's with us on the main points. But honestly, opposing suffrage? Not to mention her positively clinical attitude toward the poor. Frankly, I don't think she's much excited about democracy in the end."

"I sort of like her," said Webb. "She's practical and committed. And she sees the economic situation clearly. Things only have value if people want them. That's the cooperative approach. That's why we want productive consumers, and production for use and not profit, under democratic control."

"Tell it to the Americans," countered Shaw. "Now, about those clothes?"

Tonio had removed the overcoat before knocking, but his slacks were thin, black and pin-striped, his shirt purple and made of Chinese silk, and his jacket of brushed leather. To Annie it looked like a theatrical outfit. He claimed that his own overcoat was stolen at King's Cross Station and the outfit was the latest thing from San Francisco."

"Fashion is relative, I suppose." Annie gave it another look. "The trousers aren't practical and that shirt is completely unacceptable. Can we fix him up proper for tonight?"

A few hours later Tonio was selecting a formal shirt, pants, tie, vest, and knee-length frock coat from Shaw's closet. His host also provided a simple supper – soup, game and port – but apologized for the paucity and promised that Beatrice would provide a generous spread.

"You never said why you came by to see the editor." Shaw remembered their first exchange as they boarded a cab.

"I'm an admirer of her writing and work with the matchgirls." What else could he plausibly say? "I thought she could help with my research. It's an unusual premise and I thought an idealist like her, or you for that matter, could provide the right social context."

"Let's not mix apples with armaments," Shaw countered. "Annie is a believer and I am a professional skeptic. She is a creature of emotion and air. And I am a man of reason, and well, let's simply say that we differ on the means. But we agree on the ends, social revolution and a new society. The gathering tonight will be another small step. I guarantee you, what we are building here will reach across the whole country within a few short years.

"Of course, we'll also be raising funds tonight for the upcoming delegation to the States. But we reserve time for announcements and so forth, so I would appreciate it if you added a few words."

"I couldn't," Upton demurred. But Tonio realized that he'd better start prepping. "Could you say a bit about the Society, its aims and the like."

"Of course, it's never safe to assume," said Shaw. "The Fabian Socialist Society, but when I say Society I'm talking about something more than that. Webb and I, and of course Sydney Oliver at the Colonial Office developed the basic credo for members several years ago: reorganization of society through emancipation of land and liberation of capital from class ownership. The difference is that we intend to do it not by taking to the barricades or through parliamentary wrangling, but gradually, by spreading socialist ideas, a general, consistent and persistent dissemination of knowledge that ultimately brings us there.

"Mr. Morris, who may also attend, was good enough to host a meeting at his lecture hall in Hammersmith two years ago. Everyone came and we talked about the future, and I would describe the mood as very bright." Shaw paused for effect. "But today, especially since the bomb in Chicago, we need to be careful. A little anarchism must not become a dangerous thing.

"The moment is crucial," he confided. "We need to chart a steady course."

Beatrice Potter's home was a grand dwelling with a courtyard in front and steps leading to an entrance above the kitchen on the ground floor. Inside, he followed Shaw past a library, drawing room and gallery to a broad set of stairs leading to a saloon filled with guests.

Two hours later, when the agenda finally came around to him, the newly minted Upton Sinclair thought he was ready. He began with a recap of the gains that had been made since Henry George's New York mayoral campaign two years before. He recalled that George had been defeated but received more votes than Teddy Roosevelt, and in the aftermath the state legislature passed a series of reforms. People cheered as he listed a few – labor arbitration (enthusiastic clapping), regulating the employment of women and children (applause and cheers!), and reforming the penal system (just a smattering).

From there he moved on to a brief pitch about his imaginary book.

Adapting elements from *The Time Machine*, other science fiction and the real Upton Sinclair play he'd seen in Vermont, he launched into a lively description of a British detective who tracks a dangerous mass murderer across America. Eventually, the man disappears into a cave. The detective follows, he said, and suddenly finds himself in a different place and time.

Before he could go further a chorus of critics shouted him down with catcalls like "Bellamy's done it," "copycat" and "try again."

He stepped back, embarrassed without immediately realizing why. As the discussion proceeded to the upcoming American delegation of the British Economic Association, Annie moved in behind him and whispered a consolation, "They can be cruel and devious, these socialists, challenging everything. It's not their affection for the State that makes them so dangerous, it's all the damned questions."

He had to laugh. Then she added, "Your problem, love, is that *Looking Backward* is one of the main topics under discussion tonight. You sounded like an opportunist."

She was right. He'd come across as either a plagiarist or a fool who never heard of the most popular book making the rounds. *Looking Backward* was already a best seller in America. Edward Bellamy, an ex-lawyer and journalist, had captured the public's imagination with his tale of Julian West, a gentleman from 1887 who wakes up from hypnosis to find himself in a future socialist utopia. It was a phenomenon, with clubs being formed to discuss the book and its ideas.

Tonio listened as Webb outlined the purpose of the upcoming trip. He and Edward Pease would spend several months in the States, organizing meetings and recruiting professors, clergymen and the literary set. They would also make arrangements for the American publication of a key essay, "The Historical Aspects of the Basis of Socialism." Several people shouted out that the name needed improvement.

"A frontal attack on capitalism will not succeed," Webb argued. "The anarchists have made sure of that. We'll be fortunate if the Americans don't ban socialism altogether. But Bellamy's book provides us with an ideal springboard for a reasonable discussion. The New England states are especially ripe. We have Doctor Mulford and Reverend Gladden to thank for that.

"And largely thanks to Annie," he added with a bow in her direction, "two journalists in Boston, Baxter and Willard if I remember, have published glowing reviews of Bellamy's book that explicitly make many of our points." The plan was to coordinate the promotion of the Society's socialist manifesto with the growing popularity of Bellamy's book. Webb mentioned that a group of former soldiers had just announced plans to form a Boston club in Bellamy's name.

"It pays to understand your audience," Annie whispered. "By the way, why isn't your detective an American? You should write what you know."

For the next several minutes she stayed close to his side and provided commentary on speakers and guests, beginning with their statuesque hostess, who asserted her right to be first in the queue once Webb finished. She endorsed the plan and reinforced his arguments with snippets from her own investigations in East End slums.

"Her father was very liberal," Annie explained. "For some reason that turned all the Potter girls into moral conservatives, at least in terms of women's concerns." Tonio commented that she didn't sound that conservative. "I'm exaggerating. She simply thinks economic emancipation must come first, and that means other issues have to wait. We disagree."

"What about them?" Tonio nodded toward a young couple across the way, obviously in love and sharing a private narrative in counterpoint with the public debate.

"That's Edward," she said with an intake of breath. "Edward Aveling, a teacher and a great scholar. He's translated Marx into English."

"And her?"

"Eleanor Marx." There was obviously no love lost. "Yes, the great man's daughter. They've been together for about a year, around the same time they joined the Socialist League."

"Do you two have a problem?"

She was embarrassed but tried to conceal it. "Edward lived at my house for a bit."

"Something happened?"

"No," she said with a hint of disappointment. "He's a brilliant man. But he's with her now. It's simply a bit awkward."

"But you're all in the Society?"

While she tried to explain an upper-class gentleman followed Potter to address the room.

"That's William Morris. Wallpaper, carpets, curtains and all that. These days he's a revolutionary." Five years ago, she explained, Morris had joined the Democratic Federation, then the only active socialist organization in the country. But the businessman knew nothing about Marx or Henry George. He was an aesthete and an instinctive rebel. As a result he split from the Federation a year after joining it, and formed the Socialist League.

Last year he split again when the anarchist faction asserted itself.

"As much as I would like to join the chorus I'm afraid I cannot," Morris announced. "We have moved past the point where propaganda will turn the tide. We are on the road to revolution – or oblivion. The corruption of society is complete, is it not? Well, all right, then the time has come for a new order, not another manifesto."

"And what is this order – is it imposed by force, does it include nationalization and control of individual initiative?" It was a comment from someone in the crowd, just beyond Tonio's view. That voice, so familiar. He strained to see.

Ignatius Donnelly looked exactly as Tonio remembered him from the View Room, piercing blue eyes, stocky frame, commanding presence. "I enjoyed and appreciated *Progress and Poverty*," he said, an acknowledgement of Henry George's grand opus. "His argument is logical, and in terms of Ireland it may be correct. There is no way to justify such vast quantities of land in the hands of so few."

"Your point, sir." Morris didn't appreciate being interrupted mid-rant.

"But personally I remain too much a Jeffersonian to embrace nationalization and so-called panaceas like the single tax. Such ideas strike at basic rights and the very fundamentals of society."

"What rights?" A challenge from the crowd.

"The right of any man – or woman – to enjoy the fruits of his labor," Donnelly said defiantly. "Without that we relapse into barbarism."

"I think we've heard enough of the American position," Morris cut in. "So, what can the Society do about the individualist strain? I suspect any educational project on the other side of the pond will run a bit longer than the masses can afford."

"America will follow its own road," Donnelly insisted.

"And who will lead it, sir? You?"

"Maybe he will," blurted Tonio before he could stop himself. Dozens of faces turned his way. Realizing what he'd done, he quickly added, "as governor in the great state of Minnesota. You are the Farmer Labor Party candidate, are you not?"

"I have that honor," acknowledged Donnelly, a bit shocked that anyone in the audience recognized him. The room erupted into spontaneous applause. Donnelly basked in the moment.

"You know him?" Annie was impressed. "I do as well actually, we met briefly last spring. Interesting man – strange ideas."

Tonio thought: There goes another commandment. This is not inconspicuous.

From the balcony of Webb's home he looked out at the city, down arteries dotted with gaslights and floating lanterns, a megalopolis in the making, the first of its kind in the world. At its core was the old City, the area between the original walls and the Thames, from the Temple Bar to the Tower. But London was more than this, it was the fashionable West End and the East End slums near the docks. Beyond it, on the south side of the river, the countryside extended fifty miles, past Gravesend and the marshes of Essex and Kent, to the mouth of the Channel.

Somehow the mood of the evening was optimistic, filled with a sense of hopeful anticipation. Despite everything he'd seen that day, the murder and filth, the soul-deadening poverty, this collection of liberals and radicals, clergymen, businessmen, laborers, teachers and assorted other dreamers could envision a better future.

As the debate continued, they had retreated outside for a private moment. Donnelly needed to know something about the random American who had come to his defense. Annie re-introduced herself and apologized for Morris, insisting that there was enough room in the Fabian Society for differing views on the issues he raised.

Tonio kept his introduction vague, then inquired about Donnelly's book.

"That's why I'm here instead of campaigning at home," the politician explained. "It's my second trip this year. But this one will be brief, a few paying engagements and I'm gone. Where are you staying, we should meet."

An opportunity was staring at him, a way to avoid his likely lodging if Danny couldn't bring him back – the closest workhouse. Improvising again, he said that it actually wasn't just his overcoat those villains stole at the station. It was everything. He could certainly obtain funds eventually. But at the moment he was homeless and broke.

Donnelly gave him a quizzical stare, then glanced at Annie and inside at the animated discussion. "That's no trouble. We have a second-floor flat on Duke Street with an open room. I'll ask my companions."

He accepted immediately, but explained that he had a late appointment and would find his way sometime after midnight. After providing the address Donnelly bid them both goodnight and slowly made his way through the saloon, stopping frequently to shake hands and exchange pleasantries. Tonio returned to the view, acknowledging Annie's presence with a winning smile. After all, this wasn't the royal court, or country life with its suffocating manners.

"Are you happy with what you're doing?" He already knew she had doubts about her work.

"What a question," she replied. "But well timed. We are in the midst of an all-consuming campaign." Over the next hour she never really answered his question, but he learned more about the British labor question than he thought possible. Apparently, the Tyneside & District Laborers Union had been firmly established and the movement was spreading like wildfire along the Tyne and North East docks, pulling in scrappers, painters, helpers and other shipyard men. Factory organizing was meanwhile underway in West London, Botwell and Hayes. Within a year or two it would become a national movement, she predicted, and lead to the first general trade union.

In July, she also informed him with some pride, she had led London's matchgirls to a victory that surprised even her. After two weeks on strike, combined with considerable lobbying, several large demonstrations and letters of support from sympathetic clergy, they had won. Bryant & May capitulated and agreed to improve both pay and working conditions. A union had been formed and plans were underway for a social center. The matchstick industry, a powerful lobby before electric lighting, had been beaten.

"Someday we may look back and say, this was the start," she imagined, "a moment when young girls, with no power and little education, defeated a corporate power and achieved an historic victory for socialism and human emancipation."

"And yet?"

"And yet," she agreed. "Life has more to tell us than we know. Although sometimes I do despair that I'll ever find it. I don't believe in God, but psychology is advancing so rapidly, showing us unknown complexities in consciousness, the strange riddles of the brain."

He felt himself drawn into her world and concerns. It was an intense and colorful landscape full of causes and great goals. At one moment she would be absolutely convinced, and in the next question her conviction and wonder what Morris or Aveling might say. She had charm, incredible command of the issues, and extraordinary gifts as a communicator. Still, she was a complex mixture of defiance and suggestibility.

"George says civilization needs religion but that Darwin and materialism are destroying it," she quoted.

"And what does he think will happen?"

Annie laughed. "He's too smart to pretend to know, or at least to tell anyone that. But he has hopes, as we all do. If all of this must end," she said with an expansive wave, "at least its demise can be a prelude to something new. George would add more rational."

"And you say?"

"That there must be more, I feel it, something hidden," she told him, eyes brimming with tears. "Sometimes it drives me to the edge of distraction, like a puzzle that tortures my mind. But there is also a small voice, quite faint."

"And what does it say?"

"Take courage," she answered softly, "the time is coming, the answer is near."

The words reminded him to check Danny's pocket watch, currently attached to the borrowed vest. It said he had missed the jump.

32
Choices

Did he really just lose track of time? Not likely. Tonio had to admit it the next morning: for some reason this was where he chose to be. Tonight would be different, however. He would return to the yard with plenty of time to spare and hope for the best. In the meantime, he had another day in London, perhaps time to understand why he had stayed.

Catching the Ripper no longer seemed plausible as the only or even main reason.

Donnelly posed a related question after he bought coffee at a stall. "That was quite the presentation you made," he said with a pat of consolation.

"More like a disaster."

"None of it, that's a difficult crowd. Bright, good intentions," he judged, "but many of them have their heads in the clouds. From New York, are you? Not the usual accent."

"I grew up near…the docks."

"That must be it. But what I was wondering: Are you truly here to research a book? Somehow you seem more like a performer."

"That's good. I was an actor for a while."

"Hmm. I considered that," Donnelly recalled fondly, "I'm fairly good at stirring up a crowd."

"I know. I saw you in Chicago, talking on the Cryptogram."

"Oh, that windmill," he sighed. "The reviews, not to mention the royalties, have not been what I hoped for. Of course, the English press had bludgeons out from the start. Most would prefer to guard the rotting carcass of a national delusion than entertain a fresh idea. Nevertheless, I do find something comforting in the mathematics of the whole thing, the cipher itself, everything just seems to fit.

"But Mrs. Donnelly brought me to my senses," he sighed. "Home and security first. My primary focus these days is the state legislature and the Labor Alliance. I'm back in the House, in case you didn't hear. Before the governor's race they were accusing me of wanting a Senate seat. Now they say I'm building a private army to become House Speaker. But that's not it, I assure you. And I'll be out of the governor's race in a week."

"You're not staying in?"

"No, the family is united in the belief that a third party run this year would be a fatal error. It's been a particularly bad time for us, financially speaking. But I do see the chance of getting a reform program enacted. Last session we got the Interstate Commerce petition through. Of course the conservatives blocked us on anti-usury, said it would cost jobs and drive capital out of Minnesota.

"And we almost succeeded with clean elections." He described a tough fight over a bill that would have implemented voter registration rules, secret ballots and other measures designed to reduce intimidation and bribery. "No one had the nerve to oppose it publicly," he said. "They just killed it with amendments.

"But the fact is, Ben Harrison will probably defeat Cleveland in November, so I need to maintain decent relations with the Republicans, at least outside the state. On the other hand, I have reached the conclusion, largely due to my time here, that labor must have some protection in the form of a tariff. Free trade turns out to be a myth. But I'm a candidate for governor accidentally. It happened just after returning from the tour. To be honest, I wasn't paying enough attention to the internal dynamics and allowed myself to be seduced."

In February, he'd attended an Alliance convention but failed to notice a growing rift between farmers and the Knights of Labor. After he left for England the Alliance endorsed a St. Paul banker named Albert Scheffer as its candidate for governor. This upset the unions, which hadn't been consulted. Scheffer was playing the angles, seeking the Republican nod while talking about temperance and tariffs. The establishment sensed a split they could exploit, while Donnelly's labor friends launched a plan to draft him. A letter from one ally, reaching him in London, said he was "the only man in the state in whom the people have confidence."

"It was an awful dilemma," Donnelly lamented. "Meanwhile, savage insects ravaged the wheat. For the first time in twenty-five years we didn't have a bushel to show this season. And the Bank of Minnesota was making unpleasant noises about some debts. Still, the party leaders promised to raise a substantial war chest. In a sense I suppose my critics are right. I really can't say no to a nomination, one more chance to put my case before the people."

"Then what are you doing here?"

Donnelly flashed a devilish grin. "Money goes farther and the food is cheap. But seriously, it's all the Republican's fault. They may be many things but they are not stupid. In the end they didn't nominate Scheffer. Instead they went with Bill Merriman. Do you know who that is? Why should you? He's the man I supported for Speaker of the House just last year, a solid supporter of many of our issues, including the usury bill. Yes, he is also a banker, but I have to say he is essentially an honest fellow who seems to want fair, economical government."

He had decided to withdraw from the race after several friends in the GOP arranged an invitation by the Republican National Committee to speak on behalf of Harrison in New York. But at a meeting the pols suggested, without much subtlety, that should Harrison become President, well, Donnelly's contribution would not be ignored. He despised such vote buying and influence peddling. On the other hand, he thought James Blaine's decision to break the GOP convention deadlock and back Harrison had given him a solid edge.

"It's also really what Kate wants," Donnelly admitted with some embarrassment, "for me to be paid for all the campaigning, and perhaps to secure a federal appointment at some point."

"What did you decide?"

"I declined," he said glumly. "I had to. I'm in pretty hot water at home over that. And meanwhile, the Alliance hasn't been able raise the promised funds for the governor's campaign. So, as to why I'm here, the honest answer would be, I'm in hiding. Hopefully, by the time I start home word will begin circulating that my withdrawal is imminent. Eventually, I will have to bite the bullet and make the endorsement."

"Won't your labor friends feel betrayed?"

"I'm not looking forward to that discussion."

With a few bob in his pocket and an outfit on loan from George Shaw he felt secure enough to spend most of the afternoon exploring the City of London. One of the first things he discovered was that when people talked about "the City" they normally meant the Royal Exchange, the city's financial area. But beyond it there was more, everything really, starting with the vibrant West End, the upscale part of town, home of St. James and Whitehall, Westminster Abbey and Parliament, Downing Street and Mayfair.

Tonio walked past the expensive shops of Bond Street and the men's clubs on Pall Mall, and finally reached Park Lane, a neighborhood of glorious homes, for a look at Hyde Park and Buckingham Palace. Hearing Donnelly admit he had escaped from tough choices at home, Tonio began to think he was doing the same. In fact, he might have unconsciously blown the jump deadline to escape what he faced. Angel was angry, Danny had lied, Shelley was getting suspicious, and he hadn't been seen in days. People would be asking questions.

Then again, the reason might be Annie. By midnight he was captivated. Long before he had watched her in the stream and then seen her via the Sedona vortex. He'd studied her and read her words and stared for hours at her photo. Yet it never occurred to him that it was possible to meet. Once they were together he could barely accept the idea that the evening had to end.

Perhaps they would meet again, she'd said. That is, if he was staying in town long enough. Indeed. As the sun set he couldn't wait any longer. But the offices of *The Link* were locked and he had no idea where she lived.

On the streets a mood of suspicion and panic had taken hold since Sunday. Gossiping crowds loitered at crime scenes, hundreds of extra constables were on patrol, and the Special Branch was pursuing leads while detaining dozens of people. Bringing together various intelligence operations conducted by the Metro Police under a single command, the Branch was expanding its domain from a focus on the "Irish threat." At first Sir Robert Anderson, the well-known Christian zealot who ran the Criminal Investigations Department, suggested that the spate of killings might be a new form of Irish terrorism. But since Sunday, the public's attention had been shifting toward a different set of suspects – political extremists, Jews and other immigrants. Rachkovsky's scheme was taking effect. The "threats" were multiplying.

The first coverage in the *Illustrated Police News* didn't help matters. That morning it had fanned the latent prejudice in the wind with a front-page caricature portraying the killer as an Eastern European man with a thick nose and twisted ears, a racist epitome of a maniac Jew.

It all made him think William Morris might be correct: London did feel as if it was teetering at the edge of either a revolution or a catastrophe.

He returned to the East End a few hours early, buying a bit of bread and cheese for dinner before stopping at a pub. A final check was conducted over a glass of claret. Then he waited indoors, sheltered from the cold, until it was near midnight and time to make his way to Batty Street.

The landlady wasn't around and Tumblety's room was dark. He checked the time and walked down the alley. What a journey the last two days had been. He had seen two murders and tracked the killer to his hideout. He had met Annie Besant and her group, including George Shaw, one of the great writers of the age. He had presented himself to radical leaders of London society. Although it might have gone better, he'd turned the occasional to his advantage by defending Donnelly, a fellow outsider.

It felt almost as if the path had been created for him to reach this moment, stretching back to that night in New York when he was bored, even a bit depressed, as his crew terrorized a degenerate lawyer, a lawyer with a book collection and a familiar title on the shelf. But midnight came and went with no whirlpool forming to take him home. Looking up, he wondered whether Danny was even watching, or would ever find him again. He had stepped into the jump chamber so casually, with a mindless confidence, as if he was just boarding a bus for the airport. No big deal, just a short hop to Victorian England. No need to pack. Just wear that coat, hold onto this watch, and keep your head down. You'll be back in no time.

Would he ever return? Of course, he'd broken a few Commandments along the way. Maybe this was the cost. He'd left the stream, forgotten the time, and failed to stay inconspicuous. Was that enough to alter the future? Had he changed something, perhaps made time travel impossible and thus stranded himself? In that light the project began to seem like the height of hubris, a mistake of biblical proportions.

Still, it also felt like he was destined to be here, as if his life until recently had been mere prelude to reaching this place and time. He realized now there were clues all along. He simply hadn't noticed them. Gianni told him about Donnelly's cryptogram decades ago, during a live performance of Shakespeare no less. A few years later his death spurred Tonio's interest in criminal investigation, which brought him to the Ripper, which brought him here.

It was all connected. Yet, like the ultimate motives for the killer's crimes, the reasons continued to elude him.

33
ANOTHER NORMAL

The "double event" provided just the seasoning the press needed for juicy headlines and lurid stories. Within days they stirred roiling public fears into an even more toxic stew. By Tuesday bands of vigilantes were roaming the streets, spreading their impromptu brand of terror by chasing down and threatening anyone who looked suspicious or a bit different. As demonstrators marched and petitions circulated, a call was launched for the Home Secretary to resign.

The Central News Agency telegraphed each new twist to the world.

Any doubt or suspicion became tinder for a flare up. Some thought a deranged Royal might be on a spree. Others blamed bloodthirsty anarchists. Hearing of one gentleman who was staying near the British Museum, a reporter posted a story under the headline "Worth Inquiry." His only evidence was that the lodger "professes to be a doctor, but does not look like one. In fact, if one judged by his looks, he might be – well, a perfect ruffian.

"No one knows anything about him," he wrote. "At intervals he disappears for a time." In London even that was enough for an inquiry.

Central News had manufactured its own angle. Several days before, just prior to the Sunday murders, a letter was received and eventually forwarded to Chief Constable Williams. At first he took it as a satire. But a postcard followed, its message scrawled in red ink. The police refused to say it was from the killer, but that didn't stop the press from running with it.

Over tea and toast Donnelly read one version. "It's addressed to the Central News Office," he said, "and goes as follows. 'I wasn't codding dear old Boss when I gave you the tip.' Old Boss, who is that? Then he writes, 'You'll hear about saucy Jacky's work tomorrow double event this time number one squealed a bit couldn't finish straight off. Had no time to get ears for police. Thanks for keeping last letter back till I got to work again.' Atrocious grammar and punctuation."

"Was it signed?"

"I believe so." Donnelly read on. "It says here Jack the Ripper."

Tonio suggested that it could be false and knew for a fact it was. The messages had been concocted by Charles Moore and composed by his man Tom Bullen, both from the News Agency, forwarded to the police for release with a wink and nod by Scotland Yard.

"Why would they publish fabrications?"

"It's a catchy name," he said. "Anything to sell a threat – and a few papers."

Early that afternoon Tonio returned to *The Link*. Annie waved and kept working on correspondence, but Shaw was eager to talk. "You certainly made an impression," he began. "Morris says you're an agent provocateur."

Annie looked up, smiling. "Don't be concerned. He says that about everyone at some point or other."

"In any case, you're here at the right time: the end of civilization as we know it." The thin red-head paced as he hawked the story of the city's crisis with mock terror. "Read all about it! Lust for power and maximum profit produces deadly offspring. See the soulless evil brought to these tranquil shores by an alien plague. Superhuman bogey man on the loose -- or maybe two. Be amazed as London's intrepid police track down inhuman monsters – no matter how high the price. Sign up today for the pitchfork brigade!

"Quite the news bonanza, don't you think?" He slumped in a chair. "Sorry. It's just frustrating to see so many people manipulated; that is, unless I'm the one doing the manipulating. I don't fundamentally object to propaganda, just the bad ends to which it is so often put. This sort of thing – racial and ethnic animus, the objectification and sensationalist coverage– it can easily get out of hand."

That reminded Tonio of something Annie said. "And you blame materialism?"

"I blame the State and its organs, obviously. That includes some of the press. But I also include materialism – and let's not forget Darwin, for challenging our sense of species exceptionalism. There are large forces at work, vast historical trends and scientific discoveries of immense import. Uncontrollable, creative, but also destructive. You see, humanity has a dark side, a shadow self, an impulse toward destruction and evil that cannot be denied."

"Are you a religious man?"

"I would say so," Shaw said with slight irony. "In the sense that I find it a necessary comfort in a world buffeted by change. Most of us need something to cling to, don't you find?"

"Isn't religion the opium of the people?"

"It's opiate of the masses, but I take your point. However, what did Marx really mean? He said religion is 'the sigh of the oppressed creature, the heart of a heartless world, and' – what is it? – 'the soul of soulless conditions.' He means that it's a product of our own consciousness and self-esteem, and represents our theory of the world at a given point. And when he says it should be abolished, I think he's talking about surrendering illusions to discover real happiness. You might call that a moral stance."

Annie had stopped writing and listened with rapt attention. "Wonderful, the moral force of Marxism."

"You cannot quote me," Shaw objected. "We're merely debating the proper way to save humanity from itself. Anyway, this may not be a stand *The Link* is ready to endorse."

Annie was attempting to correct him when Sidney Webb rushed in frantically with word that a woman's body had just been discovered — found under the Metro Police building. All conversation ended and moments later they were out the door.

Down at the Thames, where a new police headquarters was under construction, a package had been discovered in an old cellar. It turned out to be a woman's decomposed torso. Once Annie caught a glimpse of the remains she next noticed the crowd gathering along the embankment.

"So dehumanizing," she said. "Yet people are fascinated, drawn to it. Let's find out why, and who people think is responsible, and what they'd like their government to do about it." Tonio tagged along at a distance. He knew better than to say much, but enjoyed being her bodyguard and second. At moments like these her defiance and strength became something else; a balance of engagement and detachment, not callous or timid, rather an ability to observe clearly while conveying empathy and compassion, and yet process it from a certain psychic distance.

Annie seemed to notice everything, recording insights and synthesizing experiences and making them her own. She was like an intelligent sponge absorbing information and processing it into knowledge. At the same time she was impressionable, and attracted to people with agile minds and original ideas – especially men of a certain age and type.

Tonio knew the type wasn't really him. But he didn't see why that should stop him. After all, he knew enough about her, and, under the circumstances, couldn't see why he should resist making use of it. If he wanted to pursue the woman of his dreams, it wouldn't hurt to have a secret weapon.

Wednesday brought an American angle to the public obsession. In addition to the fallout from yesterday's torso discovery, already being dubbed "The Whitehall Mystery," the papers carried related news from Texas.

This report was pure speculation, a suggestion that the recent London murders were the work of a Texas criminal who was never identified. The murders here did start just after the killings in San Antonio ended. And New York police had confirmed that the style of mutilation was similar. But the Police Superintendent called the killer a "monster or lunatic who has declared war literally to the knife against all womankind," and then disclaimed any suggestion it was the same person. Pointless hyperbole.

There seemed no end to it, much like the twenty-first century cable news cycle, only on street corners and in casual conversations. The worst was that Tonio knew the killer and possibly where he was. But how to explain that, and what was his evidence? Was this how Cassandra felt?

Donnelly was a pleasant host but a bit mercurial. He would begin most days like a fighter in training for a match, but then get distracted or preoccupied for hours by some minor statistic or news item. He'd then regroup and pen some letters, corresponding rapid-fire with family and friends in Minnesota and Illinois. On the other hand, he would fret over a single line in a note from Kate Donnelly saying the bank might seize a parcel of land. Then someone would call and he'd be off in fine form with a list of talking points in hand. He was a whirlwind, no vortex required.

That evening Tonio was in the sitting room on Duke Street when he returned with news of a new assault on rationality. Near Ratcliffe Highway he'd watched a crowd pursue a hapless seaman, trailing and surrounding him with curses and accusations. He was "Leather Apron," they shouted, and "the Ripper." He wasn't of course. If the police hadn't arrived in time, Donnelly thought they might have killed the fellow.

"Who was he in the end?"

"No one, just someone with red paint stains on his pants. But they held him, for his own protection. It's mayhem out there."

"Talk about déjà vu," Tonio mumbled.

"How so? I've never seen a thing like it. People are frantic, suspicious of everything. There's a smell of terror in the air."

Tonio wasn't sure how to respond. The mood actually reminded him of the period after 9/11, as well as several cities he had visited in recent years, desperate neighborhoods in tough times, and too many lives wasted. How could he explain that? "I was thinking about my novel," he answered instead.

"Really," Donnelly sounded skeptical but curious. "The one about the detective who tracks a killer into a cave? What happens next? They didn't let you get very far the other night. Do tell, where does he end up?"

What could he say? In Bellamy's book the time traveler went a century forward, "looking backward" from a future when the work week has been drastically reduced, products and services are delivered instantly and everyone retires at forty-five with healthy benefits. "The nation is the sole employer and capitalist," Bellamy wrote about the year 1988. All industrial production has been nationalized and goods are equally distributed. There is no need for dissent, and crime, though not completely eliminated, is handled as a medical issue, well on its way to the dustbin of history.

Quite a fantasy, he thought, very much the conservative Tea Party's nightmare.

"Actually, in my book the detective comes to this time to catch the killer and eventually takes him back," Tonio pitched. Technically, he wasn't breaking rules. He wasn't revealing anything about the Jump Room or claiming to be a detective. The way he saw it, there was no reason to think any fantasy he concocted would have an impact. And if it did, well, he was stuck here and would just have to do what felt right.

"Wonderful," cheered Donnelly. "What kind of future is it? Peace and harmony?"

"I wouldn't want to give away too much. That would spoil the ending. But let's begin with technology," he offered, and commenced an elaborate description of modern marvels like air travel, air-conditioning, mass communications and other features of the high-tech world he missed, a place where everything seemed possible and almost anything was for sale.

"And yet there is enormous inequality. A very few, just one percent, have almost half the wealth, while most people don't have basic security. Many are hungry and brimming with rage. Guns are everywhere. It's a heavily armed, alienated and unhappy society, I'm sorry to say, a mockery of its past, glittering on the outside but sick inside, prone to arbitrary and senseless violence, and littered with unnecessary victims. Sometimes, for no apparent reason, someone simply goes berserk and executes dozens in public, then kills himself, or commits what we call suicide by cop."

He stopped before getting to nuclear weapons and genocide, fearing they would either sound too extreme to be credible or too debilitating if believed.

"Terrible. But possible." Donnelly sat down to enjoy the performance. "Tell me about women. Are so many still forced to sell themselves on the streets?"

"On the streets? Maybe not so much. There are private clubs for that type of thing. But pimps are bigger than ever. I mean, the word has become a verb. Still, in many places women are afraid to go out alone at night."

"Why's that?"

"Fear of rape, robbery or murder." Donnelly remarked that it sounded like London these days. Tonio had to agree. "Some women have learned to defend themselves," he continued. "In fact, some are as strong or powerful as any men. But they make the same mistakes."

"Fascinating. Has humanity at least solved problems like crime, illness and poverty?"

What a question. The straight answer was no. But instead he talked about the kafkaesque criminal justice system and byzantine corrections industry, balancing that with improvements in life expectancy and medical care.

"Have we at least agreed that people have a right to end their own lives?"

"Not yet," Tonio said, taken aback by his interest. "But professionals do tell us how to live."

"You paint a grim picture, almost anti-Bellamy. And who are the rulers of this dystopia? Has royalty made a comeback?"

"Not officially, but we do have dynasties and hand out titles. First at this, best of that. And some people are celebrated just for being well-known." He'd moved from narration to role playing along the way. .

"A corrupt paradise, you might say a commons pillaged by violence and greed."

"Elementary, my dear Donnelly."

"Then it's a matter of choosing sides," the old politician concluded. "Ask yourself: What really threatens humanity, the few who break some arbitrary rules or challenge the government, or those who control the economy and the government, and enact laws causing millions to suffer and die? It's obviously a rhetorical question. But I do wonder, in this troubled future of yours, is progress and reform still possible?"

Tonio had no clever plot twist to cover that.

34
SEEDS

It was time for an inventory. With each day it felt more likely that he would spend the rest of his life here. He would never watch TV or use the Internet, and wouldn't be able to board an airplane or hear a radio broadcast for decades – if he lived that long.

That said, electric streetcars were about to make an appearance and Heinrich Hertz had just proven that radio waves existed! Thank the Lord for that. And Thomas Edison's telephone would be out commercially soon, not that he had anyone to call.

He struggled to remember more about the period in which he found himself stranded, the general state of affairs, and how he might use any knowledge of where the world and society were heading to survive, or just to his advantage. Radical ideas, sensational attitudes, shattering inventions and centralized power were all on the rise as corporations and trusts expanded their tentacles. They would soon become the dominant form of "life" on the planet, eventually claiming the same rights as people. Across the channel Eiffel's tower was rising over the Paris skyline, an icon of the age to come. In America workers and farmers were beginning to challenge a rogue's gallery of emerging capitalist titans and corrupt leaders.

It was too much to consider at the moment. Perhaps he should just take a picture of himself and have it preserved until a future time when someone who knew him could find it. George Eastman had produced a simple mass-market camera. Better yet, wait a year and use a Kodak Brownie, the cheap cardboard box that would make picture-taking possible for everyone. Yet how would he ensure that any picture reached the right hands, and whose hands would they be?

Or he could write a letter and have it delivered to himself, like Michael J. Fox in *Back to the Future*. Ok, but what should he say? Number one: When Danny Webster invites you to step into a closet for a short trip, decline. His mood hovered between panic, rage and surrender to the pure strangeness of his predicament.

Still, he had to acknowledge that without the jump he would never have met Annie or learned what he had in recent days. Being here did feel like destiny, although he was also uncomfortable with the notion. Despite any signs or synchronicities life should be an open proposition, full of options and alternatives, a series of challenges leading to a future always open to change.

Another option was to accompany Donnelly when he returned to the States in a few days. That would put him back in the country of his birth, theoretically a more familiar place, just a century ahead of schedule. Would life be any better for him there? Plus, if Danny was looking for him and trying to bring him back, the farther he went from the entrance the less likely a rescue became.

On Wednesday he had returned to Batty Street, remaining there from midnight to three in the morning to be in the back alley, with no one watching, at the three-hour points Danny had mentioned. Nothing happened. However, he did notice that Tumblety had abandoned his rooms. That brought Tonio back to why he originally came to this time and place – to identify and catch a killer. He might be missing, but Tonio knew enough to do something. The question was how to use what he had uncovered without sounding insane or dangerous.

On Thursday he took a tentative step. The landlady at 22 Batty became suspicious when Tumblety returned after the murders. She might also have seen something. He needed to convince her to talk to the cops. If he was stuck here at least he could pursue the case. Danny's Commandments were starting to feel irrelevant.

Before knocking on her front door he rehearsed an introduction. He was visiting London, he'd say, and looking for a friend who might be renting a room with her. His friend was a tall gentleman with a large mustache. He would be well-dressed and might have introduced himself as a doctor or businessman. Name of Tumblety, or maybe traveling under Townsend.

She obviously recognized the description. "That's no gentleman," she growled. "He says come back in two day. Now four and no one. Who pays?"

Tonio apologized and suggested that his friend might have been delayed. "Did he say where he was going?"

"He tells nothing," she said. "But he leaves dirty clothes."

Here was something to pursue. Perhaps he could take a look and find a clue to Tumblety's whereabouts or destination. When he asked to examine what was left behind, however, the old woman blocked his move; that is, unless Tonio was prepared to cover the debt and cleaning cost.

"What did you have to wash?"

"A shirt," she answered, "not easy. The sleeves, they was covered in blood. This messy doctor, I don't like this fellow."

It was exactly what he needed: physical evidence and an eye-witness who saw Tumblety with the bloody shirt shortly after the crimes. He had to convince her to report it. But that wouldn't be so easy. Her only concern was the money she was owed.

"Perhaps he's a victim of foul play," Tonio suggested. "You might want to let the authorities know."

"They do nothing, just bothers good peoples." He reminded her of the murders and suggested that her information might help with their investigation. She wasn't impressed, seeing nothing to gain.

"Well, do you remember anything more he said while he was here?" He was desperate for any clue. She sensed it, sneered and slammed the door.

Tonio wandered along Commercial Road, disappointed with his plan so far, and turned right on Whitechapel Road. It was only a short distance to Buck's Row and the spot where Polly Nichols died in August. Crowds no longer milled around that murder scene, which made it possible for him to walk the grid and stand in the spot from which he had witnessed the crime via RTV. He still remembered the sight, so revolting he almost ended things right there.

Next he went a mile west via Hanbury Street to visit the backyard where poor Annie Chapman met her end. Spitalfields was even more depressing in real life. He had watched her, drunk and homeless, proposition her own killer and lead him to the spot where she would die.

That was on September 8, less than a month ago. Even then he noticed the incompetence of investigators as it dawned on them that a serial killer was on the rampage. Of course, Rachkovsky was also in London and at work planting suggestions that the killer was more likely an immigrant or a Jew hiding among the East End hordes.

It occurred to him that the Russian wasn't so different from his uncle, the man he had admired as a child and mourned for decades. They were both professionals in the art of creating disinformation for their governments, misplacing blame, creating false stories, recruiting agents to destabilize political opponents. Gianni had done it in Angola and Jamaica to roll back alliances with Russia and Cuba. Rachkovsky was doing the same thing in London to scapegoat Russian radicals, Jews and their allies.

He yearned to share what he knew about Rachkovsky's covert operations and the phony Ripper clues. But he wasn't sure how to explain knowing the identity of a Russian agent whose physical appearance was practically a State Secret. They needed to know about the counter-insurgency operation underway and the potential for infiltration. But how to make them believe it?

By the time he reached Duke Street it was pitch dark. Donnelly was out, leaving him free to explore his host's drawers and closets. Several letters from a lawyer, William Eli Bramhall, informed Donnelly there was little hope of settling a $4,600 debt before the court took away 1,200 acres of the family's land. Two years of negotiating had led nowhere. Other letters suggested that more creditors were closing in.

He also found an unfinished note in which Donnelly revealed his emotional and mental exhaustion, and the difficulty he had facing the tasks ahead – especially endorsing the Republican candidate for President. He felt isolated and wanted to come home.

Why not write a letter of his own? Something to explain the journey he was on. He removed paper and began to compose, explaining that he was an American who had ended up in England as a result of an experiment in teleportation that brought him here from more than a century in the future. For those who might think this was just another Bellamy-esque parable he offered several examples – a brief tour of future events to establish his bona fides. In 1901, he told his future reader, President McKinley will be assassinated and Theodore Roosevelt will become President. In case no one found the letter for a while, he added that the first of two World Wars in the next century will begin in 1914. The other will run for much of the forties. Millions will die in each, and Germany will lose both, but make a comeback each time. The United States, England and their allies will prevail.

Over time the whole epoch will become known as the American

Century, he wrote. Long before that, however, the US will become an empire, and announce itself as the dominant power, the Big Dog on the block, by detonating weapons that can devastate entire cities and make entire regions uninhabitable for generations. He was going to bring up the rise of China but felt like he'd already said too much. He was about to close with a short section about himself and his family when he heard Donnelly on the stairs and hid the letter in a copy of *The Great Cryptogram* on the desk. A few extra pages would be undetectable under the weight of that thousand page obsession.

Back from a temperance gathering, Donnelly had more Ripper-ish news. A woman was attacked on Redman's Road but had survived. She was on her way to the same meeting as he when someone sprang at her, or so she claimed. But then the attacker hesitated and apologized. Meanwhile, a young fellow showed up, and before the first man could flee the second one noticed a long knife. The woman and her protector tried to follow but the man with the knife vanished into an alley.

"What was the description?"

"She said tall, bushy whiskers, and overcoat," Donnelly reported. "But this is odd. She also said her attacker was walking a large white dog."

The next morning Donnelly was packing before Tonio awoke. He had to board the Aurania for a six-day voyage back to New York late the same evening, he said. "It's quite the luxury experience if you aren't prone to mal de mer. A floating palace, at least if you have funds to share a stateroom." The lease on the apartment ran through the weekend, but that was just two days.

"I did receive this invitation," he added by way of consolation, passing him a hand-written note. "I can't attend, wrong night. But it might be your cup of tea, esoteric knowledge and the like, but liberal." The stationery read "Blavatsky Lodge, 17 Landsdowne Road." Donnelly had visited previously and described it as centrally located near Notting Hill Station in a tony area.

"And take your lady. Show her your soft side."

Did he have a lady? Not yet, but that could change and this sounded like a promising move. He knew Annie would become a spiritual leader eventually and had noticed her interest in the potential of humanity beyond the political domain in which she currently operated so effectively.

Donnelly and he agreed to say their goodbyes later and Tonio set off for *The Link* to make his invitation. Annie was well aware of the group and, as Donnelly predicted, sounded impressed that Upton knew about the Theosophists. In reality, he'd never heard the word before. Rather than admit it and lose ground, however, he responded with a modest smile and a pregnant silence.

Sidney Webb also wanted to come along, so the three of them agreed to meet in three hours for the train.

When Tonio returned to Donnelly's place he was outside the building supervising two porters as they loaded his cases. They clasped hands, two Americans sharing a last moment of solidarity before going their separate ways. "About that tale you told me the other night," the older man said before motioning at a cab to pull up. "It gave me nightmares, son, but also a lot to consider. One request."

"Anything," Tonio said.

"I don't disagree about where we're going, there may be terrible days ahead." He sighed. "But still, give the poor people a bit of credit. And a little hope. They will rise up someday."

"It's been an honor." Tonio watched the aging pol lift himself into the seat, close the door and tap it.

"Onward," Donnelly said.

He watched the cab and wagon rumble down the cobbled street, amazed by the series of events that had brought him here. They'd begun when he was a child, with a chance remark. Now he had a friend, and perhaps more. It felt as if he'd finally found a surrogate father he could respect.

Then he realized that his letter, unsigned yet potentially explosive, was tucked inside one of the cases, hidden deep within that strange, ungainly book.

The Blavatsky Lodge was a handsome, solid three-story building surrounded by cultivated gardens not far from the Notting Hill Station. Annie heard about the place from Stead, who wanted her to review a book by its maximum leader, the notorious occultist Helena Blavatsky, who had moved to London about a year before.

"She's very controversial," Annie announced with transparent glee at the start of the trip. "Two years ago she wrote an article saying animals have souls."

"Is that controversial these days?"

"Yes, of course. The Catholic Church has been saying they are soulless beasts for centuries, which has given good Christians just the excuse they need to overwork them to death, hunt them for sport, or skin them for adornment." He thought about their status in the so-called "modern world," the torture and grotesque treatment of countless millions; things certainly hadn't improved. In fact, few people even needed an excuse any longer. "And the way she did it, by citing St. Paul, John Chrysostom and sacred Pauline texts. The Apostles believed in an afterlife for animals and even put them on a par with us. Absolutely brilliant stroke."

But there were more critical views of Madame Blavatsky in circulation. An influential report accused her of "fraudulent phenomena," and many people in proper London society considered her no better than a charlatan. Yet she had a group of dedicated followers that included a number of wealthy acolytes. They had recently launched a journal, defiantly naming it *Lucifer*, and established the Blavatsky Lodge as the Theosophical movement's center in London. Rumor had it, according to Annie, that the relationship between Blavatsky and her old partner Olcott ended badly in India, and she was in England to establish an independent base of power.

"She was with Mabel Collins the writer for a bit," she reported, "and now here with the Keightleys. They say her book is absolutely huge and impressive. Yeats says when you meet her it's like talking with some Irish peasant woman, sad and sly and holy. Frankly, Upton, I've been curious for quite a while, so this couldn't have come at a better moment. Stead is enthusiastic, of course. But he's obsessed with automatic writing and that sort of thing, so I have to give his opinion less weight."

They arrived near sunset and entered a hive-like center still buzzing after a long day. Groups held intense discussions in alcoves and corners as volunteers went about their housekeeping tasks. After greeting them Claude Wright, an in-residence Irish theosophist, directed Annie and Tonio to the discussion in progress upstairs.

It was a truly international but generally informal affair. Stout and benignly imperious, Blavatsky simply entertained questions and directed a rambling dialogue that had been underway for an hour and seemed likely to continue for several more. It was a Socratic marathon, a meandering search for occult knowledge and random bits of obscure information.

Annie said nothing that first time, yet took in everything as usual. "Fear and imagination," Blavatsky pointed out at one point in her deep, musical accent, capturing a devotee with a piercing gaze. "Most of our diseases and ailings are caused by these two forces. The goal is to destroy the one – the fear, and give constructive direction to the other. Nature and will can do the rest."

Someone asked, "Does that mean we can manage without most of the medical profession?"

"That would be simplistic," she replied, "and would demonstrate an arrogance of will that should be avoided at all cost. Many diseases clearly require a surgeon or a physician if they are not to become fatal. Theosophists are not at war with science. But most of its efforts are directed at effects rather than causes.

"The flower of civilization is on the verge of unfolding," the Russian sage predicted. "And yet in the future, new illnesses and disorders will also arise, and many will stem from causes deep in the minds of men and women. And these disorders will be cured only by living a more spiritual life."

"Is this future determined, and can it be changed?"

"No, and yes," replied Blavatsky. "What writes history is the power of ideas. And every moment offers the potential to write something new."

She invited him back to her sitting room afterward and lit a few candles. For Annie a meeting like the one they'd just attended often produced a delayed reaction, she explained kneeling across from him on a modest quilted cushion. At such times, she said, and immediately after, there was a need to quietly process, followed later by an explosion of ideas and connections.

"That's when it's useful to have a companion," she added, "especially someone who has shared the experience."

Tonio liked where the evening was going. Donnelly's suggestion turned out to be an inspiration, and the mood felt like his romantic audition, as if she was vetting him before permitting serious advances.

"What do you believe in?" The question took him by surprise. If he was being honest, the answer was not that much. Would that be a problem? She was an atheist, or so she said, yet she seemed like someone always searching for something to believe in. Still, it was a good question.

"I believe things happen for a reason," he replied. "I just don't know what it is. But I find it hard to believe that existence, all of this, is just some random accident. I thought you were an atheist."

"Yes, but not only. And I was raised a devout Christian. And I continue to believe there is much we can learn about our existence; eternal is a large word, but certainly there must be some universal knowledge in a Gnostic sense. I think the Gnostics weren't heretics at all, even though the Church fathers insisted on it as an excuse to destroy every Gnostic text they could find. Did you know there was a time you could be put to death for admitting to it? For hundreds of years the only thing allowed was distorted versions of Gnosticism written by Christians. Over the centuries it became a symbol for religious plague, almost as if knowledge itself was evil.

"But what were the Gnostics? Maybe just those not content to worship God and read about the divine experience," she speculated with mounting excitement. "Perhaps they wanted to have the experience, a direct, personal experience of the divine." Blavatsky's radical contention, she said, was that Gnostic teaching, far from being heretical, was the dynamic original basis of Christianity, passed down from the disciples, but ultimately abandoned and condemned as too dangerous.

Tonio reached for a relevant follow up that would move things forward. The quest for knowledge needs to be balanced with an understanding that humans are still animals, he suggested. We aren't better than other animals and have the same needs and instincts. He linked that with the dangers of hubris and exaggerating our importance in the universe.

"Very good. What kind of instincts?" she asked, picking up a not-so subtle cue.

"Oh, for instance, an idea can touch you, but not in the same way a person can. So, the instinct to touch and be touched. After all, body language is the native tongue of the subconscious."

"Ah," she nodded, absorbing the odd concept, "the sub-conscious. I think I understand."

"Actually, I was thinking back massage."

She pursued her lips, mulling it over. "No, I think we can come up with something more intimate." Then she was up from the cushion and off to a shelf, returning quickly with a parchment chart. Pointing down she said, "Remove those."

A foot massage sounded fine. Tonio pulled off his boots and stretched out on two large pillows she dropped on the floor. But massage wasn't exactly what she had in mind. It was closer to therapy. "There are zones on both sides of the body, and lines of energy called meridians connecting the parts of the body," she explained, taking hold of a foot. "That chart correlates the feet with various organs and systems. If you know the problem area you want to address you can massage that zone for stimulating effect.

"So, my dear, do you have a problem we can address?"

"I have stress, a lot of it," he admitted. "What part of the foot do you –" He screamed before finishing the sentence.

"That's the solar-plexus," she said applying a bit less force to the same spot. "And this," she said pressing on his big toe hard enough to make her point, "is the Pituitary."

For the next half hour she explored the anatomy of his feet and their relationship to the rest of his body, his general emotional state and intermittent back pain. Along the way she touted the effectiveness of the technique as an anesthetic, describing it as competitive with cocaine in the right hands. Eventually, but not too soon, it was his turn. She had fierce headaches, she told him, as well as several allergies and stiff bones. It took him an hour to cover all the points.

By the time he was done they were sitting close, legs entwined as they conducted experiments with various pressure points. It was the moment he had waited for, one he'd imagined for days, if not months, and she seemed as comfortable and ready as he was. As he moved in for a kiss, however, she shifted and placed an arm over his shoulder as she pulled him even closer and whispered in an ear. "I want to show you something. Just a moment, I promise."

He frowned, not at all eager for another diversion. "Stay," she ordered, "Animal, stay." Then she laughed and sprinted to a cabinet, coming back quickly with a book. Impossible, he thought. She wanted to read now!

"It's an ancient Hindu text," she whispered with impish solemnity, "only translated into English in the last few years. There's a wonderful, funny commentary, worth investigating in depth. But I just want to talk over a few illustrations beforehand."

For a second Tonio thought he'd misread all the signals. But then she pleaded, "Humor me," and lightly caressed his feet.

35
The Edge

To say it was the most intense weekend of his life was no exaggeration. He knew the words Kama Sutra and had seen a few antique illustrations of couples wrapped in positions that looked impossible. Most guys had at least heard of it. But before that night he'd never bothered to open a copy of the obscure old book.

Annie was already an expert in its philosophy, knew some of the recommended techniques, in theory at least, and was using the volume as a personal to-do list. Kama, she said, means sensual pleasure, and Sutra refers to a set of guidelines for love, life and graceful, virtuous living. As she explained she began experimenting with various kisses and caresses, sucking, biting and scratching, generally arousing him in ways he'd never felt.

There were hundreds of verses, she explained, organized in parts and chapters covering things like how to make the best advances, sexual positions, choosing a wife and duties on the job, as well as sections on courtesan protocols and "occult practices." Basically, it sounded like a traveler's guide, India's *Let's Go Coitus*. For the moment Annie was concentrating on the chapters covering the stimulation of sexual desire, a comprehensive 64-point list covering everything from styles of moaning to maximizing a climax.

Gently urging him on, yet stressing there was no hurry, she took him on a sexual world tour that lasted until afternoon of the following day. It wasn't a tantric dance of deferred completion. It was a relaxed extended, fully satisfying, multi-faceted excursion in the realm of the senses. Before he realized it most of Saturday was gone and he'd forgotten all about the funeral of Long Liz Stride. He had planned to attend, with the intention of checking out the audience to see if Frank was the kind of guy who also enjoyed the necrophilia thrill and sadism of seeing his dead victim and her mourners.

At the moment that was the last thing on his mind.

Naked and ripe with vibrant energy Annie jumped up and vanished, only to reappear minutes later with a full plate of fruits, bread and cheese, along with some wine. They feasted and talked, and then got back to work "studying" the ancient text for plausibility. There were still many poses left to imitate.

As the sun set she finally confessed exhaustion and proposed a pause. The book also warned of dangers and pitfalls in the quest for sensual pleasure, she reminded him with a suggestive bite. "Even Shiva and Parvati needed a break."

He asked about the chapter on courtesans. "Weren't they just prostitutes in perfume and fancy clothes? Doesn't that offend you?"

"Actually no," she replied. "It's not the act of providing pleasure in exchange for money that matters . It's the treatment of women, the stigma involved, and obviously the economic conditions that make it a desperate, dangerous profession rather than the highly admired one described in the Sutra.

"Look here," she said, flipping to a page, "the text gives advice on how to wisely choose a courtesan, how to find a steady partner and stay friends with a former lover. Even money questions are handled in a direct, practical way. In context I see this as a life-affirming acknowledgement of the realities of human nature. The marriage bed has never, and I believe, can never be the only arena in which we seek sensual experience and spiritual union."

How could he disagree?

Tonio slept comfortably for the first time since landing in London. An entire week had passed since he and Danny discussed the Commandments and he made the choice to enter the Jump Room.

On Sunday morning he woke up before Annie did, threw on a robe, and sat near the window to assess things. He was safe with a woman he desired and admired. More than ever it felt like this might be his fate, the reason he was propelled down the road that took him from the Jersey shore to London. Yet this relationship – which felt like love – was founded on lies.

He was not Upton Sinclair, an American writer stranded in London while researching a book about a time-traveling detective. He was Antonio Wolfe, an American gangster's son who was stranded in London because he was teleported here from 125 years in the future. How could he begin to share who he really was?

In the end she spared him the decision. A few hours later, after an especially energetic coupling that left them spent but glowing, she confided her decision not to remain a political organizer and consider becoming a Theosophist. Christianity, Socialism, Atheism – all of them seemed inadequate, she said, and missed the ultimate answers. He just had to ask, what answers?

"Weren't you dazzled," Annie replied. "Listening to Helena talk, my riddles and puzzles vanished. It was like a bright star, a flash of illumination, the lantern in the fog, the light at the end of the tunnel."

"Really?" he said. "Is that overstating just a bit?" He was thinking of all the times his mother had said similar things about her latest New Age epiphany.

"I don't think so," she insisted. 'Why do you say that?"

"Well, you do get a bit dramatic, you could say over-zealous in your enthusiasms."

"What do you know about it? We've barely just met." She was teasing, but also miffed.

"I know you," he said. "I've been watching you since, since you walked into *The Link* that day."

"Which qualifies you to make judgments?"

"Not judgments, observations." He tried to measure each word, not wanting to betray the knowledge he had amassed over months.

She crossed her legs and folded her arms. "I'd like to hear this. Please, some observations."

Why was she putting him on the spot? Suddenly he was worried. "All right, I see you as a brilliant woman, obviously, who has lost much to get where you are. Your children, for example."

She took in a breath. "You know about them?"

"Yes, from Shaw. And I know that right now you are a key political actor in this city, and across the country. You're absolutely right about the importance of the Matchgirls' strike, how it changed things and set things in motion. Remember when you and the girls met with Bradlaugh in the Commons? Someone asked if revolution was avoidable and you said something like, 'Without justice, no.' I probably have it wrong. What did you say? Oh, I remember, "a movement of love and self-sacrifice.' What was the other part?"

"Inspiring us to give rather than take," she finished, staring at him in sad disbelief. "I've said it before. How do you know that?"

"It doesn't matter. I'm saying you are important, and you don't need to rely on people like Blavatsky to define your beliefs. You just need to trust yourself."

"But how do you know?" She was getting angry. "That was a private meeting. Only the girls, Charles and the other two, were there. How do you know what I said?"

He remembered now. It was in the View Room, the session that had caused the argument with Angel. "Not as private as you think," he tried, creating a rationale and changing the subject. "There were some observers. In fact, one extremely dangerous person I've been meaning to tell you about."

Annie was skeptical but willing to consider it.

"There is a man, a Russian agent, in London," he explained. "He was spying on your meeting in the Commons, and he also has been spreading rumors about immigrants and Jews as responsible for the murders. He has agents throughout the city. They've even planted false evidence."

She cocked her head. "That may be. But even if true, it raises another group of questions, such as who are *you* actually, and how do you know any of this? William Morris did say you were an agent provocateur. Maybe he was right."

Tonio laughed at the suggestion. "I'm an agent? That's rich. I came here to…" He wanted to say, to catch London's serial murderer and meet her. "To research my book. But along the way I've come into quite a lot of off-the-record information. I've talked to people in the neighborhoods, and even looked at some of the police reports."

"That doesn't give you permission to lecture me about my life and who I am," she shot back. "What do you know about me really, and what do I know about you? Don't be presumptuous. I know what I'm doing."

"I'm sure you think so," he said, "but there are people who mean to do you harm, and you have so much to do in life. If you only knew…"

"I suppose you know that as well."

So, here was the opening. This wasn't the way he hoped it would go, but if they had a future it needed to happen. "Yes. It wouldn't be safe to say much, at least that's what I'm told. But you will someday be an important spiritual leader and help to liberate a nation."

"Now I know you're making fun of me!" She was furious. "You think I'm that immature and impressionable?"

"No, it's true!"

"Please, stop, don't make it worse. This is insulting. Can you please tell me one thing that isn't from a novel or what you think I'd like to hear."

"This is real," he protested. "It's my life, and yours. Believe me."

"You know the future? Then you're clairvoyant."

He tried to explain. "No, I don't know my own future. But I do know certain things about yours, not everything, just what I've been able to learn…from reading."

"About my future?"

"Yes."

"You do think I'm a very stupid woman, don't you? You think you can just feed me another fantasy about some book that reveals the future and I'll roll over like a pet and say, 'Take me, stallion, possessor of the Key to the Future. Possess me.' Wait, are you a Mormon?"

"Of course not."

"I just thought, wasn't it that Joseph Smith who found mystical secrets on some plates buried in his yard?" She shrugged and stood up. "I doesn't matter, you're a liar, that's the point, and a cad. Get out!"

"No, I'm not," Tonio pleaded, trying to draw her closer. She pulled away instead, raising a hand as if to strike him. He grabbed it, she resisted and they tumbled together onto the bed. He grabbed her other arm and pinned her flat.

"Listen," he demanded.

"No. Get off me and leave."

Tonio considered refusing. But no, he thought, he could use this moment to tell her his secret. Yes, tell her everything. But that would only make things worse. She would never, could never believe the truth now. After a few seconds more, a long moment in which he drank in her essence as she struggled under his grip, he let go and silently began to dress.

She immediately leapt away and retreated to the doorway, waiting there stoically, arms locked over her breasts, eyes urging him to move faster with a silent glare. When he was finally ready she stepped aside, avoiding his glance as he passed.

He wandered for what felt like hours, re-running the argument to discover if, how and where he went wrong. Was it just a lover's quarrel, or had he blown it with the greatest woman he'd ever met? Had it ended before having a chance to begin?

In Aldgate on Mitre Street he checked his pocket watch. It was one of the few things remaining from that former life. Ten o'clock, it informed him, and also that he was under a mile from the Jump entrance. Closer than that, just a block or two away, the Ripper had grabbed Katy Kelly, a poor woman just sobering up and on her way home. How long ago was that? Eight days by his estimate.

And he had come here on February 26, which made it March 6 back in the good old 21st century. What was going on there now? Anything was possible since his disappearance. He knew he should be worried. But what could he do about it? If his actions made a difference anywhere in the world, it was here.

And this is the block where Frank Tumblety came upon Katy walking alone, the place he failed to reach in time to save her. Stopping at the entrance to Mitre Square he walked down the entry corridor. Inside it looked the same, dark except for the lonely high lantern casting its yellow cone of light. He walked the perimeter as he had that night and stood at the other end, looking through tinted fog to where he began.

A figure stood at the entrance, a man in a cape. He didn't enter but remained there for a full minute, then turned and walked on. Tonio covered the distance back in seconds and peeked around the corner. The gentleman was barely visible and heading into the East End.

On instinct he decided to follow at a distance. The man walked briskly, almost in military stride, and turned onto Commercial, a wide thoroughfare, into a neighborhood Tonio knew well. Before reaching Batty Street, he stopped and entered a pub.

Tonio hesitated. He wasn't completely certain why he had followed this far. But if there was one thing recent days had taught him, it was this: encounters and events that may look random or coincidental at first…very often aren't. The hard part was knowing the difference, and this time he believed he did.

In any case, he had long ago bought his ticket for this ride and it would be an act of cowardice not to take it to the end. He pulled on the creaking door and walked in.

36
Go Time

To one side of the hallway was a narrow barroom, to the other a large, obviously more comfortable parlor with a two-sided fireplace at the center. He peeked through the glass in both directions to find his quarry. Seeing no one familiar he surmised that, if their paths had indeed crossed, Frank Tumblety wouldn't be drinking with the proletariat.

The sign above the parlor door read "Tap Room." Inside he was struck by the plush décor and atmosphere, quite tranquil, spacious and elegant in comparison with the bustle of the bar or the rough streets beyond. Groups of men in dark suits relaxed in sturdy chairs around wooden tables served by buxom barmaids. Others convened around the fire. Farther back he noticed smaller rooms down a hallway and booths tucked in various corners. The artwork was similar to the tapestry in Shelley's den, but with more risqué depictions of round, half-naked women and their leering admirers.

He found his killer in a booth at the back, nursing a glass of sherry as he tossed dice and recorded results in a hand-sized notebook. This was his first chance for a live, unobstructed look at the villain, and to watch him at something other than committing vicious crimes. He was slightly less than six feet tall and looked to be in good shape, with smooth pink skin and the bearing of a pompous middle-aged college professor. His only distinguishing features were his eyes, more black than brown, and that over-the-top mustache, meticulously brushed and extending inches in both directions.

Tonio took an opening near the fire and contemplated a next move. The man he had been stalking for months and imagining for years, the inspiration for countless horror stories and the cause of terror for more than a century, was directly in front of him. Despite the press drumbeat and the general mood of paranoia the villain felt perfectly comfortable out for a stroll and a drink in the same neighborhood where he had butchered Long Liz just a week ago.

After several minutes Tumblety caught the arm of a barmaid, pointed across the room and handed her a note to deliver. He watched her go, waited, and then bowed to acknowledge a greeting from the young man who received it. The killer waved him over. A moment later a fellow of about twenty was standing at the table, laughing as Tumblety tried to win him over with bawdy jokes.

He was cruising, but not for a victim. Tonight he was out for a fling. Angel had uncovered his sexual preference. In a month it would lead to his arrest. But tonight's prospect apparently had other commitments. After a few minutes he offered Tumblety a consolation smile and a long, firm handshake before returning to his friends.

It was time to focus and choose. Either Tonio could wait and continue tracking him, or move in now and make direct contact. Weeks ago he and Harry discussed such a scenario, except that it was in reference to his father. They were planning the RTV demo and how to use it as an interrogation tool. "You want to think several steps ahead," Harry said. "Then, when you know enough and have the advantage and enough facts, you beat the bushes to startle the snake."

That meant administering the Psychopath Test.

Theoretically, what they planned to show Shelley with remote viewing clips would function like a Rorschach and provoke involuntary responses they could capture -- responses that would reveal his real nature. The 20-item checklist was the invention of Bob Hare, a prison psychologist who conducted remarkable experiments and codified his findings.

His father clearly exhibited several of the characteristics: He was a manipulative conman with an exaggerated sense of himself, prone to lying and self-serving distortions. His behavior problems had begun early and led to teenage delinquency, but that was apparently a plus in his own father's world. Shelley was also promiscuous, impulsive, addicted to novelty and rarely controlled his impulses. Not to mention, he'd ordered people killed.

That was already half the key characteristics and their research wasn't finished.

Using the same checklist with Tumblety in the course of a "conversation" might yield what he wanted, a profile of the killer and motives for his crimes. Where to begin? He already knew this was a versatile criminal, flexible, feral and skilled. That in itself was relatively rare. But Tonio had also witnessed a gruesome lack of control on full display, and he knew, from Angel's research, that his professional career was built on a false and parasitic foundation. Basically, he preyed on the vanity and weaknesses of his patients and clients. At first he was a backroom abortionist; now he was a medical quack with a "cure" that might do as much harm as good.

It was a good start. But to find out the rest he needed to meet the monster. It was time to step up, say hello, and look the devil in his face.

"Did I hear a friendly accent," Tonio inquired as he approached the table.

Tumblety cast the dice and raised an eyebrow.

"Sinclair," he said, extending a hand, "from Jersey. Are you, I mean, an American? I couldn't help but catch a bit of your conversation." He was playing it straight with just a touch of sexual ambiguity. He was too old for Tumblety's taste but hoped to exploit the angle to establish rapport.

"Tumblety," he replied without reaching out. "Professor Francis Tumblety of New York. Since we are technically neighbors I don't see how I can refuse. I will say, good conversation is hard to find in these parts. What are you drinking?"

Tonio had no more than a shilling and six pence, enough for drinks but nothing to spare. "Madeira for me," he said and sat.

Tumblety waved a girl over.

"So, what brings you to London?"

That was all the excuse his new drinking buddy needed for a twenty minute recitation of his accomplishments. Tumblety described himself as a well-known, even celebrated surgeon and a former soldier, which supposedly explained the medals on his richly-embroidered jacket.

"Actually, I'm not originally American. In younger years I stood for Colonial Parliament in Canada against McGee. In Ottawa they all wanted me to enter the arena, but I was intent on healing. That was prior to the Great War, terrible destruction that. I was on McClellan's staff in that fight, by the way. Union all the way!

"You're wondering why I still wear them, the medals, aren't you? Sense of pride in my service, I suppose. But I also think people here need to know what we're made of. You might say I'm a model of American esprit de corps and a good-will ambassador."

Tonio nodded supportively but Tumblety needed no encouragement. Finally getting to the original question, his next topic was the reason he was in town -- and his remarkable international success as a distributor of medical cures. And that in turn reminded him of a twenty-year-old clipping he conveniently kept folded in his notebook. It was from *The St. John Albion*, a Canadian paper, a poem about himself and titled with his name.

He called it a testimonial. Tonio got the sense he'd written it himself.

Taking the clipping back he began reciting, "Dr. Tumblety rode a white steed." In simple verses the poem explained how he had arrived in the city in the nick of time, armed with his herbal pills and accompanied by a beautiful grey hound. The next lines read:

> *Tumblety had a killing air*
> *Though curing was his professional trade*
> *Rosy of cheek and glossy of hair*
> *Dangerous man to widow or maid*

The monster laughed and added, "I love that, but it was some time ago. The hair isn't so glossy anymore."

"What about the maids and widows?" Tonio had managed to insert a question.

"More trouble than they're worth," he replied. "What I've found over the years is, frankly, that in terms of your average female, the more gifts and affections you bestow the less value they are given. In the end you get to the point where they debase themselves just to spite you.

"Sad creatures, too many of them," he contended. "I can tell you, I've seen them at their worst. You see them on the streets here, those poor polluted vessels, lost souls really, very unfortunate." Despite this persuasive display of empathy Tonio didn't believe a word of it. In fact, the glibness of this counterfeit concern was another item to check off.

He had also re-invented his biography. Angel had uncovered no Canadian political career and Tonio remembered that he never served in the military. No, he'd begged off using a bogus illness. Tonio knew the truth as well about his so-called medical "fame," all the accidental deaths and the manslaughter charges. The only thing true was the line about his "killing air." He did have some rough charm, which of course came in handy when preparing to kill.

It didn't take long to see that Frank Tumblety was a pathological liar and a manipulative con-artist, superficially attractive and fairly persuasive but irresponsible and quite callous underneath it all. Tonio also saw no self-awareness or genuine interest in others. Instead, he assumed that anyone would or should be eager to know what he thought, whatever that happened to be, and saw himself as the object of both widespread admiration and intense jealousy.

Beneath the self-aggrandizing façade, however, he also glimpsed a defensive outsider who took anything less than deference as a snub or attack. He bragged about meeting Napoleon, yet complained about every minor criticism by his business rivals. As he told it, his life was a tragic tale of grand triumphs undermined by unfair, small-minded persecution and humiliation.

"It's always been like that," he confided after several more drinks. "I always felt my path was special, but different. And they've always tried to pull me down."

"Where did you grow up?"

"Rochester mainly," he said. "I was out of there quick. But it's the same wherever you go. There's no sanctuary for the man of vision."

"Have you ever been married?"

"I must confess," he sighed with embarrassment. "Yes. I was young, which helps to explain it, and she was older and seemed more rational than most." He thought back. "I did care for her, I must say. But I haven't thought about her in years.

"Anyway, here is my sad story: this young couple gets married and goes on their honeymoon, don't you know? And he loves her, yes he does, and she pledges the same forever. But does that stop her from flirting with every handsome fellow who passes by? Not a bit. In fact, she's good at it."

He finished the drink and called for another.

"Did it end badly?" Meanwhile, Tonio thought: The first victim?

"He talked with her, softly and seriously," Tumblety slurred. "He explained how this made him look to anyone who had witnessed her infidelities. And what's she do? Just gave him a kiss and mussed up his hair, and said, 'Poor jealous little fool. There's nothing to fear.'

"And he believed her, he believed her!" Tumblety shook his head, barely able to accept that his mind could have such a blind spot. "Then one day he's out on his rounds, in a shabbier part of town, and there she is, getting out of a cab – with another man. And they enter a house, a depraved place known well around the city. And it turns out that isn't the only house she frequents."

He stared blankly at Tonio, inebriated but resolute. "You know what I'm saying, man? She was a whore!" Remembering instantly revived the old anger. Tonio could see it clearly, a murderous rage.

He waited a moment and delicately asked, "What did you do?"

Tumblety smiled. "I gave up – on women. Just kept a small souvenir. Pleasant diversions on occasion, I must admit, but not creatures you can trust. I prefer a good strong dog. They're loyal and simpler to maintain."

The profile was shaping up. Tonio still didn't know exactly how and when Tumblety went from garden-variety misogynist and sociopath to stark-raving mad, knife-wielding murderer. But he had most of the contributing factors. Along the way he continued to verify items from Bob Hare's list. Like his father, this Frank the Ripper presented a distorted and inflated view of himself, had trouble maintaining relationships, and took absolutely no responsibility for his horrendous actions.

Were his problems apparent from the start? Hard to say, but likely. He also hadn't confirmed whether Tumblety was the promiscuous type, but what he'd observed earlier clearly pointed that way. In fact, the only item he couldn't check was "revocation of conditional release," and that meant only he hadn't been caught. Then again, he had skipped out on at least one manslaughter rap.

He went back over it - superficial charm, grandiosity, lying, manipulation, the absence of affect and any true empathy, the impulsivity and irresponsibility, lack of remorse and need for constant stimulation. He was a depraved criminal, a parasite and a pervert, and his crimes attested to his utter lack of remorse. In short, the complete package.

"So, what are those notes? Do you have a system?"

Tumblety turned the dice in his hand and chuckled. "It's notation, based on the number of dice, the number of faces, and the rolls. For example, 2d6 is two six-sided dice. So 2d6x10+3 would be rolling two dice, adding the results, multiplying by ten and then adding three."

"What for?"

"You are a curious fellow," he laughed, at last taking note of the one-way conversation underway now for an hour. "To make major decisions, if you must know. I use them as a guide. One thing you can depend on is arithmetic. It's flawless, always gives the perfect, most elegant solution. But you, what brings you to the slums?"

Without thinking, Tonio launched into the cover he had used for a week, field research for a detective story. However, some of the details were very close to real life and he was describing them to the man being hunted. He should have stopped or changed the subject, except that his drinking buddy perked up and got nervous.

"The detective has been tracking this predator for years, from city to city," he explained, "a trail of bloody, disemboweled corpses stretching from Boston to Pittsburgh, then the Capital and St. Louis. He loses the killer's trail at times, but he knows the modus operandi."

Tumblety asked what any of that had to do with London.

"What drew me here were the murders, of course," Tonio admitted. "People love to talk about them, the Ripper and all that. You'd be amazed the stories you hear." He watched for a change in demeanor, any telltale sign of guilt or recognition.

"One occurred in late August I think. I read about it before I arrived.

The woman had certain organs removed, did you hear about that?" The Ripper shrugged it off. "Yes, very sexual I hear. Some people said it was the work of a surgeon. But from what I've read it really was too much of a lunatic hack job for that."

The man responsible bristled but remained silent, his only tell the occasional clearing of his throat.

"The second was pretty much the same," Tonio added casually.

"In what sense?" Now he sounded offended.

"The clumsiness of the surgery." This wasn't completely true, but Tumblety was definitely upset. Yet he still didn't budge. "I could go on, but you get the point. This is no surgeon, just a rat-catcher or some ghetto scum. The authorities are gradually coming around to that view."

"You think so," grumbled the Ripper. "Not much of a villain for you."

"Reality is often disappointing. But the procedural side is engaging, and I do have an idea for a more thrilling monster. Tell me what you think." He didn't wait for permission before beginning to profile his villain. "He is a doctor, but not accepted in the fraternity, an outsider and a man of means, which makes it possible for him to move freely. You know, I need someone more worthy of my hero's attention.

"This madman doesn't kill out of passion or lust, he doesn't violate the women. In fact, he has no interest in women except as subjects for his displays and experiments. So he stalks them, sometimes several at a time, and kills whenever the opportunity presents itself. His objective is to conduct an operation, which involves removing certain vital organs and parts of the body."

"Why do that?"

"Ah, here's the twist. He does it to display them in a private museum of horrors – in the lair my hero will ultimately discover and destroy." He waited for effect, then added, "Engaging, don't you think?"

His tall, mustachioed companion cleared his throat one more time.

"Yes, inventive. You got all that from police reports?"

"And rumors. You'd be amazed what people say. I even heard that they had a bloody shirt he'd left behind, but I haven't confirmed that yet."

"Fascinating. Well, this has been fun," he said, suddenly tired and retiring for the night. "We should meet again. How long are you here?"

"I don't know, until my research is finished."

"Right." He stood stiffly and retrieved his cape. "Mr. Sinclair, you are a singular tale-spinner."

And you, my friend, are a psychotic killer, Tonio thought, so I hope at the least I've spoiled your evening. He wanted the man to worry, to be the one frightened for once, and to know that although he might not be caught tomorrow – or next month – his secret would be exposed.

Once Tumblety was gone, however, he had some doubts. As satisfying as that felt, it was also a risky move. His quarry also might be paranoid enough to consider his little "fiction" a threat. It did, after all, incorporate details that few people knew, at this point possibly only two. The sarcastic digs were also gratuitous. The man might want to tear him open just for that. Still, he considered the snake startled.

As long as he stayed inside he was safe. But that certainly wasn't a long-term answer. He had also baited a hook and had to finish what he started. He sensed that Tumblety was waiting somewhere nearby, but knew the area well enough by now. Closing his eyes he summoned an image of the parlor and held it until the details came into focus. Then he gradually expanded his view and rose, moving to the bar across the hall, then out the front door and into the street beyond.

Peering down at Berner Street he shifted quickly around the corner for a look at Batty. There he saw a few people but, as usual, couldn't pick up their words. No one looked familiar and his nemesis didn't seem to be around.

Down the alley behind the house where Tumblety had lodged he focused more closely on the back yard. It looked empty and ready for his use. Then he opened his eyes and checked Danny's watch. The hands on the antique octagon read 11:45, good timing to give the Jump Room another chance.

The sound of boots echoed off the building walls as he walked along Commercial Road near midnight. It was cold but less foggy than usual. In minutes he reached the familiar intersection. From here it was just down one long block, then a duck into the alley to reach the backyard and wait.

He walked calmly to 22 Batty and checked the downstairs window where he had seen Tumblety last Sunday morning. The place was dark, and upstairs the old German seemed either asleep or out. Checking one more time he walked cautiously down the alleyway.

Returning to this spot had become a ritual, his moment of prayer to a "god" who might no longer be there, the absent creator of his current circumstances. Are you up there Daniel Webster, he'd ask silently, safe in our temperature-controlled paradise, watching what happens when an alien – someone who doesn't belong – is dropped, without resources except the knowledge of his origin, into this world? Are you trying to find me? Can you bring me home? He didn't doubt his god's existence, just his ability to intervene, and he was angry at him; but also at himself, for stepping into the Jump Room without thought, for the mistakes he had made since then, and most of all for blowing it with Annie.

He didn't need to close his eyes and concentrate to know someone was coming. There were faint sounds in advance, things shifting above, taps and scuffs and gusts of air. It made sense. He had decided hours ago that, if they were going to meet again, it might as well be here. Not only was it appropriate, there were at least six ways out if he found himself in trouble; three exits to alleys, two porches and the cellar door.

Days ago, he'd taken the precaution of obtaining a knife, just your basic eight-inch, doubled-edged Victorian dagger with a cross guard, brass handle and leather sheath. It would stand up to whatever Frank was packing. He pulled it out and traced a circle around himself in the dirt, repeating it several times, eight feet in diameter, a clear patch away from the buildings with access to the alleys, his personal space. If he couldn't go home he would stand his ground.

The pocket watch told him it was 11:55 and he was in the right place.

Tumblety appeared on a third floor porch connected by ladder to the rooftop. He'd been watching from above as Tonio traced the circle. Now he strode down the steps, keeping his target in sight until reaching the first floor, where he leapt over the railing and landed a few feet beyond the circle's edge.

"What were you doing there, spy?" Tumblety sounded amused. "Are you part of an occult society? It won't help, you know. I'm not impressed with peasant superstitions." He brandished his own knife, a Liston blade, the kind used for amputations. It was about the same length, eight-inches, made of high-quality metal, and named for the Scottish surgeon who designed it to cut off limbs in seconds. Amputation time could make all the difference before the advent of decent anesthetics.

"Just marking my territory," Tonio said. "Glad you made it. We do have some unfinished business."

"Do we?" He took a tentative step toward the boundary. Tonio moved into a relaxed fighting stance. "Dueling is illegal, my young friend."

"Then you stay there and let's have a conversation."

"How about a game?"

"You like games," Tonio said. "What's with the dice?"

"There's a game, the question game. You ask a question and then I ask you one. As long as we believe the answers are true, we continue asking. When we spot a lie," he said and lunged, "we fight."

Tonio caught the move, deflected it and jabbed back. "Sounds fair. So, what about the dice?"

"'All things are numbers,' that's Pythagoras. They help me make choices, notations and numbers relating to people, roles and places. My turn. What are you doing here? You're no scribbler from the States. I'm not even sure where you're from. Are you following me?"

"That's two questions. Let me just say yes, I am following you. And I have been following you for some time. You are a person of interest."

"As I told you, the hounds are always after me. Clearly you are in someone's pay. Let me tell you, I am a military veteran and these vultures you serve – "

"Could you put that in the form of a question?"

"Bastard," he snarled with a stab. "Who are you?"

"I'm an American. And I run a company that specializes in locating people like you. Special people like you, sick fucks. It's the Sick Fuck Detective Agency. As a result I know that you've never served in the military and those medals under your coat, you probably robbed them from a homeless vet. And your medical practice, that hasn't worked out very well because your patients keep dying on you."

Tumblety circled as Tonio described episodes from his life. It was a one-man celebrity roast in which the host actually did despise the celebrity.

"But you had a big idea, the Pimple Cure. What's in it, bull testicles, goat glands, calf's liver, what?"

"Lies! It's a reasonable sulfur-based cure, completely standard, with a bit of semen added. I resent your implications."

"You're a respectable businessman, I know. So you've said, except you are wanted in several states on malpractice charges. You're a butcher, not a doctor, the infamous Prince of Quacks."

"Lies spread by my enemies. Are you a Pinkerton?"

"No, I'm Croatian and Greek – and American. Upton Sinclair, private eye and public defender."

"And who pays you to harass me, Mr. Sinclair?"

"I'm freelance," he said. "You know, most of my ancestors were probably criminals and assassins, bad men, certainly no strangers to evil. But even we have standards, and you are way over the line."

"Not yet ," Tumblety snarled, slashing at his midsection, "but I will be – soon – when I know your real purpose and I cut you in half."

"I'm here because we can't have you carving up women and terrifying the whole city." Tumblety reacted, lunging and missing, opening himself up to a knee that reeled him back with a bloody nose.

"Who are you? I did nothing…"

"Oh, you did, and you were seen. And you're going down for it. The whole world is going to see exactly what kind of sick fuck you are. It's my new job. And I…"

Tumblety struck by surprise this time, slashing Tonio's knife-wielding arm as he drove into the center of the circle, tripping over to the other side. Tonio spun, wounded and bleeding, and kicked him away as the knife slipped from his hand. As he bent to pick it up the space expanded, and a whirlpool formed beneath his feet, and Tumblety, the yard, the alley and the entire East End faded as he descended into a whirlpool of light.

37

AFTERMATH

The Globe, London, October 10, 1888
DETECTIVES ON A NEW SCENT

A well-informed correspondent states that he has gleaned the following information from an undeniably authentic source, and from careful and persistent inquiries in various quarters he is able to relate the news as fact, though for obvious reasons names and addresses are for the present suppressed:

A member of the Criminal Investigation Department recently journeyed to Liverpool and there traced the movements of a man that have proven to be somewhat mysterious. Among other things he was in possession of a black leather bag. The suspect suddenly left Liverpool for London, and for some time after occupied rooms in a well-known hotel. For some reason, however, the suspect was also in the habit of 'slumming.' He would visit the lowest parts of London, take a room, and scour the slums of the East End.

After he disappeared the leather bag was sold at auction under the Innkeepers' Act to cover his unpaid expenses. Some of the contents are now in the possession of the police. Of these we cannot do more than make general mention, but certain documents, wearing apparel, and prints of an obscene description are said to form the foundation of a searching new inquiry by vigilant authorities…

The Daily News, London, October 16, 1888

According to a Correspondent, the police are watching with great anxiety a house at the East End which is strongly suspected to have been the actual lodging, or a house made use of by someone connected with the East End murders.

Statements made by the neighbors in the district point to the fact that the landlady had a lodger, which since Sunday morning of the last Whitechapel murders has been missing. The lodger, it is stated, returned home early on Sunday morning, and the landlady was disturbed by his moving about.

It is believed from the information obtained concerning the lodger's former movements and his general appearance, together with the fact that numbers of people have seen this same man about the neighborhood, that the police have in their possession a series of most important clues, and that his ultimate capture is only a question of time…

The New York Times, December 4, 1888

'Dr.' Francis Tumblety, who left his bondsmen in London in the lurch, arrived by La Bretagne of the Transatlantic Line Sunday. Chief Inspector Byrnes had no charge whatever against him, but he had him followed so as to secure his temporary address, and will keep him in view as a manner of ordinary police precaution. Mr. Byrnes does not believe that he will have to interfere with Tumblety for anything he may have done in Europe, and laughs at the suggestion that he was the Whitechapel murderer or his abettor or accomplice.

The man who is supposed to be Tumblety came over on the steamship as 'Frank Townsend' and kept in his room, refusing visitors under plea of sickness.…

1889 BOOKLET
*Dr Francis Tumblety – Sketch of the Life
of the Gifted, Eccentric and World Famed Physician*

…Now let me say a word about the attacks which certain
American newspapers recently made on me, attacks that
were as unfounded as the onslaught made on the great Irish
leader Charles Stewart Parnell. While I was not in a position
to defend myself, these papers continued their foul slanders,
but my friends will readily see, from the foregoing pages and
from the testimonials, how utterly base and wholly ground-
less these aspersions were.

Like Parnell, I have emerged from the battle totally
unscathed with my social and professional standing unim-
paired. It is gratifying to recall the pleasure with which my
friends welcomed me to my native land.

I treasure these tributes among the dearest things in my
possession.

WARDENCLYFFE

38

ROUGH LANDING

The first difference he noticed was clarity. Everything was vivid and just a bit brighter. He felt more *present*. At the same time life seemed less urgent – despite the fact that the warehouse looked abandoned. He had been gone for a week and not even Danny was here to greet him.

His voice boomed off the walls. "Anyone? Danny? Angel?"

The wound from his fight wasn't life-threatening but it would need treatment. Shaw's frock coat had also taken a beating, the left sleeve slashed midway to the elbow. He stepped out of the vault and checked the observation window. The control room seemed vacant, lit only by the glow of computer screens.

Surrounding him was the holographic stream of the London alley and Batty Street beyond projected by the view room censors. In the backyard, about fifty feet away, he could see Tumblety, alone, in utter disbelief, unable to comprehend what happened. He stood there, mouth open, checking above and below. How could he explain it – a drug-induced hallucination, a product of his imagination, dementia? He was even forced to re-consider his dismissal of the occult. This was better than any disappearing act he'd ever performed.

Tonio strolled through the scene on his way to the hall. Peeking out, he noticed a chair propped against the door to the kitchen and wing beyond. Filing that for later, he took the stairs to the mezzanine and raced to the control room. That door was wide open. It looked like someone had been sleeping there. Cushions, clothes and blankets were strewn around, along with used pizza boxes, oversized cups and bottles discarded among the papers at Danny's station. The computers were running. In the corner of a screen he saw his own face being applied to recognition software capturing images from the stream.

Retracing his steps to the blocked door he listened for sounds inside, pulled the chair away, and saw that the door was locked. Due to the renovations and their concern about soundproofing and security he needed an axe to get through. Danny was crouched in the bathroom, mouth taped shut, pants below his knees, tied to the wall near the toilet. Tonio ripped off the tape.

"My God, that was you!" Danny was a mess but better for seeing him. "I can't believe it. I heard the projection come up. I activated it days ago, linked to the IMMatch software we started testing last month. It finds faces in the stream and listens for key words."

"What the fuck happened?"

"Shelley's guys, private security," he said. "You'd been gone several days and I was frantic, especially after the call from Angel." Once freed and hydrated, the battered inventor began updating him about the week since his disappearance.

"Is she all right?"

"No idea. I've been out of the loop, you might say. But I was worried as soon as you left the crime scene. I picked you up again, about an hour later, but you never came close to the entry, and then the stream collapsed. By the time I rebooted you were gone. What happened?"

"A lot, what about here?"

After losing Tonio, Danny stayed at the lab through to the following night, searching and locking onto the alley every three hours. By the second day he was desperate enough to tell someone, but not sure who. His biggest concern was that the warehouse would be seized and shut down rather than used to bring Tonio back. Basically, he thought they would call him nuts and put him away. He rang Harry but no one answered.

On the fourth day, the day Tonio told Donnelly his "fantasy" of the future, Danny received several calls that drastically altered the dynamics. The first was from Angel, who harangued him about hanging her out to dry on the financing deal. She was also sure that Tonio was hiding from her, and suspected Danny of covering for him. She wanted to come over, certain he was in the view room ogling Annie or some London barmaid. But she never arrived.

When Harry called back, Danny spilled everything – teleportation, the Jump Room, the Commandments and protocols, where Tonio was and how long he'd been stuck there. They agreed that it didn't make sense yet for Harry to come in, but agreed to stay in touch daily. He hadn't been heard from since.

"Harry told me he had what you wanted, what we needed to deal with Shelley once and for all. I have to say, it sounded strong, something about movie stars, illegal surveillance and something called the Balkan Route. Does any of that make sense?" It did, but not in a way that helped at the moment.

The same night Paulie called Danny on behalf of the Don. He said they knew Tonio was last seen entering the building days ago and hadn't been seen since. "He was very definite about that, as if he'd personally seen you and had the place staked out."

"He didn't have to," Tonio said. "They have real time sat feeds. It's expensive but it works. Even if you escaped they could track you, hypothetically to me. And you said?"

"I said he was wrong, that you'd left days ago for a trip, and I didn't know where." Paulie didn't argue. Instead, a few hours later he showed up with muscle and demanded to check the premises for himself. Danny decided it was the best way to convince him. Bad move.

"They searched the building and didn't find anything, obviously," he continued. "But he knew things only the four of us are supposed to know, including the view room, only basics, but enough to want a demonstration. At first I thought he bought my story. But then the guy just starts wailing on me, like he took it all very personally. After that, when I came to, he had me set up an RV link with Shelley, who already had a pair of visors." They were probably the one he had given Paulie as a gift.

"Then I saw she was with him, Angel. And she looked strange, man."

It wasn't hard to piece together from there. She was angry and feeling under-valued, taken for granted, and had probably gone to Shelley thinking, if the son of bitch isn't sharp enough to see the potential of her deal, maybe the Big Dog is. After all, he's out to make a buck. But Tonio knew better. In the end Shelley Wolfe was about the power over people his money purchased. She had seriously misjudged her mark.

"How did she look?"

"I'd say sedated if I didn't know better." That also made sense. If Shelley thought Angel knew where he was after dropping out of sight for so long– or merely if she could fill in what they had been withholding – he wouldn't hesitate to spike her drink, or much worse, to find out. By now he could know everything except the existence of the Jump Room. That might be his only edge.

For the last few days Danny had been held as a hostage inside the building, released daily just to eat, check messages and take a piss while two security men patrolled the premises. Fortunately, they weren't around when the stream activated after capturing Tonio's face. At midnight the jump chamber had come online and moments later he was back. Until then it hadn't truly sunk in: For every day he had spent in London, a day also passed here. They were gone forever and could never be recovered – even with a time machine.

They cleaned up and did what they could for their various injuries. Tonio hung Shaw's coat in a locker for safe keeping. They were about to reconvene in the control room, having agreed that locating Harry and Angel was their top priority, when the lock released on the front entrance.

Tonio quickly ordered Danny to hide upstairs and returned to the kitchen to get ready.

The swath of old London filling the chamber turned it into a maze of overlapping shapes and structures. The security detail, two solid guys in insulated jackets, looked disoriented as they tried to make sense of a confusing three-dimensional jumble in which everything seemed vaguely translucent and unreal.

After seeing the open door one of them went back to check on Danny while the second made his way tentatively across the space. Tonio watched from the top of the ramp, one arm clutching a climbing rope, the other holding the longest, sharpest knife he was able to find. The blackjack and mace he'd left behind before London were stuffed in his back pockets.

When the distance looked right he launched himself, swinging down and across to knock the guy off his feet. Before he could recover Tonio kicked him several times, then beat him senseless with a series of blackjack whacks. He dragged the body to a corner and started for the door.

"You can't get out," growled a voice over the PA. He peeked up and saw the second guard watching. "There's nowhere to go we can't find you. Bro, I do this professionally," he added with an unnecessary bite of condescension. "Just a second, I'll come down." It wasn't more than ten before he was at the door.

Tonio was hidden by the projection, in slight relief from the surrounding scene. It took his quarry a while to adjust and realize that, in this place, he could walk through walls.

"Is this the missing person in question?" He was a square-built Marine-turned-merc.

"Not missing, just retiring." Tonio stepped into view, showing the knife.

"I'm not supposed to kill you," the brawler confessed, "but, you know, I am allowed to mess you up." He opened his jacket and revealed an even bigger blade of his own.

Tonio took a tentative step and lowered his weapon to indicate surrender, but watched until he saw the man's eyes follow and then maced him mercilessly to his knees. The blackjack was sufficient to finish the job, but Danny arrived in time to get in several redundant licks of his own.

His jailers had conveniently brought along handcuffs, keys and intercoms. Once they were tied, gagged and stuffed in the sauna, Tonio and Danny returned to exchanging notes. There was no time to lose; it wouldn't be long before their hostages were missed.

"We have to find Harry," urged Tonio. "If Shelley's holding Angel we need leverage. We should also warn him to watch his ass. Amazing! It turns out he wasn't paranoid enough. But where is he now?" There seemed no way to know.

Then Danny remembered, "I know where he was last Saturday. He told me."

"Where?"

"Mardi Gras, I could hear it." Harry had contacted him on a disposable phone and chided him for answering when he didn't know the number. Danny confessed why, and they spent fifteen minutes going over what had happened and what to do.

But Harry in New Orleans made no sense, and the timing was off.

"He said he couldn't resist. It wasn't far from home."

"That's impossible."

"Not in Burlington," Danny replied, "that's what he said. It was in the early afternoon and he mentioned it was cold. He was sitting in a coffee house and said something like, only a place like Burlington could get people to build floats, cheer for a mayor in gold lame, and line up outdoors to beg for plastic jewelry in the dead of winter. I definitely heard music."

That sounded better. He would blend in perfectly at Burlington's mid-winter parade, even with no costume.

"What time, close as you recall?" Danny estimated about one o'clock. The plan, as Tonio explained it on the spot, was to arrive early, catch Harry right after the call, tell him everything that had happened since, and have him try to reach Angel before her big mistake. Just as important, he could find out what Harry knew about the Don and use it to protect all of them.

Danny couldn't disagree in principle, calling it a form of "enhanced enforcement" and therefore exempt from rules about heroics and making changes. But he did have reservations. What if Tonio couldn't get back again, or the stream collapsed, or someone else arrived in the meantime? He'd been tortured enough and had no interest in repeating the experience.

"One hour," he pleaded, "you'll be tracking me. And I know the perfect entrance."

39
Human Traffic

BURLINGTON, MARCH 2, 2013

The brick monolith had been out of service for decades. Before it was shuttered, mainly due to pollution, the Moran generating station loomed over the shore for decades providing 30-megawatts of power. The same year it closed, 1986, voters backed a waterfront plan with new zoning, a public park and a bike path. They also approved legal action to extend public authority.

Various plans for the decommissioned coal plant came and went after that, most recently the former mayor's idea of transforming it into a city-owned recreation and sailing center. But the future of the 90-foot high building on the waterfront remained in doubt. The overgrown site was surrounded by a chain link fence to prevent vandalism and injuries. The new mayor, an energetic housing developer, had recently convinced voters to finance improvements for a central section of the Lake Champlain shoreline. However, he also announced that the city would no longer even try to re-purpose the hulky structure on its own.

Tonio arrived inside the building, then exited through a broken window and found a break in the fence. Except for a few die-hard skateboarders who used a rundown park on the opposite side of the building few people came to this corner of the lakefront during the winter months. But only blocks away, despite a lead-colored sky, thousands of people lined the sidewalks along Main and the Church Street Marketplace to celebrate. Harry would be nearby.

The tradition, known as the Magic Hat Mardi Gras Parade, started after he left school. The Vermont brewer had figured out how to win local backing and bring thousands of people out in the cold. It was an annual winter ritual with live performances, a lively parade and much inebriated good cheer. The night before the main event bands had performed in the heart of town to heat up the mood. Today a huge crowd was cheering the mayor, who waved back in his gold jacket, silver boots and a feathered hat as floats rolled through town.

Tonio made his way across Waterfront Park, passing a row of condos and Main Street Landing, the arts center where he'd watched *The Millennium* a few months back. When he attended school at the top of the hill most of this area was still vacant. But if Harry had come to town he wouldn't be talking with Danny on the waterfront or along the parade route. Most likely he would be in a spot where he felt at home.

Cutting across Battery Street he walked up Pearl to South Winooski and checked the area that served as unofficial gateway to the Old North End and meeting spot for the alternative set. As he suspected, Harry was having coffee at the Radio Bean as he found out the truth about the Jump Room and Tonio's disappearance.

As soon as the call ended Tonio marched into the funky coffeehouse.

"Jeez," Harry gulped, "He wasn't kidding."

"No, he wasn't." He sat down on the opposite side of the booth. "But things have gone even further south since you spoke with him."

"In ten seconds? Where did you come from?

"Next Wednesday," Tonio deadpanned, "and it's a very bad day." He rapidly retraced recent events, mostly as explained to him by Danny, including the fact that Angel had gone to visit Shelley and may have been drugged.

" Extremely unwise," Harry said, "given what we know now, which is why I was looking for you."

"Whatever it is, can we use it as a bargaining chip?"

"That, I'm not so sure. He's your blood. But sure, there's more than enough to nail him." Tonio demanded details. "We began with what we already knew and worked backward. For example, Wolfe Enterprises builds around the world, has a controlling stake in various casinos and is developing Jefferson Spaceport. We also know they have E-Global satellites.

"But here's the thing: the Feds could exercise shutter control on the satellites, just block anything they considered off limits or a national security matter. But we haven't seen evidence of that. Instead, we've got close cooperation. We also know Shelley's buying up land, in the US and elsewhere. But it's hard to see the pattern; some parcels are in the middle of nowhere and have no apparent development potential."

There was more. Harry's group also found evidence suggesting that Wolfe ran a blackmail operation targeting high rollers at the casinos and used Private Intelligence Associates (PIA), the security company it had purchased, for corporate espionage. Staffed largely by ex-military officers, PIA had contracts with NSA, managed several Air Force bases and maintained border crossing technology.

"I met two associates not long ago." Tonio meant the guys tied up in the warehouse.

"But the main thing," Harry continued, "is the link back to the old country. Your grandfather came over from Croatia, right?" As Tonio recalled the family history, Roman Lupinjak had emigrated sometime after the Second World War. "This is the key. It explains how Wolfe went from being a construction front for prostitution and gambling to what it is now, a transnational holding company. Are you aware of what's been happening in the homeland in the last twenty years or so?"

Tonio had no idea. He didn't even keep up with the headlines, and when he visited Europe his destination was normally a Mediterranean island or a beach on the Italian Riviera.

"After Yugoslavia collapsed, Croatia's new president, Franjo Tudman, started selling off state enterprises in a way that was, let's just say, not legal. It was known there as 'Privatization Robbery.' Basically, about 200 families got control over everything, and yours was one of them. It was an 'everything must go' deal, and things went at fire sale prices. Then the new owners sliced up the businesses and sold off the pieces, which was lucrative enough for them. But as a result some companies that were successful for years went bankrupt. It also led to massive unemployment. So, basically you could say the Don participated in a post-Communist gang rape of his native land."

Tonio wasn't completely shocked. But he was humbled and challenged by a growing realization that his education and most of his life had been financed by human misery.

"We've also established his ties with Ivo Sanader, the ex-prime minister, who was recently sentenced to ten years for taking bribes. When Sanader was Deputy Foreign Minister – the fight for Independence was winding down at the time – he received payments through an Austrian bank. He called them fees. At least two foreign companies were involved. One suspect was Hungary's oil and gas company, MOL. They categorically denied any involvement, which tends to suggest the opposite. The other was a front for Wolfe Enterprises.

"The judge called Sanader a war profiteer. Until a few years ago this was the most powerful man in the country. But in 2009 he resigned suddenly and designated his successor on the way out the door. Then the new PM, Jadranka Kosor, launched an anti-corruption campaign that eventually led right back to him."

"Why would Kosor turn on the guy who made him?"

"Kosor is a she, and we don't know that she really turned on him. But the Croatian elite badly wants into the European Union," Harry explained, "and for that they have to clean up their act on corruption, or at least look like it. The HDZ, the ruling party, is staking everything on EU entry. Unemployment is at least 20 percent, youth unemployment is double that. The country's per-capita debt-to-GDP ratio is one of the highest in Europe.

"From what we can see, the EU agreement will mean disaster for the country's remaining economic independence. Also say goodbye to fishing and agriculture. Fiscal policy will be decided by Euro-crats in Brussels. So will exploitation of oil and gas reserves in the Adriatic. The country will basically become another Greece, a dependent state. The US and EU have already provided a billion dollar bailout, supposedly for anti-corruption reforms. It won't be the last. But most of the money has been misused or stolen.

"What the political class wants – what Shelley wants – is access to at least four billion Euros that Brussels will provide after EU entry this summer.

"There is an opposition," he added, "a group called Croatia 21st Century led by Natasha Srdoc, one of the few politicians willing to take on corruption. She's pretty conservative on social issues –among other things, she wants to make abortion illegal – but she also wants to seize assets and prosecute any official who has amassed unexplained wealth while in office. That alone would smash organized crime in Croatia. But party supporters are already being intimidated or framed. One candidate, an anti-corruption author, documented the crimes of the Interior Minister, a thug who uses the cops as henchmen. Result – the writer, not the minister, ends up in jail as political prisoner."

Tonio interrupted. "Danny mentioned something about the Balkan Route."

Harry hesitated and then warned, "This is rough stuff. Of course, it's been a smuggling route forever – weapons, immigrants, heroin from Afghanistan. Originally, most of it went through Pakistan and Iran, now it mostly uses Balkan states. Cigarettes, oil, anything you don't want seen or taxed. Almost 90 percent of the heroin in Europe gets in that way."

The smuggling route helped organize crime get a foothold in the country, he explained. After Yugoslavia's collapse, social confusion made the whole region an easy mark. As the country moved toward democracy ties between the elite and the underworld flourished. Officials in the old regime saw a path to convert their waning political power into economic gain. Black market smuggling was already common, even encouraged. The traditional economy had never matched consumer demands. But corrupt officials and security forces helped the black market run like a well-oiled machine. Once communism was gone and privatization began, ex-cops and other officials with connections in the underground were positioned to take smuggling to the next level.

"The Serbs claim that Croatian ports have become a primary conduit for cocaine entering the region," Harry reported. "It's also believed to be the source of about a billion annually in illegal exports, everything from cars and trucks to ships, medicines, sugar and electronics. But the worst is transporting humans."

Tonio stopped him. "You're talking about human trafficking, sex slavery?"

"I'm afraid so, buddy, and Shelley has a hand in that too. It's largely Bosnian girls brought in to service the tourist trade. The offer is usually a legitimate job, but then they take away the documents and force them into sex slavery. During the last decade underage Croatian kids have been added to the mix."

It was even worse than he suspected. After months tracking down just one serial killer of women, he had been informed that his father was responsible for crimes as heinous and created even greater misery. What Harry described sounded much like the "Maiden Tribute of Modern Babylon," William Stead's expose on child prostitution in 1880s London. So little had changed.

"I need air," he announced, standing up.

Harry followed him to the sidewalk. "Let's walk and talk. I also want to know what you've been doing. And we definitely need a plan."

"Yeah, the first thing is to call Angel and stop her from going to Shelley."

"Sure, she'll listen to me."

"Try anyway. Next, get out of sight and assemble everything you have. If Truthsquad wants to shake things up this ought to do it."

Harry stopped. "Wait. You want me to expose your family?"

"I do. And you have to do it within two weeks, before the demo for Shelley. We need to turn up the heat, startle the snake, force a reaction, get him to deny some charges and then hit him with more. We need to escalate and isolate, and expose him for the lying scum and hypocrite he is."

"Harsh," said Harry, "but doable."

"Then do it with my blessings. Afterward, we meet with him and show him that, as bad as things are, they could get even worse. We re-run his past. The only thing I'm not sure about is which parts we should use. What's your call on that?"

"As much as security allows," replied Harry, "our security I mean. People first, that's what I always say. And we're people too."

They were on the top block of the Marketplace, ducking between revelers in beaded necklaces, when Tonio noticed two men on the corner who looked out of place. Wearing identical parkas and matching sunglasses they were eyeballing the crowd while the taller of the two conferred with someone on a smart phone. The shorter one occasionally glanced down to check an image on his device.

"I think they're here," he said. "More associates." He nodded across the street.

Harry noticed and cursed, "Frigging flying eyes."

"I'll draw them off. You get out of here. Now!"

Harry stepped away and turned. "It's on," he yelled, drifting into the crowd. "A week or less."

The short guy spotted Tonio and they moved to flanking positions. The order was obviously to wait for back up, so Tonio walked casually down the center of the street, not acknowledging them until he reached the entrance to the underground mall that extended toward the lake. He froze in the pedestrian flow, waiting for a moment when all the doors were wide open, then bolted inside and down the escalator, executing a quick U-turn to hide beneath.

Seconds later the two were following him down the escalator, scattering people as they headed into the structure. As soon as they rounded the first corner Tonio re-emerged, ran back up and outside. He rounded another corner, muscled through the crowd, and headed west toward the lake. Someone might be tracking him from a satellite or unmanned plane, but he had a trump card.

"I'm on my way," he shouted to Danny, tracking his movements from four days ahead. At Battery Street he crossed against the light and jogged toward the nearest connection with Waterfront Park. The two who spotted him earlier were on the opposite side after ending up inside the Hilton. Two more pairs were already positioned at Main and Pearl Streets with the intention of boxing him in. His only option was straight ahead, down a steep embankment that emptied into a parking lot. He made it halfway before tripping and tumbling to the bottom.

Ruffled but unhurt, he shot across the lot and leapt a fence. From there it was a long stretch of open land to another, higher fence around Moran. Glancing back he could see them coming, just reaching the first obstacle, and behind them two police cars screeching along Lake Street, drawn by the complaints about men causing a disturbance around the mall.

All he needed was to get there. Launching into a final sprint, he smashed into the fence, bounced off and kept going. The break was on the other side. They were still coming and one fired a warning shot, apparently meant to get his attention. He kept running until he was around the corner and saw the opening. Ducking inside the fence, he made for the building, found the broken window, and crawled back inside onto a catwalk.

Streams of pale light illuminated the dank interior. Below him several more floors were submerged in murky water. He pulled out the pocket watch and checked. It had been less than an hour, as agreed, and he was in the same spot.

"Hey," he shouted. "You guys are ex-military, right? What's it like? One day you're defending your country. The next, you're mob muscle. Can you hear me now?" The reply came in the form of several more gunshots.

"Got it," he said, moving along the catwalk, sticking to the darkest spots. By now, he assumed, the cops outside had called for backup. These guys weren't going anywhere and their actions would be hard to explain. It was time to get back to New Jersey and put things in motion.

He held his breath, hoped for the best, and hit recall. This time it worked.

40
Darcap

The vault door swung open and he lurched out, racing through the projected interior of the water-logged plant to the ramp. Danny was waiting, absorbed in the drama unfolding onscreen. A showdown was building between Burlington police officers approaching the empty power plant and the six men inside. "This is a hoot," he said. "You made me nervous once or twice, but the chase scene was radical."

More police cars joined the first, creating a blockade as officers moved around the site. One actually stood behind a car door on a bullhorn attempting to make contact with the suspects.

"Great footage for the highlight reel," Tonio said offhand, "but not our current problem. Our problem is how to get out of this building without being followed, stopped or shot. Someone's going to be looking for those two in back."

Danny shut down the projection and moved the feed to a monitor. "Oh, someone called for you. It was strange. You were gone just minutes and this guy says he's looking for you. I tell him you haven't been around for a week, and he says, 'I know, he's been busy.' Then he tells me to tell you, 'the wait and see period is over,' and he'll be around when you get back."

"Anything else, like a name?"

"Lynch. Said you met in DC."

Tonio remembered him, the sly DoD operative who attended the meeting on fabrication and finance. "Yeah, but look, I have to do something. When you brought me back – I appreciate that, don't get me wrong – I left some loose ends behind."

"Dude, what are you telling me?"

He was slightly embarrassed. "I want to go back. I need to see someone. It's personal, but important."

"Personal? Is now the time?" Danny gestured at the trashed control room to make his point. "You just said we need to get out of here. I'd like to focus that. Did you know I haven't seen the sun in five days."

"I may not get another chance." He paused for the best way to put it. "There's someone – a woman. Something happened, a real connection, she got to me big time. But the last time we spoke it ended badly and I need to …" He wasn't sure what he needed, except to see her again and make her see that he wasn't a worthless scoundrel, chauvinist and cad.

Danny shook his head. "In the grand scheme of things I'm not sure your relationship ranks high enough at this moment. Plus I really need a shower, and I'd like to catch up on the news and a ton of email. Take a breath, okay?"

Taking the hint he flopped onto a couch, letting in exhaustion after the last wild hours. The week before was no picnic either. In hindsight, the whole project looked fragile from the start. It was naïve to think they could hide such a discovery indefinitely from the Don, not to mention the world.

"Oh no! Shit!" As Danny shoved back his chair, eyes wide with disbelief, Tonio rushed over to check the article on his screen.

New York Woman Hit by Train, Apparent Suicide

Posted: Tuesday, March 5, 2013 9:30 am | *Updated: 6:13 pm, Tues March 5, 2013.*

BY RICHARD PORTO CHRONICLE STAFF |

ICELIN, NJ - A prominent New York businesswoman was struck by a high speed Acela train Friday morning, the victim of an apparent suicide.

A spokesman for the Middlesex County District Attorney's office said officials have identified the woman as Angela Brancusi, 37, of Manhattan, general manager of an aerospace and technology business. She was struck by the northbound train about 9 a.m. near the Icelin Metropark station. He did not explain why the death appeared to be a suicide.

A state medical examiner is scheduled to perform an autopsy.

The Icelin station is a commuter stop on the New York-Philadelphia rail line near the Middlesex-Essex Turnpike. Amtrak temporarily suspended train service through the station following the fatality.

One track reopened about an hour later. No injuries were reported among the passengers and crew aboard the train.

There was no doubt in Tonio's mind who to blame. No matter what the details turned out to be or what happened in the final moments of her life, a crime had been committed. Angel was dead, and he and Shelley were the reason. His lack of support had driven her to the one person she should have avoided, and that somehow led to her grisly death only days later. She'd been drugged, and what else? The Icelin station wasn't that far from Wood-Ridge.

The news was staggering. He wanted to leave the warehouse this minute, find a gun, and execute his father. He simultaneously wanted to escape to London, find Annie, plead for her forgiveness, and collapse in her arms.

"Can we stop it?"

Danny rubbed his temples. "I want to, just as much as you. But I don't think so. We talked about the consistency principle, course correction. I'm pretty certain it applies. It would happen anyway, maybe just not a train."

"If you can't stop something like this," Tonio snarled, "what's the point?"

"To know, to see…"

"It's not nearly enough."

The phone rang and Danny picked up. It was Peter Lynch again. "Hi," he said cheerily. "Would you please put your co-conspirator on?" He handed over the phone. "It's Lynch, for you. Spooky."

"That's what they say." He took the phone, "Peter, great to hear from you."

Lynch chuckled. "We need to talk about what you've been up to."

"What's that?"

"Please." He was mildly insulted. "Check your perimeter."

Tonio told Danny and they turned to the security cameras. Three identical white vans were parked in the lot and more than a dozen armed men had fanned out around the entrance. Lynch was speaking to him from right outside, looking up at a mounted security camera as he held a phone to his ear.

"We won't be disturbed," he promised. "The PIA boys won't make a move while we're here, except maybe to report to Mr. Wolfe. So, can we talk?"

Lynch glanced briefly into the view room before joining Tonio in the elevator for the short trip upstairs. "Nice digs," he offered. "I was wondering what it looked like."

Tonio gave him a once over. Lynch seemed about the same age as he was, more cautious and meticulous, tightly-wound but confident and clearly in no hurry at the moment. "This should have happened earlier," he confided. "My bad."

Once all three of them were in the same room Danny didn't conceal his discomfort. "So, who are you? FBI, NSA? Nothing we're doing is illegal."

"You mentioned Defense." On edge, Tonio acknowledged he'd never believed that. "Or is it DARPA? Remember, Danny, you told me about them, the genius network, smartest guys in any room. Am I warm?"

"Maybe it's not illegal," Lynch replied to Danny, "but fairly risky you'd have to agree, and irresponsible." He sat down and looked at the Burlington feed. "Like this," he said, pointing. "Very public. And what would have happened if they caught you? Did you think about that? And even before that, you two have been setting off alarms for a week."

"What are you talking about?" Tonio's default strategy was to admit nothing and see what the other guy knew.

"We won't get anywhere with that attitude. All right, let me paint a picture of my week," Lynch said. "Eight days ago I get a call after midnight and have to come to the office to check out a report. Apparently, some cowboy is messing with the primary stream."

Danny interrupted, "Where did you say you were from?"

"You were almost right," he admitted to Tonio. "The posting with Defense isn't my primary assignment, although much of this does fall under the general category of acquisition, technology and logistics. DARPA also isn't far from the mark, but the relationship is sub-contractual, like Lockheed Martin's management of the Sandia lab in New Mexico. Our portfolio ranges through applied research in a variety of areas, including the one you're pursuing. We're known as the Defense Applied Research Contract Associates Program, DARCAP. It's similar enough to be forgotten, that's the idea."

"And our meeting in DC?"

"As I told you, we wanted to see what you'd do. I just didn't say about what. Then you made that jump, out of the blue, an entire week. It was a shock to the system. I got the call around 1 a.m. actually, just minutes after you went through."

"Wait," Danny said. "You could see him?"

"You thought you were the only one working on this, or the first to succeed? Interesting. You may be a genius but you don't have much common sense; you should work on that. No, we've been developing the same capabilities for decades. Not me personally, the big we, or Them if you like. Come on, it's like cops and grass. You always keep the best shit for yourself."

"You can view past events?" Tonio was in denial. "And you saw me in London?"

"We knew you were there, and we could locate you if we needed to. But what were you trying to accomplish, that's what I don't get."

Danny answered first. "I was just running a test. It was supposed to be brief."

"And I wanted to expose a killer," Tonio added, "and demonstrate how this could be used to answer crucial questions, to expose criminals and find the truth about the past."

"But that is not what you've done in the last week. Let's review the record. Minutes after you teleported you upset that horse, which interrupted a documented event, that woman's murder, and scared the killer off to commit another crime."

"Are you saying I caused Katy Kelly's murder?"

"As far as we know, she would have died later, strangled by her pimp. But you changed things and you kept doing it."

"We went over that," Danny objected, "I warned him."

"Things really heated up about four days in. It was a combined effect, the impact of your absence here and what you told Mr. Donnelly there. You described the future, the actual future."

"As part of a novel."

"A novel he went on to write." He removed a volume from his attaché case. From the markings it had been withdrawn from the Library of Congress, a worn but well-preserved hardcover copy wrapped in clear, heavy plastic. The cover announced "Ceasar's Column: A Story of the Twentieth Century," credited to Edmund Boisgilbert and published in 1889 by a small Chicago publishing house, F. J. Schulte and Company.

Lynch summarized the plot. The text used the conceit of letters from the main character to his brother. The year is 1988. The whole book read like a French novel, full of hot pursuits, elaborate disguises and romantic escapes. But it also described enormous cities, vast communications systems and great ships that traveled through the air. The whole tale focused on a degraded future society where the rich have godlike power, millions live in poverty, and the only way out is violent revolution. It channeled many popular fears about the future and the failure of reform. And although it ended with the narrator and heroine escaping to a cooperative utopia the main thrust was to strip the bark from the American dream and expose the myth of progress through technology, capitalism and social Darwinism

"Does any of this sound familiar? It was published less than a year after your European vacation. Don't let the pseudonym fool you, Donnelly wrote it. The author mystery was part of the marketing strategy. He and his publisher kept the rumors going for years. But reviewers with the big city papers missed the book entirely, almost as if it wasn't meant to exist.

"It did develop what you might call a cult following in certain unions and rural enclaves. By the end of the century almost a million copies were sold. So I guess you could say you've been published, in a sense. Just don't make a habit of it. Time travel isn't your personal improv group. By the way, the only way you find that book today is virtually, via Samizdat Express. This is one of a handful of remaining copies.

"I won't go into your contact with all those London leftists or Ms. Besant. The First Amendment covers most of that, you're still free to say and do whatever or with whomever you please. That said, your contact with Mr. Tumblety did have a major effect on his life."

"Did it save Mary Jane Kelly, the last victim?"

"Sadly no. But it did contribute to his arrest. That landlady decided to contact the authorities on her own. They just couldn't hold him. And it made him extremely insecure, and thus much more cautious, for the rest of his life. The long-term effect of any change, however small, is almost impossible to calculate. We have supercomputers working on this constantly. The main concern is obviously any impact on the general direction of history. We call it the History Superhighway. It has to keep moving in the right direction and you don't get to change the route, or bend it."

"Who decides that?"

"We do. That is, people above my pay grade. The US developed this capability, this potential, and now that it exists it has to be monitored and managed. There's more than one reason we call America the indispensable nation. I wasn't with DARCAP when Secretary Albright said that. But you remember, in 1998. 'If we have to use force,' she said, 'it is because we are America! We are the indispensable nation.'

"And then she said, 'We see further into the future.' They were cheering in Virginia after that line, that's what I'm told, and some people believe it was a silent nod to what we do." He stopped to check their reactions. "You're upset, I see that. But there's good news. I'm not here to shut down TELPORT, or stop you from conducting research. The general policy isn't repression of innovation. It's smart containment, more like the Chinese approach – with verification and adjustments if necessary. But there are limits to what's allowed."

By this point in the discussion Tonio was no longer worried. Still, he wasn't pleased by what he was hearing. They appeared to have little leverage at the moment. If Lynch was telling the truth – and he sounded very convincing – their view stream and jump room were nothing more than a nuisance, a boutique enterprise that simply needed to be whipped into line. Was there any other way to explain what he knew about the London jump?

"You also said something about the impact of my absence."

Lynch explained, "Space-time is a bendable fabric, but unpredictable, and every action affects it somehow; so does not acting, not being. You vanished for eight days. That would have a profound impact even if you were just hiding out. But you were gone, removed completely from this time line. We have no model for that, but I wouldn't underestimate the effects."

While they talked Danny was working something out. "So, if you're not here to shut us down, are you here to help?"

"I'm here to discuss your options. Option one: we agree about how this facility is used and your problem with the men outside goes away."

"Don't forget the two assholes in back," Danny said.

"And the satellites tracking me," added Tonio.

"That may take longer, but the muscle can be handled. Then there's option two: I leave empty-handed and someone much less sympathetic gets a call. Not an option I recommend."

Tonio went to the point: Exactly what limits would be placed on their use of either RTV or teleportation technology?

"In simple terms, for you it's look but don't touch," Lynch explained. "We have no orders to prevent remote time viewing, although I personally anticipate a shit storm once this gets out. But that's not my department. In terms of jumping, you'll have to maintain a hands off attitude. We can get into the details. I hear you already have a do-and-don't list."

Danny handed him a business card with the Time Commandments. Lynch gave it a once over and said, "Yeah, this is a start. The main thing is not to influence, either by design or accident, the basic arc of history. And we'll know, and tell you, if that's in danger of happening."

"We have another problem," Tonio said. "My father probably knows what we've been doing, some of it anyway. And I can't predict what he'll do if he gets his hands on this."

Lynch agreed. "That's the other reason I wanted to meet you. I mentioned that we wanted to be sure this didn't get into the wrong hands."

"Can you do something about it?" It couldn't hurt to ask. "We need information about his past, any crimes you suspect and haven't proven or pursued."

"You want to take down the big bad wolf?" Lynch laughed. "Sure, we can help with that."

41
THE LOVERS

It was a huge city, perhaps the largest in the world at this moment, sprawling to the point of overflow and revolt with more than four million people. Global trade and vast industrial expansion had transformed London during the long reign of Victoria, Queen of the United Kingdom of Great Britain and Ireland, Empress of India. At her empire's heart, in the city's financial core, the god was gold. But a full third of all residents lived in abject poverty, trapped in desperate rookeries, slums as crowded and degrading as any in ancient Rome.

After a week as an accidental immigrant Tonio's attitude had profoundly changed. He'd come first as an observer, a dispassionate investigator, arrogant and disconnected from the human struggles around him, and used advanced technology to put this society under a microscope. Now he returned, no longer just trying to unravel a mystery, but connected through shared experience, deadly struggle and growing affection.

It took him a while to convince Danny to cooperate, however. After meeting Lynch and accepting his terms, the battered inventor was relieved to know it was safe to come out. He watched on a monitor as their new protector briefed his team and assigned several members to remain behind with a van. The deal was that Lynch would deal with Private Intelligence Associates, letting them know the warehouse was under federal protection, at least for the time being. But that meant playing by DARCAP's rules, and what Tonio wanted to do might veer into a grey area.

Angel was gone forever. Even if Tonio could go back and prevent her death – a question in itself – both the Time Commandments and Lynch's restrictions prohibited that. On the other hand, where was the harm in returning to see Annie and set things right? He pleaded his case with every argument he could muster. No rules would be broken. He simply wanted to see her, however brief it might be. What damage could that do?

He was worried, but not about the impact on history. What concerned him was a distinct feeling that, despite any promises Lynch made, future use of the Jump Room would be restricted or completely prohibited. If he wanted to see her, the moment was now. Danny ultimately acquiesced, but extracted a pledge to restrict his movements to her flat and the immediate surroundings. Tonio knew a courtyard in back where no one was likely to spot him materializing late at night.

Two hours after their fight he knocked on her door. Rustling within said Annie was still awake. After a few seconds she opened it a crack, peeked out and pouted, "Go away."

"Please." He wasn't too proud to beg. "Ask me anything. Only the truth, I promise."

She eyed him warily. "What's your name? Is it even Upton?"

"No," he confessed. "It's Antonio, but most people call me Tonio or T. But I am American."

"That doesn't help." The door opened a bit more. "And what's all this about knowing the future? Was that supposed to be humorous?"

"Let me in and I promise, no bad jokes." He hadn't worked out what to say beyond whatever was necessary to get inside. If he was serious, however, he needed to explain something so fantastic he hardly blamed her for considering it an insult to her intelligence.

She stepped back and allowed him to pass. But after their fight she was too overwrought to sleep. After writing for an hour she'd pulled out a Tarot deck and begun a reading. He noticed the cards spread out on the floor, arranged in a cross with another line beside it. The illustrations were similar to a deck he'd seen in Sedona. He considered it another do-it-yourself fairy tale machine, much like popular astrology. It seemed so out of character for her.

"All right, let's hear it," she demanded. "How did you know what I said in the Chamber last July? Are you a spy?"

"No, I'm not part of any government. I have a business in the States." How to put it? "And we have invented a process, a technology that allows information, objects, even human beings to be transported long distances, wirelessly and almost instantly." She was listening but still skeptical. There was no turning back, he realized, and plunged on.

"I know how this sounds, a bit absurd, impossible. But why would I say it, knowing I run the risk of losing you forever, unless it was true?"

"Because you're insane or a sadist."

"I know," he sank to the floor. "I don't blame you. Look, something happened tonight after I left here, many things really. But the one – someone died, someone close."

Annie instantly dropped her facade and took his hand. "Who? What happened?"

"A woman, a close friend, a lover once upon a time." He took a deep breath, then let it all out. "I treated her badly the last time we spoke and now she's gone. It's my fault and nothing I can do will bring her back. I can't let that happen to us. I won't."

She stared into his eyes as her own softened in the candle light.

"My father is a powerful man, a corrupt and dangerous man. He made it possible for me to run the business. And that led me here, to you. I've been following your work, but not as a spy or stalker, as a fan.

I've read articles and watched you challenge the British establishment, and win. Who wouldn't be impressed?"

She blushed at the praise. "All right, enough. You said you knew my future. What did that blather mean?"

"Isn't it possible? Remember at Beatrice Potter's, that day we met. Life has more to tell us, you said it yourself. Mysteries and complexities we haven't unraveled. And doesn't Blavatsky talk about realms beyond this one? Yes, I've seen aspects of the future, glimpses. You could even say I live there most of the time. But I choose to be here."

"So you're not a total lunatic or spy for the Special Branch?"

"No, but there is a plot brewing. I was telling the truth about that. They're exploiting the Ripper murders to turn the panic and resentment against Jews, immigrants and people like you."

"What's a Ripper?"

"It's a phrase they'll use to sell papers. They'll call him Jack the Ripper. I've been looking into this, and first of all, his name isn't even Jack, it's Frank. But the main thing is that he is living here in plain sight, an American huckster who claims to be a surgeon."

"And you know this how?"

This would be the hard part, explaining a technology so far beyond anything she had experienced or even imagined. Filmmaking was just being invented and H.G. Wells hadn't imagined *The Time Machine.* She probably knew about the phonograph, which Thomas Edison had demonstrated that June in New Jersey, and she understood that many more world-shattering inventions lay ahead. This very day in Jersey, Edison had started work on a motion picture camera. A week from now another inventor, a transplanted Frenchman called Louis LePrince, would create the first moving images in Leeds using Eastman celluloid film and his own single-lens device.

"My company invented a machine that records and replays moving images," he offered.

"Like Mr. Muybridge and his horse?"

"Very like that, but much more developed. It will revolutionize the way we see one another, at least we think so. But I don't care about any of that nearly as much as I care for you."

"You've made the case," Annie sniffled. "Just no more lies."

He had left things out, of course, but at least he'd made a start.

She insisted it was not fortune-telling. Instead, she described Tarot as an exercise in symbolic recognition, metaphorical thinking and synchronicity. Gypsies claimed the practice began in Egypt and Israel and then moved on to Greece. The Gnostics drew from a similar system, she said, but most of them were exterminated during the Crusades and Inquisition. Similar symbolic illustrations were linked to the Jewish Kabalah and Freemasons.

By the fourteenth century an astrologer and Kabalist had developed a deck for the amusement of King Charles VI in France. In England Edward IV banned their import, but decks were smuggled in and found their way into many noble houses, where readings became a popular, though illegal and hidden vice until after the French Revolution. Just two years ago the Hermetic Order of the Golden Dawn had set up shop in London and sparked the latest revival.

She laid out four cards and asked him to select one. "Pick the one that best represents you. Then ask a question." The cards she displayed were knights, each one different. One brandished a sword, a dashing, aggressive young man who seemed more like what he had been in the past than what he hoped to become. The next, holding a large goblet, looked like a dreamy fellow, a bit passive for his taste. That left a blonde knight holding a wooden staff and a darker one gazing at a coin. The first looked energetic but restless, which left the more pensive Knight of Pentacles.

"He has the right look," she agreed, "more patient and trustworthy perhaps. You don't need to discuss your question, just keep it in mind. That will give the images a context. Ready?" He nodded. "Now very gently, shuffle the deck." As he did so she explained that what he saw in the cards would depend, to some extent, on his mood.

"I'd call it hopeful, but vigilant," he injected. "Where I grew up that was known as waiting for the other shoe to drop."

She had trouble seeing the analogy."Now, when it feels right just stop and cut the deck into three piles." Once he'd done that she reassembled it, retrieving the piles in the same order. "Now the exciting part."

One at a time, she turned ten cards and arranged them, providing commentary along the way. "So, what covers you, the general atmosphere you could say, is this one, the Queen of Cups. Recognize her?" Dressed in blue and holding a lantern, he had to admit she looked a lot like Athena.

The next was the King of Swords. "The opposing force," Annie explained as she placed that card across and on top. "A family dynamic perhaps?" This King didn't look much like Shelley; he was a noble figure surveying his domain from a monolithic throne. And yet there was no doubt who it was. Next was The High Priestess, a card that didn't match any of the four suits. "These are known as Major Arcana, a series of illustrations representing principles and elements in nature. We see them in dreams and art, symbolic projections of the collective imagination. The Priestess is the daughter of the Moon, you see that. She's the eternal feminine, Isis, Eve before Adam, the power of creation, and the link between what's seen and unseen."

It sounded like the perfect woman, the woman of his dreams, Annie.

"This is beneath," she said, "something that already has been part of your experience. And this" – the next card was The Fool – "is behind you."

He judged himself foolish in many respects. "It sounds harsh," Annie admitted, "but he's more of a dreamer than an idiot, someone who wants to accomplish things but simply may not have the experience or make the right choices. Do you see the little dog at his heel? It's a wolf actually, evolving, which suggests the idea that lower life forms can improve. And those mountains in the distance, they look cold, like abstract principles that can dominate our lives."

"But that's all past."

"Waning influences, yes. But next we see what's above you, what may lie ahead." She turned over and placed the Four of Swords, a grim image, bleached of color. The sole figure was a man on a slab. "Don't worry," she said, "he's not dead, just resting. There may have been some strife before this, but now he's away from that. And things will improve."

"Where do you see that?"

"There, light coming in through the church window. He's in a sanctuary, safe."

"What's next?"

"The future, what lies ahead." She picked up the card and placed it. The number was XVI, another member of the Major Arcana. The title read The Tower and it portrayed a terrible spectacle. The central image was a tall structure, engulfed in flames and surrounded by clouds in a black sky, being struck by lightning. A golden crown fell from the building's peak, as did two figures, a man and woman screaming in terror.

"That's the future? Forget about it!"

"No, just what you may have to face. What do you see?"

"The end, Armageddon. I knew it."

She put the cards aside and turned to him. "What's happening? Tell me."

Tonio picked up The Tower and stared at it. "It's coming apart. That's her, Angel. For all I know the other one could be Danny, or me. It was selfish to come here, to take the risk."

"I don't understand."

"I know. What else?" He dried his eyes.

"Four more, fears, the influences around you, and then your hopes and the outcome. All right? I don't know the question but this one is supposed to represent your negative feelings about it." She turned over the card. More swords, nine lining the wall above a figure in bed, clearly in mourning.

"Jesus, give me a break."

"It's a woman if you look close, but the meaning is obvious. It deals with doubt, loss, even the death of someone you care about."

The next card was the opposite, a naked dancing figure floating effortlessly in a clear blue sky surrounded by a thick green wreath. It was called The World. At the corners of the card were four heads – a man, an eagle, a bull and a lion. "They represent the elements," she explained. This is about your surroundings, your friends and family. I would call that positive.

"And next come hopes." She turned over the card to reveal number VI in the Major Arcana, The Lovers. "At the top is Raphael, angel of the air, offering a benediction to the two figures below. And there, a serpent winds around a tree; that's temptation, always present." But he was focused on the lovers themselves. They gazed at each other, naked with nothing to hide. That was certainly his hope.

"I know what you're thinking," she teased. "We'll get to that. But this is about choices, attraction, and the struggle between the sacred and profane. Just one more."

The last card felt anti-climactic, the image of a lonely figure holding a long staff as he glanced at eight more lined up behind him. He didn't seem to look forward to whatever he had to do. Tonio needed an explanation.

"It's the outcome of your question," she said, "at least for now. You see his head is bandaged, and his arm. He's been in a battle, and the wooden staffs, called wands, could be a boundary he's protecting. But he's also getting ready, summoning all his strength for the fight ahead. It's about staying the course, sticking with it to the end."

"I'm exhausted," he admitted, stretching out on the floor. She joined him there, her head beside his, her body pointing in the opposite direction.

"There seem to be obstacles," she whispered sweetly. "Did you get some answers?"

"Not ones I wanted. You know I can't stay."

"I think I understand: responsibility, things left behind. But how soon?"

He turned toward her, "This morning." Reaching out he cupped her head gently in his hand and moved closer for a long kiss.

"Then we've no time to lose," she answered once their lips parted. "There are quite a few chapters left to study."

42
Overexposure

Annie was asleep when he tip-toed to the sitting room and retrieved Shaw's loaner outfit to dress and leave. If she woke before he was out the door he might not be able to do it. There was no way to know whether he would ever see her again, and he couldn't bear to admit it.

The government wasn't the only thing worrying him. Everything he'd done since last week, since choosing to experience rather than witness the past, was having profound, unintended consequences. It might look to others like nothing was altered. But they were mistaken, uninformed. Lynch had told him. From the moment he dropped into that East End alley his presence had changed things, while his absence altered lives in the here and now.

Once back in the control room, he found Danny impatient, eager to get home and uneasy about the request that he not monitor the stream. It made Tonio uncomfortable to know that, while he shared secrets or made love, someone might be watching on a computer screen. It felt like an invasion.

"Can we go now?" Danny pleaded.

Tonio thanked him and collapsed onto the closest couch. "You go. I should stay. We may be liberated, but those eyes in the sky are still watching and I'm not ready to let Shelley know where I am yet."

They checked the security cameras. Outside, the van and DARCAP unit hadn't moved. As Danny shut down the system Tonio briefed him on what had been worked out with Harry. A four day lead should be enough time to find a safe place, reach out to Angel, and fast track a set of bombshells designed to expose and discredit Wolfe Enterprises. Once alone he took a long shower and caught up on the news. It was the usual – polarization and gamesmanship, violence and unrest, the endless litany of conflict and disaster. Odd weather events were making news. Overall, the recent elections appeared to have changed little, but the weight of climate science was starting to have an impact on public opinion.

He went over the guidelines Lynch had outlined, matched them with Danny's checklist, and considered where that left them. Barring future federal restrictions, there was no threat to TELPORT's plans for release of the Visors next year. That was for the market to decide. Lynch also mentioned nothing about RTV, which suggested that they could eventually reveal that discovery to the world. The question was how to use and package it.

An idea had occurred to him on that first night in London. If nothing else, RTV recordings of their murder investigation, and particularly the visual proof that Frank Tumblety was responsible, would make one hell of a documentary. In fact, what was to stop them from producing more? Solving real crimes, revisiting crucial moments in history, this could be powerful stuff. It would make History Channel programming look even more like speculative fiction than it already did.

In the meantime, though, it was sit tight and stay indoors until Harry's bombshells began to fall.

MARCH 7, 2013
FOR IMMEDIATE RELEASE

Truthsquad says Basta Ya! Next doc dump on the way
Truthsquad builds on the pioneering work of Wikileaks, bringing scientific journalism to a world adrift in manufactured realities. Joining forces with friendly media outlets, over the next days we will release important revelations -- along with

indisputable proof that they are true – beginning with a series of document packages that focus on surveillance, blackmail and human trafficking by government-linked corporate interests.

We don't ask you to accept our version of these events on faith. Scientific journalism means you can read a news account and then click to see the original documents on which the story is based. This is true transparency!

So, decide for yourself. Is it true? And was it reported accurately?

For democracy to survive we need strong, independent media. We are part of a grassroots movement to keep both the government and media honest. That means revealing hard truths about the surveillance state, gangster capitalism and the modern scourge of human slavery.

Truthsquad is not a pacifist organization. We believe that sometimes people must defend themselves to remain free. We also believe that the biggest threat to freedom is powerful interests that lie to the people, secretive elites that ask the vast majority of us to sacrifice and die while they profit and exploit the poor, entire countries and the environment.

The best weapons we have in response are truth and the power of our ideas. If another war in the Middle East or a pipeline across the country is such a great idea, tell the whole story and let the people decide.

Truthsquad isn't the sole publisher of the material we will distribute. We work with many media outlets around the world, including The Guardian, New York Times, El Pais, De Spiegel, Rose Media, and community TV and radio stations across the country.

We've done the digging; the next step is up to you. Nothing is inevitable.

–Truthsquad Collective

The straight media didn't know what to make of the announcement.

Cable TV ran it as part of the political sideshow with little comment. But the next morning, under a bold headline shouting BASTA YA!, came the release of several thousand pages of cables, e-mails and memos linking Wolfe Enterprises – and Senoslav Wolfe personally – to forced prostitution and human smuggling in Croatia.

"Cables Link Casino Mogul to Human Trafficking," announced *The New York Times*, which had defended him only months earlier for supporting private space exploration in response to mission retrenchment at NASA. How easy it was for the media's talking heads to throw Shelley under a PR bus from hell.

Tonio watched the storm of outrage build, from shocked morning chat show hosts and a grim expose on Democracy Now! to devastating mid-day headline summaries and updates with unattractive file photos of Shelley before cosmetic surgery. The documents established that the State Department was aware that WE – an abbreviation used interchangeably for Shelley and the company – was a major player on the Balkan route, implicated in smuggling cars, commodities and people. In memos public officials expressed the pragmatic view of WE as a "necessary evil," a useful back channel liaison with the Croatian regime.

Still, the point of the dump was larger than a single man or company. It exposed the global scale of the problem – a vast international network engaged in a modern slave trade – as well as the fact that the US and other governments did little and largely looked the other way.

No response was issued by Shelley, his corporate offices or the federal government. Whatever they felt, the pressure wasn't intense enough yet. But public outrage was beginning to build. Not even the usual wing nuts leapt to his defense.

On the following Monday, the Collective followed up with a package nailing the involvement of Wolfe Enterprises in private surveillance, using PIA and satellites to conduct industrial espionage. Memos and reports indicated that WE had joint agreements with several federal agencies for the development of advanced surveillance and sub-space aircraft. In fact, it was subcontracting with DARPA on a wide-angle space surveillance telescope system that was expected to provide a 360 degree view of the sky around the Earth from a single computer screen. It would make possible the tracking of any object orbiting the planet.

The same package showed that the Pentagon was outsourcing key elements of national defense to private firms like WE in the attempt to create a global surveillance system on the cheap. The goal was the ability to watch every inch of space, the sky and the planet's surface. A space telescope system was one piece of a larger plan that featured cyber-data mining and biometric monitoring at the street level.

Civil libertarians joined the far right in condemning the developments. The public was shocked to learn that, despite talk about austerity and the need to reduce the debt and cut entitlements, billions were being funneled to private enterprises for a scheme to drastically increase questionable surveillance without public oversight. What's worse, most of this had little to do with national defense or fighting terrorism. Instead, the memos speculated about trade and the long-term economic threat posed by China's rise. One Undersecretary called the plan "an equalizer" and an "insurance policy against decline."

A note on State Department stationery was clear about the domestic implications: "Someday we may need it for crowd control."

Wolfe Enterprises issued a terse statement indicating that the reports were distorted, no laws were being violated, and Truthsquad was a terrorist organization distributing false propaganda with the goal of fomenting insurrection. It urged criminal prosecution of those who released the material. This indicated that Shelley was beginning to sweat, or possibly that some rats were abandoning ship.

It was time to call home. "How's it hanging, pops," Tonio snapped when Shelley came to the phone. He was steaming but quiet, fighting to maintain a slow burn.

"Where you been?" said the Don. "In Vermont I hear."

"And elsewhere. You know I enjoy spontaneity. I heard you were looking for me."

"Yeah."

"So, you want to see the thing, what we can do?"

"Yeah." The old man wasn't giving him anything, holding his cards close. Or else now he was the one concerned about being overheard.

"When?"

"Friday. We're having a fundraiser at the museum. Let's meet there, before." At first Tonio wasn't certain where he meant, that is, until Shelley added, "Where we met last year, the Tesla place." Then he understood completely; of course it was! "You remember, your friend got me into it, although I already knew about Mr. Tesla. Every Croat does, he's our blood. I'll have Paulie pick you up."

"Are you surviving your fifteen minutes?" Tonio couldn't resist a small poke.

"They got nothing," the Don scoffed. "Commie weasels. I just hope they step foot in Arizona. I'll have Sheriff Joe hunt them down and nail their hides on the door of the Phoenix Police Headquarters. Personal friend, you know. I'm seriously thinking about moving there."

"Right, see you Friday," Tonio said, shining him on as he thought, "Wow! He's ready to blow."

The last dump came two days before they were scheduled to meet. It was so unexpected that Harry contacted him the night before with a heads up. He called it "The Starfucker." The essence was that, in parallel with its contract work with the government and employing much of the same technology, WE also conducted private surveillance, with a special focus on patrons and talent at its casino properties. Along with an

FBI report came links to embarrassing videos, apparently recorded for purposes of extortion, including one in which movie star Maximilian Libra has sex with two under-age prostitutes in a Wolfe-owned hotel in Bangkok. The documents left the distinct impression that tapes may have been used as leverage to secure favorable contracts with marqee acts.

MAX XXX! *The New York Post* declared. The A-list star wasn't "available" for comment, the story said, but through a publicist he denied being blackmailed and protested that he didn't know the girls were thirteen and fourteen at the time. Coverage on Examiner.com added a further wrinkle.

"Momentum" Star Caught with Thai Twins

LOS ANGELES — Attorneys for Max Libra, star of the recent political blockbuster "Momentum II," said the actor will likely comment early next week on allegations he had sex with two underage girls in a Far East hotel last year.

Graham Perkins, attorney for Libra, said that he expects his client to say that the sex was consensual and dispute the age of the women. Libra, 27, has not spoken publicly about the allegations, which were revealed in documents released on the internet yesterday by an anonymous political group.

The New York Post has reported that although the Internet site hosting the video has been taken down copies can be purchased for up to $2000. One Los Angeles nightspot plans to screen it.

On the video a young man who looks like the star engages in multiple sexual acts with the two young women.

Libra's next project is expected to be a bio-picture about the life of inventor Nikola Tesla.

That night the scandal made the leap to network comedy and *The Daily Show*. Max was the latest celebrity screw up, but Shelley came off much worse. He blew up like a digital John Gotti or Al Capone, his legitimate façade melting away to expose a rogue empire built on vulture capitalist tactics, sexual exploitation and high-profile extortion. Overnight he became a punch line.

After David Letterman compared Shelley with Jabba the Hut, the slobbering *Star Wars* villain, Athena called Tonio around midnight. They hadn't spoken since the fight in December. But she was upset for a different reason and said, "He has his flaws but he doesn't deserve this." The five-day barrage of negative publicity had evidently drawn her sympathy. He wanted to tell her that it wasn't merely fair; he had helped make it happen. From past experience, however, he knew that was contra-indicated. She just couldn't be trusted to keep such a confidence.

More unsettling was the news she had flown East for Shelley's gala on Long Island. Clever move, he thought. The old man was circling his wagons, creating a media event at which he could present himself in the most favorable light, as a selfless philanthropist and family man surrounded by friends and supporters. Could such a person be an international pimp and corporate pirate?

"Ryan has been asking after you," she told him. "He asked whether you've been practicing."

"Not enough, tell him. Do you know what he means?"

"No, but I trust both of you. He also said he's sending someone your way."

"Did he say who?"

She didn't know. But the call led to questions like, was the impact on Shelley as serious as she feared -- or he hoped? Was the big bad wolf truly getting nervous, and could he focus enough for a closer look? In Arizona Tonio had generated enough energy and will to travel across distance and time, to imagine a place and then see it clearly. But that was near a vortex, which seemed to amplify his ability. In London he hadn't noticed someone stalking him at close range.

Eyes closed, sitting comfortably on a thick cushion, he waited until a speck appeared in the dark, then cracked in half and split into dozens, then hundreds, then thousands of smaller pinpoints. At this juncture the difficult transition was deciding which pinpoint to choose. It took him several attempts before he vaguely sensed Wood-Ridge and Shelley's man-cave.

Inside he found his father, flipping channels compulsively on his home theater. Conon O'Brien called him Noriega without the style. Jon Stewart had him on a list of Super-Teflon Douchebags, meaning he was one of the country's newest STDs. Shelley turned to Paulie, his faithful soldier, T's lost old friend. "You know who did this," he said with disgust, "and you know what you have to do."

For the first time Tonio could hear the words.

43
The Tower

"Let me tell you once more. I have perfected the greatest invention of all time – the transmission of electrical energy without wires to any distance, a work which has consumed ten years of my life. It is the long sought stone of the philosophers. I need but to complete the plant I have constructed and in one bound, humanity will advance centuries..."
-Tesla letter to Morgan, February 17, 1905

MARCH 15, 2013

When Nikola Tesla relocated his lab from Manhattan to Shoreham in 1902 the area was mainly open fields, just a few miles from an idyllic beach at Wading River on the Sound. Prior to the move he had worked on Houston Street, waiting for Stanford White to finish his red brick industrial cathedral of science. It was an elegant structure considering the function, with large arched windows along the front and a tall chimney at the center topped by an elegant wind vane.

Inside there was generous space for various workshops and machines, electric transformers, generators, spiral coils, a two-phase dynamo and a glass-blowing area, a remote control "telautomaton" called the Egg of Columbus and the Static Eliminator – a radio-frequency transformer, plus a research library and an office for the genius. Below the building, a conduit for the electric and hydraulic mains ran to the eighteen-story Wardenclyffe tower.

Past the spiral staircase a network of catacombs extended in several directions. Iron pipes called terrestrial grippers went down hundreds of feet further, increasing the length of the aerial and the tower's potential to transmit energy through the ground. Tesla said the tower's height and ability to radiate electrical oscillations would resonate with the natural properties of the Earth. A huge coil was calibrated to work with the wavelength of light, driving a tremendous charge into the ground and out through the iron spokes. The resulting harmonic pulse tapped a tremendous source of power, modulating and even increasing it, and creating stationary waves. At the top of the tower, a 50 foot iron and steel cupola, with hundreds of nodal points, stored and distributed the electrical charges, linked to large condensers behind the lab.

The structure was designed by a Stanford White associate and named for James Warden, a banker who had faith enough to donate the land and plan Wardenclyffe-On-Sound, a resort inspired by Telsa's vision of a "radio city" that would rise once his discoveries took hold. By the time the tower neared completion in 1903, J. P. Morgan and J. J. Astor, among others, had invested the equivalent of $3 million in the project. But Morgan became disenchanted. Marconi had jumped ahead on the next commercial breakthrough – wireless communication.

Tesla claimed to be near the ability to turn A.C. current – in competition with Edison's D.C. – into electromagnetic waves that traveled instantly from an antenna to a distant receiver. The future would be "pictures and words without wires," he promised, and even greater things were possible. In a letter to Morgan he predicted that Wardenclyffe and other towers would one day transmit not just information but cheap, abundant energy.

He had miscalculated, however. As one of Tesla's biographers, Margaret Cheney, put it, the prospect of sharing inexpensive electricity with penniless Zulus or Pygmies wasn't at all attractive to the corporate titan. After all, where was the profit? Where would the meters go?

Morgan's response was a slow, painful brush off. As he explained in one letter, "I should not feel disposed to make any further advances." His vision was a giant corporate monopoly that controlled the price and distribution of energy, not Tesla's pipe dream of a radically reorganized energy system in which abundant power could be tapped by anyone with a small receiver. Even Tesla's promise of wireless transmission was a threat to Morgan and partners like Bernard Baruch and the Guggenheim brothers, who had just bought the Utah Copper Company with plans for a $100 million a year business based on wiring the nation. Nikola Tesla had become a threat to corporate investments on several fronts.

Emotionally battered and financially under the gun, the inventor threw caution to the wind one night and tested his tower. What happened remains in dispute. But some witnesses claimed to hear a dull thunder rumble and see bolts of electricity streaming into the night sky, streaks and flashes that "seemed to shoot off into the darkness," in the words of *The New York Sun*. Reports came in from various homes along the Connecticut shore.

Years later, some researchers still insisted that the experiment failed, suggesting that Tesla hadn't anticipated problems like dissipation, the diminution of energy as it travels. Others admitted that he might well have found the key to transmitting information, but surely not energy. The wide shaft below the tower meanwhile fed rumors about the subterranean tunnels and passages. In the eyes of the world the genius had become a "mad scientist."

Subsequent decades were tough on the site. After Tesla's patents for A.C. and other forms of transmission expired, the loss of royalties made continued work on the tower difficult. Design of a turbine and commercial production of distinctive Tesla coils weren't enough to cover the mounting bills. Research stopped and layoffs began. Newspapers christened Wardenclyffe a "million-dollar folly," and by 1911 the property was abandoned.

Six years later, in the midst of World War I, new owners blew up the crumbling skeleton and sold the remains for scrap. The orders had come down from the federal government, which cited the risk that German spies might use the looming structure as a landmark for submarine attacks.

The lab was shuttered until the eve of World War II, when it was leased to Peerless Photo. After the war AGFA bought the property from Peerless and continued to use the main building for photo work. By the time it was closed in 1992 much of the site had been seriously contaminated with silver and cadmium. The cleanup cost $5 million.

Significant strides had been made since Tonio's first visit. Shelley spared no expense in the run up to his fundraiser for the proposed museum. The traditional entrance was open, the long drive leading to the lab recreated with a layer of fresh gravel. The enormous arched windows, one of White's distinctive touches, were restored and freshly painted.

Off to the side down a path off the temporary parking area stood a new Tesla tower, not as tall as the original but an impressive facsimile and a fitting memorial. The festivities would kick off later with the unveiling of an exhibit in a small renovated section of the neglected building. The program for the following week featured a panel discussion and screening of the 1977 Yugoslavian TV series, *The Genius Who Lit the World*, starring a young Rade Serbedzija as Tesla.

Another highlight was expected to be the premier of a restored print of *The Secret of Nikola Tesla*, the state-sponsored Yugoslavian film made a few years after *The Genius*, starring Demeter Bitenc, with Orson Welles in the role of J. P. Morgan. The script read as if President

Tito participated personally in writing the dialogue. Decades past his early acclaim with *Citizen Kane,* Welles accepted the part for two basic reasons: a paycheck and Oda Kodar, his muse and partner since the sixties.

A native of Zagreb, Kodar considered Tesla not just a visionary – much like Welles – but a national Croatian treasure. In the film she played Katherine Johnson, wife of *Century Magazine* editor Robert Johnson, a frustrated artist and drama queen who considered Tesla a mesmerizing, world-historical figure. More to the point, she was apparently one of few women beside Tesla's mother who could hold his interest for very long. An item in *Variety* said Kodar might attend.

Ignored in the US after its original release, *The Secret* was an ambitious failure that eventually developed a cult following and won the International UFO Congress Film Festival. The most effective aspects were its compelling visuals, convincing recreations and several revealing moments between Morgan, Tesla and Edison. But other scenes were awkward and the hero came off as remote and inscrutable, a scientific soothsayer incapable of making the world understand his prescient warnings about pollution and far-sighted philosophy of a science that worked in harmony with nature.

Whatever the truth, Tonio didn't miss the irony of Tesla's legacy being restored by Shelley Wolfe, the kind of person who once condemned it to obscurity. Tesla dedicated his life to science for the benefit of humanity. He opened the door to hydroelectric power, remote control, radar tracking, x-rays, television, radio and the Internet, right down to the remote viewing technology TELPORT had developed. But Morgan viewed his discoveries as a threat, capable of unleashing forces he might not be able to exploit. Without his patronage it became clear that other investors would withdraw and the ideas being tested at Wardenclyffe would never reach the market.

In the corporate world, Morgan's decision was essentially an economic death sentence.

Tonio thought about Tesla and the weather as they drove, another summer in March, more off the chart evidence of climate change. There wasn't much disagreement on the state of the planet: the huge departures from normal temperature ranges meant that the ground rules for discussion had finally changed. Only the responses hadn't.

Paulie was at the wheel and saying little. Tonio knew why. He was struggling with his assignment; it wasn't necessarily to kill him, but Tonio was obviously the one being blamed for the family's current troubles. Nevertheless, his instinct was that, whatever Shelley ultimately had in mind for him, it wouldn't come today, not until he knew more and had everything he wanted.

Danny was in New Jersey and Harry was in Vermont. However, they'd been conferring for almost a week to ready the demo. It was a surgical "This is Your Life" recap of Shelley's rise to power, a tale of murder and betrayal. Peter Lynch had made good on his promise to assist by offering a series of dates and locations.

Most of the original interior of Telsa's lab hadn't been touched, except to remove graffiti and debris. However, a huge tent filled one end of the building, decorated to suggest a turn-of-the-century auditorium complete with hanging chandeliers and "Tesla Power" exhibition. Shelley was reviewing cues with the technical director and crew members hired to handle sound, lights and effects.

Tonio took a seat below the stage and enjoyed the wait. It was like watching a dress rehearsal for the induction ceremonies into the Narcissist's Hall of Fame.

"You gotta see this," Shelley shouted from the podium, motioning for him to follow out the back of the tent and up a steel staircase to the second level. It was dark until Shelley grabbed a dangling control panel and switched on the power. Spotlights splayed across four metal tanks, each as big as a compact car. The riveted seams made them look antique subs.

"Batteries," Shelley announced, "and up there, the hatch to service them. But the thing is, nobody can tell me what the fuck they're for." He patted one of the tanks. "But I hear now we can go back and find out. Is that it?"

"That's the general idea, but we're working the bugs out."

"Bugs," he sniffed, "so you say. Your girl told me otherwise."

"Yeah, I hear you talked with Angel before she died. What happened with that?" He wasn't ready yet to show his cards or betray his real suspicion.

"Tragic." Shelley waved away the question. "We'll get to it. First, I want you to hear something. You need to appreciate what's happening here – this is a national reclamation project. They robbed this man, and by doing that they stole from our people, our whole country. They stole his life's work, his place in history, and then they whacked him."

As Shelley continued Tonio realized two things: even Danny didn't have some of these details, and Tesla's accomplishments (and apparently stolen glory) were much more important and personal matters to his father than he had ever imagined. As the Don described it, Tesla's last decade was a matter of vast speculation – but he had reached his own dark conclusions.

He began with what many others insisted, the idea that the inventor became mentally ill at the end. Psychologically destroyed by the collapse of his dream, Tesla supposedly sank into permanent debt and spent his remaining years living alone on the 33rd floor of the New Yorker Hotel. There was some evidence for this version. Always reclusive, Tesla never married and, according to some accounts, may have had Obsessive Compulsive Disorder for most of his life. One of the obsessions was reportedly the number three and its various multiples.

In this version Tesla spent many of his final days behind the New York Public Library feeding pigeons, his only friends at the end, while babbling about signals from distant worlds and a death ray that employed concentrated energy. It was the mad scientist story taken to the max.

But there was another scenario. In that one, the one Shelley preferred, Tesla wasn't crazy or depressed and continued working with various businesses and agencies until the end of his life. In the late 1920s, for instance, he'd worked for U.S. Steel on equipment to purify ore and conserve sulphur during processing. Later, in Buffalo, he allegedly refitted a Pierce Arrow to run with electric power. When scientists at the Carnegie Institution began attempting to split the atom they used a Tesla coil. At the end he had begun writing about cosmic rays.

A year after the US entered World War II Tesla reportedly shared some of his latest discoveries with two unidentified representatives of the federal government, Shelley claimed. The work supposedly involved stealth technology, instantaneous transmission of information and a particle beam weapon. Tesla, Einstein and John von Neumann had been investigating related ideas for a decade, according to his father. But Tesla and von Neumann disagreed about the dangers involved in the tests being proposed.

Tesla's assistant George Scherff visited the inventor for the last time on January 4, 1943. Four days later he was found dead in his apartment. Was he murdered? Shelley couldn't prove it yet, but he intended to find out with TELPORT's Telsa-inspired technology.

"They said they weren't interested in him," he rolled on, "that he was crazy, a loser. But then explain this: two days after the body was found his apartment was raided by the Office of Alien Property, on orders from Hoover's FBI. They claimed he had ties to arms merchants, Communists and the Germans. This crazy guy, this pigeon-feeding loser who didn't interest them at all, was supposed to have documents in his possession that were so sensitive to national security they had to be seized and hidden forever. Are you kidding me? They took everything. That's why we don't know what the fuck these tanks do."

He led Tonio to an elevator shaft and called for the car.

"So, you think the government killed him?"

"It's possible. But it also could have been the Nazis. That's what we'll find out. They had agents in the country. My people say it could have been planned by Otto Skorzeny. He was one of Hitler's favorites, a Waffen-SS colonel who led Operation Greif, some kind of infiltration gang. After the war the CIA set him up with a new identity. He probably used this guy Reinhard Gehlen for the hit. One source says Gehlen definitely spoke with Tesla just days before he died. He also may have stolen stuff from the safe. Most likely the old guy was suffocated, which was harder to catch in those days.

"What we know is that less than a year after Tesla died the US hid a Navy destroyer with some sort of stealth technology, they called it cloaking then. The Philadelphia Experiment – that's what happened with just one of his discoveries, and it was just the beginning."

The elevator brought them past the ground floor to a sub-basement thirty feet beneath the surface. Many of the legends were true, he was realizing.

"You should look at this as a restoration," the Don advised. "We're taking back what was stolen. I know what they say; In Belgrade he's a Serb, in Croatia he's Croat. But one thing I know for sure: Nikola Tesla was born in Smiljan in Lika province, the same place our people live to this day. He's our brother, our own blood. Our family, and many others, invested in his work. We have a claim.

"You know, I saw his birthplace once; they put up a memorial after the war. It was inspiring." He sighed and remembered. "You know, to know anything is possible."

The elevator shaft opened onto the junction of several round concrete corridors. Shelley led the way to a hurricane door at the end of one and knocked. Paulie was already inside with Pesci and Ray-Ray. It was a soundproof, temperature controlled bunker cut off from the world.

"Webster says you can do it from here." Ray-Ray pointed to a box marked with TELPORT's vortex logo. "He sent you a present." Opening it he distributed visors and handed Tonio a pre-programmed Locator.

"I just wish you'd been honest," Shelley lamented. "Maybe I should have been more straight about all this." The drift of the conversation already made Tonio nervous, while the bunker triggered his latent claustrophobia. He might not be so safe after all. He was probably the only one not carrying a gun.

"I wasn't completely in the dark when that jerk came to the casino," Shelley explained. "We already knew who he was, and the connection between his research and brother Tesla. It was related to what I'd been putting together, the land, the investments in aerospace, the satellites. But this Webster had a line to some missing pieces. Then he told me about this place and – what did he call it – the diamagnetic grid spots, some shit like that. Anyway, I saw what he was into and he needed a lab in a specific location. This was one possibility, but it wasn't available and the place in Nutley was. Kid, I made it possible to buy that building and then you shut me out."

"I didn't know any of this."

"No, you didn't trust me and you showed no loyalty to the family. But this is even bigger than that. Add what you have going to what I've put together and Wolfe will be one of the biggest names on the planet in a few years. The Spaceport you know, and you've read about some of the other divisions."

"You mean the blackmail division, the selling little girls for sex division?"

"Very funny, I mean staying ahead of the curve and getting what's ours.

Whistleblowers can blow themselves. It's just envy. And I guarantee you, the future is public-private partnerships in almost every area of life, business and government sharing the load. Everybody knows this. There's no choice, they can't handle the freight, the security and innovation costs alone, and they shouldn't. We're stakeholders too. Plus, this is still a free country, and we're not doing anything other businesses haven't done for thousands of years. We're just doing it better."

He laid out a plan to make WE one of the top ten transnational companies, combining leisure community development with elite entertainment, space tourism, a global private security network providing services to governments, and use of remote time viewing in Wolfe theme parks and "educational" centers like the future Tesla museum to sell history in a radical new way. For a premium price patrons would be able to see great moments from the past unfold before their eyes.

"If you can do it in Nutley, we can do it here," he predicted. "This is also a grid point. We're going to own history, and everyone will pay to see it." Of course, he could also exploit it to his advantage in other ways. It was a powerful vision, vast, ambitious and dangerous. If it worked, Shelley Wolfe would decide which moments from history were suitable for public consumption, and which to bury or ignore. He might even attempt to assert a legal claim, making the argument that the stream projections were his intellectual property. As troubling as any popular delusions about humanity's past might be, this sounded worse – public perception of history shaped in part by a raving sociopath. And all of it rationalized by the bizarre belief that he was reclaiming Tesla's legacy on behalf of Croatia, a country he helped destroy to build his empire.

Shelley Wolfe had aced the psychopath test. He wasn't content to be a corporate titan like J.P. Morgan. His vision was even more grandiose and devilish – to be a Don of virtual space and time. Tonio couldn't help thinking of another tower, the one that had turned up in his reading with Annie.

"Now let's take a look at what you got," Shelley said.

Everyone but Tonio was startled when they put on the visors and the room was replaced by a holographic reproduction of suburban New Jersey in 1969. "We wanted you to know that this isn't CGI or a high-end recreation," he explained. "If they can make you believe anything these days, why not this, right? But this street, on this particular day, is special. You see that guy?"

From where they were observing, one house was directly across the street. A VW van had pulled in next to its driveway and a young man jumped out. His face immediately looked familiar, but only Tonio and his father immediately knew who it was – Shelley Wolfe at the age of twenty about to commit his first capital crime.

The visors made it look real except for the data that followed each of them at the periphery – time code, GPS coordinates, camera and satellite number, and recording source.

"Is that you, boss?" Paulie was amazed. "It is! Jesus and Mary!"

Tonio explained. "We can create a link with a live event occurring at almost any time in the past. But this is a recording, a clip we selected because of its personal meaning for dad. Right? For your entertainment, the Don's first kill."

Shelley watched with mounting unease as his younger self concealed a package the size of a shoe box beneath the front porch. It was early and the street was quiet. He checked twice to be sure no one saw him, then pressed a button on the remote control, checked the package and went back to the van.

"We don't have to wait long," Tonio narrated. "He's just driving down the block." The van stopped. They looked back at the house and waited.

After a moment Shelley stood and objected, "This is shit, pointless." He was about to launch into a rant when a powerful bomb exploded, just after a young boy opened the door to check on the noise. He vanished in the blast as pieces of him and the building sprayed in all directions.

"Blew your wad – but it made the point. Joe Russo never really recovered, his only kid blown up in front of his house. And the bomb was packed with roofing nails, which was technically a violation of mob rules. But you got the job done. Russo resigned from the union leadership."

"And here you are with grandpa near the end. This is not as dramatic or visual, but it's certainly meaningful. And it shows that we can potentially pinpoint and watch even the most personal moments." The location was the Bayside home of Roman Wolfe in 1977, shortly after the stroke that eventually killed him.

"We don't need to see this," Shelley protested, returning to his seat. "I get your point. It's a fucking miracle, just what we need."

"But you should see everything, all the apps," Tonio insisted. "Specific words can be difficult to capture, especially words we don't want others to hear. It took time to find this gem, but it's a keeper."

The clip picked up in Roman's bedroom. The old Don was lying in bed as a thirty-three year old Shelley stood at the window. "Now what? G wants no part of this and you never give me a real shot or share the important shit."

The old man could barely speak, straining to lift a hand as his eyes widened.

"Always Georgie and Alek the wonderboys, all the cream for them. What made them so special? Were they more loyal, more determined? Well, I'm here to tell you they skimmed too, and dealt on the side, with no tribute. So I was justified."

Roman's expression suggested he understood what Shelley had just admitted; that he was behind the airplane crash that killed his brothers and showed not a shred of remorse. Then again, the shocked look might also have been a fleeting recognition of his own approaching death. Tonio had to wonder what Paulie and the others made of all this.

"That's enough." Shelley was on his feet again, this time heading for the door. "Open this frigging tomb."

"One more clip, so you see the full potential. You guys would enjoy one more, right?"

The crew had no idea how to respond.

"Do it quick," Shelley barked. "I got people waiting."

Tonio stepped into the middle of the projection and froze it. This was the main event, the moment to confront Shelley about Gianni's death. Lynch had provided a date and the approximate time of the last meeting between the brothers. The visors went to black and then filled with light. The GPS and time code said they were in the park where Gianni Wolfe would drop dead a week later. He and Shelley were in the midst of an argument. After waiting a few seconds for orientation Tonio hit play.

"I should break your fucking legs for Athena," shouted Shelley.

"She was lonely, and you have your whores. But you have a right to do whatever you want for that. It doesn't matter now. I'm gone, out of here, finished with all of it."

"And Tony! You had no right."

"You said it yourself, the kid has gifts and these are the people who will know how to develop them. But I don't even know where that's going. To hell with the whole fucking system. Nixon called it the Beast, you know. But Reagan's plan, which is really Casey's plan, is over the line. It was bad enough when we were whacking heads of state like we were wiseguys. Now he arms people in every hell hole on Earth, just as long as they want to kill Commies, who usually turn out to be teachers, writers, aid workers. I can't do it anymore."

"They're worried about you," Shelley warned. "Unreliable is a word I hear, a risk factor."

"How do you know?"

"I make friends. These days I'm thinking maybe some of yours can become mine, now that they're not really your friends anymore. Where's the harm?"

Gianni suddenly grabbed his brother, lifted him like a child and tossed him several feet. "You're not turning DoD into another family piggy bank," he said.

"Touchy. It's just business, man." Shelley was shaken but undeterred.

"Screw business, I'm warning you. Hands off."

"And I'm warning you," Shelley replied just as adàmantly. "You fuck my wife, you hijack my kid, and then you got the balls to tell me how to wet my beak. I should definitely kill you for that."

Tonio froze the scene. "So, did you do it?"

"You little punk." Shelley pulled off his visors and advanced on his son. Tonio was prepared for a fight if it came to that. He hadn't brought a gun but he was carrying his knife. The Don stopped five feet away and glared into the lenses. "Grow some balls. Look at me."

Tonio removed the visors. "What?"

"They wanted him dead, the feds. Okay, I said what I said. Hell, I put the pill in his water bottle. But where did I get it, ask yourself that. PEP, that's what that Agency twerp called it. The Pulmonary Embolism Pill, a perfect cure for the upset government. His words, not mine. Your heart attacks you and no one knows better. They used it for years, probably still do."

"This is the real world, kid, life and death, winners and losers. It's always been that way and always will. Your girl knew the score. She came to me with big plans, to make her deal, her own agenda. Didn't think much of you, I have to say. Even after we dosed her, she wouldn't give it up, your View Room. Then I gave her some time alone with Ray-Ray and he expanded her horizons. I also have a tape of that little scene. Want to see it? She did, but I don't think she liked the camera angle. Afterward she did tell me about your operation to keep her close up from going public. Guess she didn't want to be one of America's sexiest home videos."

Tonio was beginning to understand why Angel might have stepped in front that train. At the moment he felt fully capable of murder, even if the price might be a bullet in his brain. It would almost be worth the risk to be sure Shelley was off the planet.

"But why is all this happening, ask yourself." Shelley turned his back to leave. "The show is over, morons, take those frigging things off." The crew obeyed, a bit surprised by the revelations. "They started it, not me, the agency or whoever killed the greatest mind of the last century. When they stole from Tesla they stole from all of us. All I'm doing is taking it back."

"And how much is enough?"

"No such thing. I need your business, kid. Owning history – that's key. It will definitely fill the seats at our parks and places like this for decades. Not to mention we can get the jump on any asshole stupid enough to get in the way."

Tonio shut down the stream and addressed everyone in the room. "Guys, there have to be limits, even for people like us. You know I'm no angel. But if I say I'll burn our thing down I'm not shitting you. I can and I will. You touch that company, Danny Webster or anyone on my team everything you saw tonight – and a whole lot worse – goes to every network and web portal in the country. You'll go viral, and not in a good way."

"And if I step off?" Shelley circled, weighing the reactions of his men.

"Then I go my way, you go yours, and we're on our own. And everything you saw tonight, everything we have, remains in an undisclosed location. We're a lot alike, I can cop to that. There's part of me that would like to get it over with right now, for Angel, for all of it, all your sick shit. But I'm growing up – a little late, I admit -- so I'll settle for watching you crash and burn, with any luck behind bars. But hey, look on the bright side, now I'm motivated."

"And if I tell Ray-Ray to kill you," he asked. "Ray, point your gun at the kid."

Ray-Ray aimed at Tonio's forehead with both hands. Before he could stop himself Pauli pulled his own weapon and trained it on Ray.

"What the fuck," Shelley objected, shocked, "put that away or point it in the right direction."

Paulie thought it over, turned the gun briefly toward Tonio, then over to Pesci and back at Ray. "This feels safer," he concluded. "Can we talk about it?" He lowered the weapon just slightly, waiting for Ray to re-spond. He didn't.

Shelley scolded, "We already talked."

"But it's not like you said." His old wingman was torn between loyalty and love. "You said he was making a move, that was why we're taking the heat. He was talking to the feds you said, to get to you and take over."

"Forget what I said. Do what I tell you."

"He's just trying to get out." Paulie pressed his point with a sincere and childlike sadness. "And some of the stuff you did, it didn't look right. Did you really blow up Alek and George?"

"Shit! Will somebody just fucking shoot somebody?" Shelley cursed in frustration.

Ray-Ray thought it over only a second before firing at Paulie. He hit a shoulder and Paulie shot back. One of those bullets caught Ray-Ray in the leg. A second hit him in the chest. On the way down he fired again but his weapon jammed. Pesci crouched but didn't budge.

Seeing the Don duck behind a filing cabinet Tonio was suddenly struck by the absurdity of their pointless standoff and managed to cover his terror with enough bravado to rise from his spot on the floor, hands high in the air. "This is what happens with impulsive decisions," he said.

"And don't get me wrong, it's been big fun. But as my personal nerd keeps saying, it's important to know where the exit is, and when to use it. Right now I hear there's a party on upstairs, so come on, buddy."

Paulie was weakened and bleeding so Tonio took his gun, supporting him as they slowly backed out of the bunker, locked it and headed for the lift.

A short trip to the surface deposited them behind the tent in a storage zone, surrounded by crates and lumber. On the other side of the canvas the reception was getting underway.

"You all right?" Tonio opened Paulie's jacket for a look at the wound, a through and through. "Not bad, but let's take care of it soon."

Paulie shrugged off the pain and opted to bring around the car. "Say hello to mom. I'm sorry, man, but this is confusing shit."

Damn right it is! At first glance the situation was like a Shakespearean tragedy with Shelley as Julius Caesar, or better yet Richard III, twisted monarch of a corrupt regime who murdered his own kin to seize power. That made Tonio heir apparent, but also a threat to the crown. On the other hand, if Shelley was telling the truth, he wasn't the only villain in the piece and other forces were working behind the scenes. It was Lynch, after all, who handed him the evidence, the so-called smoking gun conversation. So Gianni's death probably did serve purposes larger than his father's rage. There was still more to the story.

The tent was filling up. Among the guests were several members of his extended family, business associates and a smattering of New York pols. Beyond that inner circle were faces he had never seen – students and teachers from local schools, Tesla aficionados from far and wide, staff from the nearby Brookhaven lab. Shelley's ploy seemed to be working and might have some positive side effects. The museum was a worthy project, and no one knew what he really had in mind. Perhaps he could rehabilitate his image. But that missed the bigger picture. Even the best publicist in the world couldn't protect him forever. The Truthsquad documents were already being mentioned in the press as the basis for a racketeering case and a Congressional investigation. It was only a matter of time before Shelley's tower came down.

He was going to need that bunker, or one of his rocket ships.

Athena noticed Tonio moving across the hall and called him over. She already considered the evening a great success, impressed that her ex was finally doing something constructive with his wealth and power. Tonio didn't have the heart to set her straight. Seated next to her was an intense red head of about twenty-five. "This is Zee Bradbury," she explained, "Ryan says you should meet." Zee didn't hesitate before reaching for his hand.

"Why's that?"

She digested the question carefully before responding, "Complementary skill sets. But I have a degree."

"Cute."

"She's too modest," gushed Athena, "it's an MBA, top of her class at Stanford. Ryan says you belong together. I assume that means business associates, but who knows?"

"If I'm still chairman next week." He handed her a card. "By the way, what's your take on Tesla?"

"Tremendous foresight," she said, "but badly in need of an accountant. Also, he probably needed to get laid. Hysteria wasn't just a woman's problem."

"Call me," he offered, moving on as soon as he noticed Shelley stepping onto the stage. The spin parade was about to start. Apologizing, he headed for the exit. There was just so much self-serving bullshit he could swallow in one day.

Still, Annie's Tarot reading was looking more prescient by the minute. The tower outside, though merely a replica of Tesla's soaring vision, suggested the unattainable, an impossible dream. As a monument to Shelley's blind ambition it also represented, in this case, a vast wasted and abused potential, manipulated into being a vehicle of one man's vanity and greed. A deadly delusion that was destined to fail and fall.

Paulie pulled up in the car and Tonio took the front seat. How could he thank this man, who in the clutch had decided to save his life at the risk of his own? It wasn't just taking a bullet, it was the real consequences. In defying Shelley his old friend had basically issued a contract on his own life. On top of that, it was the Ides of March and the Don was merely wounded. As long as he survived, could either of them afford to feel safe?

44
THE WORLD

In the sharp formulation of the causality law – "If we know the present, then we can predict the future" – it is not the consequence, but the premise that is false. As a matter of principle we cannot know all determining elements of the present.

-Werner Heisenberg,

1927 on the Uncertainty Principle

"Let's light this one up, it's a long agenda." Zee cued Danny to launch the stream. The two of them were in the control room and the others were on a deck overlooking Lake Champlain wearing stylish visors on a sunny day. No one seemed to notice that they sometimes talked to people who weren't there.

Danny predicted it would become more common in the years ahead.

"At least you exist," Harry joked. "That's more than I can say for a lot of what passes for reality these days."

The first topic for today was speeding up production. Second quarter sales were turning out better than expected. A few weeks remained until the end of June and official numbers, but Zee announced that there was little doubt. Locators were creeping up domestically on tablet PCs and other mobile devices, and as soon as FABRICO began overseas production they would launch a global marketing push. However, keeping up with demand at the moment was impossible. Customers and stores faced a two-week waiting period.

A few days after the showdown at Tesla's lab Zee had taken Tonio up on his offer to meet. Their casual conversation turned into an impromptu job interview. As it happened, Ryan Crown had read about Angel's death and immediately thought of Zee, who had studied with him after Stanford. Like Tonio, he later explained, Zee showed a natural ability to focus her will and view things and people at a distance. Beyond that, however, she was a business ace who had helped launch several undergrads into promising businesses before they had their degrees.

He introduced her to Danny and Harry at Angel's memorial service. They all immediately saw her potential. Zee had no trouble getting the larger implications and some of the risks, even before they invited her into their circle of trust. She was definitely up to it, able to stand her ground but stay loyal to the team. In her spare time she went rock climbing, pursued online avatar adventures and played lead guitar with LightSource, an indy rock group whose CD was about to drop.

Next up was a progress report on the first TELPORT documentary production, slated for released in 2014. This was Tonio's pet project. The working title was "History Live: Exposing the Ripper Cover Up." It would be a coming-out-party for RTV, the first public screening of moments from the past. For those with Locators and Visors, the latter set for release at the end of the year, it would be a killer premium, an exclusive holographic edition. But the same basic production would also be available for high-definition download and traditional 3D, 2D and Blue Ray sales.

The script wasn't set in stone, but they had the basic concept and production really began the moment Tonio took his first trip in the View Room. "History Live" would combine narration, computer animation and photo montage with RTV footage from the actual crimes, tastefully edited, and background scenes illustrating the lives of the victims and the social conditions, leading up to the revelation that the perpetrator was Frank Tumblety, American quack doctor and textbook psychopath.

Beyond the central story, the production would expose the disinformation campaign of Russia's Okhrama and the Central Branch, their cynical plot to turn latent racial animus and xenophobia against immigrants, Jews and radicals. Finally, it would show that Tumblety's guilt was covered up by authorities on two continents. The difference was that for the first time a story would be told with real scenes from another time that exposed those responsible and humanized the victims in a way that few documentaries could. The dead women would appear before the eyes of viewers, alive once again just before their brutal ends.

From subsequent meetings with Lynch he surmised there was no ban on using images streamed from the past. They simply couldn't be owned, Lynch claimed, and remained in the public domain. Words and pictures can be copyrighted, he said, but not ideas – and not past events. On the other hand, until another company developed the same technology, either by finding their own approach or licensing Danny's patented inventions, TELPORT had a de facto commercial monopoly.

After the release of "Exposing the Ripper Cover Up" Tonio's proposal was to create a "History Live" series, with each episode exploring and exposing the truth behind a different mystery, a disputed point of history – like "Did Roosevelt know about Pearl Harbor in Advance?" – or an unsolved crime.

"What could be greater transparency?" he appealed to his friends. "Talk about the ultimate disinfectant."

But Harry burst his bubble. "What mysteries, bro, and who decides, you?"

"We do, by consensus."

"And who are we? This is too much for four people, even four people I trust."

"Who then?"

Zee was practical. "Look, even before we get into that, what you're proposing is a large, ongoing commitment of time, energy and money. This isn't a media company or a TV network. If that's the direction, I think we need a partner, a company with a track record and connections in the market.

"Meanwhile, we could do some polling," Danny suggested, "find out what or who people would most like to see exposed."

"I love it," said Harry.

"How about a network?" asked Tonio, "As a partner, or maybe a merger, even a straight buy-out. Didn't Al Gore sell Current TV not long ago? Who did that go to?"

"Al Jazeera," Zee recalled, "which is owned by Qatar, which is backed by Middle East oil money. Brilliant move, Al Jazeera was frozen out of US cable for years. That's the direction, I agree."

"Yeah," Harry snorted, "and then you re-brand it as The Conspiracy Channel."

Everyone stopped, about to dismiss it, when they realized it might be the right name. Zee broke the silence. "Let's table that one until next time. Moving on, we have The Box. Who wants to get us started?"

Danny raised his hand. "We have to be just a little Steve Jobs about this. What I mean is that now, with the new fabrication possibilities, we can have a package that's compact, tactile and a total experience. We already have the Locator, which fits nicely in most pockets, and all the associated apps and accessories. In less than six months we'll have Visors. What I envision is offering them together in a cool package, a stylish, light, durable case – like a cigarette case only bigger and it won't kill you, it will liberate you. I call it The Box. 'Open the box and get there,' something like that."

There were issues but no disagreements about making something like that happen.

The big question – the elephant in the room, the vault in the back of the warehouse, the doorway to "there and then" – was what to do with the Jump Room. For the first few weeks after the Ides of March there was too much happening to even think about that.

The first shock was Paulie's death on March 26. It wasn't subtle or cinematic. He was just invited to Jimmy's, a bar he always liked, to work things out. Naïve as usual, he thought it might be a peace offering. Shelley showed up late and invited him for a ride. But when he got in the car Ray-Ray shot him twice in the head. The body was discovered the next day in a vacant lot. All that would be tough to prove, of course, but there was little doubt in Tonio's mind.

A few days later, he asked Lynch who he should talk to if he wanted to help with any current case against his father. He had the goods, even a recorded confession.

"You should ask for something in exchange," Lynch advised, "and not just because you can get it. If you don't ask your offer might look suspect."

"I may need protection."

"That could be, but I'd aim higher."

"How about an agreement that allows us to use teleportation on a, let's say, non-profit, education and research basis, within reasonable and clear parameters?"

He was surprised when Lynch said, "That's not my call, but it sounds doable. If we can't put the cork back in the bottle -- and let me tell you, we can't – I think I can say we'd rather have you running a tourist bureau to ancient Greece than let your father anywhere near Danny's funhouse."

"But he has contracts, contacts, the satellite deal."

"This isn't rocket science," Lynch explained patiently, "and I am a rocket scientist. This government, like most governments, works with many people it doesn't especially like or approve of. It's very much a 'depends' situation. He's rubbed too many people the wrong way, blackmailing high rollers, even Max Libra. He's out of control. In the end, for us he's another tin-pot dictator and there are plenty of them. We live with them and we take them out, as needed. So, it's just time for the wolf to be neutered."

Tonio asked what he thought might happen to Shelley.

"He'll be indicted, and probably convicted of something or other. There's a lot to choose from." Lynch laughed. "It's funny, the Left thinks we live in a police state, or one is on the way, and the Right thinks Obama is becoming an Emperor, so they're stockpiling weapons. Meanwhile, guys like Shelley Wolfe, real vultures and corporate killers, walk around like they're wearing Teflon.

"But Obama isn't Emperor yet," he continued, "and neither is the Big Bad Wolfe. I can't promise you we'll get to see him in a perp walk. He may just have to keep circling the Earth in one of those jets of his for the rest of his life."

As if on cue, on May 23, less than a week before his indictment was handed down, Shelley Wolfe packed his bags, emptied his safe deposit boxes, left his manicured Wood-Ridge mansion with his beautiful trophy wife, and was last spotted boarding a private jet in Newark, with a phony flight plan to an unknown final destination. The grapevine said he was holed up with a private posse in Arizona, watching for black helicopters with Sheriff Joe.

"Are we done yet?" Harry complained. "Just look at the day. I'd like to enjoy a little climate change before we all turn to toast."

"Agreed," said Zee, "but not as funny as you think. We're stuck in this office, in case you forgot, and second, we have several items to go. The Tesla project, let's start that. Based on what Harry's group found last spring I reached out to Max Libra's people and there might be something to pursue there."

"Criminal penalties for his acting," snapped Harry.

"Anyway," Zee interrupted, struggling to keep the other three on point. "The answer is yes, he was being blackmailed by Shelley to star in that Tesla movie. It was part of Shelley's whole Croatian Restoration crusade. But the point is, there was actually a script, and Max liked it. So, the question is, do we try to pick up the option? Any thoughts?"

"I say hell yes," blurted Danny. "Let's make a movie."

Tonio almost did a spit take. "It sounded like you were planning a bake sale. But money, dude! Let's go Hollywood. What's left?"

Zee paused before saying the words, "The Jump Room?"

Finally, the crucial topic and the big reveal. "I'll take it from here," Tonio told them, briefly recounting his meeting just days ago to discuss precisely that. But he had to give them the slightly censored version, at Lynch's insistence. He told them, for example, that the Jump Room could be used as long as history registers no ill effects. But what did that mean? DARCAP would keep them informed if a jump caused any "ripples." He also told them not to worry, at least if they accepted the unexplained and unsupported assertion that "history changes all the time." The trick was doing it without making things worse.

Beyond that, he was allowed to say that the government began watching events from other time periods years ago, as early as the sixties. It had also developed an early warning system, as well as teleportation capabilities likely to be far greater than their own.

At least that's some of what the man from DARCAP told him.

They parked at the east end of the National Mall near the Washington monument just after dusk. Lynch had asked to meet Tonio here and began by stressing that most small changes in history – for instance, Tonio telling Ignatius Donnelly a story that gave him an idea for his book – don't divert the superhighway of history. In fact, some changes have to be made intentionally, just for maintenance.

"Doesn't the president make that call?"

"This is beyond politics or the State," Lynch insisted. "It's advanced geo-politics, somewhere between the Bilderberg Group, the Council on Foreign Relations, the Trilateral Commission, and the Illuminati. Seriously, don't ask me, my paycheck says DoD and the only initials we use for this kind of operation is TCC. Like TCC-Wolfe, and so on. Take last year – and you can't talk about this – the Hurricane before the election, we had to make an adjustment on that."

"Hold it! What does that mean?"

Lynch raised a hand. "That means off the record. And don't get righteous. Sometimes things have to be changed, for the greater good. You know that. In this case it was a small fix."

"What?"

He got out of the car and walked toward the granite and marble obelisk, closed for repairs due to earthquake and hurricane damage. "The path of the hurricane," he said, attempting to minimize the revelation with a low tone. Tonio trailed him.

"I'm not mainly talking about time travel here," Lynch continued, "just in terms of the research, verification and access. But once you know what has happened, sometimes you have to make an adjustment. That's the term we use. You want action on climate change, we're trying – but it's touchy. In this case it was the direction of the storm, it was just adjusted a little." Tonio waited for more, nonplussed. "Come on, we couldn't let it hit the Capitol. I mean, can you imagine the White House under water? I didn't have to imagine. I saw it and believe me, that scenario did not go well."

"Wait, you changed the storm's direction, and what else? The election? Did you –"

"No!" He raised a crossing guard-like hand. "We do not decide elections. But we sometimes take steps if the future of the nation is at stake. In this case, believe me, it was."

"How did you do it?"

Lynch put a finger to his lips, leaned close and whispered, "H.A.A.R.P., High-Frequency Active Aural Research Program." Then he straightened up and laughed. "I was just kidding, it's not that secret. The main base is in Alaska, in Gokoma. It's a joint Air Force and Navy op. I haven't been up there but they say it's like a giant heater that can make incisions in the ionosphere. Most of the funding is allocated as part of space shield development."

"And how do you know when it's safe or right to change something, in the big picture?"

Lynch shook his head. "I don't have the answer to that. But you know what's possible. You were there near the beginning."

"Huh?" The remark made no sense. "Beginning of what?"

"When this kind of work began," he said, "in the seventies, and into the eighties. You were one of the whiz kids, at least for a while."

"In New Jersey, the tests, my dreams? Is that what you mean?"

"Exactly, except those weren't dreams, buddy, those were auditions and experiments in teleportation, time travel and who knows what else. You remember? Pegasus. We don't do projects with kids these days, different times. But I mean, you went to other planets, you went to the future."

Other planets, the future? It was too much for him right now, and definitely not for public consumption, or even discussion with the team at this point. Still, it did explain things; for example how someone might know in advance that the capitol would be flooded and then change the course of a hurricane. Finally, there was also verification of what he so vividly remembered seeing as a child. It wasn't a nightmare or a delusion, it was a test.

"I see by your expression this is shattering your current paradigm," Lynch said. "It's a lot to absorb. Tell your team what you need to, but my advice is not too much. The bottom line is that history changes, but it's best to be very careful. Your "History Live" idea is in the right direction. Bring people along slowly. There are plenty of mysteries to unravel. People need to know that their perceptions of the past shape their understanding of the present, and both are open to alteration.

"Everything we know is open to revision," he said.

They stopped in the shadow on the obelisk, another phallic monument to grand ambitions. Tonio couldn't help wondering: Would this one too someday have to fall. The choice of location seemed significant and possible intentional. He knew that the capstone of the Washington monument weighed precisely 33,000 pounds, a number that also preoccupied Nikola Tesla. The apex was tipped with a tiny aluminum pyramid, engraved with symbols that spell the words Laus Deo, or "Praise God," an ancient Masonic cipher. And the original opening day was October 9, 1888, the day he returned from the past. Linking Tesla's numerical obsession with the placement of censors in the View Room, Pythagoras' golden triangle, the country's founding and the 33rd degree Masonic ritual called the "killing of the king," it reminded him of the connections that had brought him this far.

At the very least, he ought to pay attention and ask. "Any particular reason we're here?"

Lynch smiled, "Oh, you mean a hidden message? Who knows? But this isn't your initiation to the Illuminati, if that's what you were hoping, although you can tell the gang one thing." He paused before offering, "It's their final secret, at least some people say so: Positive energy is as real as gravity. I know, pretty basic stuff, deceptively simple – but as they say, it has the added benefit of being true."

He let that sink in. "It kind of reminds me of something. An old Agency hand I know told me this," Lynch mused, "he worked with your uncle back in the day. I heard Gianni was quite a card and had these sayings?"

"I know about some of them," Tonio agreed.

"One was about the Middle East crisis, I think it goes like this, 'If this is the Kingdom of Heaven let God do what wants.' Kind of an anti-interventionist line, but the one I remember – because you asked why you're here, but also because it makes sense in our line of work – is this one: *God may not play dice with the universe, but if he won't roll somebody better step up.*"

Tonio didn't tell the team everything he learned that night. But he did share the last advice.

PART FIVE

ADJUSTMENTS

45
THE PRIESTESS

National Reformer, June 30, 1889
I have not had the opportunity of reading Madame Blavatsky's two volumes, but I have read during the past ten years many publications from the pen of herself, Colonel Olcott, and of other Theosophists. They appear to me to have sought to rehabilitate a kind of Spiritualism in Eastern phraseology. I think many of their reasonings wholly unsound.

I very deeply regret indeed that my colleague and co-worker has, with some suddenness, and without any interchange of ideas, adopted as facts matters which seem to me to be as unreal as it is possible for any fiction to be. My regret is greater as I know Mrs. Besant's devotion to any course she believes to be true.

The editorial policy of this paper is unchanged, and is directly antagonistic to all forms of Theosophy.

-Charles Bradlaugh, Editor

LONDON, AUGUST 4, 1889

"Since 1886," Annie told the crowd, "a conviction had been slowly growing that my philosophy wasn't sufficient, that life and mind were other than – more than – I dreamed. Psychology was advancing with rapid strides; experiments revealing unlooked-for complexities in human consciousness, strange riddles of multiplex personalities, and most startling of all, vivid intensities of mental action even when the brain was reduced to a comatose state."

She paused for effect and gazed out at her audience in the Hall of Science. It was the first of two planned talks, her much-awaited public explanation after an announcement that had shocked the nation. Annie Besant had joined the Theosophists.

"Facts hurtled in upon me," she told them, "demanding explanation I was incompetent to give. I studied the obscure side of consciousness, dreams, hallucinations, illusions, insanity, experimenting privately, finding the phenomena indubitable but the spiritualistic explanations incredible. Clairvoyance, clairaudience, thought-reading, they all seemed real."

The press was having a field day. The former Anglican church-wife, the radical secularist who had become an atheist and then a Socialist, the firebrand leader of the matchstick strike and Bloody Sunday march, was becoming something else, again. Rumors swirled that a man might be involved, another in Annie's series of strange liaisons. This time they whispered about Herbert Burrows, a recent widower who had joined the Theosophical Society and reached out to her after Tonio disappeared.

"I finally convinced myself that there was some hidden thing, some hidden power, and resolved to seek until I found it," she said. "By the early spring of 1889 I was desperate to find what I sought -- at all hazards. At last, sitting alone in deep thought, as I often do after the sun sets, filled with an intense but nearly hopeless longing to solve the mysteries of life, I heard an inner voice that bid me to take courage.

"The next day Mr. Stead handed me two large volumes. 'My young men are all shy of this,' he said, 'but you're quite mad enough on these subjects to make something of them.' I took the books, the two volumes of *The Secret Doctrine*, written by H.P. Blavatsky, and carried my burden home.

"How familiar but also so new, I thought, how subtle yet completely intelligible. I was dazzled, blinded as disjointed facts became part of a mighty new whole. All puzzles, riddles and problems seemed to disappear. The effect was partially an illusion, of course, in the sense that it had to be unraveled later, gradually sifted and assimilated from what swift intuition had grasped as truth. But the light had been seen. And in that flash of illumination I knew that the search was over and the truth had been found."

After filing her review Annie had asked for a formal introduction to the author. Back at the Blavatsky Lodge on Landsdowne Road, the folding doors were thrown wide and she was finally brought into the full and overwhelming presence of H.P.B. "My dear Mrs. Besant," said that force of nature, taking Annie's hand in her own. "I have so long wished to see you."

Annie felt a leap of primal recognition, and at the same time a fierce resistance, like an animal sensing her trainer's hand. But she managed to sit and listen. Nothing was said about the occult that night, nothing strange at all actually, just a woman of the world chatting with some visitors. Eyes partially concealed beneath a veil, Blavatsky simply discussed travel as her exquisitely molded fingers incessantly rolled cigarettes.

But as they rose to leave Blavatsky lifted the fabric and set her gaze on Annie, her voice rough with yearning. "If you would only come among us," she pleaded.

At that moment, Annie recalled, "I felt an uncontrollable desire to bend down and kiss her. But with a flash of the old pride and a jeer at my folly I bid her goodnight with an evasive remark."

Everyone was watching – Yeats, Morris, Stead, and Oscar Wilde with his green carnation, Sidney Webb and Beatrice Potter, Theosophists, unionists, members of the Fabian Society, MPs like Bradlaugh, Bryce and Montagu, the President of the Royal Academy and the men and women of the press.

Tonio was there too, listening from the back of the hall. He'd chosen this moment even though it might not give them any time together alone. He wanted to see her at this turning point in her life, doing what she did so well – inspiring people, changing lives. And it was a startling performance, but it also contained a difficult answer to the question he'd been asking himself. Could their very long-distance love affair survive? As Annie entered this new phase of her journey their prospects looked less likely than ever.

"Must I plunge into a new vortex," she asked earnestly, "again mark myself for ridicule, again fight for an unpopular truth? Perhaps it must be. Must I turn against materialism, and publicly confess that I was wrong, misled by intellect to ignore the Soul? Yes, that too. But must I leave the army that has battled beside me so bravely, and the friends who've held me near and true? That must not be!"

Stepping around the enormous podium as the room erupted in applause, red scarf draped around her throat, blond hair glowing, she tried to make even more intimate contact. "They say I sometimes allow my enthusiasms to carry me away," she joked. The audience responded with chuckles. "Possibly so, at least in the sense that my decisions come quickly. But those who know me will tell you, I have long dreamed of a higher plane, beyond the hand of death. And now I know it is real. The soul exists and it, not my body, is who I truly am.

"The soul *can* leave the body," she shouted as a low muttering began. She let it settle and pressed on. "I have seen that we can learn from others at a distance, and bring that knowledge back. It's a slow process, a process of transferring consciousness, and I've only begun to understand its secrets. It's a little like a child learning to speak, compared with perfect oratory. But I know now that consciousness, far from depending on the body, becomes more active when set free."

Tonio was amazed. Her sense of the world, of the capacities of the mind, was much the same as his. In a different time and culture, without drugs or technical assistance, she'd found the same answers. But the muttering had commenced again. "The criticisms I have seen in recent days remind me of Christian caricatures of Atheism," she said pushing back against the wave of skepticism. "I ask only this: wait and listen before you judge."

He moved up along the side of the hall for a closer look. About half-way to the stage he bumped into Shaw. "Wonderful," said the writer, "perfect timing, just as the transformation happens before our eyes. What I love about Annie is the theatrical terms in which she views her life. She inhabits a series of glorious roles, a true diva."

"That's a little rough, don't you think," Tonio objected.

"She can handle it."

Addressing Freethinkers in the audience, Annie acknowledged some of the "stumbling blocks" that made Theosophy a subject of ridicule. "For example, the assertion that beings other than men and animals exist." Tonio heard a titter. "A controversial idea, I know. But those who scoff should ask themselves this: Is it possible, throughout the mighty universe, in which our tiny planet is but a speck of sand in the Sahara, that only one planet is inhabited by living things?"

He moved closer still, now within sight from the stage.

"Can the universe be silent except for our voices, eyeless except for our vision, dead except for our life? Such a preposterous belief was acceptable in the days when Christianity proclaimed our planet as the center of the universe, and the human race as the one and only for which the Creator deigned to die."

Annie saw him then and gasped, almost interrupting herself, but pushed on. "Now we are placed in our proper position, one among countless other worlds," she said, looking into his eyes, her own brimming with sweet compassion. "Earth, air, water, all teem with living things suited to their environments. The universe pulses with life and unexplored interconnections.

"Superstition, bigots shriek. But it is no more superstition than the belief in bacteria, or in any other living thing invisible to the human eye. Spirit can be a misleading word, my friends. It connotes immateriality and a supernatural existence. But matter and spirit are connected in a web of life, and matter exists in states other than those now known to science. To deny it is to be about as sensible as the Hindu prince who denied the existence of ice because, in his own experience, water never became solid.

"Refusing to believe until proof is given is a rational position," she said. "Denying everything beyond our own limited experience is absurd."

So right, he thought, even in ways she didn't intend. He had lived in denial for years, refusing to challenge his comfortable illusions about himself, his family, the world and his place in it. The words were compelling, and the passion contagious. But Annie belonged to this world and his path pointed elsewhere.

And then he noticed something else, how she had changed in less than a year and what a toll her struggle was taking. Shaw had it right; she saw herself in dramatic terms, as waging a titanic fight to change society. But she was no plaster saint or Amazon warrior, rushing blinding and boldly into any fight. Despite her magnetic presence and her golden words she was a flesh-and-blood woman with fears, regrets and aspirations, trying painfully to make sense of her life.

"But now, as at other times, I dare not purchase peace with a lie," she announced, gazing at Tonio, as if in response, but speaking to everyone in the hall. "An imperious necessity forces me to speak the truth, as I see it, whether it please or not, whether it bring praise or blame. That one loyalty I must keep stainless, whatever friendships fail me or human ties must be broken."

Tonio bowed. Not a goodbye, merely an acknowledgement.

She noticed and went on. "It may lead me into the wilderness yet I must go. It may strip me of love yet I must pursue. I ask no epitaph but this," said this woman who'd captured his heart. "She followed truth wherever it led, without conditions."

46
END GAME

Frank Tumblety wasn't what most people expected when they thought of Jack the Ripper. He was no shrinking violet, skulking through life, unable to function in polite society, driving around alone in an unmarked cab. He also wasn't a deranged butcher, a resentful immigrant or a seductive womanizer who lured unwitting victims into his web. He was a public man, a brash self-promoter who sported flamboyant costumes, mixed with politicians and high-ranking military – although you didn't always know if the stories were real – and publicly proclaimed his contempt for the female sex.

He was a man of power and a functioning psychopath.

And like many mobile serial killers in the century since, he had an inexplicable gift. He could fade into the background, almost make himself invisible, and even "disappear" when necessary, popping up somewhere else without attracting unwelcome notice. Tumblety knew how to blend in. He was a deadly chameleon – confident, overbearing at times, but intelligent, articulate and adaptable.

He enjoyed his crimes, in a clinical sense anyway, and reveled in the controversies that swirled around his exploits. In fact, attacks provided him with a platform to protest his innocence and promote his fabricated accomplishments, another tool in his quest for celebrity. This fed his notion of himself as a special and superior man, above the common lot. At the same time he felt deeply unappreciated, robbed of the recognition and admiration that was his due.

Tumblety often said that he was constantly being cheated and humiliated despite his manly efforts to meet society's demands. He never blamed himself, of course, or acknowledged any personal shortcomings. Instead, all the slights, whether real or not, helped to justify his aggression. The only thing he did fear was bad publicity, particularly if he couldn't respond.

In some ways he was like Albert DeSalvo, the Boston Strangler, a multiple personality killer with a steady job and a normal family. Tumblety had eight sisters, one remaining brother and an extensive network of relatives, all contributing to his nonthreatening veneer. After his hasty flight from England in 1888 and success in eluding detectives in New York, he ended up in Rochester and moved in with an elderly niece. For several years he ran a medical practice out of her home.

He aged rapidly in the gay '90s, however, no longer able to travel as freely and unwilling to risk a return to England. In the final years of the century he developed a heart condition and spent more and more time at a St. Louis hospital. Eventually he moved to that city and engaged a modest room on South Euclid Avenue at St. John's Hospital, a charitable institution established by the Sisters of Mercy. He called it "a good place to die."

The room was leased under Townsend, the name he had used when escaping his crimes.

ST LOUIS, MAY 25, 1903

It was a Monday morning and Tumblety wasn't feeling well. Still, he insisted on dressing as usual and taking his daily walk, a public display of independence and determination for the staff and other patients, more proof of his superior breeding and powerful will.

He wasn't hard to track down. After the jump Tonio simply walked around the corner to Euclid Avenue and loitered across the street, watching the six-story building for the killer to emerge. These days his constitutional involved no more than a few blocks. Soon enough he would become winded and find a bench to sit. He always made certain no one from the hospital saw him in this state. Appearances – how others judged him -- remained at the twisted core of his self-image.

Tonio watched briefly and ran over his plan. He wanted the correct moment to reveal himself, when no one would notice him walk up, confront this predator and send him on his way to hell. By this time, after so many jumps, he felt relatively certain that he'd face no serious sanction from DARCAP or anyone else. Lynch had said it all. As long as the History Superhighway wasn't affected there was little risk in whacking an old man on the verge of dying anyway. Tumblety's early departure would make no ripples. He would not be missed.

But first their reunion. He crossed the street and walked up to the bench. "No dice today?"

"What?" Tumblety looked up and stiffened. "Do I know you, sir?"

Tonio sat down beside him. "Yes, we met years ago in London. Maybe you recall the name, Upton Sinclair."

Tumblety's eyes popped open as he gulped for air. He remembered it well, a name from the days when he would decide who lived and died with the code revealed by his dice, and from the night when everything changed. He remembered their barroom talk, jousting in the alley, and a disappearing act so fantastic he'd spent years struggling to work it out, to no avail. It still haunted him, like a ghost in his blind spot.

"I see you do remember." Tonio smiled. "It's good, isn't it, at least to be remembered the way you'd like to be? I read your pamphlet, your defense, quite a work of fiction. But we know the facts."

"What – what...?"

"And now the world will."

"There was never proof," he protested.

"But there are pictures. Take a look." He removed a package of photos from his shirt pocket, opened the flap, and removed a few. "Souvenirs. We call them snap shots. These were reproduced from one of the machines we have." He shared them slowly. One showed a healthier Tumblety fifteen years earlier, holding a knife over the lifeless body of Annie Chapman. Others featured mutilated corpses and time-stamped images of the killer at various crime scenes.

The photos fell from his hands. "How? Why do you persecute me?"

Tonio took back the pictures and stood. "Please. I'm not here to persecute you or even arrest you. Too late for all that. I actually came here to kill you. Even brought along a knife, a Liston blade, like the one you used to use. My plan was to gut you, maybe cut off your head, and keep it in a box at the office."

The old man shuddered in terror.

"But now that we're here I realize it's not the best punishment. I need to set aside those childish instincts and think outside the box. Hate to admit it but I need to grow up. And the world needs the appropriate adjustment, a change with some justice and bite." He began to walk away. "Your death is coming. But in the meantime, consider this. In the years ahead, long after you're worm food, millions of people will know who and what you really were, beneath all your medals and pride – Frank the Pimple, a worthless boil on the ass of humanity.

"There are fates worse than death," he said, "for guys like you it may well be bad press. So know this: you will be famous someday – but only as one of history's mistakes." He stopped at the corner and turned back. "As a pimple, well, you're busted. Now have a nice day."

Then he pulled out Danny's watch, hit recall and jumped home.

When Tumblety returned to St. John's Hospital from his walk that day he stumbled badly in front of the building and broke his nose. Retreating to his room, frightened and mortified, he never explained and never recovered from the shock. Three days later, on May 28, 1903, he died.

No will was officially filed, according to a story in the *St. Louis Post Dispatch*. But he reportedly left $10,000 each to two Catholic archdioceses, including the Minnesota church led by one of Ignatius Donnelly's foes, the powerful Archbishop John Ireland. A June 26 obituary in the *New York Herald* briefly mentioned Tumblety's arrest as a suspect in the Ripper case. It also reported that $138,000 was on deposit in his personal account with Henry Clews and Company, and ended with the suggestion that the man who had been staying at the Catholic charitable hospital didn't really need or deserve any charity.

Most of his fortune went to members of his family. But one intriguing claim came from an attorney acting on behalf of Joseph Kemp and the Home for Fallen Women, both of Baltimore. In a previous will, they wrote, Tumblety had left his jewelry to Kemp and one thousand dollars to the Fallen Women's Home. No reason was given and the application was denied.

47

THE CRYPTOGRAM LETTER

Minnesota Historical Center Library, Special Collections
Donnelly Papers: Folder M138, Microfilm 82-95
(unsigned note)

October 4, 1888
London, 20 Duke Street

To the reader,

My name is unimportant but people know me as Upton Sinclair. I'm writing this letter to leave a record of the strange situation in which I find myself.

I'm an American born in 1972 in New Jersey. If that seems off by a century please let me explain. I came here as a result of a scientific discovery that allows information and, as it turns out, people and objects to be teleported back in time. For some reason the damned thing only runs in reverse. Like many other aspects of my story, I don't know all the details. I'm more like the canary in the coalmine or a chimp in some capsule shot into space.

But that's another matter.

About five days ago, I was conducting research about London . The goal was to solve the murders that have been paralyzing the city. People in my time are more fascinated than ever with such gruesome crimes, repelled and yet incapable of resisting every fresh detail, and the crimes committed here have become influential myths. The "ripper" uses a knife and disembowels his victims in the dead of night. In 2013 young men arm themselves heavily and shoot everyone in sight in broad daylight. The results and the fascination are much the same.

In a sense I'm one of the people I've mentioned, a crime voyeur who enjoys following the process from commission of the crime to punishment of the guilty. Over the years my special area of interest has become serial killers, which ultimately brought me to the first who became what we like to call a Superstar. Where I come from there are many of both, superstars and super-killers – the fictional kind with masks and claws, and real ones in the suburbs with names like John, Ted and Scott. The one I followed here is known as Jack, but his real name is Francis.

I'm getting ahead of myself. You see, we were collecting information about the Whitechapel murders by taking pictures of them. I won't disgust you with the details. Suffice it to say, several nights ago the inventor of the recording device asked me to be a guinea pig again, and without thinking about it I agreed. Thus, I find myself in old London, glad to see London Bridge where it belongs rather than in Arizona. That's where they moved the old girl less than a century later.

Obviously, all this is difficult to accept. It would be under most circumstances, even more so now, given the success of Mr. Bellamy's book. I wish him all the success in the world. And many people I've met lately are certainly captivated by his ideas and the rosy picture he paints of the future. The problem, from my point of view, is simply this: he's almost completely wrong — not about what ought to happen perhaps, but certainly about what will.

In my time we 'd call for a spoiler alert at this point. My intention is not to "spoil" the future for anyone who may see this note prior to 2013. But it may be the only way to prove that my tale is true. So, let me share a few highlights of how it will go from here.

At the moment it may look as if Britannia will "rule the waves" forever.

Not so. The empire will crumble – but a new one will rise to replace it. In fact, before the end of the century, after defeating Spain and buying the Philippines, the American president, when asked why that was done, will explain it was accomplished "by God's grace," in order to uplift, civilize and Christianize the native peoples.

That, my friend, is empire talking.

A few years later the same president will be assassinated by a lone "crazed" gunman, the first of many. As you may have noticed, the US seems to breed this variety of the species. Over the years we have accepted it as one more price of freedom; for some reason – blame guns or culture, depending on your politics – a few people just go postal. I should explain that reference.

President McKinley's assassin claimed he was an anarchist, exactly what some people wanted to hear. The truth is that he attended a speech by Emma Goldman once or twice. Anarchism was about as responsible for his shooting McKinley as Harvard is for the nation's foreign policy since then.

My point is that it was a case of perception management, a pretext to go after people who were different or expressed "extreme" ideas, anything beyond the familiar. I've seen the same thing around London in recent days. The hunt for the man murdering those poor women in the East End is being manipulated and exploited with false evidence and propaganda. At its worst this is pure racism. It makes people watchful and suspicious, undermining trust and producing a mob mentality. Without a better understanding of evidence and motives, and with provocateurs constantly banging the drums of prejudice, this leads down false trails to unwarranted and destructive persecution.

I wish I could tell you things will improve over the next century. Alas, back to the future: When McKinley is shot and killed Theodore Roosevelt becomes president. I know that sounds unlikely right now, the man who couldn't even defeat Henry George in New York. But he is determined, an over-achiever you might say, smart and calculating, and he will construct a powerful image of himself as a happy warrior, a conservationist and straight-talker, enough to win hearts and re-election. Interesting times, but for the purposes of this proof let's jump a decade to the start of the first "world" war – a frightening but unfortunately appropriate term.

By 1914 America's "national interest" will encompass the Western hemisphere and some of the Pacific. Taking advantage of political turmoil it will establish military bases where it can, and occupy countries when banks and business interests feel it must, always insisting that the reasons are freedom, trade and the spread of democracy – a national myth that keeps Americans suspended somewhere between hope, anxiety and con-tempt. That's one man's opinion.

Millions will perish in the terrible conflict known as WWI. The US president will claim at the time it is being fought to "make the world safe for democracy." In the end, however, the victors will meet in Paris to divide and decide how to manage the "post-war" world. Within twenty years these grand schemes will crumble as Germany, loser of the War, resentfully rises in nationalistic fury, led by an ex-soldier turned char-ismatic dictator with a superman prophecy of empire and racial purity. Officially, the global conflict will last less than a decade. Its victims will number high in the millions, however, and its effects will be felt for the rest of the century.

The good news, you could say, is that a number of repressive regimes in Europe and Asia will end. In the aftermath of WWII new nations will be born and many groups will seek independence. The bad news is that 1) few will succeed, 2) there is never a shortage of dictators, and 3) to end WWII and test a new super-weapon, the US will unleash a force of mass destruction that decimates cities and makes whole regions uninhabitable for generations.

From that moment until the day I stepped into that experimental capsule in New Jersey, every human being on the planet has lived under the threat of extinction. Can you imagine the anxiety that has resulted? It's no wonder we so often imagine apocalypse around the bend.

Hopefully, this preview of coming attractions will give the reader enough information to judge whether my claim rings true. May it also motivate the reader to do something useful. The future can and certainly should be improved.

This report also ought to include a few words about the author, but that will have to wait as I hear my host approaching. I regret there isn't more time.

THE
GREAT
CRYPTOGRAM
Donnelly

THE
GREAT
CRYPTOGRAM
Ignatius Donnelly

1888

Note to Readers

How much is true? That's a fair question, but a difficult one – and also one that could be frustrating for anyone suffering from a case of irony deficiency, not to mention those who prefer more conventional wisdom. As Harry Atlas might reply, "as much as security allows."

Bibliograhpy

James Bamford, *The Shadow Factory: The Ultra-Secret NSA from 9/11 to the Eavesdopping on America*, Doubleday, 2008

Annie Besant, *Annie Besant: An Autobiography*, Henry Altemus/ Theosophical Society, 1893

Helena P. Blavatsky, *The Secret Doctrine*, Theosophical University Press, 1888

Wiliam Blum, *Killing Hope: US Military and CIA Intervention since World War II*, Common Courtage Press, 1995

Alex Butterworth, *The World That Never Was*, Pantheon Books, 2010

Carlos Castaneda, *Tales of Power*, Simon and Schuster, 1974

Sylvia Cranston, *H.P.B: The Extraordinary Life and Influence of Helena Blavatsky*, G.P. Putnam's Sons, 1993

Ingatius Donnelly, *Caesar's Column*, F. J. Schulte and Company, 1890

Ignatius Donnelly, *The Great Cryptogram*, R.S. Peale and Company, 1888

Stewart Evans & Paul Gainey, *Jack the Ripper: The First Serial Killer*, Kodansha International, 1998

Eamon Javers, *Broker, Trader, Lawyer, Spy: The Secret World of Corporate Espionage*, HarperCollins, 2010

Jill Jonnes, *Empire of Light: Edison, Tesla, Westinghouse and the Race to Electrify the World*, Random House, 2003

W. Adam Mandelbaum, *The Psychic Battlefield: A History of the Military-Occult Complex*, St. Martin's Press, 2000

Herbert Mitgang, *Once Upon a Time in New York*, The Free Press, 2000

Mark Pendergrast, *Victims of Memory*, Upper Access Books, 1995

Martin Ridge, *Ignatius Donnelly: Portrait of a Politician*, University of Chicago Press, 1962 (re-print: Minnesota Historical Society Press)

John Ronson, *The Men Who Stare at Goats*, Simon & Schuster, 2004

John Ronson, *The Psychopath Test: A Journey through the Madness Industry*, Penquin Books, 2011

Gino Segre, *Faust in Copenhagen: A Struggle for the Soul of Physics*, Penquin Book, 2007

Marc J. Seifer, *Wizard: The Life and Times of Nikola Tesla*, Citadel Press, 1998

Upton Sinclair, *The Millennium*, Seven Stories Press, 2000

John L. Thomas, *Alternative America: Henry George, Edward Bellamy, Henry Demarest Lloyd, and the Adversary Tradition*, Harvard University Press, 1983

Arnold Toynbee, Ed., *Cities of Destiny*, McGraw-Hill, 1967

Paula Uruburu, *American Eve: Evelyn Nesbit, Stanford White, the Birth of the "It" Girl and the Crime of the Century*, Penguin Books, 2008

Peter Washington, *Madame Blavatsky's Baboon*, Schocken Books, 1993

Mary Lethert Wingerd, *Claiming the City: Politics, Faith, and the Power of Place in St. Paul*, Cornell University Press, 2001

A.N. Wilson, *The Victorians*, W.W. Norton and Company, 2002

About the Author

Greg Guma grew up in New York City and moved to Vermont in 1968. Since then he has been a newspaper journalist, magazine editor, college educator, public administrator, community organizer, federal projects director, bookstore owner, self-taught historian, and CEO of the Pacifica Radio Network.

Also by Greg Guma

Fiction

Spirits of Desire
Inquisitions (and Other Un-American Activities)

Non-Fiction

The People's Republic
Uneasy Empire
Big Lies
Progressive Eclipse
Nonviolent Warriors
The Vermont Way

As editor/co-author/producer

Bread & Puppet: Stories of Struggle and Faith
Passport to Freedom (with Garry Davis)
Reign of Error (with Dan Florentino)
Celia's Land (with Georgia Davis Powers)
Informed Dissent (Pacifica Radio series)

Fomite
Burlington, Vermont

A fomite is a medium capable of transmitting infectious organisms from one individual to another.

"The activity of art is based on the capacity of people to be infected by the feelings of others."
Tolstoy, *What Is Art?*

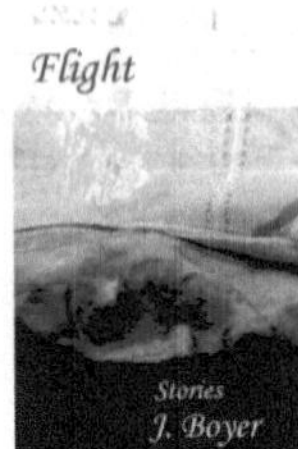

Flight and Other Stories - Jay Boyer

In *Flight and Other Stories*, we're with the fattest woman on earth as she draws her last breaths and her soul ascends toward its final reward. We meet a divorcee who can fly with no more effort than flapping her arms. We follow a middle-aged butler whose love affair with a young woman leads him first to the mysteries of bondage and then to the pleasures of malice. Story by story, we set foot into worlds so strange as to seem all but surreal, yet everything feels familiar, each moment rings true. And that's when we recognize we're in the hands of one of America's truly original talents.

Loisaida - Dan Chodorokoff

Catherine, a young anarchist estranged from her parents and squatting in an abandoned building on New York's Lower East Side, is fighting with her boyfriend and conflicted about her work on an underground newspaper. After learning of a developer's plans to demolish a community garden, Catherine builds an alliance with a group of Puerto Rican community activists. Together they confront the confluence of politics, money, and real estate that rule Manhattan. All the while she learns important lessons from her great-grandmother's life in the Yiddish anarchist movement that flourished on the Lower East Side at the turn of the century. In this coming-of-age story, family saga, and tale of urban politics, Dan Chodorkoff explores the "principle of hope" and examines how memory and imagination inform social change.

Improvisational Arguments - Anna Faktorovich

Improvisational Arguments is written in free verse to capture the essence of modern problems and triumphs. The poems clearly relate short, frequently humorous, and occasionally tragic stories about travels to exotic and unusual places, fantastic realms, abnormal jobs, artistic innovations, political objections, and misadventures with love.

Loosestrife - Greg Delanty

This book is a chronicle of complicity in our modern lives, a witnessing of war and the destruction of our planet. It is also an attempt to adjust the more destructive blueprint myths of our society. Often our cultural memory tells us to keep quiet about the aspects that are most challenging to our ethics, to forget the violations we feel and tremors that keep us distant and numb.

Fomite
Burlington, Vermont

Carts and Other Stories - Zdravka Evtimova
Roots and wings are the key words that best describe the short story collection *Carts and Other Stories,* by Zdravka Evtimova. The book is emotionally multilayered and memorable because of its internal power, vitality and ability to touch both your heart and your mind. Within its pages, the reader discovers new perspectives and true wealth, and learns to see the world with different eyes. The collection lives on the borders of different cultures. *Carts and Other Stories* will take the reader to wild and powerful Bulgarian mountains, to silver rains in Brussels, to German quiet winter streets, and to wind-bitten crags in Afghanistan. This book lives for those seeking to discover the beauty of the world around them, and will have them appreciating what they have—and perhaps what they have lost as well.

The Listener Aspires to the Condition of Music - Barry Goldensohn
"I know of no other selected poems that selects on one theme, but this one does, charting Goldensohn's career-long attraction to music's performance, consolations and its august, thrilling, scary and clownish charms. Does all art aspire to the condition of music as Pater claimed, exhaling in a swoon toward that one class act? Goldensohn is more aware than the late 19th century of the overtones of such breathing: his poems thoroughly round out those overtones in a poet's lifetime of listening."
John Peck, poet, editor, Fellow of the American Academy of Rome

The Co-Conspirator's Tale - Ron Jacobs
There's a place where love and mistrust are never at peace; where duplicity and deceit are the universal currency. *The Co-Conspirator's Tale* takes place within this nebulous firmament. There are crimes committed by the police in the name of the law. Excess in the name of revolution. The combination leaves death in its wake and the survivors struggling to find justice in a San Francisco Bay Area noir by the author of the underground classic *The Way the Wind Blew: A History of the Weather Underground* and the novel *Short Order Frame Up.*

Short Order Frame Up - Ron Jacobs
1975. America has lost its war in Vietnam and Cambodia. Racially tinged riots are tearing the city of Boston apart. The politics and counterculture of the 1960s are disintegrating into nothing more than sex, drugs, and rock and roll. The Boston Red Sox are on one of their improbable runs toward a postseason appearance. In a suburban town in Maryland, a young couple are murdered and another young man is accused. The couple are white and the accused is black. It is up to his friends and family to prove he is innocent. This is a story of suburban ennui, race, murder, and injustice. Religion and politics, liberal lawyers and racist cops. In *Short Order Frame Up,* Ron Jacobs has written a piece of crime fiction that exposes the wound that is US racism. Two cultures existing side by side and across generations—a river very few dare to cross. His characters work and live with and next to each other, often unaware of each other's real life. When the murder occurs, however, those people that care about the man charged must cross that river and meet somewhere in between in order to free him from (what is to them) an obvious miscarriage of justice.

Fomite
Burlington, Vermont

All the Sinners Saints - Ron Jacobs

A young draftee named Victor Willard goes AWOL in Germany after an altercation with a commanding officer. Porgy is an African-American GI involved with the international Black Panthers and German radicals. Victor and a female radical named Ana fall in love. They move into Ana's room in a squatted building near the US base in Frankfurt. The international campaign to free Black revolutionary Angela Davis is coming to Frankfurt. Porgy and Ana are key organizers and Victor spends his days and nights selling and smoking hashish, while becoming addicted to heroin. Police and narcotics agents are keeping tabs on them all. Politics, love, and drugs. Truths, lies, and rock and roll. *All the Sinners Saints* is a story of people seeking redemption in a world awash in sin.

Roadworthy Creature, Roadworthy Craft - Kate Magill

Words fail but the voice struggles on. The culmination of a decade's worth of performance poetry, *Roadworthy Creature, Roadworthy Craft* is Kate Magill's first full-length publication. In lines that are sinewy yet delicate, Magill's poems explore the terrain where idea and action meet, where bodies and words commingle to form a strange new flesh, a breathing text, an "I" that spirals outward from itself.

When You Remember Deir Yassin - R. L. Green

When You Remember Deir Yassin is a collection of poems by R. L. Green, an American Jewish writer, on the subject of the occupation and destruction of Palestine. Green comments: "Outspoken Jewish critics of Israeli crimes against humanity have, strangely, been called 'anti-Semitic' as well as 'self-hating Jews.' As a Jewish critic of the Israeli government, I have come to accept these accusations as a stamp of approval and a badge of honor, signifying my own fealty to a central element of Jewish identity and ethics: one must be a lover of truth and a friend to the oppressed, and stand with the victims of tyranny, not with the tyrants, despite tribal loyalty or self-advancement. These poems were written as expressions of outrage, and of grief, and to encourage my sisters and brothers of every cultural or national grouping to speak out against injustice, to try to save Palestine, and in so doing, to reclaim for myself my own place as part of the Jewish people."

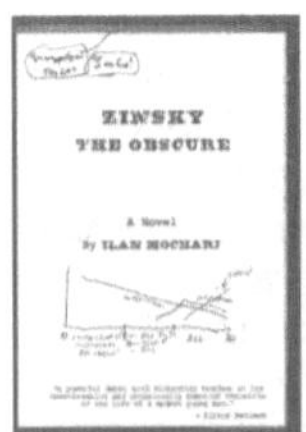

Zinsky the Obscure - Ilan Mochari

"If your childhood is brutal, your adulthood becomes a daily attempt to recover: a quest for ecstasy and stability in recompense for their early absence." So states the 30-year-old Ariel Zinsky, whose bachelor-like lifestyle belies the torturous youth he is still coming to grips with. As a boy, he struggles with the beatings themselves; as a grownup, he struggles with the world's indifference to them. *Zinsky the Obscure* is his life story, a humorous chronicle of his search for a redemptive ecstasy through sex, an entrepreneurial sports obsession, and finally, the cathartic exercise of writing it all down. Fervently recounting both the comic delights and the frightening horrors of a life in which he feels—always—that he is not like all the rest, Zinsky survives the worst and relishes the best with idiosyncratic style, as his heartbreak turns into self-awareness and his suicidal ideation into self-regard. A vivid evocation of the all-consuming nature of lust and ambition—and the forces that drive them.

Fomite
Burlington, Vermont

The Derivation of Cowboys & Indians - Joseph D. Reich

The Derivation of Cowboys & Indians represents a profound journey, a breakdown of the American Dream from a social, cultural, historical, and spiritual point of view. Reich examines in concise detail the loss of the collective unconscious, commenting on our contemporary postmodern culture with its self-interested excesses, on where and how things all go wrong, and how social/political practice rarely meets its original proclamations and promises. Reich's surreal and self-effacing satire brings this troubling message home. *The Derivation of Cowboys & Indians* is a desperate search and struggle for America's literal, symbolic, and spiritual home.

Kasper Planet: Comix and Tragix - Peter Schumann

The British call him Punch; the Italians, Pulchinella; the Russians, Petruchka; the Native Americans, Coyote. These are the figures we may know. But every culture that worships authority will breed a Punch-like, anti-authoritarian resister. Yin and yang—it has to happen. The Germans call him Kasper. Truth-telling and serious pranking are dangerous professions when going up against power. Bradley Manning sits naked in solitary; Julian Assange is pursued by Interpol, Obama's Department of Justice, and Amazon.com. But—in contrast to merely human faces— masks and theater can often slip through the bars. Consider our American Kaspers: Charlie Chaplin, Woody Guthrie, Abby Hoffman, the Yes Men—theater people all, utilizing various forms to seed critique. Their profiles and tactics have evolved along with those of their enemies. Who are the bad guys that call forth the Kaspers? Over the last half century, with his Bread & Puppet Theater, Peter Schumann has been tireless in naming them, excoriating them with Kasperdom....*from Marc Estrin's Foreword to Planet Kasper*

Views Cost Extra - L.E. Smith

Views that inspire, that calm, or that terrify—all come at some cost to the viewer. In *Views Cost Extra* you will find a New Jersey high school preppy who wants to inhabit the "perfect" cowboy movie, a rural mailman disgusted with the residents of his town who wants to live with the penguins, an ailing screen-writer who strikes a deal with Johnny Cash to reverse an old man's failures, an old man who ponders a young man's suicide attempt, a one-armed blind blues singer who wants to reunite with the car that took her arm on the assembly line— and more. These stories suggest that we must pay something to live even ordinary lives.

The Empty Notebook Interrogates Itself - Susan Thomas

The Empty Notebook began its life as a very literal metaphor for a few weeks of what the poet thought was writer's block, but was really the struggle of an eccentric persona to take over her working life. It won. And for the next three years everything she wrote came to her in the voice of the Empty Notebook, who, as the notebook began to fill itself, became rather opinionated, changed gender, alternately acted as bully and victim, had many bizarre adventures in exotic locales, and developed a somewhat politically incorrect attitude. It then began to steal the voices and forms of other poets and tried to immortalize itself in various poetry reviews. It is now thrilled to collect itself in one slim volume.

Fomite
Burlington, Vermont

My God, What Have We Done? - Susan Weiss

In a world afflicted with war, toxicity, and hunger, does what we do in our private lives really matter? Fifty years after the creation of the atomic bomb at Los Alamos, newlyweds Pauline and Clifford visit that once-secret city on their honeymoon, compelled by Pauline's fascination with Oppenheimer, the soulful scientist. The two stories emerging from this visit reverberate back and forth between the loneliness of a new mother at home in Boston and the isolation of an entire community dedicated to the development of the bomb. While Pauline struggles with unforeseen challenges of family life, Oppenheimer and his crew reckon with forces beyond all imagining.

Finally the years of frantic research on the bomb culminate in a stunning test explosion that echoes a rupture in the couple's marriage. Against the backdrop of a civilization that's out of control, Pauline begins to understand the complex, potentially explosive physics of personal relationships. At once funny and dead serious, *My God, What Have We Done?* sifts through the ruins left by the bomb in search of a more worthy human achievement.

As It Is On Earth - Peter M. Wheelwright

Four centuries after the Reformation Pilgrims sailed up the down-flowing watersheds of New England, Taylor Thatcher, irreverent scion of a fallen family of Maine Puritans, is still caught in the turbulence.

In his errant attempts to escape from history, the young college professor is further unsettled by his growing attraction to Israeli student Miryam Bluehm as he is swept by Time through the "family thing"—from the tangled genetic and religious history of his New England parents to the redemptive birthday secret of Esther Fleur Noire Bishop, the Cajun-Passamaquoddy woman who raised him and his younger half-cousin/half-brother, Bingham. The landscapes, rivers, and tidal estuaries of Old New England and the Mayan Yucatan are also casualties of history in Thatcher's story of Deep Time and re-discovery of family on Columbus Day at a high-stakes gambling casino, rising in resurrection over the starlit bones of a once-vanquished Pequot Indian tribe.

Suite for Three Voices - Derek Furr

Suite for Three Voices is a dance of prose genres, teeming with intense human life in all its humor and sorrow. A son uncovers the horrors of his father's wartime experience, a hitchhiker in a muumuu guards a mysterious parcel, a young man foresees his brother's brush with death on September 11. A Victorian poetess encounters space aliens and digital archives, a runner hears the voice of a dead friend in the song of an indigo bunting, a teacher seeks wisdom from his students' errors and Neil Young. By frozen waterfalls and neglected graveyards, along highways at noon and rivers at dusk, in the sound of bluegrass, Beethoven, and Emily Dickinson, the essays and fiction in this collection offer moments of vision.

Visiting Hours - Jennifer Anne Moses

Visiting Hours, a novel-in-stories, explores the lives of people not normally met on the page——AIDS patients and those who care for them. Set in Baton Rouge, Louisiana, and written with large and frequent dollops of humor, the book is a profound meditation on faith and love in the face of illness and poverty.

Fomite
Burlington, Vermont

Travers' Inferno - *L.E. Smith*

In the 1970's, churches began to burn in Burlington, Vermont. If it was arson, no one or no reason could be found to blame. This book suggests arson, but makes no claim to historical realism. It claims, instead, to capture the dizzying 70's zeitgeist of aggressive utopian movements, distrust in authority, escapist alternative lifestyles, and a bewildered society of onlookers. In the tradition of John Gardner's *Sunlight Dialogues*, the characters of *Travers' Inferno* are colorful and damaged, sometimes comical, sometimes tragic, looking for meaning through desperate acts. Travers Jones, the protagonist, is grounded in the transcendent—philosophy, epilepsy, arson as purification— and mystified by the opposite sex, haunted by an absent father and directed by an uncle with a grudge. He is seduced by a professor's wife and chased by an endearing if ineffective sergeant of police. There are secessionist Quebecois involved in these church burns who are murdering as well as pilfering and burning. There are changing alliances, violent deaths, lovemaking, and a belligerent cat.

Still Time - Michael Cocchiarale

Still Time is a collection of twenty-five short and shorter stories exploring tensions that arise in a variety of contemporary relationships: a young boy must deal with the wrath of his out-of-work father; a woman runs into a man twenty years after an awkward sexual encounter; a wife, unable to conceive, imagines her own murder, as well as the reaction of her emotionally distant husband; a soon-to-be-tenured English professor tries to come to terms with her husband's shocking return to the religion of his youth; an assembly line worker, married for thirty years, discovers the surprising secret life of his recently hospitalized wife. Whether a few hundred or a few thousand words, these and other stories in the collection depict characters at moments of deep crisis. Some feel powerless, overwhelmed—unable to do much to change the course of their lives. Others rise to the occasion and, for better or for worse, say or do the thing that might transform them for good. Even in stories with the most troubling of endings, there remains the possibility of redemption. For each of the characters, there is still time.

Raven or Crow - Joshua Amses

Marlowe has recently moved back home to Vermont after flunking his first term at a private college in the Midwest, when his sort-of girlfriend, Eleanor, goes missing. The circumstances surrounding Eleanor's disappearance stand to reveal more about Marlowe than he is willing to allow. Rather than report her missing, he resolves to find Eleanor himself. *Raven or Crow* is the story of mistakes rooted in the ambivalence of being young and without direction.

Entanglements - Tony Magistrale

A poet and a painter may employ different mediums to express the same snow-blown afternoon in January, but sometimes they find a way to capture the moment in such a way that their respective visions still manage to stir a reverberation, a connection. In part, that's what *Entanglements* seeks to do. Not so much for the poems and paintings to speak directly to one another, but for them to stir points of similarity.

Fomite
Burlington, Vermont

Signed Confessions - *Tom Walker*

Guilt and a desperate need to repent drive the antiheroes in Tom Walker's dark (and often darkly funny) stories:

-A gullible journalist falls for the 40-year-old stripper he profiles in a magazine.

-A faithless husband abandons his family and joins a support group for lost souls.

-A merciless prosecuting attorney grapples with the suicide of his gay son.

-An aging misanthrope must make amends to five former victims.

-An egoistic naval hero is haunted by apparitions of his dead wife and a mysterious little girl.

The seven tales in *Signed Confessions* measure how far guilty men will go to obtain a forgiveness no one can grant but themselves.

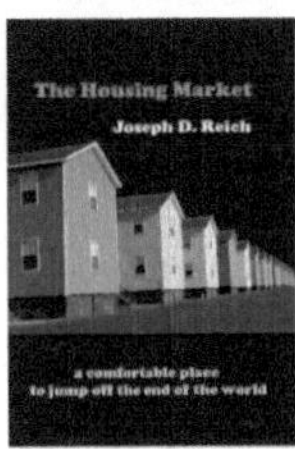

The Housing Market - *Joseph D. Reich*

In Joseph Reich's most recent social and cultural, contemporary satireof suburbia entitled, "The Housing market: a comfortable place to jumpoff the end of the world," the author addresses the absurd, postmodern elements of what it means, or for that matter not, to try & cope & function, and survive and thrive, or live and die in the repetitive and existential, futile and self-destructive, homogenized, monochromatic landscape of a brutal and bland, collective unconscious, which can spiritually result in a gradual wasting away and erosion of the senses or conflict and crisis of a desperate, disproportionate 'situational depression,' triggering and leading the narrator to feel constantly abandoned and stranded, more concretely or proverbially spoken, "the eternal stranger," where when caught between the fight or flight psychological phenomena, naturally repels him and causes him to flee and return without him even knowing it into the wild, while by sudden circumstance and coincidence discovers it surrounds the illusory-like circumference of these selfsame Monopoly board cul-de-sacs and dead ends. Most specifically, what can happen to a solitary, thoughtful, and independent thinker when being stagnated in the triangulation of a cookie-cutter, oppressive culture of a homeowner's association; a memoir all written in critical and didactic, poetic stanzas and passages, and out of desperation, when freedom and control get taken, what he is forced to do in the illusion of 'free will and volition,' something like the derivative art of a smart and ironic and social and cultural satire.

Body of Work - Andrei Guruianu

Throughout thirteen stories, Body of Work chronicles the physical and emotional toll of characters consumed by the all-too-human need for a connection. Their world is achingly common — beauty and regret, obsession and self-doubt, the seductive charm of loneliness. Often fragmented, whimsical, always on the verge of melancholy, the collection is a sepia-toned portrait of nostalgia — each story like an artifact of our impermanence, an embrace of all that we have lost, of all that we might lose and love again someday

Fomite
Burlington, Vermont

Love's Labours - Jack Pulaski

In the four stories and two novellas that comprise *Love's Labors* the protagonists, Ben and Laura, discover in their fervid romance and long marriage their interlocking fates, and the histories that preceded their births. They also learned something of the paradox between love and all the things it brings to its beneficiaries: bliss, disaster, duty, tragedy, comedy, the grotesque, and tenderness.

Ben and Laura's story is also the particularly American tale of immigration to a new world. Laura's story begins in Puerto Rico, and Ben's lineage is Russian-Jewish. They meet in City College of New York, a place at least analogous to a melting pot. Laura struggles to rescue her brother from gang life and heroin. She is mother to her younger sister; their mother Consuelo is the financial mainstay of the family and consumed by work. Despite filial obligations, Laura aspires to be a serious painter. Ben writes, cares for, and is caught up in the misadventures and surreal stories of his younger schizophrenic brother. Laura is also a story teller as powerful and enchanting as Scheherazade.Ben struggles to survive such riches, and he and Laura endure.

Meanwell - *Janice Miller Potter* *Meanwell* is a twenty-four-poem sequence in which a female servant searches for identity and meaning in the shadow of her mistress, poet Anne Bradstreet. Although Meanwell herself is a fiction, someone like her could easily have existed among Bradstreet's known but unnamed domestic servants. Through Meanwell's eyes, Bradstreet emerges as a human figure during the Great Migration of the 1600s, a period in which the Massachusetts Bay Colony was fraught with physical and political dangers. Through Meanwell, the feelings of women, silenced during the midwife Anne Hutchinson's fiery trial before the Puritan ministers, are finally acknowledged. In effect, the poems are about the making of an American rebel. Through her conflicted conscience, we witness Meanwell's transformation from a powerless English waif to a mythic American who ultimately chooses wilderness over the civilization she has experienced.

Four-Way Stop - Sherry Olson

If *Thank You* were the only prayer, as Meister Eckhart has suggested, it would be enough, and Sherry Olson's poetry, in her second book, *Four-Way Stop*, would be one. Radical attention, deep love, and dedication to kindness illuminate these poems and the stories she tells us, which are drawn from her own life: with family, with friends, and wherever she travels, with strangers – who to Olson, never are strangers, but kin. Even at the difficult intersections, as in the title poem, *Four-Way Stop*, Olson experiences – and offers – hope, showing us how, *completely unsupervised*, people take turns, with *kindness waving each other on*.

Olson writes, knowing that (to quote Czeslaw Milosz) *What surrounds us, here and now, is not guaranteed.* To this world, with her poems, Olson brings – and teaches – attention, generosity, compassion, and appreciative joy.

—Carol Henrikson

Fomite
Burlington, Vermont

Dons of Time - Greg Guma

"Wherever you look…there you are." The next media breakthrough has just happened. They call it Remote Viewing and Tonio Wolfe is at the center of the storm. But the research underway at TELPORT's off-the-books lab is even more radical -- opening a window not only to remote places but completely different times. Now unsolved mysteries are colliding with cutting edge science and altered states of consciousness in a world of corporate gangsters, infamous crimes and top-secret experiments. Based on eyewitness accounts, suppressed documents and the lives of world-changers like Nikola Tesla, Annie Besant and Jack the Ripper, Dons of Time is a speculative adventure, a glimpse of an alternative future and a quantum leap to Gilded Age London at the tipping point of invention, revolution and murder.

Alfabestiario

AlphaBetaBestiario - *Antonello Borra*

Animals have always understood that mankind is not fully at home in the world. Bestiaries, hoping to teach, send out warnings. This one, of course, aims at doing the same.

Writing a review on Amazon, Good Reads, Shelfari, Library Thing or other social media sites for readers will help the progress of independent publishing. To submit a review, go to the book page on any of the sites and follow the links for reviews. Books from independent presses rely on reader to reader communications.